AN AMERICAN MARRIAGE

WINNER OF THE WOMEN'S PRIZE FOR FICTION 2019

A *NEW YORK TIMES* BESTSELLER

OPRAH'S BOOK CLUB 2018 SELECTION

CHOSEN BY BARACK OBAMA
AS ONE OF HIS FAVOURITE SUMMER READS OF 2018

LONGLISTED FOR THE 2018 NATIONAL BOOK AWARD FOR FICTION

'It's among Tayari's many gifts that she can touch us soul to soul with her words.'
Oprah Winfrey

'A moving portrayal of the effects of a wrongful conviction on a young African-American couple.'
Barack Obama

'This is a marvellous feat of storytelling, told with the type of light touch that can only be achieved through hard work.'
Guardian

'Nuanced and evocative… A compelling exploration of the thorny conflicts that drive us apart and bind us, the distorting weight of racism, and how commitment looks across time – and generations.'
BBC Culture

'If you haven't read it yet, now is the time.'
Sunday Times

'Quietly powerful… [Jones's] writing illuminates the bits and pieces of a marriage: those almost imperceptible moments that make it, break it, and forcefully tear it apart.'
The Atlantic

'Another incredible love story, though fraught with greater challenges for the couple at the centre, which makes the story all the more moving. Jones's prose is chock-full of lyricism, grace and wisdom. You will never forget the story of Celestial and Roy.'
Observer

'Suspenseful and compelling. *An American Marriage* delivers on all fronts, raising questions both intimate and epic about the intersections of race and class, the burdens and joys of shared history, and what it means to commit to a future together.'
Salon.com

'A searing, gut-wrenching, page-turning read.' *Sun*

'Tayari Jones's wise and compassionate new novel, *An American Marriage*…is a clear vision of the quiet devastation of a family. It is beautifully written, with many allusions to black music and culture – including the everyday poetry of the African-American community that begs to be heard.'
The New York Times Book Review

'Powerful… The story…is both sweeping and intimate – at once an unsparing exploration of what it means to be black in America and a remarkably lifelike portrait of a marriage.' *The New Yorker*

'Subtle, well-crafted, and powerful.' *Kirkus* (starred review)

'Compelling… spun with tender patience by Jones, who cradles each of these characters in a story that pulls our sympathies in different directions. She never ignores their flaws, their perfectly human tendency toward self-justification, but she also captures their longing to be kind, to be just, to somehow behave well despite the contradictory desires of the heart.' *Washington Post*

'A wonderfully deep and moving novel…powerful and exciting.'
Kate Williams, Chair of Judges, The Women's Prize for Fiction

'A blend of thoughtful drama and social issues.' *Independent*

'A nuanced dissection of love, race, class, family and gender…the sharp simplicity of Jones's writing unleashes her characters' vulnerabilities, and facilitates a remarkably intimate portrait of a corrupt justice system, and the irreversible effects of wrongful conviction.' *Irish Times*

'A magnificent, painful story of love and justice.'
Sainsbury's Magazine, Book Club Choice

'Moving and thought-provoking.' *Irish Examiner*

'This moment, right here in February 2018, feels like exactly the right time for Tayari Jones to be writing – and for us to be reading Tayari Jones. In the years since her debut, she has been getting better, and…added heft and substance to the rich and necessary stories she weaves.' *BuzzFeed*

'One of America's finest writers, Tayari Jones has offered up another masterpiece with her latest novel, a tremendously powerful story about love, injustice, inequality, and strength. *An American Marriage* reveals how quickly dreams can be derailed due to systemic malignant forces all around us. It's a novel of vision and grace, and it will bury itself in your consciousness.'

Nylon.com

'A tense and timely love story. Told in letters and from alternating perspectives, packed with brave questions about race and class, *An American Marriage* is the perfect book-club book – one the whole group will finish and discuss with conviction.' *People* (Book of the Week)

'Tayari Jones is a bard of the modern South, a writer whose skill at weaving stories is matched only by her compassion for her characters. While *An American Marriage* confronts thorny issues around race and the criminal justice system it is, at heart, a love story. It's also a meditation on the creation of art, the meaning of family and the conflict between duty and desire. Jones has crafted a complex, layered story that's both intimate and broad, a literary page-turner that's impossible to put down.' *The Los Angeles Times*

'*An American Marriage* is that rare treasure, a novel that pulls you under like a fever dream, a novel whose pages you start to ration midway through, a novel you miss like a lover the minute you kiss its final page goodbye. *An American Marriage* is a gripping, masterfully crafted message in a bottle, at once a dispatch from the past and a foreshadowing of the future, bringing exquisite reading pleasure and painful, crucial news.' *San Francisco Chronicle*

'Tayari Jones is blessed with vision to see through to the surprising and devastating truths at the heart of ordinary lives, strength to wrest those truths free, and a gift of language to lay it all out, compelling and clear. That has been true from her very first book, but with *An American Marriage* that vision, that strength, and that truth-telling voice have found a new level of artistry and power.' Michael Chabon, author of *The Amazing Adventures of Kavalier & Clay*

'A heartbreaking and genuinely suspenseful love story… Tayari Jones has written a complex and important novel about people trapped in a tragic situation, struggling to reconcile their responsibilities and desires.' Tom Perrotta, author of *Little Children*

'Heart-wrenching… *An American Marriage* poses profound questions about what we owe each other, and what injustices we allow to persist.'

Huffington Post

'Jones writes brilliantly about expectations and loss and racial injustice, and how love must evolve when our best laid plans go awry.'   *Esquire*

'I love *An American Marriage* and I'm so excited for this book to be in the world. Tayari's novel is timely, thoughtful, and beautifully written. Reading it, I found myself angry as hell, laughing out loud, choking up and cheering. A gem of a book.'   Jacqueline Woodson,
author of *Another Brooklyn* and *Brown Girl Dreaming*

'This utterly gripping novel from Tayari Jones explores marriage in an intimate and realistic way, making it an engaging read for both married and single audiences alike. This stirring love story is a profoundly insightful look into the hearts and minds of three people who are at once bound and separated by forces beyond their control.'   *Paste Magazine*

'Tayari Jones is a great storyteller. *An American Marriage* holds the reader from first page to last.'   Amy Bloom, author of *Lucky Us*

'Brilliant, timely…heartbreaking… With spare and shimmering prose that can strike with the shock of a shiv, Jones captures the life-altering losses Roy and Celestial endure in this unforgettable American marriage.'   *USA Today*

'A stunning epic love story filled with breathtaking twists and turns… Skilfully crafted and beautifully written, *An American Marriage* is an exquisite, timely, and powerful novel that feels both urgent and indispensable.'
Edwidge Danticat, author of *Breath, Eyes, Memory*

'Breathtaking… Jones is a master with words and *An American Marriage* is the wordsmith at the top of her game.'   Bitch Media

'*An American Marriage* is a masterpiece of storytelling, an intimate look deep into the souls of people who must reckon with the past while moving forward – with hope and pain – into the future.'   *The Rumpus*

'[A] very insightful, touching story about contemporary relationships.'

Book Riot

An American Marriage

TAYARI JONES

ONEWORLD

A Oneworld Book

First published in Great Britain by Oneworld Publications, 2018
This paperback edition published 2019
Reprinted six times in 2019

Copyright © Tayari Jones, 2018

The moral right of Tayari Jones to be identified as the author of this work has been asserted
by her in accordance with the Copyright, Designs and Patents Act 1988

ISBN 978-1-78607-519-2
ISBN 978-1-78607-517-8 (eBook)

Book design by Steve Godwin
Printed and bound in Great Britain by Clays Ltd, Elcograf S.p.A.

Epigraph by Claudia Rankine from *Citizen: An American Lyric*, © 2014
by Claudia Rankine. Used by permission of Graywolf Press. All rights reserved.

This is a work of fiction. Names, characters, places, and incidents are either the product of
the author's imagination or are used fictitiously, and any resemblance to actual persons,
living or dead, businesses, companies, events or locales is entirely coincidental.

Oneworld Publications
10 Bloomsbury Street
London WC1B 3SR
England

For my mother's sister, Alma Faye,
and for Maxine & Marcia, my own

What happens to you doesn't belong to you,
only half concerns you. It's not yours. Not yours only.

—CLAUDIA RANKINE

ONE

---+---

Bridge Music

ROY

There are two kinds of people in the world, those who leave home, and those who don't. I'm a proud member of the first category. My wife, Celestial, used to say that I'm a country boy at the core, but I never cared for that designation. For one, I'm not from the country per se. Eloe, Louisiana, is a small town. When you hear "country," you think raising crops, baling hay, and milking cows. Never in my life have I picked a single cotton boll, although my daddy did. I have never touched a horse, goat, or pig, nor have I any desire to. Celestial used to laugh, clarifying that she's not saying I'm a farmer, just country. She is from Atlanta, and there was a case to be made that she is country, too. But let her tell it, she's a "southern woman," not to be confused with a "southern belle." For some reason, "Georgia peach" is all right with her, and it's all right with me, so there you have it.

Celestial thinks of herself as this cosmopolitan person, and she's not wrong. However, she sleeps each night in the very house she grew up in. I, on the other hand, departed on the first thing smoking, exactly seventy-one hours after high school graduation. I would have left sooner, but the Trailways didn't stop through Eloe every day. By the time the mailman brought my mama the cardboard tube containing my diploma, I was all moved into my dorm room at Morehouse College attending a special program for first-generation scholarship types. We were invited to show up two and a half months before the legacies, to get the lay of the land and bone up on the basics. Imagine twenty-three young black men watching Spike Lee's *School Daze* and Sidney Poitier's *To Sir with Love* on loop, and you either will or will not get the picture. Indoctrination isn't always a bad thing.

All my life I have been helped by leg-up programs—Head Start when I was five and Upward Bound all the way through. If I ever have kids, they will be able to pedal through life without training wheels, but I like to give credit where it is due.

Atlanta is where I learned the rules and learned them quick. No one ever called me stupid. But home isn't where you *land*; home is where you *launch*. You can't pick your home any more than you can choose your family. In poker, you get five cards. Three of them you can swap out, but two are yours to keep: family and native land.

I'm not talking bad about Eloe. Obviously there are worse native lands; a big-picture mind can see that. For one, Eloe may be in Louisiana, not a state brimming with opportunity, but it is located in America, and if you're going to be black and struggling, the United States is probably the best place to do it. However, we were not poor. Let me make that extra-strength clear. My daddy worked too hard at Buck's Sporting Goods by day plus handymanning in the evenings, and my mother spent too many hours fixing trays at the meat-and-three for me to act like we had neither pot nor window. Let the record show that we had both.

Me, Olive, and Big Roy were a family of three, and we lived in a sturdy brick house on a safe block. I had my own room, and when Big Roy built an extension, I had my own bathroom. When I outgrew my shoes, I never waited for new ones. While I have received financial aid, my parents did their part to send me to college.

Still, the truth is that there was nothing extra. If my childhood were a sandwich, there would be no meat hanging off the bread. We had what we needed and nothing more. "And nothing less," my mama would have said, and then wrapped me in one of her lemon-drop hugs.

When I arrived in Atlanta, I was under the impression that I had my whole life ahead of me—endless reams of blank paper. And you know what they say: a Morehouse Man always has a pen. Ten years later, my life was at its sweet spot. When anybody said, "Where are you from?" I said, "The A!"—so intimate with the city that I knew her by her nickname. When asked about my family, I talked about Celestial.

We were properly married for a year and a half, and we were happy for that time, at least I was. Maybe we didn't do happy like other people, but we're not your garden-variety bourgeois Atlanta Negroes where the husband goes to bed with his laptop under his pillow and the wife dreams about her blue-box jewelry. I was young, hungry, and on the come-up. Celestial was an artist, intense and gorgeous. We were like *Love Jones*, but grown. What can I say? I always had a weakness for shooting-star women. When you're with them, you know that you're deep into something, none of that hi-and-bye stuff. Before Celestial, I dated this other girl, also born and raised in the A. This girl, as proper as you can picture, pulled a gun on me at an Urban League gala! I'll never forget that silver .22 with a pink mother-of-pearl handle. She flashed it inside her purse under the table where we were enjoying steak and au gratin potatoes. She said she knew I was cheating on her with some chick from the Black Bar Association. How can I explain this? I was scared, and then I wasn't. Only an Atlanta girl could be so classy while doing something so hood. It was love-logic, granted, but I wasn't sure if I should propose or call the police. We broke up before daybreak, and it wasn't my decision.

After Pistol Girl, I lost my touch with the ladies for a minute. I read the news as same as anyone, and I heard about some supposed black man shortage, but it seemed that the good news had yet to make an impact on my social life. Every woman I took a shine to had someone else waiting in the cut.

A little competition is healthy for all parties involved, but Pistol Girl's departure got up my skin like chiggers and sent me to Eloe for a few days to talk things over with Big Roy. My father has this alpha-omega way about him, like he was here before you showed up and he would be sitting in his same recliner chair long after you left.

"You don't want no woman that brandished a firearm, son."

I tried to explain that what made it remarkable was the contrast between the streetness of the pistol and the glitter of the evening. Besides: "She was playing, Daddy."

Big Roy nodded and sucked the foam from his glass of beer. "If that's how she plays, what's going to happen when she gets mad?"

From the kitchen, as though speaking through a translator, my mother called, "Ask him who she is with now. She might be crazy, but she's not crazy. Nobody would dismiss Little Roy without somebody on the back bench."

Big Roy asked, "Your mother wants to know who she is with now." Like we weren't all speaking English.

"Some attorney dude. Not like Perry Mason. Contracts. A paperwork sort of person."

"Aren't you a paperwork person?" Big Roy asked.

"Totally different. Being a rep, that's temporary. Besides, paperwork isn't my destiny. It's just what I happen to be doing now."

"I see," Big Roy said.

My mother was still peanut-gallerying from the kitchen. "Tell him that he is always letting these light-skinned girls hurt his feelings. Tell him he needs to remember some of the girls right here in Allen Parish. Tell him to lift somebody up with him."

Big Roy said, "Your mother says—" before I cut him off.

"I heard her and didn't nobody say that girl was light-skinned."

But of course she was, and my mama has a thing about that.

Now Olive came out of the kitchen wiping her hands on a striped dish towel. "Don't get mad. I'm not trying to get in your business."

Nobody can really satisfy their mama when it comes to the ladies. All my buddies tell me that their mothers are steady warning them, "If she can't use your comb, don't bring her home." *Ebony* and *Jet* both swear up and down that all the black men with two nickels to rub together are opting for the swirl. As for me, I'm strictly down with the brown, and my mama has the nerve to fret about which particular shade of sister I was choosing.

But you would think that she would have liked Celestial. The two of them favored so much that they could have been the ones related. They both had that clean pretty, like Thelma from *Good Times*, my first TV crush. But no, as far as my mama was concerned, Celestial looked right, but she was from a different world—Jasmine in Bernadette's clothing. Big Roy, on the other hand, was so taken by Celestial that he would have married her if I didn't. None of this scored any points with Olive.

"There is only one thing that will win me any ground with your mother," Celestial once said.

"And what might that be?"

"A baby," she said with a sigh. "Whenever I see her, she looks me up and down like I might be holding her grandbabies hostage in my body."

"You exaggerate." But the truth was, I knew where my mother was coming from. After a year, I was ready to get this show on the road, creating a new generation with an updated set of rules and regulations.

Not that there was anything wrong with the way either one of us was brought up, but still, the world is changing, so the way you bring up kids had to change, too. Part of my plan was to never one time mention picking cotton. My parents always talked about either real cotton or the idea of it. White people say, "It beats digging a ditch"; black people say, "It beats picking cotton." I'm not going to remind my kids that somebody died in order for me to do everyday things. I don't want Roy III sitting up in the movie theater trying to watch *Star Wars* or what have you and be thinking about the fact that sitting down eating some popcorn is a right that cost somebody his life. None of that. Or maybe not much of that. We'll have to get the recipe right. Now Celestial promises that she will never say that they have to be twice as good to get half as much. "Even if it's true," she said, "what kind of thing is that to say to a five-year-old?"

She was the perfect balance in a woman, not a button-down corporate type, but she wore her pedigree like the gloss on a patent-leather shoe. In addition, she popped like an artist, without veering into crazy. In other words, there was no pink pistol in her purse, but there was no shortage of passion either. Celestial liked to go her own way and you could tell that from looking at her. She was tall, five nine, flat-footed, taller than her own father. I know that height is the luck of the draw, but it felt like she chose all that altitude. Her hair, big and wild, put her a smidge over my head. Even before you knew she was a genius with needle and thread, you could tell you were dealing with a unique individual. Although some people—and by "some people," I mean my mama—couldn't see it, all that's what was going to make her an excellent mother.

I have half a mind to ask her if we could name our child—son or daughter—Future.

If it had been up to me, we would be all aboard the baby train on our honeymoon. Picture us laid up in a glass-bottom cabana over the ocean. I didn't even know they *had* shit like that, but I pretended to be all about it when Celestial showed me the brochure, telling her it was on my bucket list. There we were, relaxing up over the ocean, enjoying each other. The wedding was more than a day behind us because Bali was twenty-three first-class hours away. For the wedding, Celestial had been done up like a doll-baby version of herself. All that crazy hair was wrangled into a ballerina bun and the makeup made her seem to blush. When I saw her floating down the aisle toward me, her and her daddy both were giggling like this whole thing was only a dress rehearsal. There I was, serious as four heart attacks and a stroke, but then she looked up at me and puckered her pink-paint lips in a little kiss and I got the joke. She was letting me know that all of this—the little girls holding up the train of her gown, my morning jacket, even the ring in my pocket—was just a show. What was real was the dance of light in her eyes and the quick current of our blood. And then I smiled, too.

In Bali, that slick hair was long gone and she was rocking a 1970s *Jet* magazine fro and wearing nothing but body glitter.

"Let's make a baby."

She laughed. "That's how you want to ask me?"

"I'm serious."

"Not yet, Daddy," she said. "Soon, though."

On our paper anniversary, I wrote on a sheet of paper. "Soon like now?"

She turned it over and wrote back, "Soon like yesterday. I went to the doctor and he said all systems are go."

But it was another piece of paper that hemmed us up—my very own business card. We were back home after our anniversary dinner at the Beautiful Restaurant, a half diner, half cafeteria on Cascade Road. Not fancy, but it was where I popped the question. She'd said, "Yes, but put that ring away before we get jacked!" On our wedding anniversary, we returned, for a feast of short ribs, mac and cheese, and corn pudding. Then we headed home for dessert, two slices of wedding cake that had been sitting in the freezer for 365, waiting to see if we would stick through the year. Not content to leave well enough alone, I opened my wallet to show the photo of her that I kept there. As I pulled the picture from its sleeve, my business card floated free, landing softly beside the slabs of amaretto cake. On the back, in purple ink, was a woman's first name and phone number, which was bad enough. But Celestial noticed three more digits, which she assumed to be a hotel room number.

"I can explain this." The truth was straightforward: I liked the ladies. I enjoyed a little flirtation, what they call *frisson*. Sometimes I collected phone numbers like I was still in college, but 99.997 percent of the time it ended there. I just liked to know that I still had it. Harmless, right?

"Get to explaining," she said.

"She slipped it into my pocket."

"How did she slip you your own business card?" Celestial was mad, and it turned me on a little, like the click on the stove before the flame took.

"She asked me for my card. I thought it was innocent."

Celestial stood up and collected the saucers, weighed down with cake, and dropped them in the trash, wedding china be damned. She returned to the table, picked up her flute of pink champagne and slammed the bubbly like a shot of tequila. Then she snatched my glass out of my hand, drank my share, and then tossed the long-stemmed glasses into the garbage, too. As they broke, they rang like bells.

"You are so full of shit," she said.

"But where am I now?" I said. "Right here with you. In our home. I lay my head on your pillow every night."

"On our fucking anniversary," she said. Now her mad was melting into sad. She sat on her breakfast chair. "Why get married if you want to cheat?"

I didn't point out that you had to be married in order to cheat at all. Instead, I told her the truth. "I never even called that girl." I sat beside her. "I love you." I said it like a magic charm. "Happy anniversary."

She let me kiss her, which was a positive sign. I could taste the pink champagne on her lips. We were out of our clothes when she bit me hard on the ear. "You are such a liar." Then she stretched across to my night-stand and produced a shiny foil pack. "Wrap it up, mister."

I know that there are those out there who would say that our marriage was in trouble. People have a lot of things to say when they don't know what goes on behind closed doors, up under the covers, and between night and morning. But as a witness to, and even a member of, our relationship, I'm convinced that it was the opposite. It meant something that I could make her mad with just a scrap of paper and she could make me crazy with just a rubber.

Yes, we were a married couple, but we were still young and smitten. One year in and the fire was still burning blue hot.

The thing is this: it's a challenge being 2.0. On paper, we're *A Different World: Where Are They Now?* Whitley and Dwayne all grown up. But Celestial and me are something Hollywood never imagined. She was gifted and I was her manager and muse. It's not like I lay around in my birthday suit so she could draw me. No, I simply lived my life and she watched. When we were engaged, she won a competition for a glass sculpture she created. From a distance, it looked to be a shooter marble, but when you got up close and looked from the right angle, you could make out the lines of my profile swirled inside. Somebody offered her five thousand dollars for it, but she wouldn't part with it. This isn't what happens when a marriage is in danger.

She did for me and I did for her in return. Back in the day, when you worked so your wife didn't have to, they called that "sitting your woman down." It was a goal of Big Roy's to sit Olive down, but it never quite worked out. In his honor, and maybe for my own, I worked all day so Celestial could stay home making dolls, her primary art medium. I'm into the museum-quality marbles and the delicate line drawings, but the dolls were something that an ordinary person could get behind. My vision was a line of cloth dolls that we were going to sell wholesale. You could display them on a shelf or hug the stuffing out of them. There would still be the high-end custom jobs and art pieces. Those could fetch five figures, easy. But the everyday dolls were going to make her mark, I told her. And you see, I turned out to be right.

I know that all of this is water under the bridge, and not a sweet little creek either. But to be fair, I have to tell this whole story. We were married only a year and some change, but it was a good year. Even she would have to admit that.

A METEOR CRASHED our life on Labor Day weekend when we went to Eloe to visit my parents. We traveled by car because I liked a road trip. Planes, I associated with my job. Back then, I was a rep for a textbook company, specializing in math books, even though my way with numbers ended with my 12 times tables. I was successful at my gig because I knew how to sell things. The week before, I closed a nice adoption at my alma mater, and I was in the running for one at Georgia State. It didn't make me a mogul, but I was looking forward to a bonus hefty enough to start talking about buying a new house. Nothing was wrong with our current abode, a solid ranch house on a quiet street. It's just that it was a wedding gift from her parents, her childhood home, deeded over to their only daughter, and only to her. It was like white people do, a leg up, American style. But I kind of wanted to hang my hat on a peg with my own name on it.

This was on my mind but not on my spirit as we drove up I-10 on our way to Eloe. We settled down after our anniversary skirmish and we were back in rhythm with each other. Old-school hip-hop thumped from the stereo of our Honda Accord, a family kind of car with two empty seats in the back.

Six hours in, I clicked on the blinker at exit 163. As we merged onto a two-lane highway, I felt a change in Celestial. Her shoulders rode a little higher, and she nibbled on the ends of her hair.

"What's wrong," I asked, turning down the volume of the greatest hip-hop album in history.

"Just nervous."

"About what?"

"You ever have a feeling like maybe you left the stove on?"

I returned the volume on the stereo to somewhere between thumping and bumping. "Call your boy, Andre, then."

Celestial fumbled with the seatbelt like it was rubbing her neck the wrong way. "I always get like this around your parents, self-conscious, you know."

"My folks?" Olive and Big Roy are the most down-to-earth people in the history of ever. Celestial's folks, on the other hand, were not what you would call approachable. Her father was a little dude, three apples tall, with this immense Frederick Douglass fro, complete with side part—and to top it off, he is some sort of genius inventor. Her mother worked in education, not as a teacher or a principal but as an assistant superintendent to the whole school system. And did I mention that her dad hit pay dirt about ten or twelve years ago, inventing a compound that prevents orange juice from separating so fast? He sold that sucker to Minute Maid and ever since, they have been splashing around naked in a bathtub full of money. Her mama and daddy—now *that's* a hard room. Next to them, Olive and Big Roy are cake. "You know my folks love you," I said.

"They love *you*."

"And I love you, so they love you. It's basic math."

Celestial looked out the window as the skinny pine trees whipped by. "I don't feel good about this, Roy. Let's go home."

My wife has a flair for the dramatic. Still, there was a little hitch in her words that I can only describe as fear.

"What is it?"

"I don't know," she said. "But let's go back."

"What would I tell my mother? You know she has dinner cooking at full tilt by now."

"Blame it on me," Celestial said. "Tell her everything's my fault."

Looking back on it, it's like watching a horror flick and wondering why the characters are so determined to ignore the danger signs. When a spectral voice says, GET OUT, you should do it. But in real life, you don't know that you're in a scary movie. You think your wife is being overly emotional. You quietly hope that it's because she's pregnant, because a baby is what you need to lock this thing in and throw away the key.

WHEN WE ARRIVED at my parents' home, Olive was waiting on the front porch. My mother had a fondness for wigs, and this time she was wearing curls the color of peach preserves. I pulled into the yard close up to the bumper of my daddy's Chrysler, threw the car in park, flung open the door, and bounded up the stairs two at a time to meet my mama halfway with an embrace. She was no bigger than a minute, so I bent my back to sweep her feet up off the porch and she laughed musical like a xylophone.

"Little Roy," she said. "You're home."

Once I set her down, I looked over my shoulder and didn't see anything but dead air, so I trotted back down the stairs, again two at a time. I opened the car door and Celestial extended her arm. I swear, I could hear my mother roll her eyes as I helped my wife out of the Honda.

"IT'S A TRIANGLE," Big Roy explained as the two of us enjoyed a corner of cognac in the den while Olive was busy in the kitchen and Celestial freshened up. "I was lucky," he said. "When I met your mama, we were both a couple of free agents. My parents were both dead and gone, and hers were way in Oklahoma, pretending like she was never born."

"They'll get it together," I told Big Roy. "Celestial takes a minute to get used to people."

"Your mama isn't exactly Doris Day," he said in agreement, and we raised our glasses to the difficult women we were crazy about.

"It'll get better when we have a kid," I said.

"True. A grandbaby can soothe a savage beast."

"Who you calling a beast?" My mother materialized from the kitchen and sat on Big Roy's lap like a teenager.

From the other doorway Celestial entered, fresh, lovely, and smelling of tangerines. With me nestled in the recliner and my parents love-birding on the couch, there was no place for her to sit, so I tapped my knee. Gamely, she perched on my lap and we seemed to be on an awkward double date circa 1952.

My mother righted herself. "Celestial, I hear you're famous."

"Ma'am?" she said, and jerked a little to get up off my lap, but I held her fast.

"The magazine," she said. "Why didn't you tell us you were making waves in the world?"

Celestial looked shy. "It's just the alumnae bulletin."

"It's a magazine," my mother said, picking up the shiny copy from under the coffee table and flipping it to a dog-eared page featuring Celestial holding a cloth doll that represented Josephine Baker. "Artists to Watch," announced a bold font.

"I sent it," I admitted. "What can I say? I'm proud."

"Is it true that people pay five thousand dollars for your dolls?" Olive pursed her lips and cut her eyes.

"Not usually," Celestial said, but I spoke over her.

"That's right," I said. "You know I'm her manager. Would I let somebody shortchange my wife?"

"Five thousand dollars for a baby doll?" Olive fanned herself with the magazine, lifting her peach-preserve hair. "I guess that's why God invented white folks."

Big Roy chuckled, and Celestial struggled like a backside beetle to get free from my lap. "The picture doesn't do it justice," she said, sounding like a little girl. "The headdress is hand-beaded and—"

"Five thousand dollars will buy a lot of beads," my mother noted.

Celestial looked at me, and in an attempt to make peace, I said, "Mama, don't hate the player, hate the game." If you have a woman, you recognize when you have said the wrong thing. Somehow she rearranges the ions in the air and you can't breathe as well.

"It's not a game; it's art." Celestial's eyes landed on the framed African-inspired prints on the walls of the living room. "I mean real art."

Big Roy, a skilled diplomat, said, "Maybe if we could see one in person."

"There's one in the car," I said. "I'll go get it."

THE DOLL, SWADDLED in a soft blanket, looked like an actual infant. This was one of Celestial's quirks. For a woman who was, shall we say, apprehensive about motherhood, she was rather protective of these cloth creations. I tried to tell her that she was going to have to adopt a different attitude for when we opened up our storefront. The *poupées*, as the dolls were called, would sell for a fraction of the price of the art pieces, like the one I was holding. They would have to be sewn with a quickness and, once it caught on, mass production all the way. None of this cashmere blanket stuff. But I let her slide with this one, which was a commission for the mayor of Atlanta to be given as a gift to his chief of staff, who was expecting a baby around Thanksgiving.

When I parted the blanket so my mother could see the doll's face, she pulled in a loud breath. I gave Celestial a little wink, and she was kind enough to reset the ions in the air so I could breathe again.

"It's you," Olive said, taking the doll from me, taking care to support its head.

"I used his picture," Celestial piped up. "Roy is my inspiration."

"That's why she married me," I joked.

"Not the only reason," she said.

You know it was a charmed moment if my mother didn't have a single word to say. Her eyes were on the bundle in her arms as my father joined her and stared over her shoulder.

"I used Austrian crystals for the hair," Celestial went on, getting excited. "Turn it to hit the light."

My mother did and the doll's head shimmered as light from our every-day bulbs bounced off the little cap of black beads. "It's like a halo," my mother said. "This is how it is when you really have a baby. You've your own angel."

Now my mother moved to the couch and laid the doll on a cushion. It was a trippy experience because the doll really did favor me, or at least my baby pictures. It was like staring into an enchanted mirror. In Olive, I could see the sixteen-year-old she had been, a mother way too soon but as tender as springtime. "I could buy this from you?"

"No, Mama," I said, pride barreling up from my chest. "That's a special commission. Ten K. Quick and dirty, brokered by yours truly!"

"Of course," she said, folding the blanket over the doll like a shroud. "What do I need a doll for? Old lady like me?"

"You can have it," Celestial said.

I gave her the look that she calls my Gary Coleman expression. The contract specified delivery by the end of the month. The deadline was more than firm; it was black-ink-notarized in triplicate. There was no CPT proviso.

Without even looking at me, Celestial said, "I can make another one."

Olive said, "No, I don't want to set you back. It's just that he's so much like Little Roy."

I reached to take the doll from her, but my mother wasn't exactly releasing it and Celestial wasn't exactly making it easy. She's a sucker for anybody who appreciates her work. This was something else we were going to have to work on if we were going to make a real business out of this.

"Keep it," Celestial said, like she hadn't been working on this doll for three months. "I can make another one for the mayor."

Now it was Olive's turn to stir the ions.

"Oh, the mayor. Well, excuse me!" She handed me the doll. "Put it back in your car before I get it dirty. I don't want you sending me a bill for ten thousand dollars."

"I didn't mean it like that." Celestial looked at me in apology.

"Mama," I said.

"Olive," Big Roy said.

"Mrs. Hamilton," Celestial said.

"It's dinnertime," my mother said. "I hope y'all still eat candy yams and mustard greens."

WE ATE DINNER, not in silence, but nobody talked about anything. Olive was so angry that she messed up the iced tea. I took a deep sip, expecting the soft finish of cane sugar, and choked on the hot taste of kosher salt. Shortly after that, my high school diploma fell off the wall, and a crack starred across the glass. Signs? Maybe. But I wasn't thinking about missives from above. I was too distracted by being accidentally caught between two women I treasured beyond question. It's not that I don't know how to handle myself when I'm in a situation. Every man knows what it is to spread himself around. But with my mother and Celestial, I was actually split down the middle. Olive brought me into this world and trained me up to be the man I recognized as myself. But Celestial was the portal to the rest of my life, the shiny door to the next level.

Dessert was sock-it-to-me cake, my favorite, but the tussle with that ten-thousand-dollar doll stole my appetite. Nevertheless, I pushed my way through two cinnamon-swirled helpings because everybody knows the way to make a bad matter worse with a southern woman is to refuse her food. So I ate like a refugee and so did Celestial, even though we both had pledged to stay away from processed sugar.

Once we cleared the table, Big Roy said, "Ready to bring your bags in?"

"No, Big Man," I said, my voice light. "I got us a room in the Piney Woods."

"You would rather stay in that dump than your own home?" Olive said.

"I want to take Celestial back to the first beginning."

"You don't have to stay there to do that."

But the truth was that I did. It was a story that needed telling away from my parents' revisionist tendencies. After a year of marriage, she deserved to know who she was married to.

"Was this your idea?" my mother asked Celestial.

"No, ma'am. I'm happy to stay here."

"This is all me," I said, although Celestial was glad we were staying in the hotel. She said she never felt right about us sleeping together under either of our parents' roofs even though we were lawfully wedded, et cetera. Last time we were here she put on a Little House on the Prairie nightgown, although usually she slept au naturel.

"But I made up the room," Olive said, reaching suddenly for Celestial. The women looked at each other in a way that a man never looks at another man. For a beat, they were alone together in the house.

"Roy." Celestial turned to me, strangely frightened. "What do you think?"

"We'll be back in the morning, Mama," I said, kissing her. "Biscuits and honey."

HOW LONG DID it take for us to leave my mother's home? Maybe it's the looking-back talking, but everyone except me seemed to have stones in their pockets. As we made our way through the door at last, my father handed Celestial the shrouded doll. He carried it awkwardly, like he couldn't decide if it was an object or a living thing.

"Give him some air," my mother said, pulling back the blanket, and the sinking orange sun lit up the halo.

"You can have it," Celestial said. "For real."

"That one is for the mayor," Olive said. "You can make me another one."

"Or better yet, the real thing," Big Roy said, tracing an invisible pregnant belly with his big hands. His laughter broke whatever sticky spell bound us to the house, and we were able to leave.

Celestial thawed as soon as we climbed into the car. Whatever bad mojo or heebie-jeebies were bothering her vanished once we were back on the highway. She undid the French braids over her ears, nesting her head between her knees, busy unraveling and fluffing. When she sat up, she was herself again, riot of hair and wicked smile. "Oh my Lord, that was awkward," she said.

"Word," I agreed. "I don't know what that was all about."

"Babies," she said. "I believe that the desire for grandchildren makes even sane parents go left."

"Not your parents," I said, thinking of her folks, cool as icebox pie.

"Oh yes, mine, too," she said. "They keep it in check in front of you. All of them need to go to therapy."

"But we're trying for kids," I said. "What difference does it make if they want kids, too? Isn't it good to have something in common?"

ON OUR WAY to the hotel, I pulled over on the side of the road right before we crossed a suspension bridge that was out of scale with what maps called the Aldridge River but was basically a hearty stream.

"What do you have on your feet?"

"Wedges," she said, frowning.

"Can you walk in them?"

She seemed embarrassed by her shoes, an architectural construction of polka-dot ribbon and cork. "How was I supposed to impress your mother in flats?"

"No worries, it's close," I said, shuffling down a soft embankment as she baby-stepped behind me. "Hold my neck," I said, picking her up like a bride and carrying her the rest of the way. She pressed her face into my neck and sighed. I would never tell her, but I liked being stronger than she was, the way I could literally sweep her off her feet. She wouldn't tell me either, but I know that she appreciated it, too. Reaching the bank of the stream, I set her down on the soft earth. "You getting heavy, girl. You sure you not pregnant?"

"Ha ha, very funny," she said, looking up. "This is a lot of bridge for a little slip of water."

I sat on the ground and pressed my back against one of the metal pillars like it was the big hickory tree in our front yard. I scissored my legs and patted the space between them. She sat there and I crossed my arms across her chest and rested my chin where her neck met her shoulder. The stream beside us was clear; the water gushed over smooth rocks, and twilight outlined the little waves with silver. My wife smelled like lavender and coconut cake.

I said, "Before they built the dam and the water went low, me and my daddy came out here on Saturdays with our lines and bait. In a way that's what fatherhood is about: bologna sandwiches and grape soda." She giggled, not knowing how serious I was. Above us, a car passed over the metal mesh, and the sound of the wind passing through the holes played a musical note, like when you blow softly over the mouth of a bottle. "When a lot of cars pass over, it's almost a song."

There we sat, waiting on cars, listening for the bridge music. Our marriage was good. This isn't just memory talking.

"Georgia," I said, using her pet name. "My family is more complicated than you think. My mother . . ." But I couldn't manage the rest of the sentence.

"It's okay," she promised. "I'm not upset. She loves you, that's all."

She swiveled and we kissed like teenagers, making out under the bridge. It was a wonderful feeling to be grown and yet young. To be married but not settled. To be tied down yet free.

—

MY MOTHER EXAGGERATED. The Piney Woods was about on the level of a Motel 6, a star and a half by objective measure, but you have to throw in another star just for being the only hotel in town. A lifetime ago, I had taken a girl here after prom, hoping to get that virginity thing out of the way. I bagged a lot of groceries at Piggly Wiggly to pay for the room, the bottle of Asti Spumante, and a few other accoutrements of romance. I even swung by the Laundromat for a stack of quarters to operate the Magic Fingers. The night ended up being a comedy of errors. The bed massager ate six quarters before it finally kicked on, rumbling as loud as a lawn mower. Furthermore, my date wore a plantation-era hoop dress that flipped up and hit me in the nose when I was trying to get better acquainted.

After we checked in and settled into our room, I told this story to Celestial, hoping she would laugh. Instead, she said, "Come here, sweetie," and let me rest my head on her bosom, which is kind of exactly what the prom date did.

"I feel like we're camping," I said.

"More like study abroad."

Locking my eyes with hers in the mirror, I spoke. "I was almost born right in this hotel. Olive once worked here, cleaning." Back then, Piney Woods Inn was named the Rebel's Roost, clean, but the confederate flag hung in every room. Scrubbing a bathtub when labor pains kicked in, my mama was determined that I would not start my life under the stars and bars. She clamped her knees shut until the motel owner, a decent man despite the decor, drove her the thirty miles to Alexandria. It was 1969, April 4, a year to the day, and I slept my first night's sleep in an integrated nursery. My mama was proud of that.

"Where was Big Roy?" Celestial asked, as I knew she would.

The question was the whole reason we were here at all, so why did I have such a difficult time answering her? I led her to this question, but once it was asked, I went as noiseless as a rock.

"Was he working?"

Celestial had been sitting in bed sewing more beads onto the mayor's doll, but my silence got her attention. She bit the thread, tied it off, and twisted to look at me. "What's the matter?"

I was still moving my lips with no sound. This wasn't the right place to start this story. *My* story may begin the day I was born, but *the* story goes back further.

"Roy, what is it? What's wrong?"

"Big Roy is not my real father." This was the one short sentence that I promised my mother I would never say aloud.

"What?"

"Biologically speaking."

"But your name?"

"He made a junior out of me when I was a baby."

I got up from the bed and mixed us a couple of drinks—canned juice and vodka. As I stirred the cups with my finger, I couldn't bring myself to meet her eyes, not even in the mirror.

She said, "How long have you known this?"

"They told me before I went to kindergarten. Eloe is a small town, and they didn't want me to hear it on the school yard."

"Is that why you're telling me? So I don't hear it in the street?"

"No," I said. "I'm telling you because I want you to know all my secrets." I returned to the bed and handed her the thin plastic cup. "Cheers."

Not joining me in my pitiful toast, she set the cup on the scarred night-stand and carefully reswaddled the mayor's doll. "Roy, why do you do things like this? We've been married more than a year, and it never occurred to you to share this with me before now?"

I was waiting for the rest, the terse words and tears; maybe I was even looking forward to it. But Celestial only cast her eyes upward and shook her head. She breathed air in, she breathed air out.

"Roy, you're doing this on purpose."

"This? What *this*?"

"You tell me that we're making a family, that I'm the closest person to you, and then you drop a bomb like this."

"It's not a bomb. What difference does it make?" I flipped it as a rhetorical question, but I craved a real true answer. I needed her to say that it didn't make a difference, that I was myself, not my gnarled family tree.

"It's not this one thing. It's the phone numbers in your wallet, the way you don't always wear your ring. Then this. As soon as we get over one thing, there's something else. If I didn't know better, I would think that you were trying to sabotage our marriage, the baby, everything." She said it like it was all my fault, as though it were possible to tango alone.

When I was mad, I didn't raise my voice. Instead, I lowered it to a register that you heard with your bones, not your ears. "Are you sure *you* want to do this? Is this the out you've been waiting for? That's the real question. I tell you that I don't know my daddy and you're having second thoughts about our whole relationship? Look, I didn't tell you because it didn't have anything to do with us."

"There's something wrong with you," she said. Her face in the streaked mirror was wide awake and angry.

"See," I said. "This is why I didn't want to tell you. So now what? You feel like you don't know me because you don't know *my exact genetic profile*? What kind of bourgie shit is that?"

"The issue is that you didn't tell me. I don't care that you don't know who your daddy is."

"I didn't say that I didn't know *who* he is. What are you trying to say about my mother? That she didn't know who she was pregnant for? Really, Celestial? You want to go there?"

"Don't flip the script on semantics," Celestial said. "You're the one who kept a secret the size of Alaska."

"What is there to tell you? My real daddy is Othaniel Jenkins. That's all I got. So now you know everything I know. That's a secret as big as Alaska? More like Connecticut. Rhode Island, maybe."

"Don't twist this around," she said.

"Look," I said. "Have some sympathy. Olive wasn't even seventeen yet. He took advantage of her. He was a grown man."

"I'm talking about me and you. We are married. *Married*. I don't care what the hell his name is. Do I look like I care what your mother . . ."

I turned to look at her without the mediation of the mirror, and what I saw worried me. Her eyes were half-shut and she pressed her lips, preparing to speak, and I instinctively knew I didn't want to hear whatever she was about to say.

"November 17," I said before she could complete her thought.

Other couples use safe words to call a time-out from rough sex, but we used it as a time-out from rough words. If either of us says "November 17," the anniversary of our first date, then all conversation must cease for fifteen minutes. I pulled the trigger because I knew that if she said one more word about my mama, one of us would say something that we couldn't come back from.

Celestial threw up her hands. "Fine. Fifteen minutes."

I stood up and picked up the plastic ice bucket. "I'll go fill this up."

Fifteen minutes is a nice chunk of time to kill. As soon as I was out the door, Celestial was going to call Andre. They met in a playpen when they were too young to even sit up, so they are thick like brother and sister. I know Dre from college, and it was through him that I met Celestial in the first place.

While she fumed to Dre, I walked up to the second floor and set the bucket on the machine and pulled the lever. Ice cubes tumbled out in fits and starts. As I waited, I encountered a woman about Olive's age, heavyset, with a kind, dimpled face. Her arm was trussed up in a cloth sling. "Rotator cuff," she said, explaining that driving was a challenge, but a grand-baby waited on her in Houston, a grandbaby she planned to lift with one good arm. Being the gentleman my mama raised me to be, I carried her ice back to her room, number 206. Because of her injury, she had trouble operating the window, so I lifted the frame and propped it open with the Bible. I had another seven minutes to go, so I went into the bathroom and played plumber, fixing the toilet that was running like Niagara. Leaving, I warned her that the doorknob was loose, that she should double-check to make sure it was locked when I left. She thanked me; I called her ma'am. It was 8:48 p.m. I know this because I checked my watch to see if it was late enough for me to return to my wife.

I tapped on the door at 8:53. Celestial had made us two fresh Cape

Codders. Reaching into the bucket with her naked hand, she added three cubes for each of us. She shook the drinks to spread the chill and then she extended her beautiful arm in my direction.

And this was the last happy evening I would experience for a very long time.

CELESTIAL

Memory is a queer creature, an eccentric curator. I still look back on that night, although not as often as I once did. How long can you live with your face twisted over your shoulder? No matter what people may say, this was not a failure to remember. I'm not sure it is a failure at all.

When I say that I visit the Piney Woods Inn in my waking dreams, I'm not being defensive. It's merely the truth. Like Aretha said, *A woman's only human. . . . She's flesh and blood, just like her man.* No more, no less.

My regret is how hard we argued that night, over his parents, of all things. We had fought harder even before we married, when we were playing at love, but those were tussles about our relationship. At the Piney Woods, we tangled about history, and there is no fair fight to be waged about the past. Knowing something I didn't, Roy called out "November 17," stopping time. When he left with the ice bucket, I was glad for him to go.

I called Andre, and after three rings he picked up and talked me down, sane and civil as always. "Ease up on Roy," he said. "If you lose it every time he tries to come clean, you're encouraging him to lie."

"But," I said, not ready to let go. "He didn't even—"

"You know I'm right," he said without being smug. "But what you don't know is that I'm entertaining a young lady this evening."

"Pardon moi," I said, happy for him.

"Gigolos get lonely, too," he said.

I was still grinning when I hung up the phone.

And I was still smiling when Roy appeared at the door with the ice bucket extended in his arms like a bouquet of roses, and by then my anger had cooled like a forgotten cup of coffee.

"Georgia, I'm sorry," he said, taking the drink from my hand. "This has been burning a hole in my pocket. Think how I feel. You have this perfect family. Your father is a millionaire."

"He didn't always have money," I said, something that I seemed to say at least once a week. Before my father sold his orange juice solution to Minute Maid, we were like any other family in Cascade Heights, what the rest of America thinks of as middle-middle class and what black America calls upper-middle class. No maid. No private school. No trust fund. Just two parents, each with two degrees and, between them, two decent jobs.

"Well, as long as I've known you, you have been a rich man's daughter."

"A million dollars doesn't make you rich-rich," I said. "Real rich people don't have to earn their money."

"Rich-rich, nouveau rich, nigger rich—any kind of rich looks rich from where I'm sitting. There is no way I was going to roll up on your father in his mansion and tell him that I've never met my daddy."

He took a step toward me and I moved toward him.

"It's not a mansion," I said, making my voice soft. "And I told you, my daddy is literally the son of a sharecropper. An Alabama sharecropper at that."

These conversations always caught me off guard, although after a year I should have been accustomed to this fraught song and dance. My mother cautioned me before I got married that Roy and I were from two separate realities. She said that I would constantly have to reassure him that we were, in fact, "equally yoked." Amused by her language, I shared this with Roy, along with a joke about pulling a plow, but he didn't even crack a smile.

"Celestial, your daddy ain't sharing no crops now. And what about your mom? I wasn't going to have her seeing Olive as a teenage mother, left by the side of the road. No way was I going to set my mama up like that."

I closed the space between us, resting my hands on his head, feeling the curve of his scalp. "Look," I said with my lips near his ears. "We're not blackface *Leave It to Beaver*. You know my mother is Daddy's second wife."

"Is that supposed to be some kind of shocker?"

"That's because you don't know the whole story." I took a breath and pushed the words out fast before I could think too much more about them. "My parents got together before Daddy was divorced."

"You saying they were separated . . . or?"

"I'm saying that my mother was his mistress. For a long time. I think like three years or so. My mother was a June bride at the courthouse because her pastor wouldn't perform the ceremony." I have seen the photos. Gloria wears an off-white suit and a veiled pillbox hat. My father looks young and excited. There is no indication of anything but effortless devotion in their smiles. There is no evidence of me, but I'm in the frame, too, hiding behind her yellow chrysanthemum bouquet.

"Damn," he said with a low whistle. "I didn't think Mr. D had it in him. I didn't think Gloria—"

"Don't talk about my mama," I said. "You don't talk about mine, and I won't talk about yours."

"I'm not holding anything against Gloria, like I know you wouldn't hold anything against Olive, right?"

"There's something to hold against my daddy. Gloria says that he didn't tell her he was married until they had been dating a whole month."

She explained this to me when I was eighteen, when I was leaving Howard University after a messy love affair. Helping me seal cardboard cartons, my mother had said, "Love is the enemy of sound judgment, and occasionally this is in service of the good. Did you know that your father had certain obligations when we met?" I think of this as the first time my mother had ever spoken to me as one woman to another. Wordlessly, we swore each other to secrecy, and until now, I had never betrayed her confidence.

"A month, that's not a lot of time. She could have walked away," Roy said. "That is, if she wanted to."

"She didn't want to," I said. "According to Gloria, by then she was *irreversibly in love*." As I told this to Roy, I imitated my mother in the tone she used in public, elocution-class crisp, not the shaky register in which she had shared this detail.

"What?" Roy said. "Irreversibly? The warranty was up after thirty days and she couldn't send him back?"

"Gloria said that looking back on it, she's glad he didn't tell her because she never would have gone out with a married man and Daddy turned out to be the One."

"I can get that, in a way." Roy raised my hand to his lips. "Sometimes when you like where you end up, you don't care how you got there."

"No," I said. "The journey matters. Let my mama tell it. My daddy lied to her for her own good. I never want to feel grateful about being deceived."

"Fair enough," he said. "But think about it 2.0. If your daddy didn't hide his situation, you wouldn't be here. And if you weren't here, where would I be?"

"I still don't like it. I want us to be on the up-and-up. I don't want our kid to inherit all of our secrets."

Roy pumped his fist in the air. "Did you hear yourself?"

"What?"

"You said 'our kid.'"

"Roy, stop being silly. Listen to what I'm trying to say."

"Don't try and take it back. You said '*our kid.*'"

"Roy," I said. "I'm for real. No more secrets, okay? If you got anything else, spill it."

"I got nothing."

And with that, we reconciled, as we had so many times before. There is a song about that, too: *Break up to make up, that's all we do.* Did I imagine that this was our pattern for all time? That we would grow old together, accusing and forgiving? Back then, I didn't know what forever looked like. Maybe I don't even know now. But that night in the Piney Woods, I believed that our marriage was a fine-spun tapestry, fragile but fixable. We tore it often and mended it, always with a silken thread, lovely but sure to give way.

We climbed into the small bed, a little buzzed from our jerry-rigged cocktails. Agreeing that the bedspread was suspect, we kicked it to the floor and lay facing each other. Lying there, tracing his brow bone with my fingers, I thought of my parents and even Roy's. Their marriages were cut from less refined but more durable cloth, something like cotton-sack burlap, bound with gray twine. How superior Roy and I felt that night in this rented room of our own, enjoying the braid of our affection. I am ashamed at the memory and the hot blood heats my face, even if I'm only dreaming.

Then, I didn't know that our bodies can know things before they happen, so when my eyes suddenly filled with tears, I thought this was the unpredictable effect of emotion. It washed over me sometimes when I was browsing fabric stores or preparing a meal—I would think about Roy, his bowlegged walk or the time he wrestled a robber to the ground, costing him a precious front tooth. When memory tapped me, I let go a few tears, no matter where I was, blaming it on allergies or an eyelash gone rogue. So when my emotion filled my eyes and closed my throat on that night in Eloe, I thought it was passion rather than premonition.

When we planned the trip, I'd thought we'd be staying at his mother's, so I didn't pack lingerie. Instead, I wore a white slip, which would have to do for our game of undressing. Roy smiled and said he loved me. His voice caught, like whatever had taken hold of me had grabbed him, too. As silly as we were, young as we were, we thought it was merely desire. This thing we enjoyed in abundance.

So there we were, not sleeping yet spent, occupying some in-between restful affection state, full of possibility. I sat up in bed next to him, inhaling the odors of the day—river mud, the musk of hotel soap, and then the scent of him, the marker of his personal chemistry, and then my own. It's a fragrance that burrowed into the fibers of our sheets. I eased close to him and kissed his shut lids. I was thinking that I was lucky. I didn't mean that I was lucky in the way that single women made me feel when they reminded me how fortunate I was to find a marrying man these days, and not lucky in the way of magazine features lamenting how few "good" black men there were remaining, providing a bullet-point litany of the ineligible—dead, gay, in jail, married to white women. Yes, I was fortunate by all those measures, but in my marriage to Roy, I felt blessed in the old-fashioned sense, in the way that anyone would be in finding someone whose smell you enjoyed.

Did we love so forcefully that night because we knew or because we didn't? Was there an alarm from the future, a furious bell without its clapper? Did this hopeless bell manage to generate a breeze, causing me to reach to the floor to find my slip and use it to cover myself? Did some subtle warning cause Roy to turn and pin me to his side with his heavy arm? In his sleep, he mumbled something but did not wake.

Did I want a child? Did I lie in bed that night imagining an eager clump of cells dividing and then dividing again until I was somebody's mother and Roy was somebody's daddy, and Big Roy, Olive, and my parents were somebody's grandparents? I did wonder what was going on inside my body, but I won't say what I hoped for. Is motherhood really optional when you're a perfectly normal woman married to a perfectly normal man? When I was in college, I took on a volunteer position at a literacy organization and tutored teen mothers. It was hard work and tended to be disheartening, as the young women seldom earned their diplomas. My supervisor said to me over espresso and croissants, "Have a baby and save the race!" He was smiling, but he wasn't kidding. "If girls like this are having all the kids, and girls like you stay childless and fancy-free, what's going to happen to us as a people?" Without thinking, I promised to do my part.

This is not to say that I didn't want to be a mother. It's not to say that I did. This is only to say that I was certain that the check would come due.

So while Roy slept with confidence, I closed my eyes with trepidation. I was still awake when the door burst open. I know they kicked it in, but the written report says that a front-desk clerk handed over the key and the door was opened in a civilized manner. But who knows what is true? I remember my husband asleep in our room while a woman six years older than his mother says she slept lightly in room 206, worried because the door didn't seem quite secure. She told herself she was being paranoid but couldn't convince her eyes to stay closed. Before midnight, a man twisted the knob, knowing that he could. It was dark, but she believed she recognized Roy, the man she met at the ice machine. The man who told her he had been fighting with his wife. She said that this was not her first time finding herself at the mercy of a man, but it would be the last. Roy, she said, may be smart, and he may have learned by watching TV how to cover his tracks, but he couldn't erase her memory.

But she couldn't erase mine either. Roy was with me all night. She doesn't know who hurt her, but I know who I married.

I MARRIED ROY Othaniel Hamilton, whom I met for the first time when I was in college. Our connection wasn't immediate. He considered himself a playboy in those days, and even at age nineteen, I was not one to play with. I'd come to Spelman as a transfer student after the one-year disaster at Howard University in DC. So much for me leaving home. My mother, an alumna herself, insisted that this was where I would cultivate new, bone-deep friendships, but I stuck close with Andre, who was literally the boy next door. We had been close since we were three months old, bathing together in the kitchen sink.

Andre was the one who introduced me to Roy, although it wasn't quite on purpose. They had been next-door neighbors in Thurman Hall, on the far side of campus. I often stayed nights in Andre's room, strictly platonic, although no one believed us. He slept atop the covers, while I huddled under the blankets. None of it makes sense now, but this is how Dre and I always were.

Before Roy and I were properly introduced, a sex-breathy voice on the other side of the wall pronounced his whole name. Roy. Othaniel. Hamilton.

Andre said, "You think he asked her to say that?"

I snorted. "Othaniel?"

"Doesn't strike me as a spontaneous utterance."

We giggled as the twin bed thumped against the wall. "I think she's faking it."

"If she is," Andre said, "then they all are."

I didn't meet Roy in person for another month.

Again, I was in Andre's room. Roy came by at 10 a.m., trying to hustle up some change to do his laundry. He came in without the courtesy of a knock.

"Oh, excuse me, ma'am," Roy said in a way that sounded like a surprised question.

"My sister," Andre said.

"Play sister?" Roy wanted to know, sizing up the dynamic.

"If you want to know who I am, ask me." I must have looked a sight, wearing Andre's maroon-and-white T-shirt and my hair tucked beneath a satin bonnet, but I had to speak up for myself.

"Okay, who are you?"

"Celestial Davenport."

"I'm Roy Hamilton."

"Roy *Othaniel* Hamilton, from what I hear through the wall."

After that, he and I stared at each other, waiting for a cue to show us what type of story this was going to be. Finally, he looked away and asked Andre for a case quarter. I flipped over on my stomach, bent my knees, and crossed my legs at the ankle.

"You something else," Roy said.

When Roy was gone, Andre said, "You know that Gomer Pyle thing is an act."

"Clearly," I said. Something about him was dangerous, and after my experience at Howard, I wanted no part of danger.

I suppose it wasn't our time because I didn't speak with or even think about Roy Othaniel Hamilton again for another four years, when college felt like a photo album memory from another era. When we reconnected, it wasn't that he was so different. It's just that what felt like peril then now morphed into something that I labeled "realness," something for which I developed a bottomless appetite.

—

BUT WHAT IS real? Was it our uneventful first impression? Or the day in New York, of all places, where we found each other once again? Or did things "get real" when we married, or was it the day that the prosecutor in a little nowhere town declared Roy to be a flight risk? The state declared that though he may have roots in Louisiana, his home was in Atlanta, so he was held without bond or bail. At this pronouncement, Roy spat out a caustic laugh. "So *now* roots are irrelevant?"

Our lawyer, friend of my family but paid handsomely just the same, promised me that I wasn't going to lose my man. Uncle Banks made motions, filed papers, and objected. But still, Roy slept behind bars one hundred nights before he was brought to trial. For one month, I remained in Louisiana, living with my in-laws, sleeping in the room that could have saved us this trouble. I waited and I sewed. I called Andre. I called my parents. When I sent the mayor his doll, I couldn't bring myself to seal the flaps on the sturdy cardboard box. Big Roy did it for me and the memory of ripping tape troubled my sleep that night and many nights to come.

"If this doesn't go the way we want it to," Roy said the day before his trial, "I don't want you to wait for me. Keep making your dolls and doing what you need to do."

"This is going to work out," I promised. "You didn't do it."

"I'm looking at so much time. I can't ask you to throw your life away for me." His words and his eyes were speaking two different languages, like someone saying no while nodding his head yes.

"No one is going to throw anything away," I said.

I had faith in those days. I believed in things.

ANDRE SHOWED UP for us. He had been a witness at our wedding and a character witness at trial. Dre let me cut his hair, handing me the scissors to saw through the dreads he had been growing for the last four years. At our wedding, they had been rebellious little nubs, but when I cut them off they were finally responding to gravity, pointing toward his collar. When I was done, he walked his fingers through the choppy curls that remained.

The next day we took our seats in the courtroom, costumed to seem as innocent as possible. My parents were there, and Roy's, too. Olive was dressed for church, and Big Roy sat beside her looking poor-but-honest. Like Andre, my own father groomed himself, and he, for once, appeared to be "equally yoked" to my elegant mother. Watching Roy, I could see he was an obvious match for us. It wasn't just the cut of his coat or the break of his hem against the fine leather of his shoes; it was his face, shaven clean, and his eyes, innocent and afraid, unaccustomed to being at the mercy of the state.

The time in the county jail shrank him; the boyish chub of his cheek was gone, revealing a squared-off jaw that I didn't know he had. Strangely enough, the leanness made him look more powerful than wasted. The only thing that gave him away as a man on trial, rather than a man on his way to work, was his poor fingers. He'd chewed his nails down to the soft meat and started in on his cuticles. Sweet Roy. The only thing that my good man ever hurt was his own hands.

WHAT I KNOW is this: they didn't believe me. Twelve people and not one of them took me at my word. There in front of the room, I explained Roy couldn't have raped the woman in room 206 because we had been together. I told them about the Magic Fingers that wouldn't work, about the movie that played on the snowy television. The prosecutor asked me what we had been fighting about. Rattled, I looked to Roy and to both our mothers. Banks objected, so I didn't have to answer, but the pause made it appear that I was concealing something rotten at the pit of our very young marriage. Even before I stepped down from the witness stand, I knew that I had failed him. Maybe I wasn't appealing enough. Not dramatic enough. Too not-from-around-here. Who knows? Uncle Banks, coaching me, said, "Now is not the time to be articulate. Now is the time to give it up. No filter, all heart. No matter what you're asked, what you want the jury to see is why you married him."

I tried, but I didn't know how to be anything other than "well spoken" in front of strangers. I wish I could have brought a selection of my art, the Man Moving series, all images of Roy—the marble, the dolls, and a few watercolors. I would say, "This is who he is to me. Isn't he beautiful? Isn't he gentle?" But all I had were words, which are as light and flimsy as air. As I took my seat beside Andre, not even the black lady juror would look at me.

It turns out that I watch too much television. I was expecting a scientist to come and testify about DNA. I was looking for a pair of good-looking detectives to burst into the courtroom at the last minute, whispering something urgent to the prosecutor. Everyone would see that this was a big mistake, a major misunderstanding. We would all be shaken but appeased. I fully believed that I would leave the courtroom with my husband beside me. Secure in our home, we would tell people how no black man is really safe in America.

Twelve years is what they gave him. We would be forty-three years old when he was released. I couldn't even imagine myself at such an age. Roy understood that twelve years was an eternity because he sobbed right there at the defendants' table. His knees gave way, and he fell into his chair. The judge paused and demanded that Roy bear this news on his feet. He stood again and cried, not like a baby, but in the way that only a grown man can cry, from the bottom of his feet up through his torso and finally through his mouth. When a man wails like that you know it's all the tears that he was never allowed to shed, from Little League disappointment to teenage heartbreak, all the way to whatever injured his spirit just last year.

As Roy howled, my fingers kept worrying a rough patch of skin beneath my chin, a souvenir of scar tissue. When they did what I remember as kicking in the door, what everyone else remembers as opening it with a plastic key, after the door was opened, however it was opened, we were both pulled from the bed. They dragged Roy into the parking lot, and I followed, lunging for him, wearing nothing but the white slip. Somebody pushed me to the ground and my chin hit the pavement. My slip rode up showing my everything to everyone as my tooth sank into the soft of my bottom lip. Roy was on the asphalt beside me, barely beyond my grasp, speaking words that didn't reach my ears. I don't know how long we lay there, parallel like burial plots. Husband. Wife. What God has brought together, let no man tear asunder.

Dear Roy,

I'm writing this letter sitting at the kitchen table. I'm alone in a way that's more than the fact that I am the only living person within these walls. Up until now, I thought I knew what was and wasn't possible. Maybe that's what innocence is, having no way to predict the pain of the future. When something happens that eclipses the imaginable, it changes a person. It's like the difference between a raw egg and a scrambled egg. It's the same thing, but it's not the same at all. That's the best way that I can put it. I look in the mirror and I know it's me, but I can't quite recognize myself.

Sometimes it's exhausting for me to simply walk into the house. I try and calm myself, remember that I've lived alone before. Sleeping by myself didn't kill me then and will not kill me now. But this is what loss has taught me of love. Our house isn't simply *empty*, our home *has been emptied*. Love makes a place in your life, it makes a place for itself in your bed. Invisibly, it makes a place in your body, rerouting all your blood vessels, throbbing right alongside your heart. When it's gone, nothing is whole again.

Before I met you, I was not lonely, but now I'm so lonely I talk to the walls and sing to the ceiling.

They said that you can't receive mail for at least a month. Still, I'll write to you every night.

Yours,
Celestial

Roy O. Hamilton Jr.
PRA 4856932
Parson Correctional Center
3751 Lauderdale Woodyard Rd.
Jemison, LA 70648

Dear Celestial, aka Georgia,

I don't think I have written a letter to anyone since I was in high school and assigned a French pen pal. (That whole thing lasted about ten minutes.) I know for sure that this is the first time I ever wrote a love letter and that's what this is going to be.

Celestial, I love you. I miss you. I want to come home to you. Look at me, telling you the things you already know. I'm trying to write something on this paper that will make you remember me—the real me, not the man you saw standing in a broke-down country courtroom, broke down myself. I was too ashamed to turn toward you, but now I wish I had, because right now I would do anything for one more look.

This love letter thing is uphill for me. I have never even seen one unless you count the third grade: Do you like me __ yes __ no. (Don't answer that, ha!) A love letter is supposed to be like music or like Shakespeare, but I don't know anything about Shakespeare. But for real, I want to tell you what you mean to me, but it's like trying to count the seconds of a day on your fingers and toes.

Why didn't I write you love letters all the while, so I could be in practice? Then I would know what to do. That's how I feel every day here, like I don't know what to do or how to do it.

I have always let you know how much I care, right? You never had to wonder. I'm not a man for words. My daddy showed me that you *do* for a woman. Remember that time when you damn near had a nervous breakdown because it looked like the hickory-nut tree in the front yard was thinking about dying? Where I'm from, we don't believe in spending money on pets, let alone trees. But I couldn't bear to see you fret, so I hired a tree doctor. See, in my mind, that was a love letter.

The first thing I did as your husband was to "sit you down," like the old folks say. You were wasting your time and your talents doing temp work. You wanted to sew, so I made it happen. No strings. That was my love letter to say, "I got this. Make your art. Rest yourself. Whatever you need to do."

But now all I have is this paper and this raggedy ink pen. It's a ballpoint, but they take away the casing so you just have the nib and this plastic tube of ink. I'm looking at it, thinking, *This* is all I have to be a husband with?

But here I am trying.

Love,

Roy

Dear Georgia,

Hello from Mars! That's not really a joke. The dorms here are all named for planets. (This is the truth. I couldn't make this up.) Your letters were delivered to me yesterday. Each and every one, and I was very happy to receive them. Overjoyed. I am not sure even where to start.

I haven't even been here three months, and already I have had three cell partners. The one I have now says he's here for good, and he says it like he has some type of inside track. His name is Walter. He's been incarcerated for most of his adult life, so he knows what's what around here. I write letters for him but not gratis. It's not that I'm not compassionate, but you get no respect when you do things for free. (This I learned in the workforce, and it's ten times as true in here.) Walter doesn't have money, so I let him give me cigarettes. (Don't make that face. I know you, girl. I don't smoke them. I trade them for other things—like ramen noodles. I kid you not.) The letters I write for Walter are to women he meets through personal ads. You would be surprised how many ladies want to pen-pal with convicts. (Don't get jealous, ha ha.) Sometimes I get irritated, staying up so late answering all his questions. He says he used to live in Eloe, so he wants me to bring him up to date. When I said that I haven't lived in Eloe since before I went to college, he says he has never set foot on a college campus and he wants me to tell him all about that, too. He was even curious about how I got the name Roy. It's not like my name is Patrice Lumumba, something that needs explaining, but Walter is what Olive would call "a character." We call him the "Ghetto Yoda" because he's always getting philosophical. I accidentally said "Country Yoda" and he got mad. I swear it was an honest mistake, and it's one I won't make again. But it's all good. He looks out for me, saying that "us bowlegged brothers got to stick together." (You should see his legs. Worse than mine.)

So that's all I got in terms of atmosphere. Or all that I want you to know about. Don't ask me questions about the details. Just suffice it to say that it's bad in here. Even if you killed somebody, you don't deserve to spend more than a couple of years in this place. *Please tell your uncle to get on it.*

There is so much here that makes you stop and say, "Hmm . . ." Like there are about fifteen hundred men in this facility (mostly brothers), and that's the same number of students at "Dear Morehouse." I don't want to be some kind of crazy conspiracy nut, but it's hard not to think about things in that way. For one, prison is full of people who call themselves "dropping science," and second, things here are so bent that you think somebody must be bending it on purpose. My mother wrote to me, too, and you know her theory—"the devil stays busy." My dad thinks it's the Klan. Well, not the Klan specifically with hoods and crosses but more like Ameri–KKKa. I don't know what I think. Besides thinking that I miss you.

I finally got to make my visitors' list and right at the top is you, Celestial GLORIANA Davenport. (They want your full government name.) I'll put Dre on, too—does he have a middle name? It's probably something religious like Elijah. You know he's my boy, but when you come the first time, come by yourself. Meanwhile, keep the letters flowing, baby. How did I forget that you have such a pretty handwriting? If you decide not to be a famous artist, you could go be a schoolteacher with that penmanship. You must bear down on the pen because the paper buckles. At night, when the lights are out—not that they are ever really out—they make it dark enough that you can't read but too light to really sleep—but when they cut the lights off, I run my fingers over your letters and try to read them like Braille. (Romantic, right?)

And thank you for putting money on my books. You have to buy everything you think you might want in here. Underwear, socks. Whatever you need to try and make your life a little better. This isn't a hint, but it would be nice to have a clock radio, and of course the main thing that would make my life a little better would be seeing you.

Love,
Roy

PS: When I first started calling you Georgia, it was because I could tell you were homesick. Now I call you that because I'm the one missing home and home is you.

Dear Roy,

By the time you get this letter, I will have already been to visit because I'm mailing it on the way out of town. Andre has filled the tank and the car is stocked with snacks. I have practically memorized the visitors' guide. There are clothing regulations and they are extremely specific. My favorite detail is that "gauchos and culottes are strictly prohibited." I bet you don't even know what those are. I recall them being very fashionable when I was in the fourth grade, and thankfully, they have never come back in style. To summarize the dress code: show no skin. Don't wear an underwire bra unless you want to fail the metal detector test and get sent home. I imagine it's like going to the airport . . . on your way to a convent. But I'm ready.

It goes without saying that I know this country and I know history. I even remember a man who came to speak at Spelman who had been wrongfully imprisoned for decades. Did you see him? He spoke along with the white woman who pointed the finger at him in the first place. They both got saved or something. Even though they stood right there in front of me, they felt like a lesson from the past, a phantom from Mississippi. What did it have to do with us, college students piled in the chapel for convocation credit? Now I wish I could remember what they said. I'm bringing this up because I knew that things like this happen to people, but by *people*, I didn't mean us.

Do you ever think about the one who accused you? I wish I could have a sit-down with her. Somebody attacked her in that room. I don't think she's making that up, you could tell that just from her voice. But that somebody wasn't you. Now she's gone back to Chicago or whatever, wishing she never stopped in Eloe, Louisiana, and she isn't the only one. But you don't need me to tell you this. You know where you are and you know what you didn't do.

Uncle Banks is preparing the first appeal. He reminds me that it could be worse. Many people have run-ins with the law and they don't live to tell the tale. There's no appealing a cop's bullet. So at least there's that, but it's not much.

Do you know that I'm praying for you? Can you feel it at night when I get down on my knees beside my bed like I did when I was a little girl? I close my eyes and I can picture you the way you were when we were last together, all the way down to the freckle over your eyebrow. I have a notebook where I wrote down every word that we said to each other before we fell asleep that night. I wrote it down so when you get home, we can pick up where we left off.

True confession: I am extremely nervous. I know it's not the same, but it reminds me of when we were first going out, when we were trying to be a long-distance couple and you sent me a ticket. After all the buildup with our phone conversations and email, I wasn't sure what to expect when we finally saw each other again. Obviously it all worked out, but I feel the same way writing this letter. So I want to say in advance that even if things are awkward between us when we finally lay eyes on each other, please know that it's because it's all very new and I'm so agitated. Nothing has changed. I love you as much as I did the day I married you. And I will always.

Yours,
Celestial

Dear Georgia,

Thank you for coming to visit me. I know it wasn't easy to get here. When I saw you sitting there in the visitor's room, all classy and out of place, I have never been happier to see anyone. I could have cried like a little girl.

I won't lie. It was strange to have to see each other for the first time in front of so many people. And the truth is that I was quiet because you said that you didn't want to talk about what was really on my mind. I didn't push it because I didn't want to ruin our time together. And it wasn't ruined. I was very glad to see you. Walter teased me all the next day about being lit up like a Christmas tree. But I'm sorry, Celestial. I have to tell you what has been troubling my soul.

I know that I said that I didn't want any son of mine having to say his daddy was in jail. You know I don't know much about my biological father except his name and that he is probably a criminal. But since Big Roy raised me as his own, I didn't have to wear shame around my neck like a giant clock. Sometimes, though, in the back of my mind I could hear that clock ticking. I was also thinking about this kid I knew named Myron whose father was in Angola. Myron was teeny-tiny and his clothes were all donated by the church. One time I saw him in one of my cast-off jackets. They nicknamed him "Chickie" because his daddy was a jail*bird*. To this day, he answers to "Chickie" like it's his real name.

But our kid would have had Mr. D and Gloria, Andre, and my family, too. That's a village and half right there to take care of him until I win my freedom. He would have been something else for me to look forward to.

I can see why you didn't want to talk about it. What's done is done. But I can't stop thinking about him. Of course, I don't know that the baby was a boy, but my gut is telling me he was my junior.

This is painful to ask, but if we had more faith, would things have worked out differently? What if it was a test? What if we kept the baby? I could have made it home in time to see him crown into the world, innocent and bald-headed. This whole ordeal would just be a story we would tell him when he was older, to teach him how to be careful as a black man in these United States. When we decided to have the abortion, it was like we were accepting that things weren't going to work out in the courtroom. And when we gave up, God gave up on us, too. Not that He ever gives up, but you know what I mean.

You don't have to answer this. But tell me, who knows about it? It doesn't matter, but I'm curious. I put your parents on my visitors' list and I wonder if they know what we did.

Georgia, I know I can't make you talk about what you don't want to talk about, but you should know what it was that was blocking my throat so I couldn't hardly talk.

Still, it was beautiful to see you. I love you more than I can say here.

Your husband,
Roy

Dear Roy,

Yes, baby, yes, I think about it, but not constantly. You can't sit with something like that every single day. But when I do, it is with sadness more than regret. I understand that you're in pain, but please do not ever send me another letter like the one you sent last week. Have you forgotten the county jail? It smelled like pee and bleach and all these desperate women and kids surrounding

us. Your complexion was so gray that you looked like you had
been powdered over with ashes. Your hands were rough like alliga-
tor skin, and you couldn't get any cream to stop the cracking and
bleeding. Have you forgotten all of that? Uncle Banks had to find
you a new suit because you dropped so much weight waiting for
your "speedy trial." You were your own ghost.

When I told you I was pregnant, it wasn't good news, not in the
way it should have been. I hoped the idea would stir you, bring you
back to this life. You did come back but only to moan into your
tight fists. Remember your own words: *You can't have it. Not like
this.* This is what you said to me, your grip on my wrist so tight
my fingers tingled. You can't tell me that you didn't mean what
you said.

You didn't mention a boy named Chickie or your "real" dad, but
I saw the forest, if not the trees. This is something that I was sure
about at the time, and I'm still mostly sure about now: I don't want
to be a mother of a child born against his father's wishes, and you
made your wishes clear.

Roy, you know I hated to do it. However much it hurts you,
remember that I am the one it happened to. I am the one who
was pregnant. I'm the one who isn't pregnant anymore. Whatever
you feel, think about what I must feel. Just like you can say I don't
know what it is like to be in prison, you don't know what it's like to
go to a clinic and sign your name in the book.

I'm dealing with it in the way that I do, through my work. I've
been sewing like a crazy person, late at night. The dolls remind me
of a doll I had when I was little, when you could go to Cleveland,
Georgia, and adopt a "baby." They were a little beyond our means,
but Gloria and I went out there to at least have a look. When we
saw all the dolls on display, I said, "Is this summer camp for dolls?"
And she said, no, it was like an orphanage. I was so sheltered, I

didn't even know what an orphan was, and when she explained, I sobbed and asked to take all the dolls home.

I don't think of my dolls as orphans; they're babies that happen to live in my sewing room. I've made forty-two so far. I'm thinking I'll try and sell them at craft fairs, at cost, about fifty dollars each. These are for children, not collectors. And truth be told, I want to get them out of the house. I can't have them staring at me all day, but I can't stop making them either.

You asked me who knows. Are you asking me who knows what I did or who knows that you asked me to? Do you think I took out a billboard? If you're a grown woman and you have more than ten dollars in the bank, nobody understands why you can't have a baby. But how could I think about being a mother with my husband in prison? I know you're innocent, there is not one doubt in my mind, but I also know that you're not here. This isn't a game, a drill, or a movie. I don't know that it hit me until I was two weeks late and getting ready to pee on a stick.

I didn't tell anyone but Andre. All he said was, "You can't go by yourself." He drove me and he covered my head with his jacket as we made our way past the chanting demonstrators and their disgusting signs. When it was done, he was waiting for me. Afterward, in the car, he said something that I want to share with you. He said, "Don't cry. This isn't your last chance." Roy, he's right. You and I will have babies in the future. We will be parents. Like they say, "A girl for you, a boy for me," or was it the other way around? But when you get out, we can have ten babies if that's what you want. I promise you that.

I love you. I miss you.

Yours,
Celestial

Dear Georgia,

I know I said that I would let this go. But I have one more thing to say. We took our family and pulled it out by the roots. Reading your letter, you make it sound like I forced you, like you came into the county jail excited to be having my child. You said, "I'm pregnant," like it was cancer. What was I supposed to say? And besides, let's say that I did push you in one particular direction, don't act like you were being an obedient little woman. I'll never forget our wedding when, in front of everyone, you got into a stare-down with the minister who asked you to say the word *obey*. If he didn't back down, we would still be standing at the altar, on the outskirts of matrimony.

That day at the County, we had a discussion. You and me. Two grown people. It was not about me telling you what to do. As soon as I mentioned the idea of not keeping the baby, I saw the relief on your face. I loosened my grip and you snatched the ball and ran with it. Everything you remember is true. I said what I said, but you didn't try and argue the other side. You didn't say that we could make it. You didn't say that this was a child *we* created. You didn't say that maybe I could be free by the time he was born. You tucked your head and said, "I can do what has to be done."

Yes, I get it. Your body, your choice. All of that they taught you at Spelman College. Fine.

But we should have known there would be some consequences. I'll take responsibility for my role in it, but it wasn't me by myself.

Love,
Roy

Dear Roy,

Some background:

In college, my roommate told me that men want a woman to be a "virgin with experience," and therefore you should never talk about your past relationships with a man because he wants to pretend like they never happened. So I know that you're not going to want to hear this, but I feel like you're forcing me to share this sad story.

Roy, you know that I spent a year at Howard University before Spelman, but you don't know why I left. At Howard, I took Art of the African Diaspora, and my teacher, Raul Gomez, was the diaspora himself. A black man from Honduras, he spoke Spanish when he was excited and he was always excited about art. He said that the reason he didn't finish his dissertation was because he couldn't bear to write about Elizabeth Catlett in English. He was forty, married, and handsome. I was eighteen, flattered, and dumb as a box of rocks.

When I figured out that I was pregnant, we were unofficially engaged. I had no ring, but I had his word, but—there is always a "but" isn't it? *But* he needed to get divorced and he didn't think that after twelve years of marriage, his wife should have to bear the shame of a "love child." (And here I was, encouraged that he used the word *love*.)

I believe that you know where this story is going. It's clear to me, too, looking back on it. I was recovering when he came to my dorm room to tell me that we were done. He was all dressed up in a dark blue suit and a tie the color of ashes. I was wearing sweatpants and a baggy T-shirt. He showed up outfitted like the Harlem Renaissance and I didn't even have shoes on my feet. He said, "You're a beautiful girl. You turned my head and made me forget right from wrong." And then he left.

He was gone, and I was gone, too. It was like I slipped on a patch of ice on a dark road inside my own mind. I stopped going to his class and then I stopped going to all classes.

After a couple of weeks, one of my dad's friends from the chemistry department alerted my parents. Black colleges are serious about that in loco parentis thing. My folks were up to DC faster than you can say "civil lawsuit." (Yes, Uncle Banks was the attorney. The suit was frivolous, but the goal was for Raul to lose his job.)

The experience broke me down, Roy. I came back to Atlanta and just sat there for a month. Andre would come over and I didn't even want to talk to him. My parents were seriously thinking about sending me somewhere. It was Sylvia who snapped me out of it. (Every girl needs a wise and reassuring aunt.) I was telling her the same kinds of things that you're telling me now—how I thought I jinxed my own life. That if I had been brave enough to keep the baby, I would have been rewarded with what I really hoped for, which was to be Mrs. Gomez. That life was a test that I kept failing.

Sylvia said, "I am not about to judge you. That's between you and Jesus. Sugar, tell me the honest truth—do you wish you had a baby right now?" I really couldn't say. The main thing was that I didn't want to feel the way I was feeling. Then Sylvia said, "When you took the test, were you hoping for a plus or a minus?" And I said, "Minus."

So she said, "Look. What is over with is over with. What are you going to do? Get in a time machine? Go back to last fall and un-fuck him?"

And then she pulled out a dozen socks, embroidery thread, and cotton batting. This part of the story you know, everyone does. She showed me how to make the sock dolls that would be donated to Grady Hospital to comfort the crack babies. We went over there sometimes and held the poor little ones who were so strung out that they rattled in my arms.

It wasn't charity. I sewed those first dolls to work the guilt out of my system. I never thought of *poupées*, commissions, contests, or exhibitions. I felt like every time I made something to comfort a motherless infant, I was repaying the universe for what I did. After a while, the dolls and DC weren't connected anymore. I had a weight pressing on my soul and I dolled my way out from under it.

But I didn't forget, promising myself I would never find myself in that predicament again. For a while, I was scared to try, thinking that maybe I ruined myself, not in a medical way but in a spiritual one.

Roy, I know that we had a choice, but really, we didn't have a choice. I mourned as though I had miscarried. My body apparently was fertile soil, but my life was not. You may feel that you're carrying a burden, but I shoulder a load as well.

So now you know. We are bearing two different crosses.

And can we please please please stop talking about it. If you care for me at all, you will never bring this up again.

Yours,
Celestial

Dear Georgia,
Two years down and ten to go. (This is my idea of a joke.)
Finally, Banks will go forward with the appeal. I hate thinking

about how much money your parents are shelling out for this. They are getting a "friends & family" rate, but still, I imagine the number clicking by like an odometer. But if things go well with the state appellate court, I'll be out of here and I'll take whatever job I can find and pay your daddy back. Seriously. I don't care if I have to bag groceries.

See, this is why I like letters better than email. Anything I write down is a promissory note and a paper receipt, signed, sealed, delivered. We can only get email in the library for sixty-five minutes a week and there is always someone waiting or someone looking over your shoulder. Besides, I like to use that time to write emails for hire. You know what I got paid with last week? An onion. I know you're going to think this is crazy, but onion is rare to come by in here and prison cuisine tastes better with a little bit of flavoring. To get it, I wrote a long email for this guy; it was part mash note and part fund-raising pitch. If it yielded the cash he was hoping for, he was going to get me an onion. Of course I split the onion with Walter, since he acted as a broker for the whole exchange. You should have seen it. If the hunchback of Notre Dame could be a vegetable, it would be that funky little onion. You don't want to know what we cooked up in our cell that night, but I know you're curious, so I'll try and explain. It's a casserole that you make out of ramen noodles, crunched-up Doritos, onion, and Vienna sausages. Everybody chips in what they have, and when it's done, you divide it up. Walter is the chef. I promise that it tastes better than it sounds.

Another thing about paper letters is that I can write them at night. I wish more folks were in the market for old-fashioned mail, because it could be a little cottage industry. The problem is that people on the outside don't write back and the whole point of sending a letter is to get something in return. Email is different. Most anyone will at least shoot back a response, no matter how short. You always answer my letters and you know I appreciate it.

Can you send me some pictures? I want some photos from before and a couple of new ones.

Love,
Roy

Dear Roy,

I got your letter yesterday—did you get mine? As promised, here are a few photos. The snapshots from back in the day, you will recognize. I can't believe how thin I was. Since you asked for them, here are some new ones. Andre is into photography these days, so that's why they look so artsy and serious. He's not about to quit his day job, but I think he's good. I think this is all due to his girlfriend—a twenty-one-year-old who thinks she can make a living making documentaries. (But who am I to talk? I'm in my thirties and I earn my living doll making!) Besides, if Dre likes it, I dig it, and Dre is smitten. But twenty-one? She makes me feel like a senior citizen.

Speaking of old: these pictures. You can see that I have put on some weight. My parents are both so slim, but it's like some recessive gene snuck up on me and smacked me on my behind. It's my own fault. I've been sewing like crazy, which means I spend the whole day sitting down. But I have so many orders to fill!

Things have reached critical mass and I've taken steps to secure a retail space. It's not quite like you imagined—more boutique than toy store. Think of it as high end for toys but low end for art. I have to say that it's rewarding to give a pretty brown doll to a pretty brown girl and watch her squeeze and kiss it. It's different from watching a collector take it away in a wooden crate.

I wonder if maybe I'm compromising. It's art but not Art.

Look at me, worried about selling out before I even hang out my shingle.

And speaking of money, I think you know what I'm going to say next. I have exactly one investor, and it is my father. Because he is sinking so much capital into it, we put everything in his name. I had to remind him that a silent partner is supposed to be quiet. He wanted the sign to say "Pou-Pays" so people would know how to pronounce it. (Ha! No.)

I know that we planned to start a business ourselves, without assistance, but things happen, and besides, my parents *want* to do this for me. All this hardheaded independence isn't helping me or anyone else. Daddy and I went to the bank; we talked to a real-estate broker. Assuming there are no hiccoughs, Poupées will open up in about six months. It's not our dream, but it's dream-adjacent. Like Daddy says, I "could make some real money."

Okay, back to the pictures. I keep changing the subject because I don't really like the way that they came out. I feel like they show too much. Maybe you know what I mean? This is what I appreciate about Dre's work, as long as the photos are of other people. He took a picture of my father and you could see the last fifty years in the lines of his forehead. Everything was there, Alabama, fatherhood, his whole black Horatio Alger thing. (He doesn't like his portrait either, but I think it's stunning.)

The pictures I chose are all rated PG so you can pass them around, but when I look at them, I really hope you will keep them to yourself. Show your friends the old pictures.

Please tell your friend Walter that I said hello and I hope to meet him. He sounds like a good guy. Does he have family? If you want me to, I can send some money for his books. I don't like to think about folks in there without any little creature comforts. I can do it under Andre's name if you want it to be anonymous. I know how proud people can be. Tell me what you think is best.

Yours,
Celestial

Dear Georgia,

You are the greatest gift of my life. I miss everything about you, even your sleeping bonnet that I used to complain about. I miss your cooking. I miss your perfect shape. I miss your natural hair. More than anything, I miss your singing.

The one thing I don't miss is how we fought so much. I can't believe we wasted so much time fussing over nothing. I think about every time I hurt you. I think about the times when I could have made you feel secure, but I let you worry simply because I liked being worried about. I think about that and I feel like a damn fool. A damn lonesome fool.

Please forgive and please keep loving me.

You don't know how demoralizing it is to be a man with nothing to offer a woman. I think of you out there and there are so many dudes in Atlanta with their Atlanta briefcases and Atlanta jobs and Atlanta degrees. Trapped in here, I can't give you anything. But I can offer up my soul and that's the realest thing.

At night, if I concentrate, I can touch your body with my mind. I wonder if you can feel it in your sleep. It's a shame that it took me being locked up, stripped of everything that I ever cared about, for me to realize that it is possible to touch someone without touching them. I can make myself feel closer to you than I felt when we were actually lying in bed next to each other. I wake up in the morning exhausted because it takes a lot out of me to leave my body like that.

I know it sounds crazy, but I'm asking you to try it. Please try to touch me with your mind. Let me see how it feels.

Love,
Roy

Dear Georgia,
Please forgive me if my last letter was a little "out there." I didn't mean to freak you out (ha). Please write me back.

Roy

Dear Roy,
I'm not freaked out. I'm just really busy these last few weeks. Things are really looking up for my career. I hate using that word, *career*. It always feels like the word *bitch* is hiding out between the letters. But I know that I'm being paranoid. The point is that things are really heating up. There is talk about a solo show. I didn't want to tell you about it until things were set in stone, but now they are set in, say, Play-Doh. But here is my news: Remember my Man Moving series? Now it's called I <u>AM</u> a Man. The show is all of the portraits I have made of you over the years, starting with the

marble. They might give me a show in New York. The key word is *might*, but I'm very excited and very busy. Andre's doing all my slides and graphic design stuff. Everything looks perfect, but I wish he would accept a real payment. I know we are like family, but I don't want to take advantage of him.

It has been demanding, but working all day with images of you makes me feel like I'm spending time with you and sometimes I forget to write. Please forgive. And know that you're on my mind.

Yours,
C

Dear Georgia,
My mother says you're famous. Confirm or deny.

Love,
Roy

Dear Roy,
I must be famous if word has made it to Eloe, Louisiana. I guess the entire Negro Nation subscribes to *Ebony*. I don't know if you have seen the article, but even if you have, let me explain. Even if you haven't, I want you to understand exactly what happened.

I told you that my doll won a contest at the National Portrait Museum. What I didn't tell you was that the portrait was of you. Your mother asked for a doll based on your baby picture, the black-and-white studio portrait in your bedroom. I promised it to her and I worked on it for three months to get the chin right. She even provided your original outfit. It was surreal, dressing the doll in the clothes your mother had intended for her grandson to wear. (The whole thing was deep.) I promise that I was going to give it to her, but I left it at home. Just a stupid mistake. So I was going to send it to her for Valentine's, but I couldn't let it go. You know how I am, a perfectionist on the commissions. Something about it was too easy, too on the nose. She asked me about it a thousand times and I kept telling her it was coming.

What's next is complicated, so let me back up.

Since you've been away, my mother and I have been spending more time together. At first, it was just so I wouldn't be alone in the house, but now we visit like girlfriends, talking and drinking wine. Sometimes she even sleeps over. One night, she told me how she and her family came to live in Atlanta. It was a long story, and I was tired, but every time I drifted asleep she tapped me awake.

The story starts when my mother was a baby in a pram. Nana had taken her grocery shopping, which was always stressful because my grandparents had a lot of needs and not a lot of money. Sometimes they took credit at the general store and that hurt my grandmother's dignity, and you know how debt can spiral out of control. While Nana was in the store trying to calculate the least amount of food she could buy to take care of the whole family, they crossed the path of a white woman and her child. (My mother talks bad about these white people and she talks about them in detail, as if she could actually remember them. She says that they were trashy, smelled of camphor, and the little girl didn't even have shoes.)

But anyway, the little girl pointed at my mother and said, "Look, Mommy! A baby maid!" And for my grandmother, this was the last straw. By the end of the month the family packed up and moved to

Atlanta, living with my grandfather's brother until my granddaddy found a job. But the whole point is that in that instant in that store, my mama *was* a baby maid, and this is what made my grandparents move, just that inevitability.

Kind of remember that, okay? It's important.

I never told you this, but about a year ago I had an incident. Not a breakdown, just an incident. I didn't tell you because you have enough to think about. Don't get mad about that. I'm okay.

Andre and I were walking nearby to Peeples Street because we had installed my show at the Hammonds House—these dolls are very ornate, almost baroque, lots of raw silk and tulle. The process was grueling because the topsy-turvy dolls were displayed on movable platforms that I built myself. Andre helped me, but it was hard work and I was about cross-eyed by the time we got it all set up. So the main thing is that I was exhausted.

We were on Abernathy on our way to buy fish sandwiches from the Muslims, which is another factor. I was hungry.

Near an intersection, we passed a little boy walking with his mother. He was teensy and adorable. Kids that size always get my attention. If things were different, maybe we would have a boy that age. His mother looked young, maybe twenty-one, but you could tell she was conscientious, just from the way she held his hand and chatted with him while they walked. Clear as water, I could imagine myself in her position, feeling his sweet little hand, answering his bright-eyed questions. When they got closer, he smiled—those little straight teeth—and I felt a jolt of recognition. That little boy looked like you. A voice in my head that was not my own said, *A baby prisoner.* I clamped my hands over my mouth and looked to Andre who seemed confused. "Did you see him? Was it Roy?" Dre said, "What?" I feel embarrassed even writing this. But I'm trying to explain what happened. Next thing I knew I was on my knees on the sidewalk in front of a water hydrant, embracing it like a small stout child.

Andre knelt beside me and we probably looked like we were having some sort of domestic dispute. He peeled my hands off the hydrant, one finger at a time. Somehow we made it to the fish place. He called Gloria, then he grabbed me by the shoulders. "You cannot let this destroy you," he said. Finally Gloria showed up and gave me one of those "nerve pills" that all mothers stash in their pocketbooks. Long story short: I slept it off, whatever possessed me. I recovered and went to my opening at the Hammonds House the next day. I can't really explain it, but the idea got inside me like a hookworm.

So I dolled it. I stripped the doll out of the john-johns and used waxed cotton to make a diminutive pair of prison blues. Dressing the doll in these clothes was just as difficult, but it felt more purposeful. In the baby clothes, it was only a toy. In the new way, it was art. That's the doll that won the contest. I hate that you had to hear it from your mother and not from me.

When I was interviewed on stage, I didn't tell them about you. They asked about the inspiration and I talked about my mother being a baby maid and I spoke about Angela Davis and the prison-industrial complex. What is happening with you is so personal that I didn't want to see it in the newspaper. I know you will understand what I mean.

Yours,
Celestial

Dear Georgia,

A few months ago, you said you were dream-adjacent, but it looks like you have been living your real dream behind my back. The shop, that was *my* idea, but your fantasy involved galleries, museums, and white-glove installations. Don't treat me like someone who doesn't know you.

I understand what you're saying and I understand what you're not saying. Are you ashamed of me? You are, aren't you? You can't go to the National Portrait Museum and tell them that your husband is in prison. You *could*, actually, but you *won't*. I empathize—it's a lot to get used to. Before, we were living that Huxtable life. But now where are we? I know where *you are* and I know where *I am*, but *where are WE?*

Send me a picture of the doll. Maybe I'll like it better when I can actually see what it looks like, but I must tell you that I don't care much for the concept. And even if what you said in the article is true, about how you "want to raise consciousness about mass incarceration"—let's say this wasn't bullshit—please explain to me what a baby doll is going to do to help anybody in here. Yesterday, a dude died because nobody would give him his insulin. I hate to break it to you, but no amount of *poupées* is going to bring him back.

Look, you know I have always supported you in your art. Nobody believes in you more than me, but don't you think you crossed a line here? And to not even tell me or mention me? I hope that prize from the National Portrait Gallery means a lot to you. That's all I'll say.

You know, if you're not comfortable telling people that your husband, an innocent man, is incarcerated, instead you can tell them what I do for a living. I've been given a promotion. I push a trash can around Mars, picking up garbage with giant tongs. It's a sweet gig because Parson prison is also an agri-business site; before, I was picking soybeans. Now I work inside, and although I'm not wearing a white shirt and tie, I do have a white jumpsuit. Everything is relative, Celestial. You still have your upwardly mobile husband. In here, I'm white collar. No need to be ashamed.

Your husband (I think),
Roy

PS: Was Andre there? Were the two of you going around telling everybody how you have been best friends since you were two little babies taking a bath in the sink? Was everybody saying how cute that is? Celestial, I may have been born yesterday but not last night.

Dear Roy,

Your last letter upset me so much. What can I say to make you see that this isn't about shame? Our story is too tender to explain to strangers. Don't you see? If I say that my husband is in prison, that's all anyone can focus on, not me or my dolls. Even when I explain that you're innocent, all they remember is the fact that you're incarcerated. Even when I tell the truth about you, the truth doesn't get delivered. So what's the point of bringing it up? This was a special occasion for me, Roy. My mentor flew in from California, and even Johnnetta B. Cole showed up. I couldn't bring myself to talk about something this painful on the microphone during the Q&A.

Maybe it was selfish, but I wanted to have my moment to be an artist, not the prisoner's wife. Please write me back.

Yours,
Celestial

PS: As for your remarks about Andre, I will not even dignify that silliness with a response. I'm sure by now you have come to your senses and I am accepting your apology in advance.

Dear Georgia,

According to Walter, I am being a jackass for not looking at things from your side of the bed. He says it's unreasonable for me to expect that you would constantly reiterate that your husband is incarcerated. He said, "This ain't *The Fugitive*. You want her to go running after the one-legged man?" (See why we call him the Ghetto Yoda?) He says that your potential for advancement in your profession will be greatly diminished by having your brand associated with incarceration, which evokes troubling stereotypes of African American life. Except he said it like this: "She is a black woman and everybody already thinks she got fifty-eleven babies with fifty-eleven daddies; that she got welfare checks coming in fifty-eleven people's names. She got that already to deal with, but she got the white folks to believe that she is some kind of Houdini doll maker and she even got them thinking that this is an actual job. She is working her hustle. You think she supposed to get up there talking about her man is in the hoosegow? Soon as she say that, everybody will start looking at her and thinking about the fifty-eleven everythings and she might as well go on back home and work for the phone company." (Again, these are his exact words.)

My exact words should be *I'm sorry*. I didn't mean to guilt-trip you. But it's heavy, Georgia. You don't know what it is like in here. And trust me, you don't want to know.

I went to the library and pulled up the article and the photo one more time. You wore a smile on your face and my ring on your finger. I don't know how I didn't see it before.

Love,
Roy

Dear Celestial,

Didn't you get my letter last month? I said I was sorry. Maybe I didn't make it plain. I'm sorry. So write back? Even email is fine.

Roy

Roy O. Hamilton Jr.
PRA 4856932
Parson Correctional Center
3751 Lauderdale Woodyard Rd.
Jemison, LA 70648

Dear Mr. D,

I don't suppose that this is what you pictured when I came to you and asked for Celestial's hand in marriage. There I was, all serious, trying to do things the right way, and you said, "Her hand is not mine to give." At first I thought you were kidding, but when I determined that you were serious, I tried to backtrack, pretending it was all a joke, but inside I was mad and embarrassed. I felt like I was eating with my fingers when everyone else was using a knife and fork. Her hand wasn't yours to give, like you said. But at the same time, I needed to approach you as a man to another man. I was asking if I could be your son-in-law.

I am very close to my own father. Maybe Celestial shared with you that technically he is my stepfather, but he is the only father I have ever known and he has been a positive male influence. I am his "junior" in every way. But he doesn't know much about the world I was living in in Atlanta, even though his sacrifices made it achievable. Big Roy has always lived in one small southern town or another. He didn't finish high school, yet he provided a secure home for our family. I respect my father more than anyone else in the world.

I came to you because we have a lot in common. We are both immigrants to Atlanta, if you know what I mean. You've been there longer, and I'm just off the boat, but our backgrounds are almost the same. You are rags to riches and I was rags on my way to riches. Or at least that's the way it felt at the time. With my present condition, who knows what will happen to me. But when I asked for her hand, I was seeking your blessing, as her father, but also as a mentor. With Celestial, I was punching above my weight, and I guess I was hoping for a clap on the back, but I ended up feeling like a dummy.

And maybe I'm a dummy for writing this letter at all.

Mr. Davenport, Celestial has not come to Louisiana to visit me in two months now. We have not had any significant arguments or disagreements. I was expecting her in September, but she didn't show. She sent word that she was having car trouble, and I expected her the following weekend. But I have not seen her at all, nor have I received any correspondence. Mr. D, I'm hoping that you will speak to her on my behalf. I know you will say that I should reach out to her myself. Trust me, I have tried.

When you sent me away, you said that maybe I didn't know her well enough to marry her. This is why I'm turning to you now. I obviously do not know her as well as I thought. You, on the other hand, have known her all her life, and maybe you will know what to say to her to bring her back to me.

Please tell her that I understand that being married to an incarcerated man is a major sacrifice. I am not accustomed to asking for things. I have worked for everything I have. I wouldn't have been bold enough to show my face in your house if I hadn't put in the effort. In my current position, there is no work that I can do to win her love. There is no work I can do to convince you, as her father, that I'm worthy. Before, I had my good job and my gold cuff links. What do I have today? Only my character. I know she can't wear my character on her left hand, and I know it doesn't pay bills or father children. But it's what I have and I believe that it should count for something.

Thank you, sir, for reading this. I hope you will consider my request. And please do not share this with Celestial or her mother. Let this please stay between us as men.

Sincerely,
Roy O. Hamilton Jr.

Franklin Delano Davenport
9548 Cascade Rd.
Atlanta, GA 30331

Dear Roy,

I am pleased to hear from you, as I think of you often. My wife fancies herself a "prayer warrior," and she pleads with the Lord for you on a regular basis. No one here has forgotten you. Not me. Not my Gloria. Not Celestial.

Son (and I use the word deliberately), I think you are misremembering our exchange when you came asking for Celestial's hand. I didn't refuse you. I merely explained to you that my daughter is not my property. I almost chuckle to remember it. You came here as proud as a peacock's daddy with that velvet box tucked in your jacket pocket. For one bewildered second, I thought you were about to propose to me! (That is meant to be humor, by the way.) I was glad to see that you were serious in your intentions, but I didn't think I should see the ring before Celestial did. I could tell that your feelings were a little bruised when you left that day, and frankly, that was a positive development. You said in your letter that you are not accustomed to asking for things, and that was apparent, not from your gold cuff links (Authentic! Who knew!) but from the sway in your walk. You were not asking me for her hand (and I still assert that it wasn't mine to give). Instead, you were telling me that you were marrying her—and she hadn't even agreed. I surmised that your strategy was to get on your knee, whip out the ring (and I assumed it was a whopper), and announce that she had won the marriage sweepstakes. I was honest when I said that you didn't know her very well if you believed this approach would be successful.

Here is an anecdote from my personal history: I proposed to Gloria three times before she said yes. The first instance was, admittedly, a bit awkward as I was encumbered with my first wife. Gloria is a refined woman, but these were her exact words: Hell no. The second rejection was kinder: No, not yet. The third time I wasn't down on my knees—neither literally or metaphorically. I presented my modest token and asked her to share my life. I apologized for my transgressions. I laid myself low. I didn't involve her father and I didn't ask her best friend to help me make the scene right. I took her hand, telling her the truth of my soul. She answered with a nod. It wasn't this hooting and hollering and jumping up and down you see on TV. None of this proposing via billboard or at halftime at the Rose Bowl. Marriage is between two people. There is no studio audience.

All that said, I'll speak to Celestial about why it is that she has put her visiting schedule on hiatus. In the spirit of disclosure, I admit that I was not aware of this until now. But I must make it clear to you that I cannot speak "on your behalf." I can only talk to her on behalf of myself, as her father.

I hope you will not interpret this as rejection, because that is not my intention. You are a part of our family and every one of us holds you in highest regard.

I feel obligated to tell you as well that I will be sharing your letter with Celestial. I am her father and I cannot collude against her. She is the joy of my world and my only living blood relative. But I can tell you this: I know the sort of woman we have raised her to be. Her mother was loyal to me, even when I didn't deserve it, and I feel confident that my daughter will be no less steadfast.

Please write to me again, son. I'm always glad to hear from you.

Sincerely,
Franklin Delano Davenport
cc: C. G. Davenport

Dear Celestial,

By the time you get this letter, Mr. D will have narced on me. I hope that you're not upset that I wrote to him. I've felt close to your daddy since the first time he invited me to that big house (I always think of it as the Mothership), back when you and I were feeling each other out. I'll never forget it. It was cold outside, but Mr. D wanted to sit out on the wraparound porch. I was freezing, but I didn't want to be a chump. I was ready to tell him that my intentions were honorable and all of that, but he didn't even want to talk about you. I got there, sat down, and he promptly started rolling a blunt! It was crazy, I felt like I was on *Candid Camera*. Then your old man said, "Don't act like you don't smoke. I can see it in your eyes!" Then he whipped out this tall fireplace lighter and damn near singed off my eyebrows, blazing me up. I took a hit with him and it was like Welcome to the Family.

Celestial, you know I have a thing about fathers.

That's the real reason that I'm writing. I planned to send you another letter begging you to come visit. But for one thing, I'm sick of begging. You'll come see me when you come see me. That's what I got between the lines of your daddy's letter. You're grown and nobody can make you do anything you don't want to do (like I needed somebody to tell me that).

I'm writing to you now because something has happened that has my head all messed up. I know that you're on "hiatus," like your daddy said, but what I'm telling you is burning a hole in my pocket. I got to tell it to somebody, and Georgia, the only person I trust with it is you.

You remember the last day we were together and I carried you down to the stream to hear the bridge music? I planned to tell you then and there that Big Roy wasn't my biological father. I lost my nerve, but I had to eventually come correct because it wasn't fair for us to be talking about growing a family without you knowing about a genetic joker in the pack. I wanted to do what was right, although I know I should have told you before we even got married. I started to bring it up a couple of times, but I could never make myself spit it out. We fought hard over it and that particular disagreement led up to the predicament that I find myself in now. I have to confess that although I apologized to you for not telling you sooner, it's not until now that I see how it feels to not know somebody that you think you know.

Forgive the cliché, but I hope that you are sitting down. You might want to pour yourself a glass of wine because this will blow your mind. *Not only is my Biological incarcerated in this very same prison, he is none other than Walter, the Ghetto Yoda.*

This is how I found out: As you know, a brother with my verbal skills is in high demand in prison. I can write letters, decipher documents, and even do a little jailhouse lawyering. By a little, I mean a little. But I can do better than most (my Morehouse education at work—Benny Mays would be so proud). Anyway, I was doing some work for Walter and I happened upon his face sheet and there across the top was his full government name: Othaniel Walter Jenkins. There is only one man in the world with that name, but there once were two. Before Big Roy made me Roy Jr., I was Othaniel Walter Jenkins II. My mother kept Othaniel as my middle name for the sake of history, I guess.

When I saw the name, I knew it was him. Remember what he said to me when I first got moved into his cell? "Us bowlegged brothers got to stick together." And he looked at me to see my reaction. I didn't think much of it at the time, but he was pointing out the family resemblance. You know, they call him my pops, but I thought it was some prison shit. People make families in here, and Walter did look after me like I was his own.

Let me back up. This is the story that Olive told me: She said that when she was sixteen, she finished high school in Oklahoma City, hopped on the Greyhound with the intention of living in New Orleans. She had taken a typing class and figured she was qualified to be a secretary. On her way through, she met my Biological and got sidetracked in a little town called New Iberia. She was almost seventeen and he was thirty or something like that. He wasn't married, but he was a father many times over, so Olive stressed that I should be careful when I meet girls from Louisiana, Mississippi, or east Texas. (When she said that, I pictured him Johnny Appleseeding all over the region.) Long story short—he took off and left her broke and pregnant. But you know Olive wasn't going to go out like that. She stayed in New Iberia until she was ready to pop, then she went off in search of her man. She went all over town, leading with her stuck-out stomach until sympathetic old ladies gave her whatever little information they had. Finally, someone at the butcher's told her that somebody said he was in Eloe, working at the paper mill. (Mama said she should have known it was faulty information since it involved the word *work*.) When she got to Eloe, Walter was long gone—but she hit upon the three things she says a woman needs: Jesus, a job, and a husband.

And as far as Olive was concerned, that was all the story that I needed to have. For me, that was all the story I required. I had Big Roy, and everybody in Eloe knows me as Little Roy. Why would I feel compelled to chase down some rolling stone?

Well, sitting there, it was like that stone rolled right upside my head. When library time was over, I went back to my cell. Where else was I going to go? Not like I could go sit under a bridge and think. When I got there, he was using the commode. Life ain't right, Georgia. I find out the man is my Biological and he's standing there with his dick in his hand. (Pardon my French, but this is a story that must be told in full.)

He finished his business, turned to look at me, and read me like a newspaper. He said, "What? You found out?" I told him about the face sheet, and he said, "Guilty as charged," and even smiled a little bit like he had been waiting all his life for this conversation.

I wasn't even sure what it was that he was "guilty as charged" about. Was it that he was guilty of being my father or guilty of not telling me? He was over there grinning like all of this was good news, but I felt like a sucker.

He asked for a chance to tell his side of the story, and that's what he did. You have no privacy in prison, and let me tell you, these dudes in here gossip like bitches. Walter was talking loud, like he was saying his Easter speech. His version was not all that much different from my mother's. They met on the run—Olive from her father and Walter from a woman (or the woman's husband, to be precise).The scene is the colored section of a Greyhound bus. Fifteen hours is a long time to be elbow-to-elbow, and by the time they passed into Louisiana, my mama was gone, head over heels over head. Walter sweet-talked her into staying with him for a while in New Iberia. (At this point he said, "I was a pretty nigger in my day." He actually said that.) Olive and Walter literally shacked up. *In a shack*. Running water was the only amenity. Anyway, it was a matter of a couple of months before she got pregnant. Like any pregnant girl, she wanted to get married, and like any trifling motherfucker, he ran off and left her. When he was telling me this, he switched into Ghetto Yoda mode: "When a woman tells you she is having your baby, your first mind is to get the hell out. It's like if the house is on fire. You don't *think* to escape, you just *do*. It's human nature because you know she is asking you for your whole life. And a man don't have but one life."

It was bullshit and I knew it was bullshit, but something about his little soliloquy stuck in my throat like a fish bone.

Celestial, I think it was because I know I wasn't there for you when you told me the test was positive. I said, "What do you want to do?" What I did was the same as leaving town.

Anyway, Walter saw me sitting there snuffling back my thug tears and he tried to defend himself, swearing up and down that he never beat my mama, never stole from her—even though her pocketbook was *right there* on the chifferobe. He said it wasn't even personal, that he had left other women with big bellies. That this was the way things were then. But I wasn't thinking about him, Celestial, I was thinking about you and what a piece of shit I am. This is the truth.

I was sitting on the bed, having my own private come-to-Jesus, while Walter was getting more and more agitated. He said, "You think it's a coincidence that we are in this cage together?" He said his buddy Prejean, who is from Eloe, told him who I was, and he checked me out on the sly. He said, "They say that fruit doesn't fall far from any particular tree. But I didn't know which tree you fell from, me or your mama's." Then he said that he saw me and decided that all I got from him was "bowlegs and nappy hair." And then he paid good money to get me moved to his cell before I was beat up any more than I already was. He said: "Admit it. Things got better for you once you moved in with me. You got to give me some credit."

Celestial, I want to be mad at him. He left my mama like a two-dollar trick, but he would have been a terrible father to me in my real life. He wouldn't have sacrificed to get me to Morehouse.

Still, I have to give him the credit he asked for. If it wasn't for him, I could be dead by now or at least a lot worse off. Walter isn't the Don Corleone of the prison, but he is an old head and people stay out of his way. He didn't have to take me in, but he did.

It's complicated. Last night, when lights were out, he said, "I can't believe she let that nigger change your name. That's disrespectful."

I pretended like I didn't hear him. To say even one word would be a crime against Big Roy. He made me his junior with more than his name. He was my father, or should I say he *is* my father. But Walter is my old man in here.

This world is too much for me, Celestial. I know I said I wasn't going to do any begging in this letter, but I will ask you once more. Please come and see about me. I need to see your face.

Love,
Roy

Dear Roy,

I'm writing this letter to ask you to forgive me. Please be patient. I know it has been a long time. At first it was because I was going through a lot, but now my reason for staying away is boring and uncomplicated. It's just that the holiday season is here and I'm slammed at the shop. My assistant, Tamar, is going to cover for me weekend after next. (She's a student at Emory, with talent to burn. She has a gorgeous gift for quilts. Just breathtaking.)

So while Tamar minds the store, Gloria and I are going to drive up. She wants to give your mother one of her famous blackberry jam cakes, and I could use the company.

I know that you're mad at me. You have a right to be frustrated. But I hope that we don't waste our visit being angry. When we sit down together, our time is precious. If you can forgive, please forgive me. If I explain, will you listen? Tell me what I need to do to make it better.

What does Walter have to say about all of this? I hope you haven't talked about me too badly. I don't want to meet my father-in-law for the first time and make an unfavorable impression. (I'll get to meet him, won't I?) How are you two dealing with this shocking development? I guess you're the only one who's shocked, but I'm sure that it has changed things between you. Did you tell Olive? There's so much to unpack here. In the meanwhile, give me his information and I can put something on his commissary for the holidays.

I know you're proud, but let me do that for him and for you. He's family. I'll see you soon.

Yours,
Celestial

Dear Celestial,

Thank you for coming to see me; I know the journey is long and I know that you are a busy woman. You look different. I thought maybe you lost weight because your face had more shape to it. But I don't think the shift is on the physical plane. Are you all right? Is there something happening that I should know about? This isn't a backdoor way for me to ask if you're seeing somebody else. That's the last thing on my mind. I'm just asking what is going on. When I saw you, I was looking into your face, but I didn't really see *you*.

I don't have the right words to explain.

Roy

Dear Roy,

How am I expected to respond to your last letter? Yes, I have dropped a few pounds. Some on purpose—I've been flying to New York a lot these days and you know they are a little bit leaner up there. I don't want to show up looking like the unsophisticated chick from "down south" with the folk art. If my dolls are going to be taken seriously, I have to look the part. But I don't think my waistline is what you're talking about.

Am I different? It has been close to three years, so I guess I have changed. Yesterday I sat under the hickory tree in the front yard. It's the only place where I find rest and just feel fine. I know *fine* isn't a lot, but it's rare for me these days. Even when I'm happy, there is something in between me and whatever good news comes my way. It's like eating a butterscotch still sealed in the wrapper. The tree is untouched by whatever worries we humans fret over. I think about how it was here before I was born and it will be here after we're all gone. Maybe this should make me sad, but it doesn't.

Roy, we're getting older. Every week or so I pluck one or two gray hairs from my head. It's a little early for dye, but still. Obviously, we are not elderly, but we're not teenagers either. Maybe that's what you saw—time getting away.

Am I seeing someone else? You say you aren't asking that, but you asked it anyway if only to say you weren't asking. Your ring is on my finger. That's what I will say.

Celestial

Dear Celestial,

Olive is sick. On Sunday, Big Roy came to visit without her. As soon as I saw him sitting on that little bitty chair, looking like a bear sitting on a mushroom, I could tell that there was news and it was bad. He says she has lung cancer, although she hasn't touched a cigarette in twenty-three years.

I want you to go and see about her. I know it's been a long time since I have been able to do for you in return. I feel like I'm running up a tab, just like with Morehouse and my student loans. At one point I estimated how much it cost me per day, then per hour, then per minute. I know you aren't keeping a scorecard, but I am. I need you to come see me. I need you to put money on my books. I need you to keep your Uncle Banks on his toes. I need you to remind me of the man I once was so I don't forget and become another nigger in here. I feel like I need and need and need and it's wearing a hole in the fabric. I'm not crazy, I can see it. I know you don't come around like you used to. I know what true feeling looks like, but I know what obligation looks like, too. What's in your face, that's all duty.

This that I am asking you, I know it's a lot. I know the drive is far and I know that you and my mother have never been friends. But please look in on her and tell me what my daddy won't.

Roy

Dear Roy,

This is the letter I promised that I would never send. Before I go any further, I want to tell you that I am sorry. I want to tell you that even typing these words is killing me. I won't say that this will hurt me more than it hurts you because I know how much you're hurting every day and no matter what is happening to me, it will never compare. I understood that I'm not in the same agony as you are, but I'm in pain and I cannot continue to live this way.

I can't go on being your wife. In some ways I feel like I never even got to try my hand at that role. We were only married a year and a half before lightning struck, counting off the time in months like you do with a baby. I have done my best to be married without actually being a wife for three years now.

You're going to think that this is about another man, but this is about the two of us, about our delicate cord that has been shredded by your incarceration. At your mother's funeral, your father showed what the connection is between husband and wife. If he could have, he would have gone into the grave instead of her. But they lived under one roof for more than thirty years. In some ways they grew together and grew up together, and had she not died, they would have grown old together. That's what a marriage is. What we have here isn't a marriage. A marriage is more than your heart, it's your life. And we are not sharing ours.

I blame it on time, not on you or me. If we put a penny in a jar for each day we have been married, and we took a penny away every day we've been apart, the jar would have been depleted a long time ago. I've been trying to find ways to add more pennies, but our visits in that busy room at that sad table send me home with empty hands. I know this and you do, too. The last three times I have visited, we said almost nothing to each other. You can't bear to hear about my days and I can't bear to hear about yours.

I'm not abandoning you. I will never abandon you. My uncle will continue to file appeals. I'll continue to keep your commissary up to date and I'll visit you every month. I can come as your friend, as your ally, as your sister. You're a part of my family, Roy, and you will always be. But I can't be your wife.

Love (and I mean it),
Celestial

Dear Georgia,

What do you want me to say? Am I supposed to say that I'm okay with us just being friends? Maybe it's me, but I made a different interpretation of "till death do us part." Because the last I checked, I wasn't dead yet. But you do what you have to do. Be an empowered woman or whatever they taught you in college. Leave a brother when he's down. I never thought you would be this kind of person. There are women around here who have been coming to see their men for *decades*, riding buses that leave Baton Rouge at 5 a.m. Walter has women he never even met in person and they come to see him, and when they get here, they do more than talk. Some women bunk in their cars in the parking lot so they can be in the visiting room as soon as it opens. Before she died, my mother was here every week. What is it that makes you think that you're so much better than all of them?

Don't come here talking about you're here to be my friend. I don't need friends.

ROH

Dear Roy,

I didn't expect you to receive my *very honest* letter with confetti and a ticker-tape parade, but I did at least expect you to take a moment to consider my perspective. Are you really comparing me with the women who crowd the crack-of-dawn bus to prison? I know them, too. I've met them myself. They organize their whole lives around coming to Parson; besides working, it's all they do. Every week they are strip-searched. More than once, I've had to let some guard put her hand in my panties just so I can sit across the table from you. This is what you want for me? This is what you want for my life? Is this the way you love me?

You always talk about how you understand that this is hard. You slump in your chair, admitting that you can't give me what I need. But now you act like you're confused. For more than three years, I've been there in body and in spirit. But I've got to change the way I'm doing things, or I won't have any spirit left. I said in my last letter and I'll say it again. I'll support you. I'll visit you. I just can't do it as your wife.

C

Dear Celestial,
I am innocent.

Dear Roy,
I am innocent, too.

Dear Celestial,
I guess it's my turn to send a letter I said I'd never write. I want you to know formally that I am discontinuing our relationship. You're right. This marriage isn't a two-way street. How can I argue with that? But you cannot argue with this: I only want you in my life as my *wife* because in my head and heart I'm your *husband*.

Please do not come visit me. If you disregard my wishes, you will be turned away because I have taken you off my visitors' list.

I'm not being spiteful, I'm trying to figure out how to live with this new reality.

ROH

> Roy O. Hamilton Jr.
> PRA 4856932
> Parson Correctional Center
> 3751 Lauderdale Woodyard Rd.
> Jemison, LA 70648

Dear Mr. Banks:

This will be your last act as my attorney. Please remove the following person from my visitors list:

Davenport, Celestial Gloriana

Sincerely,
Roy O. Hamilton Jr.

> Robert A. Banks, Esq.
> 1238 Peachtree Rd., Ste. 470
> Atlanta, GA 30031

Dear Roy:

This is a response to your letter of last week. Without violating privilege, I have spoken with the Davenport family, who indicate that they will continue to retain me in my capacity as your attorney. If I don't hear otherwise from you, I will continue in my duties on your behalf. As per your request, I have drafted the documents amending your visitors' list, although I urge you to reconsider.

Roy, in my years as an attorney, I have won cases and I have lost them, but none of them upsets me as much as yours, not only because it has left my niece disconsolate but because of the damage done to you. You remind me, actually, of Celestial's father. He and I have been friends ever since he had holes in his shoes. We worked the graveyard shift at a box factory, clocking out just in time to run to school. Franklin got where he is by the sheer force of his determination. Your will is like his. And so is mine.

I know it was disheartening to have our appeal denied by the state appellate court. It is disappointing but not surprising. I know Mississippi is the favored contender for "worst of the South," but Louisiana isn't far behind. The federal courts are much more promising because there is a chance of encountering a judge who isn't drunk, corrupt, racist, or some unpleasant cocktail of these variables.

There is hope. Do not give up.

Pride should not cut you off from the Davenports. Prison, as you know, is very isolating. You are staring down the barrel of a long sentence, and while I am working to find a solution, I urge you not to disconnect from the people who remind you of the life you once had and the life you want to live again. That said, I am including here the document I mentioned that will bar my niece from coming to visit. If you choose to post it yourself, you may. As your attorney, our correspondence will be confidential, of course, but I felt that I must offer my advice.

Sincerely,

Robert Banks

Roy O. Hamilton Jr.
PRA 4856932
Parson Correctional Center
3751 Lauderdale Woodyard Rd.
Jemison, LA 70648

Dear Mr. Banks:

I know that you are right, and with this letter I am unfiring you as my lawyer. I will leave Celestial on my visitors' list, but I am asking you, as my attorney, not to mention this to her. Should she come to visit me, she will find her name there. But to tell her implies that I'm asking for a visit and I'm not asking her to do anything.

These years have been rough on her, I am sure. But you know that they have been rougher on me. I try to see her side of things, but it's hard to weep for anyone who is out in the world living their dream. All I wanted from her is that she honor the promise we made when we said to have and to hold, etc. I asked this of her, but I won't plead (anymore).

Please continue pursuing my case, Mr. Banks. Don't forget me in here or think I am a lost cause. You warned me not to be surprised by the outcome of the appeal, but how can I keep hope alive if I'm not allowed to be optimistic? I feel like people are constantly asking me for things that are impossible.

And, Mr. Banks, I know that your services are not free. Any more the Davenports pay you, I'll repay to them, and after that I'll give you the same sum as soon as I am able. You're my only hope. I never thought I would be saying this to you, someone I really don't know that well. My mother is gone and my father is here, but what can he do? He's a hardworking man with values but without money. Celestial seems to have moved on. All I have is you, and it pains me to know that you're being paid with her daddy's money, but you're right: it's stupid to put pride ahead of common sense.

So this is my letter saying thank you.

Sincerely,

Roy O. Hamilton Jr.

Dear Roy,

Today is November 17, and I am thinking of you. Maybe on this anniversary of our first date, you will answer my letter. When it was our "safe word," we used it to bring communication to a halt. Now I hope it can restore our connection in some small way. This isn't how I want things to be between us. Let me care for you in the way that I can, as one human being to another.

Love,

Celestial

Dear Roy,

Merry Christmas. I haven't heard from you, but I hope you are okay.

Celestial

Dear Roy,

If you don't want to see me, I can't force you. It is unkind that you would cut me off because I can't be exactly the way you want me to be. I'll say it again: I'm not abandoning you. I would never do that.

C

Dear Celestial,

Please respect my wishes. Up until now, I have lived in fear of this happening. Let me be. I can't dangle from your string.

Roy

Dear Roy,

Happy birthday. Banks tells me that you're fine, but that's all he will say. Will you give him permission to give me news?

C

Dear Roy,

You will get this around Olive's anniversary. I know you feel all alone, but you are not. I haven't heard from you in so long, but I want you to know that I am thinking of you.

Celestial

Dear Celestial,

Can I still call you Georgia? That will always be my name for you in my head. So, Georgia, this is the letter I have been waiting five years to write, the words I have been practicing. I even scratched it into the paint on the wall beside my bed.

Georgia, I am coming home.

Your uncle came through. He went over the heads of these local yokels and ran it straight to the fed. "Gross prosecutorial misconduct" basically means they cheated. The judge vacated the conviction and the local DA didn't care enough to retry. So, as they say, "in the interest of justice," I will soon be home free.

Banks can explain it all to you in more detail. I have given him permission, but I wanted you to hear it from *me*, to see it in my own handwriting, that I will be a free man one month from today, in time for Christmas.

I know that things have not been right between us for some time now. I was wrong to take you off my list and you were wrong not to fight me about it. But this is not a time for blaming each other for what we cannot change. I regret not answering your letters. It has been a year since I have received any word, but how can I expect you to keep writing when you thought I was ignoring you. Did you think I forgot you? I hope I didn't hurt you with my silence, but I was hurt myself, and also ashamed.

Will you hear me when I say that the last five years are behind me and behind us? Water under the bridge. (Remember the stream in Eloe, the way the bridge makes a song?)

I know that we can't "start love over." But this is what I do know: you have not divorced me. All I want is for you to tell me why you have chosen to remain my lawfully wedded wife. Even if someone else is occupying your time, you have chosen to keep me as your husband these many years. In my mind, I picture us at our same kitchen table, in our same comfortable house, passing quiet words of truth.

Georgia, this is a love letter. Everything I do is a love letter addressed to you.

Love,
Roy

TWO

———+———

Prepare a Table for Me

ANDRE

This is what it must be like to be married to a widow. You give her bandages for her wounds; you offer comfort when memories sneak up and she cries for what looks like no reason. When she reminisces about the past, you don't remind her of the things she has chosen not to recollect, all the while telling yourself that it's unreasonable to be jealous of a dead man.

But what can I do other than what I've done? I've known Celestial Davenport all my life, and I have loved her at least that long. This is the truth as natural and unvarnished as Old Hickey, the centuries-old tree that grows between our two houses. My affection for her is etched onto my body like the Milky Way birthmark scoring my shoulder blades.

On the day we got the news, I was aware that she didn't belong to me. I don't mean that, on paper at least, she was another man's wife. If you knew her, you would know that she never belonged to him either. I'm not sure if she even realized it herself, but she's the kind of woman who will never belong to anyone. This is the truth that you have to lean close to see. Picture a twenty-dollar bill. You think it's green, but when you get up close you find that it's beige linen with dark green ink. Now consider Celestial. Even while she wore his ring, she wasn't *his wife*. She was merely a married woman.

I'm not making excuses for myself. I know that there are men in this world, better men than me, who would cut these feelings off and burn the stump the day that Roy went to prison, especially with him being falsely convicted. His innocence is something that I have never doubted. None of us did. Mr. Davenport is disappointed in me, believing that I should have been a gentleman and left Celestial alone, letting her be a living monument to Roy's struggle. But anyone who can't understand doesn't know what it means to have loved someone since you first figured out how to bend your tongue to talk, how to flex your feet to make steps.

I was a witness at their wedding, you know. The day she married Roy, I signed my name, Andre Maurice Tucker, even though my right hand trembled so badly I had to steady it with my left. At the church, when the preacher asked if anyone could say why these two should not wed, I kept my own counsel there at the altar, cummerbund strapped around my waist and a sloppy fist beating in my chest. She meant what she said on that spring day, but now you have to consider all the days that came after as well as those stacked up before.

Let me start again. Celestial and I grew up on the same narrow street in Southwest Atlanta. The street was Lynn Valley, off of Lynn Drive, which branched off of Lynhurst. The dead end was considered a plus because we could play in the road without getting run over. Sometimes I envy the children today with all their tae kwon do, psychotherapy, and language immersion, but at the same time, I appreciate that back then being little meant you really didn't have to do anything but stay alive and have fun.

We ran loose straight through the seventies, but we got stopped short when a serial killer terrorized the city. We tied a yellow ribbon around Old Hickey in memory of the twenty-nine missing and murdered. It was a rough couple of years, but the threat passed; the yellow ribbons frayed and fell like leaves and were burned like leaves. Celestial and I continued to live, love, learn, and grow.

When I was seven, my parents tangled in a nasty divorce back when nice families didn't split up. Once Carlos moved out—a grand performance involving his three brothers, an off-duty cop, and a U-Haul—Celestial volunteered her own father. I'll never forget her pulling me by the hand down to the basement lab. Mr. Davenport wore a white coat, like a doctor; his goggles burrowed in his asymmetric afro. "Daddy," she said. "Andre's daddy ran off, so I said you could be his daddy, too, sometimes." Mr. Davenport fired up a Bunsen burner, pulled down his goggles, and said, "I'm amenable to the proposition." To this day, this remains the greatest gift that anyone has ever extended to me. Mr. Davenport and I never became like father and son; the chemistry wasn't quite right. Still with that gesture of generosity, she lifted the covers, I crawled under, and we became a family.

To lay it all on the table, we were not quite like brother and sister. We were more like kissing cousins. Our senior year in high school, we went to the Valentine's Ball together, for lack of other options. She had her eye on a bass drummer, and I had my eye on this one majorette. As luck would have it, they had their sights on each other. I wasn't surprised to be dateless. In a world that prized tall, dark, and handsome, I was little, light, and cute. After the prom, we kissed each other in the back of the limo from Witherspoon's. Then, back at her house, we snuck down to the basement and made out on the little sofa her father crashed on when he needed a break from his work. The room smelled like rubbing alcohol, and the sofa cushions smelled like weed. Celestial glided over to a shiny file cabinet and produced a flask filled with something that might have been gin. We passed it back and forth until the courage kicked in.

Then I was such a mama's boy that I confessed everything to Evie. The next morning. She had two things to say: (a) it was inevitable and (b) it was my duty to go next door, ring the bell, and ask Celestial to be my girlfriend. Like her daddy had said all those years ago, I was "amenable to the proposition," but Celestial was not. "Dre, can we pretend like we didn't do that? Can we just watch TV?" She was asking me a real question, wanting to know if it were possible for us to reverse the clock. Could we shift away from the memory of the night before, grow toward some other sun. I finally said that we could try. She broke my heart that afternoon, like how Ella Fitzgerald could shatter a glass with a song.

I'm not telling this to say that I planted my flag way back in high school. All I want to get across is that there is real history between us, not just an accident of time and place.

After high school, we went our separate ways, seeking our fortunes like the three little pigs. My seeking only took me seven miles up the road, to Morehouse College. I was a third-generation legacy, and this was enough for Carlos to pony up the tuition even though he hadn't paid Evie half of what she asked for in child support. My first-choice school was Xavier University in New Orleans, but I had to go where Carlos was willing to send a check. I'm not complaining. Morehouse was a good fit, teaching me that there were dozens of ways to be a black man. I only had to choose which one was right for me.

Celestial picked Howard University, although her mother voted for Smith in Massachusetts and her dad endorsed Spelman. But whatever Celestial wanted, Celestial got, so they bought her a gray Toyota Corolla she named Lucille, and she set out for the nation's capital. I halfheartedly tried to meet up with her when Morehouse played Howard for homecoming. My girlfriend at the time wasn't keen on meeting Celestial; even she could tell from the way I pronounced her name that my feelings were more than friendly.

About three weeks after I didn't see her in DC, she came back home, shattered. Her family kept her essentially sequestered for nearly six months. I visited twice and I would have come by every week, but her aunt Sylvia sent me away. Something shadowy and female happened between them, as mysterious and primal as witches' brew.

Come September, Celestial was ready to live again, but she didn't go back to DC. Strings were pulled and she enrolled at Spelman College after all. Evie told me to keep an eye on her, and I did. Celestial was the same girl I had always known but with a little bit of risk about her, like she might cut you. Her sense of humor was ratcheted up a few notches, and she stood even taller.

All that was a long time ago, when things were different. I know that nostalgia is a hell of a drug, but I can't help recalling those days when we were underage and broke; she would sometimes come stay with me in my dorm room and we feasted upon wing-on-wheat, a chicken-and-bread combination that cost only two dollars and some change. After we ate, I would mess with her, asking why she never brought around any of her friends to meet me.

"I notice that you never talk about me bringing anybody until *after* the food is all gone."

"I'm serious," I said.

"Next time," she said. "I promise." But she was never going to bring anyone around and she would never tell me why not. On these evenings, near 1 a.m. or so, I always offered to escort her back to her own campus and she would say, "I want to stay here." We slept in my twin bed—her under the covers and me beside her with a sheet between us, for modesty's sake. I would be lying if I didn't say sharing the bed with only a stretch of cotton separating our bodies didn't rile me up from time to time. But looking back, I attribute that to my youth. Once she woke up before the sun and whispered, "Andre, sometimes I feel like I'm not all the way together." That was the one time I joined her underneath the sheet, but it was only to quiet her trembling. "You're good," I told her. "You're good."

And if I may say another thing to color the record, they met through me. She had slept over and Roy came by at 8 a.m. trying to hustle up some quarters to do his laundry. He came busting in with no warning, like there was no way I could be doing anything private. In college, I was a hard guy to categorize. I wasn't militant enough to be an Afrikan with a *k*, I wasn't peculiar enough to be a nerd, and it goes without saying that I didn't have the moves to be a Rico Suave. So I may not have had a natural female constituency, but I did well enough. Roy, as per usual, was drowning in attention. *He* was tallish, dark, and handsome but unpolished enough that it made him appear wholesome. Since our dorm rooms shared a wall, I knew that the clodhopper act was a technique. Not that he wasn't country as sugar on grits, but he wasn't stupid or harmless.

"I'm Roy Hamilton," he said, staring at Celestial like he was hungry.

"Roy *Othaniel* Hamilton, from what I hear through the wall."

Now Roy looked at me like I had shared classified information. I held my hands up. Then he turned his eyes to Celestial again and kept them there. At first, I think it was the challenge of it all. He couldn't believe that she had less than no interest in him. Even I was confused.

That's when I realized that her transformation was permanent. This was the new Celestial, straight ahead and direct, the by-product of all that time she spent recuperating with her aunt. Six months in Sylvia's care taught her two things: how to sew dolls from socks and how to tell immediately when a man was coming at her from the wrong side of the street.

ROY CAME TO my room three or four times to ask after her. "Ain't nothing up with y'all, right?"

"Nothing at all," I said. "I been knowing her since we were little."

"Okay," he said. "Then give me some intel."

"Like what?"

"If I knew, would I be asking you?"

There was insight I could have given him, no doubt. However, I wasn't going to give Roy the map to the core of her. He was a cool dude; even back then I liked him. He and I were almost frat bothers. Part One of my father's conditions in sending me to school was that I pledge—in his mind, only his first-born son could keep the legacy going. When I showed up for the "informational meeting," Roy was there, too. Being first-generation *everything*, he didn't have too much to write on the index cards, whereas the rest of us were busy inking our bona fides. I was sitting right next to him, so I saw a little blemish of panic bloom on his face. When the brothers came around and asked for his card, he handed it back as blank as the moon. "I didn't feel those questions could tell you who I am." He didn't put the bass in his voice when he said it, but there was a little something there. The Big Brother snorted at him and said, "Fool, fill out the card." Yet he won a little ground for himself there. Roy glanced over at my card on which I block-lettered my dad's whole entire family tree.

"It's in your blood," Roy said.

I waved the card and said, "Ask me how many times I have seen these people in the last ten years."

Roy shrugged. "It's your family."

I handed my card in and sat beside him again. Things got silly. I won't go into detail because secrets are secrets, but let's just say there was ceremonial garb but no sacrificial chickens or other livestock.

"We should break up out of here." Roy poked me with his elbow, testing the waters.

And when I think back on it, I wish we had headed for the door, escaping with our dignity intact. Flash forward: short version—neither of us made line. Slightly more detailed version—they kicked our asses for three weeks straight and we still didn't make line. Super-secret version—when we didn't make line, I was privately relieved, but Roy wiped his eyes with his sleeve.

He and I were friendly, if not friends, but I wasn't going to present Celestial on a silver platter. Evie raised me better than that. It took another three or four years for them to find each other on their own, and then the time was right. Was Roy the kind of guy you want your sister to marry? The truth is that you never want your sister to marry at all. But they were good together, Celestial and Roy. He took care of her, and to my knowledge, when he promised to have and to hold, he was sincere. Even Evie approved, to the point that she played piano at the wedding. It was an uplifting story: boy chases girl until she catches him and all of that. At the wedding reception, I sat at the head table, wishing them the best. When I raised my glass to their happiness, my words were heartfelt. Anyone who would say different is a liar.

All this is a true story. But life happens. Trouble happens, and good luck, too. I'm not trying to sound all *que será* about it, but how can I apologize for the nearly three years Celestial and I have spent as partners in life? And besides, if I was going to start apologizing, to whom would I make amends? Would I go to Roy repentant and red-handed? Maybe in his mind it would seem appropriate, but Celestial isn't something you can steal like a wallet or even a bright idea. She is a living, breathing, beautiful human being. Obviously, there are more sides to this story than just mine and hers, but what can't be questioned is this: I love her and she loves me. She is the first thing I think about in the morning whether I wake up beside her or wake up by myself in my own pitiful bed.

When I was growing up, Grandmamma used to say, "The Lord works in mysterious ways" or "He might not be there when you want Him, but

He's always right on time." Evie used to say, "God will do to you what He feels like needs to be done to you." Then Grandmamma would tell Evie to hush and remind her that getting left by a man was not the worst thing that ever happened to somebody. And Evie would say, "It's the worst thing that ever happened to *me*." She said it so much that she came down with lupus. "God wanted me to see what misery really was," Evie said. I didn't like all this God talk, like He was up there toying with us. I preferred more of the tenderness and acceptance my grandmother promised in her hymns. I told this to Evie when I was a little boy and she said, "You got to work with the god you were given."

You also have to work with the love you are given, with all of the complications clanging behind it like tin cans tied to a bridal sedan. We didn't forget Roy. Celestial and I both sent money to his account every month, but it was like sending thirty-five cents a day to feed an orphan in Ethiopia, something and nothing at the same time. Still, he was always there, a shimmering apparition in the corner of the bedroom.

On the fourth Wednesday in November, I came home from work to find Celestial in my kitchen, wearing her sewing smock and drinking red wine from a bubble glass. I knew she was agitated from the sharp click of her nails against the tabletop.

"Baby, what's wrong?" I asked, taking off my coat.

She shook her head and offered a sigh I couldn't interpret.

I sat next to her and took a sip from the glass. This was a thing with us, sharing a single drink.

Celestial ran her hands over her hair, buzzed short since we first got together. The close cut made her older, and not in a negative way. It was the difference between a young lady and a grown woman.

"You okay?" I said.

With the hand not holding the wine to her lips, she produced a letter from her pocket. Before I unfolded the lined paper, I knew exactly what it was, knew exactly what it said, as though the meaning bypassed language and found its way into my blood, uncut.

"Uncle Banks worked a miracle," she said, rubbing her hands over her naked head. "Roy's getting out."

She rose from the table as I got up and went to the cupboard and got my own bubble glass and sloshed it half full of cabernet, wishing for something a little bit stronger. I raised my glass. "To Banks. He said he wouldn't give up."

"Yeah," Celestial said. "Finally. It's been five years."

"I'm happy for Roy. He was my friend."

"I know," she said. "I know you don't wish anything bad on him."

We stood before the kitchen sink gazing out the window at the brown grass covered with fallen leaves. Against the far wall at the edge of the property grew a fig tree that Carlos planted to celebrate my birth. Not to be outdone, Mr. Davenport set out a jungle of rosebushes for Celestial's first birthday, and to this day, they creep up a dozen trellises each summer, fragrant and undisciplined.

"You think he wants to come back here?" Celestial asked. "In his letter he doesn't mention any plans."

"How could he have plans?" I said. "He has to start over."

"Maybe he could come here," she said. "You and I could stay in my house and we could set him up in your house. . . ."

"No man is going to go for that."

"He might?"

I shook my head. "Nope."

"But you are glad he's out," she said. "You don't begrudge him that?"

"Celestial," I said. "What kind of person do you think I am?"

Of course, I was happy to hear that he was being set free. Nothing would change the fact that my chest filled with gratitude on behalf of Roy Hamilton, my friend, my Morehouse brother. Still, there were things that Celestial and I needed to discuss. Yes, last month she finally agreed to talk to Banks about divorce papers, and yesterday I went to the jeweler and selected a ring, something my mama had been predicting since I was three years old. My idea was to wake her with it tomorrow, Thanksgiving Day. The stone wouldn't put your eye out; Celestial had already been down that yellow brick road. I didn't even go for a diamond at all, choosing instead a dark oval-cut ruby, shot through with fire, mounted on a plain gold band. It was as though her singing voice had been solidified into a jewel.

To buy it, I walked out on faith, because Celestial says she doesn't believe in marriage anymore. "Till death do us part" is unreasonable, a recipe for failure. I asked her, "So what *do* you believe in?" She said, "I believe in communion." As for me, I'm modern and traditional at the same time. I, too, believe in intimacy—who doesn't? But I also believe in commitment. Marriage is, as she says, "a peculiar institution." My parents' divorce made it clear what kinds of raw deals are brokered at the altar. But right now, in America, marriage is the closest thing to what I want.

"Look at me," I said to Celestial, and she shifted, showing on her open face the places where her features give her away. She bit the left corner of her bottom lip. If I pressed my lips up against her neck, I would feel her pulse pounding against her skin.

"Dre," she said, turning her eyes back to the yard strewn with leaves. "What are we going to do?"

In response, I positioned myself behind her and circled my arms around her waist, crouching a little to rest my chin against her sharp shoulder.

Celestial said it again: "What are we going to do?" I liked that she used the word *we*. It wasn't much to grab hold of, but let me tell you, I gripped it with both hands. I said, "We have to tell him. That's first. The question of where he will live—all that comes later. That's details." And she nodded but didn't say anything else.

"Four weeks?" I said.

She nodded. "Give or take. December 23. Merry Christmas."

"Let me go talk to him," I said.

I turned toward her, hoping she would see this offer as what it was, not a bottom-of-the-ninth bunt but a gentlemanly gesture; I was laying myself down like a coat over a mud puddle.

She said, "In the letter, he says he wants to talk to me. Don't you think I owe him that?"

"You do, and you will," I said. "But not right away. Let me give him a broad outline, and if he wants the face-to-face, I will drive him to Atlanta. But he might not even need to come here after he knows."

"Dre," she said, touching my cheek so softly that it felt like a kiss or an apology. "But what if I want to talk to him? I can't send you to Louisiana to handle him like he's a flat tire or a traffic ticket. I was married to him, you know? It's not his fault that things didn't work out."

"It's not about fault," I said. But of course there was that nagging voice insisting that being with Celestial was a crime like identity theft or tomb raiding. *Go get your own woman*, it scolded me in Roy's voice. Other times it was like my father reminding me that "all you have is your good name," which should have been a joke coming from him. But alongside all the clutter in my head was my grandmother's advice: "What's for you is for you. Extend your hand and claim your blessing." I never told Celestial about the voices, but I'm sure she hosted a choir of her own.

"I know that nobody is to blame," she said, "but the relationship is sensitive. I know we weren't married long, but it did happen."

"Listen," I said, not dropping to one knee; we were way past such formalities. "I don't want to talk about him before we talk about us. This isn't how I planned to do this, but look."

She regarded the ring centered in my palm, shaking her head, confused. When I purchased the ruby, it seemed perfect and personal, so different from what she had before, but now I wondered if it was enough.

Celestial said, "Is this a proposal?"

"It's a promise."

"You can't do this like that," she said. "This is too much on me at one time." She pulled away and walked to my bedroom and closed herself in with a little click of the knob. I could have pursued her. A paper clip could best the catch, but when a woman shuts you out, picking the lock won't let you back in.

In the den I poured myself a splash from the bottle of smoky scotch Carlos had given me when I graduated. For almost fifteen years, I stored it unopened in the liquor cabinet, waiting for an occasion. A year ago, Celestial asked about it, and her presence seemed occasion enough. We opened the bottle in celebration of each other. Now it was nearly empty and I would mourn when it was gone. Then I took my glass outside and sat at the base of Old Hickey. There was a little nip in the air, but scotch burns going down. Over at Celestial's, all the lights were on and the drapes parted. Her sewing room was crammed with dolls, prepared for the holiday rush. All of them looked a little like Roy to me, even though they were of varying complexions, and most of them were girl dolls. Each and every one was Roy. I made my peace with this reality a long time ago. She was a widow. Widows are entitled to mourn.

She called for me as the moon rose. I hesitated, waiting for a second overture. I sensed the worry as she wandered the house. If she slowed down and thought about it, she would know where to find me. My name reverberated through the vacant rooms only a few moments more. At last, she appeared on the front porch, wearing a floral gown and robe, looking like we had been married a couple hundred years.

"Dre," she said, walking across the cold, damp lawn, her feet bare. "Come in the house. Come to bed."

Without speaking, I walked past her and headed to my bedroom. The sheets were in disarray, as though she had fallen asleep only to find a nightmare waiting for her. As I would on any other night, I prepared myself for bed, washing up and changing into pajama pants and a T-shirt. Then I returned the sheets to the mattress, and the blankets. I smoothed the covers, folded them back, switched off the light, and then made my way over to where she stood by the closet with her arms crisscrossed over her chest. "Come here," I said, embracing her like a brother.

"Dre," she said. "What do you want me to do?"

"I want to get married, make everything legit, aboveboard. You have to tell me, Celestial. You can't leave me hanging."

"The timing's not right, Dre."

"Just tell me what you want. Either you want to marry me, or you don't. Either we've been playing house for almost three years, or we've been here building something real."

"Is this an ultimatum?"

"You know me better than that. But, Celestial, I need to know and I need to know now."

I loosened my grip and she went to her side of the mattress and I went to mine, like boxers in our corners.

NOBODY TALKED; NOBODY slept. I wondered if this would be the end of us. I considered rolling over to join her in her territory, the side of the bed that smelled like lavender. We often slept close, sometimes sharing a single pillow. But this night, I felt like I needed to be invited, and it didn't look like an offer was coming. You can never know another person's mind; this is one thing I have learned. But regardless, she extended herself to me before dawn, barely ahead of the deadline ticking in my chest. She reached for me with her hands, her legs, her lips, her everything. I was right there, ready, like I was spring-loaded.

As far as the state was concerned, she was another man's wife, but if the events of the last five years have taught us anything, it is that you can't trust the state to know anything about the truth of people's lives. In my bed, in the exhausted, sweaty tangle of us, you couldn't tell me that this was not communion.

"Listen," I whispered into the perfume of her skin. "Roy being locked up isn't why we came together. You hear me?"

"I know," she said, sighing. "I know, I know, I know."

"Celestial. Please, let's get married."

In the dark, she spoke with her lips so close to mine that I could taste her words, rich and peaty.

CELESTIAL

A t the time, I was a newlywed, combing rice from my hair. Eighteen months in, I danced the line between wife and bride.

Marriage is like grafting a limb onto a tree trunk. You have the limb, freshly sliced, dripping sap, and smelling of springtime, and then you have the mother tree stripped of her protective bark, gouged and ready to receive this new addition. Some years ago, my father performed this surgery on a dogwood tree in the side yard. He tied a pink-blooming limb stolen from the woods to my mother's white-blooming tree secured from a nursery lot. It took yards of burlap and twine and two years for the plants to join. Even now, all these years later, there's something not quite natural about the tree, even in its amazing two-tone glory.

In my marriage, I never determined which of us was rootstock and which the grafted branch. The baby we were trying for might have rendered this irrelevant. Three takes you from being a couple to being a family, upping the consequences for walking away, upping the pleasure quotient for staying home. It wasn't as calculated as all of that at the time. The chilly rationale of hindsight is what exposes the how and why of something that once seemed supernatural. It's the magician's manual that shows you how the tricks are done, not with sorcery but with careful cues and mysterious devices.

This is not an excuse, just an explanation.

I WOKE UP on the morning of Thanksgiving beside Andre, wearing his ring. I never imagined myself to be the kind of woman who would find herself with both a husband and a fiancé. It didn't have to happen this way. I could have asked Uncle Banks to draw up divorce papers the instant I knew that I couldn't be a prisoner's wife. In the wake of Olive's funeral, I knew I wanted Andre, sweet Dre, who had been there all along. Why didn't I set this thing right on paper? Did some dormant love for Roy sleep inside me? For two years, that was the question in Andre's eyes, just before bed. It is the question just beneath the words in Roy's letter, like he wrote it down, erased it, and scribbled over it.

There are many reasons. Guilt seeps in through the cracks in my logic. How could I serve him with the divorce papers, subjecting him to yet another state decree, another devastating development? It seemed gratuitous to make official what he certainly already knew. Was I being kind, or was I just weak? A year ago, I asked this of my mother, who offered me a glass of cold water and assured me that everything works for the good.

I placed my hand on Andre's sleeping shoulder, cupping my fingers over his birthmark. He breathed deeply, trusting that the world would keep spinning until he had gotten his rest. Life was less daunting at five in the morning when only one of us was awake. Andre had grown into a handsome man. His long and lanky solidified into slim but strong. He was still leonine, with his sandy hair and reddish complexion, now like a lion full grown and not just an adorable cub. "You two are going to have some pretty babies," strangers said to us from time to time. We smiled. It was a compliment, but thinking of babies raised a knot in my throat that threatened my air.

Jolted by a dream, Andre caught my hand with his, so I rested against him a while longer. Today was Thanksgiving. One of the hurdles of adulthood is when holidays become measuring sticks against which you always fall short. For children, Thanksgiving is about turkey and Christmas is about presents. Grown up, you learn that all holidays are about family, and few can win there.

How would my mother, the dreamy romantic, interpret this ring on my finger, deep red like an autumn leaf? According to the ruby, Andre is my fiancé, but Roy's diamond, so white that it's blue, insists that this is impossible. But who listens to the wisdom of jewelry? Only our bodies know the truth. Bones don't lie. What else hides in my jewelry box? A small tooth, ivory like antique lace, with a serrated edge like a steak knife.

EVERYONE IN SOUTHWEST Atlanta knows my parents' house. It's a landmark of a sort, although no plaque marks the spot. Situated at the junction of Lynhurst Drive and Cascade Road, right before Childress Street, the grand Victorian stood abandoned for almost a half century before my father rescued it from the squirrels and chipmunks. Set back from the street, partially hidden by a green wall of unkempt shrubbery, it stood like a turn-of-the-century cautionary tale in this community of tidy brick houses. When I was little, we passed it on our way to Greenbriar Mall, and Daddy used to say, "We're going to live right there. That monster was built after the war, a consolation prize for losing Tara." When I was very small, I took him seriously and pleaded against it: "But it's haunted!" "Yes little lady," he said. "Haunted by the ghost of history!" At this point my mother would intervene. "Your father is being rhetorical." Then Daddy might say, "No. I'm being prescient." And Gloria would say, "Prescient? Try delusional? Or maybe optimistic. But stop it. You're scaring Celestial."

And Daddy did stop it, until his money came in. After that, he rekindled his fascination with the crumbling mansion on the hill with its cupolas and stained glass. Uncle Banks discovered that the property was in the hands of the old-money family who had owned it since Reconstruction. They couldn't bear to live in it since Southwest Atlanta had become all black, but they couldn't bear to sell it either. Or at least they couldn't until Franklin Delano Davenport showed up three generations later with a briefcase full of cash money handcuffed to his arm. Daddy says that he knew that a cashier's check would do, but sometimes it was all worth it for the gesture.

Gloria didn't think that the white folks would relent, but she knew better than anyone that her husband was capable of hitting a long shot. Who would have thought that he, a high school chemistry teacher, would land upon a discovery that would make them *comfortable*, as she likes to put it. When he returned sans briefcase, she discarded the brochures for modern stucco manses just outside the perimeter and started researching contractors that specialized in historic renovations. She says she is happier here, anyway, on the fringe of the old neighborhood, a community of schoolteachers, family doctors, and other salary-and-benefits jobs that were put into play by the civil rights movement. In one of the swanky subdivisions farther west, her neighbors were likely to have been rappers, plastic surgeons, or marketing executives. For his part, Daddy says he's glad not to be under the thumb of some homeowners' association that would try to tell him what he could and couldn't do with his own damn house.

Daddy is headstrong and persistent; these qualities are the key to his unlikely success. For twenty years he retreated to his basement laboratory tinkering with compounds after long days of teaching high school.

Most of my childhood memories of him involve him wearing a lab coat ornamented with a mishmash of vintage slogan buttons. "FREE ANGELA!" "SILENCE IS CONSENT!" "I AM A MAN!" Daddy let his afro thrive, wild and uncontrolled, even after "black is beautiful" mellowed into "black is just fine." Few women would have hung in with this sort of unkempt, dreamer husband, and never mind the peculiar odors that floated up from downstairs, but Gloria encouraged Daddy's experiments. She, too, worked all day, but she found time to fill out his patent applications and mail them in. When he is asked how he went from being a barefoot boy from Sunflower, Alabama, to the mad-scientist millionaire he is today, he explains that he was too ornery to fail.

I never imagined that he would ever turn his inflexible nature against me and Dre. After all, Dre had been my father's first choice. Roy, with his aspirations raw and pink like the skin underneath a scab, made my father like him as a person but not as a husband for me. "I bet he showers in a coat and tie," my father said. "I respect his ambition; I had mine. But you don't want to spend the rest of your life with a man who has something to prove." For Dre, on the other hand, Daddy had nothing but fondness. "Give ole Andre a chance," he said every so often, all the way up until the morning of my engagement party. When I insisted that we were like brother and sister, Daddy said, "Ain't nobody your sister but your sister." When he was on the wrong side of a fifth of Jack Black, he said, "Me and your mama, we came at our marriage the hard way. But you don't have to be smacked around by circumstance in order to live your life. Consider Andre. You know what he's about. He's already part of the family. Take the easy way for once."

But now it was all he could do to greet Dre with a curt nod hello.

Thanksgiving morning, Andre and I arrived at my parents' home light-handed, bearing little more than the news of our new commitment and Roy's upcoming release. I had promised two desserts—German chocolate cake for my father and chess pie for my mother, but I was too shaken to bake. Sweets are curious, temperamental, and moody. Any cake mixed by hand on this day would slump in the oven, refusing to rise.

We found my father out front struggling with his Christmas decorations. With so much acreage, he had space enough to properly express the full scope of his holiday spirit. His T-shirt was on backward, so ONLY IN ATLANTA ran across his narrow back as he squatted in the middle of the vast green yard, using a straight razor to open three cardboard boxes of wise men.

"Remember those shirts?" Dre said as we inched up the steep driveway.

I did remember. Only in Atlanta was one of Roy's many entrepreneurial ventures. He hoped it would be like a southern version of the I Love New York craze that made somebody somewhere extremely wealthy. Roy had only gotten as far as ordering a few T-shirts and key chains before he was taken away. "He always had a plan," I said.

"Yeah. He did," Dre said, turning to me. "You okay?"

"I'm good," I said. "What about you?'

"I'm ready. But I can't lie. Sometimes I feel guilty as hell for just being able to live my life."

I didn't have to tell him that I understood, because he knew that I did. There should be a word for this, the way it feels to steal something that's already yours.

We watched my father for a couple of minutes, gathering ourselves to perform holiday cheer. From each box, Daddy extracted Balthazar—the swarthy wise man—and stuffed the others back where they came from. What he planned for the six discarded white kings, I had no idea. Awaiting his attention were a crèche, two blow-up snowmen, and a family of grazing deer covered in lights. On the porch was Uncle Banks, halfway up a ladder, situating what looked like dripping icicles.

"Y'all," I said, throwing my arms wide and embracing the entire scene.

"Celestial," Daddy said, not ignoring Dre but not acknowledging him either. "You bake me a cake?"

"Hey, Mr. Davenport," Dre said, pretending to be welcome. "Happy Thanksgiving! You know we weren't going to come over here with our arms swinging on the holiday! I brought you some Glenlivet."

My father jutted his chin in my direction, and I leaned in and kissed his cheek. He smelled like cocoa butter and cannabis. He finally extended his hand to Andre, who accepted it with an optimistic face. "Happy Thanksgiving, Andre."

"Daddy," I whispered, "be kinder." Then I took Dre's hand, the one not holding the bottle, and we walked toward the front porch, which wrapped around the entire house. Before we made it to the doorway, my father called, "Thank you, Andre, for the libation. We'll sit down with it after dinner."

"Yes, sir," Andre said, pleased.

Uncle Banks was ahead of us on the porch, untangling a clump of lights.

"Hey, Uncle Banks," I said, hugging his legs on the ladder.

"Hey, baby girl," said my uncle. "And how are you, my man?" he said to Dre.

Just then Aunt Sylvia popped her head out the front door. My earliest memory of Sylvia was when she and Banks first started dating and they took me to the Omni for ice skating. As a souvenir, she bought me a pale yellow candle, set into a wineglass. My mother confiscated it immediately. "You can't give a child fire!" But Sylvia pleaded with my mother on my behalf. "Celestial won't light it, will you?" I shook my head no, and my mother paused. "Trust her," Sylvia said to Gloria, but her attention was on me. For my wedding, she walked the aisle before me, beaming as matron of honor, although technically she wasn't a married woman.

"Celestial and Andre! I am so glad you made it. Your mother wouldn't put the rolls in the oven until you got here." Angling her face toward Andre, she said, "Give me some sugar, nephew."

She pulled the door wide and Dre followed her in. I hung behind and stood at the base of the ladder. "Uncle Banks?"

"No," he said, reading my mind. "I didn't tell anybody but Sylvia. It's your call about breaking it to your folks."

"I want to thank you," I said. "You didn't give up."

"No, I did not. Those peckerwoods didn't know what hit them." Wearing his Sunday shoes, Uncle Banks took several careful steps down the ladder and landed on the porch beside me. "Your daddy is my oldest friend. We came to Atlanta in '58 without a penny between us. I'm more loyal to him than to my own brothers. But I want you to know that I don't agree with him on everything. As an attorney, I have seen it all, so I have some perspective. Frank, on some topics, he has the same ideas he was born with. But he treasures you, Celestial. You have all these people loving you—your daddy, Andre, Roy. Try to think of it as a high-class problem."

DINNER WAS SERVED on the heavy oak table, which was covered with a lace cloth to hide years of everyday use. While everything else in my parents' meticulously renovated dream home was lovely and polished, this table had a story to tell. It was a wedding gift from my grandmother, one of a few my parents received after their courthouse wedding. "You will pass this on to your children and their children," she had said. When the movers delivered it to the house, Gloria said, "Be careful. That table is my mother's blessing."

Only at holidays did my father reveal his training as a preacher's son. "O Lord," he boomed, and we all bowed our heads. I took Daddy's hand on my left side and Andre's on my right. "We are gathered here to give thanks for all the blessings you have heaped upon us. We thank you for this food and the table upon which it rests. We thank you for freedom. We pray for those behind bars tonight who cannot enjoy the balm and succor of family." Then he recited from memory a lengthy scripture.

Before we could all say "Amen," Andre spoke. "And we thank you for one another."

My mother raised her bowed head. "Amen to that."

Immediately, the room came to life with a pleasant racket. My father sliced through the turkey with the electric carving knife, which resembled a chain saw in miniature, as Gloria served iced tea from a gleaming pitcher. Banks and Sylvia sat at their places, as calm as a pretty day, but I was convinced that under the table Banks's hand rested on Sylvia's thigh. It was quite a tableau, the room stuffed with flowers as candles burned in the candelabras. I took a lemony sip of iced tea from a heavy glass, which reminded me of Olive. She adored crystal and bought her goblets one at a time. I wondered what happened to all her things after she passed, since she never had a daughter to bless with her approval or glassware. I bowed my head and said a prayer for her. *May heaven be filled with elegant objects.* Then I whispered to the air, "Please forgive me."

I shifted my eyes to my mother, hoping that she would grace me with at least a smile. Gloria is outrageously beautiful. I used to warn Roy not to see my mother as a guarantee on my future looks, although I share many of her features. We are both tall, deep brown, large-eyed, and full-lipped. She is Gloria Celeste and I am Celestial Gloriana. When I was a girl, she often kissed my forehead and called me her "love child."

I heaped my plate, but I was unable to eat. The secrets blocked my throat like a tumor. Anytime I said anything other than *Roy will be out before Christmas, and Andre and I are getting married*, it was a lie, no matter how true. Across the table, Uncle Banks cut his food but didn't have much appetite either. I was overcome with tenderness for my sweet uncle. He had done his best, and for all these years, until now, his best hadn't been enough. He deserved to be able to share the news with his friends. He deserved thanks and honest congratulations.

I felt Gloria studying me. I gazed at her with a question on my lips and she gave me a subtle nod, like she knew what she couldn't know.

Dessert was blackberry jam cake, a recipe passed to my mother from hers. To have a cake ready to serve on Thanksgiving, you have to bake it on the last day of summer, douse it in rum and seal it away when the fireflies are still thick on the breeze. This dessert figures into my parents' courtship. Gloria, at the time teaching social studies, offered a crumbling slice to the new chemistry teacher. "I was bewitched!" he claims to this very day.

Gloria placed the cake on the table and the aroma of rum, cloves, and cinnamon rose to meet me. I looked up at her over my shoulder and she said, quietly, "Whatever it is, you know I'll always be your mother." I turned my eyes to my plate, to the cake centered on the paper doily and to the tiny spoon balanced on the rim. It reminded me of our rehearsal dinner. Roy asked for my mother's specialty as his groom's cake. As everyone else ate duck and drank cava, Gloria pulled me outside the restaurant. Standing in the parking lot, beside a fragrant gardenia bush, she pulled me close. "I'm happy today because you're happy. Not because you're getting married. I don't care about all the top-shelf details. All I care about is you." And this was my mother's blessing. I hoped that she would extend it once more.

I turned to Andre, who radiated confident excitement. Then I glanced at Uncle Banks, who was deep into a murmured conversation with Sylvia. Finally I faced my father. For so many years I was Daddy's girl, his little Ladybug. When I married Roy, I wore ballerina flats, not so I would be shorter than Roy but so I wouldn't tower over my father. Even though I insisted that the pastor omit the word *obey*, for Daddy's sake we kept the line "who gives this woman" so he could say "I do" in his surprisingly deep voice.

At the table, when I lifted my glass, only a splash of tea remained. "I would like to make a toast." Five glasses rose as if of their own accord. "To Uncle Banks, whose tireless efforts have borne fruit. Roy will be released from prison before Christmas."

Sylvia let out a sweet cheer and pushed her glass forward through the silent air, hoping that someone would clang theirs against it. Uncle Banks said, "Thank you." My mother said, "Won't He do it!" And my father said nothing.

Andre pushed back from the table. Tall and narrow, he stood like a lighthouse. "Everyone, I've asked Celestial to marry me."

Roy and I announced our engagement at this same table, much in the same way, but our news had been greeted with Bordeaux and applause. This time, my father turned to me. "And what," he asked mildly, "did you say, Ladybug?"

I stood beside Andre. "Daddy, I said yes." I tried to make my words decisive, but I could hear the question in it, the need.

"We can work this out," my mother said with her eyes on my father. "We can talk it through."

Andre circled his arm around my shoulder and I felt myself breathing deep, calming breaths even as water burned my eyes. There was comfort in the truth, no matter how difficult.

My father set his dry glass beside his untouched cake. "It's not right," he said casually. "Ladybug, I can't cosign this one. You can't marry Andre if you already have a husband. I'm willing to take responsibility for my part in this. I indulged you since you were a little girl, so you think every day is supposed to be the weekend. But this is reality. You can't always get what you want."

"Daddy," I said. "You should know more than anybody that love doesn't always obey the rule book. When you and Mama got married—"

"Celestial." Gloria wore an expression I couldn't decipher, a warning in a foreign tongue.

Daddy broke in. "Entirely different scenario. When I met Gloria, there were extenuating circumstances. I was in a marriage that I rushed into too young. Your mother is my soulmate and helpmeet. Water always finds its own level."

"Mr. Davenport," said Andre. "Celestial is that for me. She is the one I want forever."

"Son," my father said, gripping the dessert spoon like a pitchfork. "I have one thing to say to you, as a black man: Roy is a hostage of the state. He is a victim of America. The least you could do is unhand his wife when he gets back."

"Mr. Davenport, with all due respect—"

"What's all this Mr. Davenport this, Mr. Davenport that. This ain't complicated. You want this man to come home after five years in the state penitentiary for some bullshit he didn't even do, and you want him to come back and see his wife with your little ring on her finger and you talking about you love her? I'll tell you what Roy is going to see: he is going to see a wife who wouldn't keep her legs closed and a so-called friend who doesn't know what it is to be a man, let alone a black man."

My mother was on her feet now. "Franklin, apologize."

Andre said, "Mr. Davenport, do you hear yourself? Hate me all you want. I came here hoping for your blessing, but I don't need it. But Celestial is your daughter. You can't say things like that about her."

"Don't cuss me, Daddy," I said. "Please don't cuss me."

Uncle Banks didn't rise, but he projected a calm authority. "You had to see this coming. Franklin, what do you want the girl to do?"

"I want her to be the girl we raised her to be."

Gloria said, "I raised her to know her own mind."

My father attached his hands to the sides of his head like he was trying to secure it on his neck. "What is all this stuff about love and her own mind? I don't mean to be harsh, but this is bigger than any little romance. She had her whole life to lay up with Andre if that's what she wanted to do. But that juncture has passed. What did Roy do to deserve any of this? He didn't do anything but be a black man in the wrong place at the wrong time. This is basic."

There was no easy comeback to this accusation. Andre and I were still standing, stranded in the crowded room. My father dug his spoon into the jam cake, self-satisfied, I could tell, with his performance, enjoying having spoken the last word.

Across the table, Sylvia whispered to Uncle Banks, her earrings tiny mirrors catching the light. Harnessing her nerve, she took an audible breath and spoke in a rush. "Technically, I'm not part of this family, but I've been here long enough. Y'all are way out of line. Every single one of you. First off, we need to take at least a minute to give Banks a round of applause. He worked like an animal these last five years. All anybody else did was write checks and pray. Banks was the one who got it done. He's the one who was fighting city hall."

We all mumbled embarrassed thanks, which Uncle Banks accepted with a charitable nod. Then he reached for Sylvia's hand, a signal for her to stand down. But she didn't.

"Now, Franklin." She cocked her head toward the head of the table. "You didn't ask my opinion, but I am giving it anyway. Look, Celestial already has to choose between Andre and Roy. Don't add your weight to this. Don't force Gloria to choose between her daughter and her husband, because you can't win that. Don't make your daughter feel like she got to lay with who you want her to lay with, like you're some kind of pimp. That's street fighting, Franklin, and you know it."

ROY

In the short/long weeks between when I got news that I was leaving until I actually left, Walter hardly slept at all, talking through the night, 1,001 life lessons for the recently un-incarcerated. "Remember," he said, "your woman has been in the world this whole time."

"You don't know her," I said. "How are you going to tell me what she's been doing?"

He said, "I can't tell you what I don't know—which is what she has been up to. I have no idea, and neither do you. The only thing I know for sure is that everyone else's life has moved forward, just not yours."

According to him, the key is to wipe your mind clean. The future is what I should think about. But he never explained how I was supposed to not pine for what I used to have. Walter didn't understand because there is nothing behind him but missed opportunities and regret. For him, the chance to start anew would be a reprieve, but for me it would be the mother of all setbacks.

Until they slapped a twelve-year sentence on me, I had hit everything I aimed for: a job that more than paid the bills, a four-bedroom house with a big lawn I cut myself on Sundays, and a wife who lifted me up like a prayer. My job was good, but in a couple of years, I would look for a better one. Our place on Lynn Valley Road was a starter house. Next on the agenda was children. It takes being together to another level when you go to bed for a purpose larger than your own feelings. Even after what happened next, I'll never forget that night and all our sweaty intentions.

"Walter, you tell me to forget what I had and to focus my mind on what I want going forward, but for me, it's the same thing."

"Hmm," he said, buckling his face like he was thinking some deep Ghetto Yoda thoughts. "Well, somebody in your situation needs to look at life like a newborn baby. Pretend like you have never been in the world before and you're waiting for it to show you what's what. Keep your head in the right now."

I surveyed my pitiful surroundings. "You can't tell me to live in the present when the past was so much better."

He clucked his tongue. "You know what you have right now? Right now you have to clean that sink."

Even in prison where everything is upside down, I could see how weird it was—him giving me chores. My Biological threw a small sponge at me and I caught it. "It's your turn," I told him, tossing it back.

"Fathers don't have a turn," he said, batting it back in my direction.

I rubbed a little bar of soap against the yellow sponge and started wiping down the sink, which wasn't really that dirty.

"Country Yoda," I said.

"Watch your mouth."

WHAT WALTER DIDN'T tell me was that innocent or not, I wouldn't be allowed to leave through the front door, a modest expectation from a man who should have known better than to expect much. Banks warned me not to look for any kind of formal apology, no envelope outfitted with the state seal. Hell, I didn't even know the names of the officials I should have demanded this apology from. I wasn't getting any restitution other than the twenty-three sorry dollars that everybody gets when they walk out of the Louisiana State Penitentiary. But was it unreasonable for me to think that I, as an innocent man, having paid somebody else's debt to society, would be allowed to exit through the front door? I pictured myself making my way down a big marble stairway with the sun shining on my face, entering a little grassy lawn where my whole family would be waiting for me, even though Olive was two years dead and Celestial was two years gone. Big Roy would be there. This much, I could take to the bank. But for true, only a woman can truly welcome a man back home, wash his feet, and fix his plate.

KNOWING THAT I wasn't walking out anyone's front door, my father waited in the back parking lot, leaning on the hood of his Chrysler. I walked toward him, and Big Roy straightened his collar and ran his palm over his hair. As I shielded my eyes against the late afternoon sun, his face broke into a smile.

A dozen of us were released that day. For a young cat, no more than twenty, a family waited with metallic balloons shaped like Christmas ornaments; a little boy wearing a red rubber nose squeezed the bulb on a bicycle horn, somehow causing the nose to glow. Another dude didn't have anybody. He didn't look left or right but walked straight to the gray van that would carry him to the bus station, as though pulled by a leash. All the rest were picked up by women: some mamas, others wives or girlfriends. The ladies drove to the gate but made sure to let the man take the wheel as they left. I was the last one out the door on that bright winter day. My shoes felt foreign on my feet—leather wingtips. My dress socks got lost somewhere, so I settled my feet in the shoes raw. The texture of the asphalt was rough beneath the leather soles as I walked to my father. *Father*, what a clumsy word now, as I approached Big Roy, afraid to want anything at all. Not that I would ask for much. When I was in high school, too old for Roy to punish me for cutting up, the way boys do, he would say, "Listen here, boy, get yourself arrested, don't call me. I'm not into prodigals. I don't do welcome-back parties." But that was when we thought incarceration had something to do with being guilty or at least being stupid.

If anybody deserved a party, it was me, the other son, the one that didn't get the fatted calf. Or Job. Or Esau or any of the many people in the Bible left hanging. When I went to fill a bucket with ice on that fateful night, every smart decision I'd made suddenly became irrelevant.

Somebody raped that woman—that was clear from her shaky fingers twitching in her lap—but not me. I remember feeling tender toward her when I met her that night at the ice machine. I told her that she reminded me of my mother and she said she always wanted a son. Walking to her room, I spilled my guts, telling her about my stupid fight with Celestial, and she promised to light a candle for me.

At the trial, I was a little sorry for her as she marched her way through her awful story, ruining my life. She spoke carefully, as though she memorized her statement, using textbook terms to describe her own body and what had been done to it. She stared at me in the courtroom with a mouth quivering with fear but also with hurt and rage. In her mind, I was the one who did it, just after she prayed for me and for my marriage and the baby we were trying for. When they asked her if she was sure, she said she would know me anywhere.

Sometimes I wonder if she would know me now. Would anybody who knew me then recognize me today? Innocent or not, prison changes you, makes you into a convict. Striding across the parking lot, I actually shook my head like a wet dog to get these thoughts out of my mind. I reminded myself that the point was that I was walking out the door. Front door, back door. Same difference.

So this is me. A free man, as they say. Don't nobody care about shiny balloons, cognac, or fatted calves.

BIG ROY DIDN'T rise from his place leaning on the fender and run across the lot to meet me. He watched me approach, and when I was in striking distance, he opened up his arms and pulled me in. I was thirty-six years old. I knew I had a lot of years left, but I couldn't stop counting those I'd forfeited. I bit down on my lip and tasted the hot flavor of my own blood as I rested there, feeling the weight and safety of my father's arms. "Good to see you, son," and I enjoyed the feel of the word, for the truth in it.

"You, too," I said.

"You're early," he said.

I couldn't help but smile at that. I didn't even know what part of *early* he was talking about. Was he talking about the five-day bump-up that was announced three days ago? Then, of course, there was the fact that I got away with putting in less than half of a twelve-year bid. So I said, "You the one who taught me that five minutes early is late."

He smiled, too. "Glad to know you were listening."

"My whole life."

WE SETTLED INTO the Chrysler, the same car he drove when I went in. "Want to go visit Olive? I haven't been there today yet."

"No," I said, because I wasn't ready to confront the rectangle of land with my mother's name scraped deep into cold marble. The only "her" I wanted to see was Celestial, but she was in Atlanta, 507 highway miles away, and she didn't even know yet that I was free.

Big Roy let his shoulders fall. "I suppose it's all right. Olive ain't going nowhere."

I believe he meant it in an offhand way, but the words burrowed in deep. "No, she's not," I said.

We drove the next mile or so quietly. To the right, the casino's neon lights competed with the sunshine and won. Cars ant-hilled around, looking for parking. Up ahead, a highway patrol car's nose stuck out from a stand of bushes, speed trap, the same as always.

"So when you going to see her?"

This time *her* was Celestial. "In a couple of days."

"She know you coming?"

"Yeah. I sent a letter. But she didn't hear that the date was moved up."

"How would she hear it if you didn't tell her?"

I didn't really have much to say back but the truth. "Let me get my constitution straight first."

Big Roy nodded. "You know for sure she still your wife?"

"She didn't divorce me," I said. "That's got to mean something."

Big Roy said, "She's doing well for herself."

I nodded. "In a way, I guess." I almost added that an artist can only be so famous in America, but I didn't want to sound jealous or petty. I added, "I'm real proud of her."

My daddy didn't look up from the road. "I haven't seen Celestial since your mama's funeral, with your friend Andre. It was good to see her there."

I nodded again.

"That was two years ago, actually a little more. No sign of her since."

"Me either, but she put money on my account," I said. "Every month."

"That's something," Big Roy said. "I won't disrespect that. When I get home, I'll show you the magazine with her picture."

"I already saw it," I said. Posing with a pair of dolls that look like her parents, Celestial smiles like she never suffered a day in her life. I read the article three times. Twice silently and once aloud to Walter, who conceded that the article didn't mention me, but he also observed that there was no mention of another man either. Still, I was in no hurry to see the magazine again. "They have a subscription to *Ebony*, the jail does. *Jet, Black Enterprise*. The whole trifecta."

"Is that racist?" Big Roy asked.

"Maybe a little." I laughed. "My cell mate liked to read *Essence*. He would fan the magazine and say, 'There are a lot of women out there in need of a man!' He was an older cat. Walter was his name. He looked out for me." An emotion I hadn't booked on shook my words.

"He did?" Big Roy lifted his hand from the steering wheel like he was going to adjust the rearview, but then he scratched his own chin and set his hand back on the wheel. "That's a blessing. A small blessing." The light changed, but Big Roy hesitated. Behind us, cars beeped their horns, but timidly, like they didn't mean to interrupt. "I'm glad for anything or anybody that helped to get you home alive, son."

The drive to Eloe was only about forty-five minutes, plenty of time for a man to get things off his chest, but I didn't share any of the news that had been bouncing off the walls of my skull for the last three years. I told myself that the story wasn't like a carton of milk; it wouldn't go bad if I kept it to myself a little longer. The truth would remain true for a week, for a month, for a year, ten years, however long it was before I felt like talking to Big Roy about Walter, if I ever did.

Big Roy drove the car up into the yard. "It's getting bad around here," he said. "Somebody tried to steal the Chrysler. Came in the yard with a tow truck when I wasn't home, told the neighbors that I asked them to do it. It was lucky that my partner, Wickliffe, was home from work and run them off with his pistol."

"Wickliffe is what? Eighty years old?"

"You're as young as your gun," Big Roy said.

"Only in Eloe," I said.

It felt strange coming home with no bags to bring in. My arms felt useless as they swung by my side.

"Hungry?" Big Roy asked.

"Starving."

He opened the side door and I stepped into the living room. Everything was laid out the same way—sectional situated so that every seat provided a view of the television. The recliner was new, but it was placed where the old one had been. Above the couch was a large piece of art that Olive prized, showing a serene woman wearing an African head scarf, reading a book. Olive bought it at the swap meet and paid extra for the gilded frame. The room was so clean that a faint lemony smell rose up from the vacuum tracks in the carpet.

"Who fixed up the house?" I said.

"Your mama's church ladies. When they heard you were coming home, they came over here like a cooking-cleaning army."

I nodded. "Any one church lady in particular?"

"No," Big Roy said. "It's too soon for all of that. Come in. Go on in the bathroom and wash up."

While I was lathering my hands in the sink, I thought of Walter washing his hands in his obsessive way. I wondered if he had a new cell partner by now. I gave Walter everything I owned—clothes, hairbrush, my few books, and my radio. I even left my deodorant. What he could use he would keep, and what he could trade or sell would be swapped or sold.

The hot water felt good, and I left my hands under the faucet until I couldn't stand the heat.

"On your bed are some essentials. Tomorrow you can go to Walmart and get whatever else you need."

"Thanks, Daddy."

That word, *Daddy*. I never used it with Walter even though I think he would have liked it. He even said it himself a couple of times, "Listen to me. I'm your daddy." But never did I let the word escape my lips.

Once I was washed up, Big Roy and I heaped our plates. It was the same fare they brought out when somebody died—baked chicken, string beans boiled slow with ham, clover rolls, macaroni and cheese. Big Roy placed his dinner in the microwave, pushed a few buttons, and the plate revolved under the light. Sparks flew as the metal rim popped like a cap gun. Using oven mitts, he removed his food, covered it with a paper towel, and held his hand out for mine.

We sat together in the living room with our plates resting on our laps.

"You want to say the blessing?" Big Roy asked me.

"Heavenly," I began, choking again on the word *father*. "Thank you for this food that will nourish our bodies." I tried to find other things to say, but all I could think about was how my mother was gone forever and my wife wasn't here either. "Thank you for my father. Thank you for this homecoming." Then I added, "Amen." I kept my head down waiting for Big Roy to echo. When he didn't, I looked up to find him rocking slightly with his hand over his mouth.

"All Olive wanted was to see this day. That was all she ever asked for and she's not here to experience it. You're home and we're sitting here eating other women's food. I know the Lord has a plan, but this isn't right."

I should have gone over to him, but what did I know about comforting a grown man? Olive would have sat beside him, pulled his face into her chest and shushed him in a woman's way. Even though I was hungry, I didn't pick up my fork until he was able to pick up his. By then, the magic of the microwave had worn off, leaving the food tough and dry.

Big Roy stood up. "You tired, son? I would like to go to bed early. Start fresh in the morning."

It was only seven o'clock, but in winter the days are short, if not warm. I

went to my room and dressed in the pajamas Big Roy or maybe the church
ladies set out for me.

FIVE YEARS WAS a long time in real-life time. In inside life, it
wasn't forever. It was a stretch of time with an end you could see. I wonder
what I would have done differently if I had known that five years was all
I was looking at. It was hard being behind bars when I turned thirty-five,
but would it have been so hard if somebody told me that the next year
I would be a free man? Time can't always be measured with a watch or a
calendar or even grains of sand.

"Celestial." I did this every night, chanting her name like a plea, even
after her letter written on paper the color of the palms of my useless hands.
Even when I did the things that it embarrasses me to recollect, I was always thinking of her, wondering what I would tell her about what I had
done, what was given me, what was stolen, who I touched. Sometimes I
thought she would understand. Or even if she didn't, she would come to
empathize. She would know that I thought that I was gone away forever.

Celestial was a tricky woman to figure out; she almost didn't marry
me, although I never doubted her love. For one thing, I made a couple of
procedural errors with my proposal, but more than that, I don't think she
planned on getting married at all. She kept this display she called a "vision
board," basically a corkboard where she tacked up words like *prosperity*,
creativity, passion! There were also magazine pictures that showed what
she wanted out of life. Her dream was for her artworks to be part of the
Smithsonian, but there was also a cottage on Amelia Island and an image
of the earth as seen from the moon. No wedding dress or engagement ring
factored into this little collage. It didn't bother me, but it bothered me.

It's not that I was planning a wedding like a twelve-year-old girl, nor
was I some clown fantasizing about fathering ten sons, handing out cigars

every eighteen months. But I pictured myself with two kids, Trey and then a girl. Spontaneity and playing it by ear is fine for those who can afford it, but a boy from Eloe had to have a strategy. This was something that Celestial and I had in common; neither of us believed in letting chips fall where they may.

About a year ago, in the throes of hopelessness, I destroyed every letter she ever sent me, except for her carefully composed Dear John. And yes, Walter warned me against wadding all that scented paper into a ball and plunking it into the metal commode. Why I chose to save the one letter that hurt me most, I don't know. But now, on my first night of breathing unfettered air, here I was about to read it again.

If I could have stopped myself, I would have. Unfolding the page carefully so that it wouldn't give way at the softened creases, I ran my fingers under the words, feeling for the hope I sometimes found sheltered there.

CELESTIAL

Ours was a love story, the kind that's not supposed to happen to black girls anymore. This was vintage romance made scarce after Dr. King, along with Negro-owned dress shops, drugstores, and cafeterias. By the time I was born, Sweet Auburn, once the richest Negro street in the world, was split in two by the freeway and left to die. Stubborn Ebenezer was still standing, a proud reminder of her famous son, whose marble tomb and eternity flame kept watch next door. When I was twenty-four, living in New York City, I thought that maybe black love went that way, too, integrated into near extinction.

Nikki Giovanni said, "Black love is Black wealth." On a drunk night in the West Village, my roommate Imani tattooed this on her right hip, hoping for the best. She and I were both HBCU alums, so grad school was culture shock and dystopia at the same time. In art school there were only two of us who were black, and the other one, a guy, seemed to be mad at me every day for spoiling his uniqueness. Imani was in the same boat, getting her poetry degree, so we took jobs waiting tables at Maroons, a restaurant in Manhattan that specialized in black comfort food from all over the globe: jerk chicken, jollof rice, collard greens, and corn bread. Our boyfriends were our supervisors, smoldering men with colonial accents. Too old, too broke, and too handsome, they were as faithless as the weather, but like Imani said, "Black and alive is always a good start."

Back then, I was trying to fit into the New York artsy scene. I was always on a diet, and I tried to stop saying "y'all" and "ma'am." For the most part, I was successful, unless I was drinking. After three gin fizzes, all that Southwest Atlanta came pouring out like I never had an elocution lesson. Roy, back then, lived in Atlanta metro but only barely, renting an apartment so far out that he could hardly catch the R&B station on the radio. He worked a cubicle job that compensated him fairly well for agreeing to integrate their workplace. He didn't like or dislike it; for him, a job was a means to an end. The travel part of it he did enjoy, since before signing on he hadn't ventured west of Dallas or north of Baltimore.

Of course, I wasn't aware of any of this when Imani seated his party at a big round table in my section. All I knew was that table 6 was a party of eight, seven of whom were white. Expecting him to be *that* kind of brother, I was all business. As I recited the specials, I could feel the black guy staring at me, even though the redhead to his left appeared to be his girlfriend, leaning toward him as she read the menu. Finally, she ordered a sorrel caipirinha. "And what will you have, sir?" I asked him, chilly as a tax auditor.

"I'll have a Jack and coke," he said. "Georgia girl."

I flinched like someone slipped an ice cube down the back of my shirt. "My accent?"

All the people at his table grinned, especially the redhead. "You don't have a southern accent," she declared. "All *of us* are from Georgia. You're all Yankee."

Yankee was a white word, the verbal equivalent of the rebel flag, leftover anger about the civil war. I turned back to the black guy—we were a team now—and gave the tiniest of eye rolls. In response, he gave an almost imperceptible shoulder shrug that said, *White folk gonna white folk.* Then he leaned slightly away from the redhead, this time communicating, *This is a work dinner. She isn't my date.*

Then, in words, he said, "I think I know you. Your hair is different, but didn't you go to Spelman? I'm Roy Hamilton, your Morehouse brother."

I never really bought into the SpelHouse mentality about us being brothers and sisters, maybe because I had been a transfer student, missing out on the Freshman Week rituals and ceremonies. But at that twinkle, it was as though we discovered that we were long-lost play cousins.

"Roy Hamilton." I said the name slowly, trying to jog some sort of memory, but he looked too much like a standard-issue Morehouse man, the type who declared his business major in kindergarten.

"What was your name again?" he asked, squinting at my name tag, which read IMANI. The real Imani was across the room wearing a CELESTIAL tag.

"Imani," the redhead said, clearly annoyed. "Can't you read?"

Roy pretended like he didn't hear her. "No," he said. "That's not it. Your name was something old timey, like Ruthie Mae."

"Celestial," I said. "I'm named for my mother."

"I'm surprised you don't go by Celeste now that you're up here in New York City. I'm Roy, Roy Othaniel Hamilton, to be exact."

At the sound of that middle name—talk about old timey—I did remember him. He had been a playboy, a mack, a hustler. All those things. My manager, who only yesterday insisted that he was not my man, cleared his throat. Game recognize game and all of that.

Is this nostalgia? Is this how it really happened? I wish we had taken a photo so I could remember how we looked later that evening standing outside the restaurant. Winter arrived early that year. Roy wore a lightweight wool coat, with a puny little scarf that probably came with it. I was bundled against the elements in a down coat Gloria sent me, so convinced was she that I would die of hypothermia before I finished my "artist phase" and came back home to get a master's in education. Snow fell in wet clumps, but I didn't tie my hood, wanting Roy to see my face.

Much of life is timing and circumstance, I see that now. Roy came into my life at the time when I needed a man like him. Would I have galloped into this love affair if I had never left Atlanta? I don't know. But how you feel love and understand love are two different things. Now, so many years down the road, I recognize that I was alone and adrift and that he was lonely in the way that only a ladies' man can be. He reminded me of Atlanta, and I reminded him of the same. All these were reasons why we were drawn to each other, but standing with him outside of Maroons, we were past reason. Human emotion is beyond comprehension, smooth and uninterrupted, like an orb made of blown glass.

ROY

Standing on the sidewalk outside the restaurant, I memorized her—the shape of her lips and the purple tint of her lipstick, which matched the streaks in her hair. I knew her accent, southern but not too much, and I knew her shape, thick through the hips but slim on top. I had said her name was "something old timey," but I should have said "something classic." I could remember the feel of her name in my mouth, like the details of a dream.

"Want to see Brooklyn?" she asked. "My other roommate works at Two Steps Down. If we go there, we can drink for free."

My first mind was to tell her that we didn't need free cocktails, but I had a feeling she would be more annoyed than impressed, so I said, "Let's get a taxi."

"You won't get a taxi tonight."

"How come?" By way of question, I tapped the brown skin peeking out between my camel-hair coat and my soft leather gloves.

"That," she said, "and it's snowing. Meter's double. We better take the subway." She pointed at a green orb, and we descended a staircase into a world that reminded me of that dark scene in *The Wiz*.

"After you," she said, depositing a token at the turnstile, nudging me through.

I felt like a blind man who left his cane at home. "You know," I said. "I'm here on business. Sales meeting in the morning."

She smiled in a polite way. "That's nice," she said, but she didn't care at all about my professional standing. Hell, I didn't even care about it all that much, but the point was to remind her that I had something going on in my life.

I'm not a fan of public transportation. In Atlanta, there was the bus or the MARTA train, and you only took those if you couldn't afford a car. When I first got to Morehouse, I had no choice, but as soon as I gathered four nickels at the same time, I bought myself the last remaining Ford Pinto. Andre called it the "Auto Bomb" on account of the safety issue, but it never stopped him or anybody else from bumming a ride.

The A train was nothing like you would think from the song. The New York subway was packed with people, and you could smell whatever stuffed their damp sleeping bag coats. The floor was covered with the kind of linoleum that you only find in the projects, and the seats were a fixed-income shade of orange. And do not get me started on the able-bodied men sprawled out, taking up two seats sometimes while ladies were left standing.

For the jerky ride, we stood in front of a black lady who clinched a large shopping bag to her chest and slept like she was at home in the bed. Beside her was a light-skinned dude, the type we used to call "DeBarge." He had a portrait gallery inked all over his head. Over his cheekbone was a woman's face, and she appeared to be weeping.

"Georgia," I said into her hair. "How can you live up here?"

She turned around to answer me, and our faces were so close that she leaned back to keep from kissing me. "I'm not really living here, living here. I'm in grad school, paying dues."

"So you're pretending to be a waitress?"

She adjusted her grip on the strap and lifted her foot to show me a black shoe with a thick rubber sole. "Somebody needs to tell my feet I'm pretending, because they are killing me like I'm really working."

I chuckled with her, but I felt sorry, thinking about my mama back in Louisiana who was always complaining about her arches. She claimed it was because of the high heels she wore on Sundays, but it was really from being on her feet all day, fixing trays at the meat-and-three.

"What are you in school for?" I hoped that she wasn't getting a PhD, an MBA, or a law degree. It's not like I had anything against women getting ahead in the world, but I didn't want to have to explain why it was that I decided to cool my heels with just my BA.

"Fine arts," she said, "concentrating on textiles and folk art." I could see from the little turn-up at the corner of her eyes that she was so proud that she could have been her own mother, but I had no idea what she was talking about.

"Is that right?" I said.

"I'm an artisan," she said, not like she was explaining but like she was sharing the good news. "I'm a doll maker."

"That's what you're going to do for a living?"

"Haven't you ever heard of Faith Ringgold?" I hadn't, but she kept on. "I want to be like her. With dolls instead of quilts. I want to get a tax ID and go into business."

"What's the name of the corporation?"

"Babydolls," she said.

"Sounds like a strip club."

"No, it doesn't," she said, loud enough that it woke up the lady dozing on the seat in front of us. The guy with the face tattoos twitched a little bit.

"It's just that my degree is in marketing," I said. "It's my job to think about things like that."

She kept looking like she was offended in a pretty meaningful way.

"Maybe another name might be more effective." Since it seemed like I was moving in the right direction, I kept going. "You could call it Poupées. That's French for dolls."

"French?" she asked, eyeing me. "You're Haitian?"

"Me?" I shook my head. "I'm a standard-issue American Negro."

"But you speak French?" She sounded hopeful, like she had a translation job that needed doing. For a second, I considered throwing down my Louisiana credentials, because women dig it when you claim to be Creole, but I didn't feel like lying to her. "I studied French in high school and took a few hours toward a minor at Morehouse."

"My supervisor, Didier," she said. "He's Haitian. Kind of Haitian. He was born in Brooklyn but still Haitian. You know how it is up here. He speaks French."

I may seem like I fell off a turnip truck, but I knew enough to know that it's never a good sign when a woman brings up another brother out of the blue like that.

After we changed trains, she finally said, "This is our stop," and led me up a filthy little staircase tiled like a public restroom. As we emerged into the Brooklyn night, I was surprised to see trees up and down the sides of the road. As I looked up at their stripped branches, chubby snow-flakes floated down. I'm a southern boy by birth and constitution, so a real snowfall was something to see. It was all I could do not to stick my tongue out to taste one. "It's like TV," I said.

"Tomorrow it will be all filthy and stacked up on the side of the road. But it's nice when it's fresh like this."

We turned down the next street and I wanted to take her hand. The buildings on each side of the road were light brown, like pencil shavings, and the walls of one touched the other so that the road appeared to be flanked by castles. She explained that each of the brownstones was built to be houses for one family, all four stories, but now they were cut up into apartments.

"I live right there," she said, pointing across the street and down. "Garden level. See?"

I followed her arm with my eyes.

"Oh, hell no," she said. "Not again."

I was squinting in the light, trying to peek between the snowflakes to see what she was worried about. Before I could figure out what from what, she hollered, "Hey," and took off like she had been snapped from a slingshot. She got four or five seconds on me, just from the surprise factor. When I took off after her, I still wasn't 100 percent sure what was going on. I gave it all I had, but I was still pulling up the rear. Like Spike Lee said that time: *It's the shoes.* What I wore on my feet were for styling, not striding— oxblood Florsheims that would make a preacher covetous. Leather upper *and* sole. Celestial had on glorified nurse's shoes, ugly as newborn puppies, but a plus in a street race.

When I spotted the dude running, I assessed the situation. In between her calling him all kinds of motherfuckers, she ordered him, "Put my shit down!" Apparently, we were chasing a burglar, one who could really move. She was going pretty good, but this dude was booking. He had on a pair of Jordans he probably stole from somebody, and like I said, it's the shoes.

Carlton Avenue is a long street. Brownstones on each side, all the way, and trees with roots that buckled the sidewalk, turning the chase into an obstacle course. Apparently, I was the only one without prior experience. Celestial was hopping over the exposed roots without missing a beat. The burglar was even better, graceful even. You could tell this wasn't his first rodeo.

He knew she wasn't going to catch him. *I knew* she wasn't going to catch him. As a sensible man, I'm not one to chase wild geese, but I had to keep running as long as she did. How would it look if I hung back while my date chased a criminal? So I kept pushing, even though I was struggling to breathe. A man does what he has to do.

How long did this chase go on? Forever. Between the cold air icing up my lungs and shoes pinching my feet, it occurred to me that I might be killing myself. Ahead, Celestial focused on the kid, and cussing like a longshoreman. I caught a charley horse, only it was in my heart. Even though all the profanity slowed her down a hair, it wasn't looking good for me. I was bigger, late to start, and to cap it off, I was dressed like Louis Farrakhan. I'm no follower of the Nation, but the thought of Farrakhan gave me a little boost. He may be outrageous on some matters, but he has a grip on some basic things. No matter what Minister Farrakhan happened to be wearing, there was no way he would let a sister apprehend a burglar while he sat back and watched.

I swear, just then, the gods smiled on me. As I dug down in my inner reserve for strength and endurance, Celestial's foot snagged on a chunk of jagged sidewalk and she went sprawling. In three strides, I caught up and jumped over her like Carl Lewis. For me, the race was over right then, before my dress shoes hit the ground. They could have played the theme music and rolled the credits with me in midair.

Too bad this wasn't a movie. I landed, slid a few inches in the wrong direction, got my bearings back and kept moving. The kid was only a couple of sidewalk squares ahead, looking back. Now I went for the grand prize. I pumped my arms and legs harder, trying to recall anything I learned from high school track. Then he stumbled, costing him some ground. He was close enough now that I could read the label on the back of his shirt: Kani. My fingers closed around his skinny ankle as I hit the asphalt with my right knee taking the lead. He gave his leg a couple of vigorous shakes, but I was holding on for dear life.

"What the hell is wrong with you?" he marveled. "What if I had a gun?"

I honestly stopped a second to think about it, and in that second, he jerked his foot free and kicked me in the face. To his credit, I will say that he didn't kick me as harshly as he could have. He didn't stomp my head into the sidewalk. As kicks go, it was more like a love tap, delivered straight to my mouth, knocking loose one of my bottom teeth.

Behind me, I could hear Celestial's rubber-soled footfalls. I was scared that she was going to play me like a hurdle and continue this crazy chase, but she stopped and knelt beside me.

"I didn't get your stuff back," I said, gasping for breath.

"I don't care. You're my hero," she said. I thought she was being funny, but her hands on the side of my face said that she wasn't.

The dentist who fitted me for a bridge told me that he could have saved my tooth if I had gone to the hospital. Celestial even suggested it at the time, but I waved it away as we headed back to her small apartment that she shared with three people and a dozen baby dolls. She gave me a cold compress and called the police. The officer didn't arrive for another two hours, and by then my nose was wide open. I was giddy like the Jackson 5. *Do re mi. ABC.* On the police report, she signed her full name and I would have tattooed it on my forehead: Celestial Gloriana Davenport.

ANDRE

The whole truth wasn't anybody's business but mine and Celestial's.

On the Sunday before we laid Olive to rest, I visited the prison while Celestial stayed with Roy's father. I say *visit* for lack of a better term. Maybe it's best to say that I went to see him. As we shared three bags of chips from the vending machine, Roy asked me to take his place on Monday morning and carry his mother's casket from the hearse to the altar. I agreed but not gladly; this wasn't a task you take on with pleasure. Big Roy had drafted an extra deacon to carry the right-hand corner load, but I was to explain to him that Roy sent me and the deacon would step aside. We shook on it, like we were finishing a business deal. When we let go, I stood up to leave, but Roy didn't move.

"I got to stay here until visiting hours are over."

"You'll just sit?"

He curled up one side of his mouth. "It's better than going back in there. I don't mind it."

"I can wait another minute," I said, returning to the plastic chair.

"You see that dude?" He pointed to a skinny man with a flat-top fade and Malcolm X glasses. "That's my father. My Biological. I met him in here."

I stole a glance at the older man who was speaking to a chubby brunette wearing a flowered dress.

"He met her from the classifieds," Roy explained.

"I wasn't looking at his lady," I said. "I'm tripping. Your actual father?"

"Apparently so." He went over my face, slowly, like he was searching a grid. "You didn't know," he said. "You didn't know."

"How would I know?"

"Celestial didn't tell you. If she didn't tell you, she didn't tell anybody." As he was pleased, I felt a little sting somewhere between a mosquito and a yellow jacket.

"You look like your pops," I said, pointing with my chin.

"Big Roy is my pops. Him over there, we're cool now, but back in the day, nigger went for a pack of cigarettes and never came back. Now I see him every day." He shook his head. "I feel like it's supposed to mean something—like in the whole scheme of things—but I don't know what."

I sat there silent, uncomfortable in the gray suit I would wear to the wake later in the day. I had no idea what it could mean. Fathers were complicated beings. I was seven when my father met a woman at a trade show and defected, creating a new family. My dad had pulled this sort of trick before, falling stupid in love with a stranger and threatening to set up house with her. His business—running an icehouse—required that he travel to conventions, where he got caught up in the excitement. He was a passionate man, clearly. When I was three, he fell for a woman who hailed from the world of dry ice and shipping, but she decided not to leave her husband, and he returned to Evie and me. After that, there were other zealous flirtations, but nothing stuck. He met the Ice Sculptress at an overnight trade show in Denver. After just under thirty-six hours in her marvelous company, he came home, packed up all his shit and was gone for good. For whatever it's worth, they have a son and a daughter together and he hung tight and watched them grow up.

I spread my hands. "The Lord works in mysterious ways?"

"Something like that," he said. "My mama is gone."

"I know," I said. "I'm sorry."

He shook his head, and contemplated his palms. "I appreciate you," he said. "Carrying her for me."

"You know I got you," I said.

"Tell Celestial I miss her. Tell her I said thank you for singing."

"No problem," I said again, pushing up from my chair.

"Dre," he said. "Don't take this the wrong way. But she's my wife. Remember that." Then he smiled, big and broad, revealing a dark gap. "I'm just kidding, man. Tell her I asked after her."

CELESTIAL ISN'T THE kind of singer you would want at your wedding. While her mother is a gravity-defying soprano, she is a scotch-and-Marlboros alto. Even when she was a little girl, her voice was like the middle of the night. When she gives a song, it isn't entertaining; rather, it sounds like she is telling secrets that are not hers to reveal.

Just as Roy asked me to be a pallbearer, he asked Celestial to offer up a hymn. She walked to the front of the congregation not looking at all like herself. With her hair ironed straight and a navy-blue dress borrowed from Gloria, she seemed humbled. Not brought low, but there was respect in her decision not to be gorgeous.

"Miss Olive loved two things." The microphone gave her words a ghost echo. "She loved the Lord and she loved her family, especially her son. Most of you know why Roy is not here. But he's not absent." As Celestial stepped back a few paces, the nurse ushers communicated with hand signals, ready to swoop in, in case she was about to break down, but she was stepping back only because her voice was too big for her to stand so close to the sound system.

She sang "Jesus Promised Me a Home" without the benefit of a piano accompaniment, looking past the casket of dark wood. Staring right at Roy Senior, she gave it all she had until women stood up and raised their fans, and a gentleman in the front room repeated, "Thank you, Jesus." Singing, she wounded and healed both. "If He said it, I know it's true." She wasn't grandstanding or trying to break him down, but she hollered out that melody, delivering both the Holy Spirit and earthly emotion until Big Roy's shoulders bucked and the cooling waters came down. I'm no theologian, but there was Love in that room. She said that Roy was not absent, and when she finished, not one soul doubted this.

Celestial returned to the pew beside me, exhausted, and I took her hand. With her head on my shoulder she said, "I want to go home."

After the eulogy, which was standard fare about wives and mothers, with talk of the book of Ruth, it was time for the pallbearers to take our places. Roy Senior insisted that we bear her weight in the formal way, balanced on our shoulders without the benefit of hands. The mortician directed us like he was conducting an orchestra, and at his command the six of us settled Miss Olive upon our shoulders and inched our way out of the sanctuary. There is no weight like the burden of a body. The load was shared by six, but I felt alone in my labors. With every step, the casket bumped my ear, and for a superstitious second, I thought I was maybe receiving a dispatch from the other side.

The three of us—Roy Senior, Celestial, and me—rode in a limousine driven by the undertaker's son, who asked if we wanted air-conditioning. "No, Reggie," Roy Senior said. "I prefer fresh air." And he lowered the window, letting in a humid breeze, as thick as blood. I sat still, concentrating on breathing. Celestial was wearing a perfume that smelled like romance. Roy Senior sucked on peppermint, strong and sweet. On my left side, Celestial took my hand, and I enjoyed the cool feel of it.

"I would appreciate it if you wouldn't do that," Roy Senior said. She pulled her fingers away, leaving me with a vacant palm.

After a few miles, the hearse led the small processional down a bumpy, unpaved road. The jostling unlocked something in Roy Senior, who said, "I love Olive in ways you young people can't even picture. I was the best husband I knew how to be and the best father I could manage. She showed me how to join with a woman. She taught me to take care of a little boy."

I flexed my hand. "Yes, sir," I said, and Celestial hummed a tune I recognized but didn't know the title of. She was like a different person, deeper and broader, like she perceived something about life and death and love that I had the luxury of not knowing yet.

At the cemetery, we hefted the coffin again. As we made our way to the grave, I marveled at how a town so small had accumulated so many dead. Near the front were the modern headstones, polished granite, but in the distance stood timeworn markers, limestone probably. For this leg of Olive's journey, we were allowed to use our hands to steady her, and then we set her down on the straps stretched across the gaping hole in the earth.

The minister was behind us, chanting as he took his place. He spoke about the corruptible body that worms would destroy and the immaculate, untouchable spirit. We all said *dust to dust*. The small crowd of mourners pulled apart the floral arrangements, tossing the bright flowers into the hole as workers loosened the straps and lowered Olive into the ground.

Under the green tent, Celestial sat next to Roy Senior, soothing him as the top of the cement vault was thumped into place. She dabbed at her eyes with wadded tissue while the workers unrolled the AstroTurf from the pile. They hung back, not wanting to start up the earth-mover tractor while the family was still there. It troubled me a little to think that Celestial, Roy Senior, and I constituted "the family," but there we were.

I stood up. "I think it's time for us to go, sir. People will be waiting for us at the church."

Celestial stood, too. "Everyone will be there."

"Who is everybody? Ain't no everybody without my wife."

Behind us, the grave diggers were antsy and ready to do what they had been hired to do. I could smell the grave, fertile and musty, like fishing bait. Finally Roy Senior stood and went over like he was going to grab a handful of soil and toss it over the coffin, already settled six feet down. Celestial and I walked close behind and were surprised when he sat down on the mound in a deliberate way, almost like a protest.

Celestial said, "Sir?"

And Roy Senior didn't say anything. Celestial followed him and sat, too. I swiveled my head looking for someone to help us out here, but the few mourners had gone, likely heading back for the repast supper. Taking her lead, I joined them. The dirt was wet and the moisture seeped in through the seat of my trousers as the grave diggers spoke to each other in hushed Spanish.

Although I was close on his right flank, Roy Senior spoke only to Celestial, explaining to her that she was the one responsible now. "Olive went to see Little Roy every week right up until she was too sick to make the journey. She stays on top of Mr. Banks. She calls him every Wednesday around lunchtime. I can't say what he has done so far, but she kept on him. She's gone now, so it's up to you, Celestial. I'll do what I can," he explained, "but a man needs a woman to care after him."

Celestial nodded with wet eyes. "Yes, sir," she said. "I understand."

"Do you?" he said, regarding her with wary eyes. "You think you know everything, but you're too young, girl."

I stood up and brushed the back of my clothes. I held out a hand to Celestial and she pulled herself up. Then I extended my hand to Big Roy. "Sir, let's go and let these men do their work."

Roy Senior got up, but he didn't use my arm for support. He is a big man, and beside him I felt narrow as a switch.

"It ain't their work," he said. "It's mine." Then he strode over to a tree and picked up the shovel resting against the bark. Though not a young man, Roy Senior moved the earth in heaping shovelfuls and heaved it onto Olive's vault. I'll never forget the sound of the landing dirt.

I picked up the other shovel, thinking of Roy and that I should be his understudy here. Roy Senior barked that I should put the shovel down, but then, kinder, he said, "This isn't your job. I know you call yourself stepping in for Little Roy, but even if he was here, this wouldn't be none of his work either. This is personal. Just me and my wife. I need to cover her with my own hands. You and Celestial take the Cadillac; I'll meet you when I'm done with what I need to do."

We obeyed him like he was our own father. We walked away, weaving through the headstones until we reached the sedan idling on the path. When we opened the door, we surprised the driver, who hastily shut off the dance music bumping through the speakers. As we pulled away, like children, we twisted to look through the back windshield, watching Roy Senior John Henry his wife's grave.

Celestial sighed. "You'll never see anything like that again, no matter how long you live."

"I don't want to."

"Roy has been away so long," she whispered. "I've done everything I'm supposed to do. I haven't *thought* about any other man, let alone touched one. But when I look at Mr. Roy out there, at his wife's grave, I feel like I've been playing at marriage. That I don't know what it is to be committed." And then she sobbed a wet spot onto my dirty white shirt. "I don't want to go to the church. I just want to go home."

I shushed her and tilted my head in the direction of the driver and made my voice low. "This is a small town. No need broadcasting anything that could get misinterpreted."

A quarter of an hour later, we walked into Christ the King Baptist Church, as filthy as coal miners, and ate a meal fit for royalty. People talked about us; I know they did, but to our faces they were polite and kept pouring more fruit punch. I looked Celestial in the eye and knew that, like me, what she wanted was a vodka martini, extra dry, but we made our way through the soul-food dinner, and we didn't leave until it was clear that Roy Senior wasn't going to show.

IT TOOK US a while, but we found a bar where we could crash. It would have been quicker to drive thirty miles up the road to the casino, where the drinks were cheap and the bartenders heavy-handed. When I steered the car in that direction, Celestial stopped me. "Don't go that way," she said. "I don't want to pass the prison."

"That's cool," I said.

"Is it?" Celestial said. "It's shameful that I can't even *look* at the barbed-wire fence while he has to *live* behind it. Do I love him, Dre?"

I couldn't answer her. "You married him."

She turned toward the window, tapping her forehead against the glass. I reached in my jacket pocket and gave her my handkerchief, driving one-handed, on the lookout for a bar we could belly up to.

It's not like there was any shortage of booze in Eloe. There were package stores and churches every hundred feet. Men stood on corners, tipping brown bags. If I didn't find something soon, we would buy a bottle and pass it back and forth like winos.

Finally we ended up at Earl Picard's Saturday Nighter, a joint that looked like it had been a 7-Eleven in its last incarnation. We chose two wobbly barstools and watched hot dogs ride around a red lightbulb. The windows were painted over, so although it was only two o'clock in the afternoon on the streets, it was perpetually 2 a.m. inside. Hardly anyone was there, but I guess that people with jobs were at work, and the unemployed weren't wasting their money on liquor by the glass. When we sat down, the bartender looked up from the book she was reading with the help of a pocket flashlight.

"What can I get you?" she asked, setting down the flashlight and sending a circle of light to the ceiling.

This was not exactly a martini sort of establishment, so Celestial asked for a screwdriver and the bartender poured a good four fingers of Smirnoff into a flimsy cup before opening a can of juice. She rummaged under the counter and produced a jar of cherries, spearing them with a plastic sword.

We drank without tapping our cups together; we were so dirty that I tasted grit in my drink. "Do you think that Roy Senior is still out there with his shovel, or do you think he let the machines take over after we left?"

"He's out there," Celestial said. "He's not going to let a tractor bury her." Shaking her drink to chill it, she asked, "What about Roy? How's he holding up?"

"He was okay, I guess. He said to tell you that he misses you."

"You know that I love him, right, Dre? His mother never believed me."

"Well, she didn't know you, did she? Maybe she didn't think anybody was good enough for her son. You know how black mamas are."

"I want another round," she said, and the bartender mixed more vodka and orange juice. I rooted in my pocket, fishing out some quarters. "Slow your roll, cowboy," I told her. "Go put something on the jukebox."

She took the money and walked to the back, unsteady, like she was walking on someone else's legs. Her hair responded to the humidity, losing that funeral lankness and drawing up around her ears. The men sitting at the other end of the bar noticed her figure as she bent at the waist to peer into the jukebox.

"That's your wife?" the bartender asked me, with what might have been a flirtatious flicker in her eye.

"No," I said. "We're old friends. We drove up from Atlanta for a funeral."

"Oh," she said. "Olive Hamilton?"

I nodded.

"So sad. Is she the daughter-in-law?"

I had a feeling she already knew. That little glint wasn't anything more than small-town nosiness.

As Celestial made her way back to me, the bartender retreated like she was embarrassed. Suddenly Prince sang out of the jukebox, "I wanna be your lover." I said to her, "Remember in the eighth grade? When we thought Prince was saying '*I want to be the only one you cook for*'?"

Celestial said, "I never thought that."

"You knew what 'come' was? In the eighth grade?"

"I guess I knew it was *something*."

We didn't talk for a while. She pounded cheap vodka and I switched to beer and then to Sprite.

"She hit me," Celestial said, rattling the ice in her cup. "Roy's mother. When I stayed away too long. Next time she saw me, she slapped the tar out of me. We were having dinner at the casino and she waited until Gloria got up to go to the bathroom and she reached over and *pow*." Celestial clapped her hands. "Right across my face. Tears came to my eyes and she said, 'Listen here, little girl, if I don't get to cry, nobody cries. I have suffered more just this morning than you have in your whole life.'"

"What?" I said, touching her cheek. "What the hell was that all about?"

"It was about everything. Olive slapped all the tears right out of me." Then she covered my hand on her cheek with her own. "All through the services, except when I was singing, my face was on fire. Right here." She rubbed my hand over the soft place. Then she turned her head and kissed my palm.

"Celestial," I said. "You are so drunk, baby girl."

"I'm not," she said, reaching again for my hand. "Well, I am. But I'm still me."

"Stop it." I pulled my hand back. "People in here have figured out who we are." I gave her a stern look with my head cocked to the side.

"Oh yeah," she said. "Small town."

I nodded as her face fell a little. "Microscopic."

Now the Isley Brothers were on the jukebox. There was something about those vintage, slow jams. Those old cats sang about a kind of devotion long since out of style. "I always liked this song," I told her.

"You know why?" Celestial said. "It's because this is the music we were conceived to. It speaks to you on a primal level."

"I prefer not to imagine my conception."

She was a little mopey now as she twirled the ice cube with her fingernail that was chewed down to the meat. "Dre, I'm so tired of this. Of all of this. This dirty little town. I'm tired of having in-laws. And prison. Prison isn't supposed to be part of my life. I was married a year and half—that's it. Roy got snatched up and my daddy was still writing checks to pay for my wedding."

"I never got used to you as a Mrs. Hamilton." I signaled for the check and asked for two glasses of ice water.

She rolled her eyes. "When you went to see him, did he seem mad at me? When I went last, he said he didn't like my vibe, that I was coming out of obligation." She set her glass down. "He wasn't wrong, but what was I supposed to do? I work crazy hours at the shop, then I drive for hours to get to Louisiana and spend the night with his parents, who don't really even like me. Then I go through . . ." She fluttered her fingers. "Go through everything, and he doesn't think my smile is cheery enough? This isn't what I signed up for."

She was serious, but I laughed anyway. "I didn't know there was a sign-up sheet. That's not how it works."

"You can laugh," she said with angry eyes. "You know how I feel when I'm here? Black and desperate. You don't know what it's like to be standing in the line to get in to see him."

"I do," I said. "I was there yesterday."

"It's different for women. They treat you like you're coming to visit your pimp. Every single one of them smiles with a little smirk like you should know better. Like you're a delusional victim. If you try to fix yourself up and look respectable, it's worse in a way. They treat you like you're an idiot because it's clear you *could* do better if you weren't such a fucking fool." She popped her fingers to the music like she was trying to snap herself out of the spell of feelings coming over her, but she was buzzed enough that her emotions weren't hers to control.

Had we been alone, I would have touched her, but under the eyes of the bartender and the three other men present, I didn't lift my hands. I just said, "Let's go."

WHEN WE GOT back to the hotel, it was light out, but the casino parking lot was full. Apparently a ten-car giveaway was scheduled for this evening. When we were safe behind the doors of the elevator, I faced her.

She fastened her arms around my torso, reminding me of our childhood when she used to hug the breath out of me. She smelled like vodka but also like lavender and pine trees. I held her until we reached the fifth floor, even as the doors opened revealing a family patiently waiting to get on board.

"Newlyweds," the mother explained.

We stepped out of the elevator and stood facing the hall leading to our rooms.

"Everyone thought we would get married one day," she said.

"You're drunk," I said. "Way drunk."

"I disagree." She made her way to her room and slid the key into the door. Tiny green lights twinkled. "I'm something, but I'm not drunk. Come in? Do you want to?"

"Celestial," I said, though I felt myself leaning in her direction like someone tipped the world. "It's me, Dre." She laughed and it sounded playful like we hadn't watched Roy's daddy bury his wife with an old-fashioned spade. She laughed like this was a time before anything bad had ever happened.

"It's me, too," she said with a grin. "Celestial."

I tried to laugh back, but no sound came. Besides, any laugh would be fake, and I never faked anything when it came to her.

It was all over when I stepped over the threshold and heard the door click shut behind me. We didn't fall into each other's arms like in a movie, with furious deep kissing and groping. For the first slow moments, we just looked at each other, like what we had chosen was a package that we couldn't quite figure how to open. She sat on the bed and I did, too, and it reminded me of the other time when we crossed the line, in high school. Then, like now, we were dressed up and frazzled. Back then we had been in the dark basement, yet I could make out the outlines of the ruffles of her party dress. But now we were in the full light. Her hair swelled around her head in a dark halo; both our mouths were hot with alcohol and our clothes stained with graveyard soil.

I moved closer to her and wound my fingers in her thick hair. "We've always been together," she told me. "Not like this. But always."

I nodded. "I want to be the only one you cook for."

We laughed, a real laugh, a shared laugh. This is when our life changed. We came to each other with joy on our lips. What came next may not have been legally binding; there was no clergyman or witness. But it was ours.

ROY

In Eloe, if you want to know who you're supposed to be, you don't have to go further than the family Bible. Right there, on a blank page, before "In the beginning . . ." is all you need to know. There were other truths in the world, but they weren't often written down. These unofficial records of kin were passed from lips to ear. Much was made of white relatives, whispered about sometimes in shame, sometimes in satisfaction, depending on the details. Then there was other family on the right side of the color line, but the wrong side of the property line. I was the rare soul in Eloe with no family ties outside of my parents. Olive was born in Oklahoma City and there was family there, but I never met them. Big Roy was from Howland, Texas, and wandered to Eloe on his way to Jackson. Our family Bible they received as a wedding gift from Big Roy's landlady. When you lift the leather cover, there are only our three names spelled out in Olive's careful cursive.

Roy McHenry Hamilton   +   Olive Ann Ingelman
Roy Othaniel Hamilton Jr.

Olive never wrote Celestial's name beside mine, but there was a lot of room on the page, space to list all the Hamiltons of the future, connected with diagonal lines and dashes.

Davina Hardrick was different. At least a dozen black Hardricks lived in town, even a few Hardriks, without the *c*, who changed their names when the family split like a feuding congregation. I envied her these robust roots, thick enough to buckle the sidewalk. She said she was living in Miss Annie Mae's house, and I tried to remember who Miss Annie Mae was to her, what Bible lines connected them. I remembered Davina's grandfather, Mr. Picard, or maybe he was her uncle? There had been something extended about her family, that much I did remember. Once I had known who all was kin to anybody else.

I had run into Davina at Walmart when I had gone to buy flowers for Olive. Davina, dressed in a blue uniform, unlocked the floral refrigerator and helped me select a bouquet that I couldn't bring myself to deliver. Wrapping my purchase in clean white paper, she asked me if I remembered her from high school, even though she was a couple of years ahead of me. I told her that I did. She asked me if I would like to have a home-cooked meal. I told her I would. A few hours later I stood in front of the clapboard house outfitted for Christmas with multicolored lights and metallic ribbon.

I climbed up the three concrete steps and stood on the sloping porch. The little house must have been seventy, maybe eighty years old, built probably by Miss Annie Mae's husband. This neighborhood was known as the Hardwood, where the colored mill workers lived, back when there was a mill, back when *colored* was a word of respect. I rapped on the silver-wreathed door, almost wishing I wore a hat so I could take it off and hold it in my hands.

"Hey," she said through the screen door, looking inviting in a holiday apron that set off her skin tone, a lush brown with red underneath like a nice pair of loafers. She tilted her head to the side. "You look nice."

"You, too." Kitchen aromas spiced the air all the way out here, and I wanted more than anything in this world to cross her threshold.

"You're early," she said with a little smile, not like she was annoyed, but letting me know. "Give me a minute to fix my hair." Then she shut the door. I sat down on the front stairs and waited. Five years away and you get good at that sort of thing. I sat there, but I didn't turn my face on the diagonal to the orange-brick funeral home where they had taken care of my mother. Instead, I sat with my eyes on my own fingers, so much like Walter's, knotty with yellowish calluses. I went in with bankers' hands and came out looking like a mill worker. But at least I was out. Something you learn in there: keep your mind on what's important.

Edwards Street was mostly quiet. A cluster of little boys used bacon and string to catch crawfish in the ditch that ran along the sides of the road. In the distance, I could see the reflection of the neon lights in the liquor store window and feel the faint vibration of the subwoofers that shook the air. This was my hometown. I skinned my knees on these streets; I learned to be a man on these same corners, but I didn't feel like I was home.

WHEN DAVINA CAME to the door the second time, she wasn't wearing the apron, and I missed it, though the burgundy dress she changed into highlighted everything captivating about a woman's body. In high school, she had a perfect figure—small and thick at the same time, what we used to call a "brick house." Big Roy warned me those girls that are fine at fifteen get fat by thirty, so you shouldn't marry them. Thinking of

Davina, that advice seemed childish and cruel. Yes, she had a lot going on in the bust and the hip, but she looked delicious.

"You still married?" she asked through the screen door.

"I don't know," I said.

She smiled, cocking her head, showing a tuft of tinsel tucked behind her ear like a gardenia. "Come on in," she said. "Dinner will be ready in a minute. You want something to drink?"

"What you think?" I watched her splendid curves as she walked the few steps to the kitchen.

The old me, and I don't mean the me before I went to prison, I mean the old me from way before I started going out with Celestial, the me I was in my early twenties and running through women like water—*that* me would have known what to say. Back then, I knew how to focus. *Keep my mind on my money and my money on my mind.* I used to say that to myself under my breath, no matter what it was that I was zooming in on. One thing at a time. That's how you win. But here I was, in front of one woman, one *fine* woman, and I was sitting here thinking about a wife I hadn't talked to in two years.

I'm not saying that I was anybody's angel during my marriage. As they say, mistakes were made and feelings were bruised, like that one time when Celestial happened upon a receipt for two pieces of lingerie, not just for the one I gave her for her birthday. She wasn't livid, but it was going that way. I said to her, "Celestial, I don't love anybody but you." It didn't necessarily explain the little piece of paper in her hand, but it was God's truth, and I suspect that she understood that.

Sitting in Davina's living room drinking up her liquor, I held Celestial's face in my mind, her scent in my nose, her song in my ear. Even still, I looked at Davina and my mouth went wet. "When did Miss Annie Mae pass?" I asked her. "She was a nice lady. I remember when she sold sour pickles for a dime. When we were little. You remember that?"

"She's been gone four years now. I was surprised that she left everything to me, but we were always close, and her son lives in Houston now. His name was Wofford. Remember him?"

I did remember him as the local boy made good who came to speak to us when we were in high school, telling us not to drop out, get anybody pregnant, or smoke crack. "Yeah, I recall."

Davina smirked. "With Miss Annie Mae gone, I don't expect we will ever see him again in this town." She shook her head. "My daddy was the same way. Halfway to Dallas before I even turned five years old."

I said, "You don't know for sure why he went."

She smiled again, a real smile like she appreciated me trying to look on the bright side. "All I know is that he's gone. Same trifling story everybody tells."

"Don't call him trifling," I said. "Men have reasons."

She shushed me. "You didn't come here to talk about my daddy, did you?" And there was a question in her question. Women have that way of asking you more than what they want to know.

"Food smells good," I said, trying to lighten the mood. "Louisiana women. I swear y'all come out of the womb gripping a skillet."

I hoped that I would get to the table and see a bowl of crowder peas, pulled from the vines that grew along the fence that separated Davina's property from the neighbors'. When I was coming up, Mr. Fontenot, the language teacher, had lived there. I ended up enrolled in French class by accident, the only black kid in the room. Me and Mr. Fontenot were close, both being onlies.

He told me about the French Club, how they met after school and practiced the language in preparation for a ten-day trip to Paris. I asked Mr. Fontenot if there were black people in Paris, and he said, "Both local and imported." He gave me a novel by James Baldwin, *Go Tell It on the Mountain*, that had nothing to do with France, but he assured me that the author was there as we spoke. I turned the book over and studied the sad but intelligent face. James Baldwin was plenty black. "Learn the language," Mr. Fontenot said, "and I will help sponsor your journey." But three things happened: I would have been the only black kid going on the trip and nobody thought much of that idea. "Something goes wrong over there and it will be your word against theirs," Big Roy said. Another thing was the money. Seven hundred fifty dollars would have been my share even with Mr. Fontenot sponsoring me. That's why no black kids were going. And the last thing was Mr. Fontenot himself.

When he hipped me to *Go Tell It on the Mountain*, he didn't say one word about Jimmy being a homosexual. "Jimmy" is how Mr. Fontenot always talked about him, like they went way back. According to Mr. Fontenot, Jimmy started saving his papers for posterity when he was only eleven years old because he knew he was going to be important and that he was going to need "documentation of his trajectory." He had then given me a little black notebook. "You should keep a journal for future generations," he said. "When you get out of this town, people are going to want to know how you did it." It was this journal that ended all my plans, more than the money. Big Roy didn't like the look of the little book and neither did my mother. Eloe is a small town, claustrophobic and mean sometimes. Didn't take more than a couple of phone calls for my parents to find out that Mr. Fontenot was "funny like that," and there was no way they were sending me to Paris under his sponsorship.

"What happened to Mr. Fontenot?"

"He passed away in the early nineties," Davina said.

"From what?"

"You know what I'm talking about," she said. "Come on, you need to eat."

I got up and headed to the oval-shaped table, like the one I grew up eating on. Six people could fit easy. I pulled back the chair and was about to sit down when she asked me if I would like to wash my hands. Shamefaced,

I asked her where the bathroom was. Lathering up with soap that smelled like girls, I felt a little prickle of anger along the underside of my jaw, but I splashed water on my chin until it settled. Tilting my head under the faucet, I filled my mouth with the soft water and swallowed it down. It had been a long time since I could look into a real glass mirror, but what I saw I could have done without. My forehead was creased like the fan Olive kept in her purse. But at least I was clean; I was shaved. As soon as I got my money right, I would see a dentist and get fitted for a new bridge. Using a fluffy brown towel dangling from a hook, I dried my face and returned to the table, which Davina piled with a righteous feast.

It was like something out of the Bible. Pork chops swimming in gravy, macaroni and cheese—brown on the top and shiny with butter. Mashed potatoes heaped in a striped blue bowl and next to that a stack of the white rolls Olive used to make. When you tugged them, they came apart in buttery sections. There, snug in a shiny silver bowl, were a few of the crowder peas I had been craving.

"You want to say the blessing?" she said, reaching out for my hand.

I closed my eyes and bowed my head, but I didn't get past "Dear Lord" when my throat started twitching. It took me two breaths to give up on talking. I clamped my eyes shut and swallowed hard against whatever it was that was trying to rise up and get out of me.

"Dear Lord," Davina picked up. "Thank you for this food that will nourish our bodies. We thank you for this fellowship. In the name of your son, Jesus Christ, Amen." She squeezed my hand at the *Amen*, like the period at the end of the sentence, but I kept squeezing, even when she tried to pull away. I managed to say, "Bless the hands that prepared it," before I let her go.

AS DAVINA SPOONED mounds of everything onto my plate, I imagined myself—a man just out of the joint, about to do some serious damage to some pork chops. I felt a little bit like a punch line, more self-conscious than I had ever been in corporate America, right here in my own hometown. Davina set the food down in front of me, and at the last moment I remembered my manners and didn't touch my fork until she picked up hers.

"Bon appétit," she said with a little smile.

I said it back and remembered Celestial, who said just that before she ate anything, even her morning cereal.

I was working my way through a second helping of food and a third round of sweet lemonade when Davina said in a tone that was too breezy for a question she asked twice already, "You still married?"

I slowly finished chewing, swallowed, and washed it all down with lemonade. "How you want me to answer that? This is what I got: I was married when I went in, and she didn't divorce me."

"You don't have to talk in circles like a lawyer." She seemed hurt, like I came here and ate her dinner under false pretenses.

I took a breath and gave her as much truth as I had on me. "I haven't seen her in two years. Not since my mama passed."

"You talk to her on the phone?"

"Not lately," I said. "What about you? You with somebody?"

She looked around the room. "You see anybody up in here?"

We let the subject drop, like we were both satisfied that we had done our due diligence.

AFTER WE ATE, I jumped up to help clear the table. I scraped the plates and stacked them in the sink. Davina gave a little smile, like the way you might smile at a baby that tried to do something grown, like play the piano. "Don't worry about the kitchen. You're company."

I swear to God, I didn't come over here just to have sex with Davina. I swear to God that it wasn't what I came over here planning for. Did I come here hoping for it? I can't lie and say I wasn't starving for a woman, like Walter warned me not to be. But I was also starving in general. I was starving for my mama's cooking, been starving for it since the day I left for college. Davina Hardrick had invited me to dinner. If all we had done was eat, I would have left with more than I arrived with.

"You want coffee?" she asked me.

I shook my head no.

"Another drink?"

"Yeah," I said, and she poured me another one, paler this time.

"Don't want you to get a DUI," she said, and I was disappointed that she was already thinking about sending me home.

"Can I ask you something," she said. "About when you were gone?"

"You know I didn't do it."

"I know," she said. "Nobody around here thought you did it. It was just the wrong race and the wrong time. Police are shady as hell. That's why everybody is locked up."

As a salute, I tipped my drink and finished in one hot gulp. I held out my glass to Davina.

"One question." As she fell serious, I braced myself for another question about Celestial.

"Yes?"

"When you were gone, did you know someone named Antoine Guillory? Full name Antoine Fredrick Guillory?"

"Why," I said. "That's your man?"

She shook her head. "My son."

"No," I said, with condolence in my voice. If he was her son, he couldn't be more than seventeen or eighteen at the most. "I never met him."

"They call him Hopper? Or Grasshopper?"

The nickname I did know. Hopper wasn't the youngest person there but still too young for adult prison, too frail and too pretty. I remembered his rouged lips and hair flattened with homemade lye.

"I don't know him," I said again.

"You sure?"

"I'm sure," I said. "No Hopper." I held my glass out to her again. "Please, ma'am?"

She shook her head. "I'm cutting you off. It's for your own good."

"Girl, I ain't worried about no DUI. I walked over here. This town ain't no bigger than a minute."

"Roy," she said. "A lot of things have changed. You're not trying to be walking around at night. I don't know what's worse, police or everyday people. Hopper got caught up on a weapons charge. He was only trying to protect himself. Sixteen years old and they charged him as an adult."

"Trust me. I am not afraid. You know where I been the last five years?" I said, this time with a laugh that scraped my throat. "You think I'm scared of some country motherfucker jumping out from behind the bushes talking about boogety-boogety?"

"If it's a country motherfucker with a *gun*, yes." Then she slapped my arm and gave me a real smile, one with dimples. "Boogety-boogety. You so crazy. I'll get you one more. But I won't make it strong."

"Fix yourself another one, too. I can't stand drinking by myself."

She came back with the drinks poured into two little glasses like the ones my mama used for orange juice. "Ran out of ice," she said. I held my glass up and we toasted without saying what to and then threw it back like a shot. It felt good, reminded me of my first job; at the company holiday party, the white folks poured top-shelf liquor and we sucked it down like water, like there was no end to money.

Davina got up and switched on some music, Frankie Beverly talking about "happy feelings." She popped her fingers a couple of times as she made her way back. This time she folded herself back onto the cushion like she was showing off all her hinges. "Hey," she said with a little play at the edge of her words.

I can't say whiskey made her beautiful. Davina wasn't a PYT any more than I was a young executive. But I used to be, and she used to be; something of it was left in us both, I think. Davina was everything I ever missed, transformed into warm brown flesh.

"You okay?"

I shook my head no because that was all I could do.

"What's the matter?"

I shook my head again.

"It's okay," she said. "You just got home. It's always tiring when you get back." She said it like I had been released from the army or the hospital.

In a motion like a librarian, Davina touched her hand to her lips, and I leaned in behind it. Celestial—I couldn't help thinking of her—isn't a small woman; she is big-boned and stacked, but not soft like Davina, who felt like the robes at a four-star hotel. I tried holding myself back because I didn't want to reach for her like a caveman, and I can say that every moment I spent fully clothed was a miracle. I kissed her deep when I let myself go, driving my tongue in her mouth, finding the spicy flavor of whiskey and liking it. She let her fingers roam around my body, as dainty as a firefly but with healing in her hands like a storefront preacher. She worked her way under my shirt and the feel of her very cool palms on my hot back was electric.

In the bedroom, we didn't undress each other. We took off our clothes in our own separate patches of darkness. Davina hung her dress in the closet with a tinkle of hangers, and then she slid herself in bed beside me, smelling of whiskey but also like cocoa butter. She turned on her side and let her hair tumble into my face. I pulled back from its plastic texture because I didn't want to touch anything that wasn't real. I yearned to rub against something breathing. I craved something alive. She raised her thigh up to rest on my hip. "You okay?" she whispered.

"Yeah," I said. "You?"

"I'm okay."

"I'm sorry about your son."

"I'm sorry about your mother."

For normal people, talking about the lost would put out the fire, but for me it was like kerosene, gasoline, and a blast of pure oxygen. I kissed her again, shifting to position myself over her. Looking down at her outline in the dark, I felt myself wanting to explain again. But I could never tell her that I didn't want to fuck her like a man who just got out of jail. I wanted to do it like a man who was home visiting his family. I wanted to do it like a local boy made good. I wanted to fuck like I had money still, like I had a nice office, Italian shoes, and a steel watch. How can you explain to a woman that you want to fuck her like a human being?

I wouldn't call myself scared, but I hovered there, supporting my weight on my forearms, honestly unsure as to what to do next. I wanted to please her—not make her holler my name or anything ignorant like that. I wanted to make a good impression. She said she didn't believe that I raped that woman in the Piney Woods Inn, but isn't there always a little seed? The second side that every story is supposed to have?

"Baby," Davina said, reaching up and crossing her arms over my back, pressing us together. Relying on muscle memory, I used my knee to spread her legs, but she escaped me, lying on her side, facing me. She pushed my chest with her index finger and I lay on my back. "Not yet," she said, using the flat of her hand to nudge me down when I tried to sit up and reach for her.

Davina took care of me. That's the only way that I can tell it. Two days after I got out of prison, she laid me out on her bed and took care of me. With hand and mouth, she touched my entire body, leaving no small parcel of skin unloved. She moved over, and under, and maybe even through me. Whichever part of me she wasn't loving was on fire, hoping it would catch her attention next. You don't know what you need until somebody gives it to you exactly the way you need it gave.

When she was twined around me in such a way that her foot was near my face, I dipped my head to kiss the arch. How someone that grew up here in Eloe could have such baby feet, I didn't know. Celestial had smooth feet, too. The thought of my wife stirred something in me and I sprang up, like I was waking up from a nightmare. Davina paused, and whatever light was in the room reflected from her eyes. "You all right?"

"Naw," I said.

"Come here," she said, lying on her back and holding out her arms. Then she called me "baby" in the way that some women do, making it their own one-word language, meaning whatever she needed it to mean. This time it was an invitation. It was as though she said "please." She wrapped her legs around my waist and I held on to her because my life depended on it. "Baby," she said again.

"You got a rubber?"

"I think so," she said. "In the medicine cabinet."

"In the bathroom?"

"Yeah."

"Do I have to?"

Davina was quiet in the dark. I rose up on my elbows and tried to see her, but the moonlight didn't fall on her face. "You want me to, I'll get up and get it," I promised, but I was kissing her again, biting softly on her sweet bottom lip. "Do we need it?" I was begging her, whether she knew it or not. I ached to do this, touch another person, no plastic in between. It was like it felt to touch her real hair, growing crinkly at the base of her scalp. It was the difference between talking on the phone and speaking breath to breath. "Please," I heard myself say. "I'll pull out. I promise. Please." We were still touching. She hadn't shoved me off of her or even drawn her knees together. "Baby," I said, and it was me speaking the secret language this time.

"It's okay," she said at last. "It's okay, baby. I'm safe."

CELESTIAL

Gloria taught me to pray when I was three years old. She knelt beside me, showed me how to press my palms together under my chin like a cherub. Church was her thing, not my father's. There is a certain type of Christian woman who can't resist a godless man, keeping his soul safe on her knees. Sometimes I wish I were like her, born to save a man; then I could follow my mother's bread crumb trail.

"Now I lay me down to sleep." Gloria almost sang the words, and I repeated, a little baby echo, eyes screwed tight. Before "Amen," I opened my eyes and asked her to explain "I pray the Lord my soul to take." She said that it was up to God to see if you got to wake up the next morning, to decide if you're afforded another day. If you died in the night, you asked to go with Him back up to heaven. Or at least this is how I took it.

Stricken, I lay in my canopy bed, afraid to even blink my eyes for fear of falling into an eternal sleep.

Every night, she put me to bed this way, the two of us chanting. As she knelt beside me, I prayed the way she expected, but when Gloria had gone, I recanted, negotiating to keep my soul for myself.

Somewhere it is written that your sins fall on your parents, mostly on your mother, until you're twelve years old. After that, your trespasses are on your own scorecard. Once I had a choice in the matter, I seldom accompanied my mother to services, preferring the easy company of my father. But always, I say my prayers.

When I lived alone, I spoke the prayers aloud, but now that Andre shares my bedroom, I move my lips around the words, but I don't give them air. I pray for Roy. I ask for his safety. I ask for his forgiveness, although in the clean light of morning, I know I have done nothing wrong. I also pray for Andre, and I ask him to forgive me for asking for forgiveness. I pray for my father, and I pray that I'll figure out how to be his daughter again.

My mother taught me that we have no secrets from God. He knows our feelings because He made them. When you confess your sins, He will bless you for your courage. He will bless you for your humility. He blesses you when you're on your knees.

God must know that in the bottom of my jewelry case, snapped into a felt box, is Roy's missing tooth. A root woman would know what to do with it; even I, not talented in the unseen, can feel its blazing comet energy in the palm of my hand. But I have no way to harness this power or command it to my will.

ROY

I spent about thirty-six hours straight with Davina Hardrick in what used to be Miss Annie Mae's house. Life is full of wonders. Who would have predicted that a girl I knew only a little bit in high school would capture me so completely that I hardly remembered my way home? The only reason I left her bed at all was that she put me out so she could go to work. Between her good cooking and her good loving, I could have stayed there forever. When I finally showed up in the rumpled clothes I had been wearing (or not wearing) for the last day and a half, Big Roy was waiting on the front porch. The two Huey Newton chairs stood unoccupied while he sat on the concrete floor with his legs hanging over the side, his feet planted in the flower beds. His left hand was curled around my mama's yellow coffee cup and the other was gripping a honey bun he ate straight from the wrapper. "You alive?"

"Yes, sir," I said, bounding up the stairs. "Alive and *well*."

Big Roy pulled his eyebrows up a couple of inches. "What's her name?"

"I am sworn to secrecy to protect the innocent."

"Long as she's not married. I would hate to see you go through all you been through just to get shot by some hard-leg over a woman."

"You're right. My story is tragic enough as it is."

"More coffee is on the stove," he said, jerking his head in the direction of the front door.

I fixed myself a cup, then returned to the porch and sat down next to my father. I looked up and down the road thinking about myself, a habit I picked up when I was gone. You sit there thinking about where you want to be, who you want to be with. What you wish you could eat. I used to sit there for as long as twenty minutes or so thinking about Kalamata olives and what I would eat them on. Now I was thinking about Davina and wondering if I could go back over there tonight.

Was I cheating on Celestial, or was I cheating on my memories of her? I suppose a man in my position should receive some sort of special consideration. I won't say that Davina Hardrick saved my life with her plush thighs and her "baby" language, but she salvaged my *something*, if not my life, maybe my spirit.

Big Roy spoke over the rim of the yellow coffee cup. "You need to learn how to use the telephone, son. You can't just disappear. Not after everything that has happened."

I felt my shoulders round as I tucked my head almost to my chest. "I'm sorry, Daddy. I didn't think about it."

"You got to remember how to consider about other people."

"I know." I slurped some more coffee, and he handed me the half-eaten honey bun. I tore it in two pieces and stuffed the sweet bread in my mouth. "Trying to get used to being myself."

Big Roy said, "You need to get in touch with your wife today. Let her know."

"Let her know what?"

"Not about whoever got you over here grinning like Jiminy Cricket. But you got to let her know you're back home. Trust me on this, son. Whoever you been with, she may seem special right now, but she's not your wife."

I threw my hands up. "I know. I know." I hadn't had a little scrap of happiness in five entire years and he wasn't even going to let me have an hour of basking in the sun.

"But wait until you wash up," he said.

He was right. I needed to make some plans to get back to Atlanta, to greet Celestial skin-to-skin and ask her whether we were still married. A part of me said, if you have to ask, the answer is no. Maybe I was setting myself up. Two years of no visits is a message; why did I need to hear it from her own lips? Whatever she had to say for herself would draw blood, and it wouldn't be a clean cut. The truth would hurt jagged, like a dog bite.

But there was still the simple and undisputed fact that she didn't divorce me. If she didn't get out of the marriage officially, it was only because she didn't want to. That carried some weight in my book. Besides, even a dog bite can heal.

WHEN THE PHONE started ringing, I hadn't gotten dressed any further than my shorts. The outdated telephone rang with a loud metallic jangle. "Tell Wickliffe I'm waiting on the porch," Big Roy shouted from outside.

Pussyfooting to the kitchen, half-naked and barefoot, I picked up the phone and said, "He's waiting on the porch."

The man on the other end said, "Excuse me?"

I said, "Sorry. Hello? Hamilton residence."

The man on the other end said, "Roy, is that you?"

"Little Roy. You want Big Roy?"

"It's Andre. What are you doing answering the phone? I thought you weren't getting out until Wednesday."

The last time I saw Dre, he wore the gray suit he would wear to Olive's wake. I could feel the crowd in the visitors' room watching him as we talked, trying to figure out the deal with us. I knew how I looked: like everyone else in there, worn jumpsuit, black skin. Everything else about me was details. In his dress clothes, Dre didn't look like a lawyer; he presented more like a musician who moved to Europe because "cats in the States don't get jazz."

I had been glad to see him. Dre was my boy. He introduced me to Celestial the first time, even though it didn't take until much later. When we got married, he stood up with me, signed his name. Now here he was on the last Sunday Olive would be aboveground.

"Will you carry her for me?" I asked.

Dre breathed deep and nodded.

It's painful to even recollect it, but when he agreed, I felt thankful and furious all at once. "I appreciate you," I said.

He whisked my words away with his piano-player fingers. "I'm sorry about all of this. You know, Banks is still working. . . ."

Now it was my turn to wave him quiet. "Fuck Banks. Even if he got me out tomorrow, it would be too late. My mama is already dead."

HEARING HIS VOICE now, I felt that same mix of shame and rage I felt when he said he would carry Olive's casket. It made my throat itch, and I had to clear it twice before I spoke.

"What's up, Dre? Good to hear from you."

"Likewise, man," he said. "But you're early. We weren't expecting you for a few more days."

We, he said. *We weren't expecting you.*

"Paperwork," I said. "Bureaucracy. Someone in the Department of Corrections said it was time for me to go and so I went."

"I hear you," said Dre. "Does Celestial know?"

"Not yet," I said.

"No problem," Dre said after a beat. "I hope you don't mind holding steady for a couple of days."

"Y'all are driving down together?"

"Just me," said Dre.

I hung up the phone and went back out to the porch and stood over Big Roy. From this angle, I could see the little scars on the top of his balding head. I remember my mother kissing them when he would whack his head on the light fixture that hung a little too low over the dining-room table. She was crazy about that dinky little chandelier, and my father never asked her to take it down.

"It wasn't Wickliffe," I said. "It was Andre."

"What did he say that got you so shook up that you're standing outside in your drawers?"

I looked down at my bare legs, turning ashy already. "He says he's coming down to get me. Just him."

"That sound right to you?"

"I don't know what's right."

Big Roy said, "You better get to Atlanta and see if you have any marriage left." He paused. "If that's what you want."

"Hell yeah, it's what I want."

"I had to ask because ten minutes ago you didn't seem so sure."

The phone rang again and Big Roy jutted his chin toward the house. "Answer it. It's either going to be Wickliffe or Celestial. If it's Wickliffe, tell him I'm calling in. If it's Celestial, you're on your own."

I let it jangle until she gave up.

I RETURNED TO the kitchen dressed in the best apparel Walmart had to offer, khaki pants and a knit shirt with a collar. At least I had good shoes. In the mirror, I looked like a budget Tiger Woods, but I didn't look like an ex-con. "I want to go home."

Big Roy was stooped in front of the refrigerator rummaging inside. "Atlanta, you mean?"

"Yeah."

"You made up your mind quick," he said. "Andre lit some kind of fire under you."

"I always knew I was going to go, but I didn't know when. Now I know that *when* is as soon as I can."

"You set to drive?"

I reached in my back pocket and pulled out my wallet. After all these years in prison storage, the leather was still soft and supple. Stuck to a punch card for lattes, was my driver's license. The photo was of the successful me; cocky and sure in my button-down shirt and burgundy tie, I grinned, showing two rows of strong square teeth. According to the state of Georgia, I was clear to drive a vehicle for another six months. The Peach State also was under the impression that I lived at 1104 Lynn Valley Road. This license was the only thing I had left from before. I held it up and let the light play off the state seal. "All set, but I don't have a car."

"You can take the Chrysler," Big Roy said, opening an egg carton and finding only one lonely egg. "I need to go make groceries. Two grown men need to eat breakfast."

"Daddy, how you going to get to work without a car?"

"Wickliffe will ride me around if I help him with gas."

"Let me think about it."

"I thought you said you were ready to go."

"I said I'm thinking about it."

"You know, sometimes you can make up with bacon what you don't have in eggs." Big Roy opened the fridge wider and bent himself low enough to rummage in one of the drawers. "One sorry strip of bacon. I guess you could have the egg and I could have the bacon." He went to the cabinet and opened it, showing neat rows of tin cans. "I got it! Salmon croquettes. You eat them, right?"

I looked at Big Roy like I was meeting a stranger. His body was too large for my mother's kitchen, but he did all right, cracking the single egg one-handed and whipping it with a dainty fork.

"What?"

"Nothing, Daddy. It's just that the entire time I was growing up, I never knew you to touch a pot or a pan. But now you putter around the kitchen like Martha Stewart."

"Well," he said, with his back to me as he kept whipping that solitary egg, "losing Olive left me with two options: learn to cook or starve to death."

"You could marry somebody else." I hardly got the words out. "It's legal."

"When I want somebody else, I'll find somebody else," Big Roy said. "But if all I want is a meal, then I'll cook." He held up the can of salmon and smiled. "They don't tell you, but a lot of foods have recipes on the back of the can to tell you how to fix it."

I watched him for a while longer, and I wondered if this is what it meant to move on, to learn to live in a new way without someone. He was busy over the little bowl and sprinkled in some cayenne pepper. "The problem is that they don't tell you how to season it right. It's a smart rule of thumb to shake some pepper anytime you dealing with a can recipe."

"Mama cooked from the top of her head," I said.

Big Roy glugged some oil into a cast-iron skillet. "I still can't believe she's gone."

When he finished cooking, he divided the food onto our plates. We each got two good-size croquettes, one-half of the bacon slice, and an orange cut into triangles.

"Bon appétit," I said, reaching for my fork.

"O Lord," Big Roy began, saying grace, and I set the fork down.

The food wasn't bad. It wasn't good, but it wasn't bad.

"Tasty, right?" Big Roy said. "The can asked for bread crumbs, but I crunched up Ritz crackers instead. Gives a nutty flavor."

"Yes, sir," I said, eating my half slice of bacon in one bite.

I couldn't help thinking of Olive, a virtuoso in the kitchen. On Friday nights, she baked cakes, pies, and cookies to sell on Saturday afternoon, to be served after Sunday dinners at homes all over town. Other women practiced the same hustle, but Olive had the nerve to charge two dollars above the going rate. "My desserts are worth a little extra," she used to say.

We ate slowly, engrossed in our thoughts.

"You will need a haircut before you go," Big Roy said.

I ran my hand over my woolly head. "Where can I get a haircut on a Monday?"

"Right here," Big Roy said. "You know I cut hair when I was in the army. I always keep my barber papers current. Worse come to worse, you can always make money cutting heads."

"All these years?"

"I cut your hair every Saturday night until you were ten years old." He shook his head and bit into one of the orange slices. "Seems like fruit used to have more taste to it."

"That's the thing I missed most when I was in there. Fruits. I paid six dollars one time for a pear." As soon as I said it, I gave a quick shake of my head to dislodge the memory, but it was dug in. "I can't forget that pear," I said to Big Roy. "I drove a hard bargain for it. I sold this one dude a garbage bag. He wanted to give me just four dollars, but I kept pushing."

"We tried to provide for you when you were in there. We may not have put as much on your commissary as your in-laws, but what we gave was more to us."

"I'm not comparing," I said. "I'm trying to tell you something. Let me tell you this, Daddy. I sold a garbage bag and I didn't ask myself why someone would want to pay good money for it. I just worked him till I had every cent he had, because I needed cash to get a piece of fruit. I was craving that fresh taste." The pear had been red like an autumn leaf and it was as soft as ice cream. I ate the whole thing: seeds, core, and stem—all of it. I ate it in the filthy bathroom because I didn't want anybody to see me with it and take it from me.

"Son," Big Roy said, and I knew just from the loosening of his face that even *he* knew the rest of the story. It felt like I was the only person in the world who didn't understand how a man in prison uses a garbage bag. I had tried to share the pear with Walter, but he wouldn't touch it, not when I told him how I got it.

"How was I supposed to know?" I asked my father.

In prison, you learn quick that anything can be a weapon to be used against the other man or yourself. A toothbrush becomes a dagger, a chocolate bar can be melted into homemade Napalm, and a garbage bag makes a perfect noose. "I didn't know. I wouldn't have given it to him, let alone taken his money."

I remembered myself retching over the metal commode, hoping the foul odor would help me vomit that pear, but nothing came up but my own stomach juices, bitter and sharp.

"I'm not blaming you, son," Big Roy said. "Not for anything."

THEN THE PHONE started up, like it knew that we were sitting there and it refused to be ignored.

"That ain't Wickliffe," Big Roy said.

"I know."

It rang until she got tired. And it rang again.

"I don't want to talk to Celestial until I have something to tell her."

"You just told me that you're going up there. That's something to tell."

Now was the time to say the words I didn't want to say. "I don't have money."

Big Roy said, "I can help you some. It's close to payday, but you're welcome to what I have. Maybe Wickliffe can spot me a few."

"Daddy, you already offered me your car. You can't take money from Wickliffe."

"This is no time to be pigheaded. You either drive up there with what money I can scrape together for you, or you wait for Andre to come get you. It may hurt your ego to take money from a senior citizen, but it's going to hurt you more if you wait till Wednesday."

It was amazing how much Big Roy reminded me of Walter right then. I missed my Biological something terrible. I wondered what he would have to say about all of this. I always figured that Walter was as far away from Big Roy as two people could get, and not just that Big Roy was the kind of man to make a junior out of another man's son, while Walter was a borderline deadbeat. Knowing them both, I can see that my mama had a type, and I guess we all do. Her type of man is one with a point of view. Somebody who thinks he has figured out how this life thing works.

"YOU KNOW," BIG ROY said, "There's the money your mother saved for you when you were just born. Might be a couple hundred dollars in your name. With your driver's license and your birth certificate, you should be able to draw it down. Olive kept all your papers in her dresser drawer."

The bedroom was set up the way it was when Olive was alive. Spread on the bed was the quilt with the overlapping circles she bought at the swap meet. On the west wall was a framed picture of three girls wearing pink dresses, jumping rope. I'd bought it for her with money from my first check. It wasn't an original, but the print was signed and numbered. On top of the dresser, like a mischievous angel, was the *poupée* dressed in my john-johns.

When Big Roy said the bank book was in "her" dresser drawer, he meant the one on the top right, where she kept her most personal things. I positioned my hand on the brass drawer pull and froze.

"You see it?"

"Not yet," I said. Then I yanked the drawer like I was snatching off a bandage. The draft in the room collided with the neatly folded clothes, releasing the scent I'll always associate with Olive. If you were to ask me what it smelled like, I couldn't answer any more than you would know what to say if someone asked you to describe the fragrance of coffee. It was the scent of my mother and it couldn't be broken down into parts. I lifted up a flowered scarf and held it to my face. Pressure amassed behind my eyes, but nothing came. I inhaled deep from the cloth in my hand, and the strain became heavier, almost a headache, but the cry wouldn't come. I tried to fold the scarf, but it looked rolled up, and I didn't want to disrupt the orderly stacks.

A clutch of papers fastened with a green rubber band fit into the back corner of the drawer. I gathered the little stack and took it back to the kitchen where Big Roy was waiting.

"You never cleared out her things?"

"I couldn't see the purpose," he said. "Not like I needed the extra room."

I took the rubber band off the bundle. On the top was my birth certificate, indicating that I was a Negro male born alive in Alexandria, Louisiana. My original name was on it, Othaniel Walter Jenkins. Olive's signature is small and cramped, like the letters were hiding behind one another. Underneath that was the revised document with my new name and Big Roy's signature laid down in a flourish of blue ink, and my mother's handwriting is loopy and girlish. The first page of the bank book showed a $50 deposit the year I was born and $50 every year thereafter. The deposits picked up when I was fourteen and I added $10 every month. When I was sixteen I pulled down $75 to get the passport I now held in my hands. Opening the little blue booklet, I gazed at the black-and-white photo taken at the post office in Alexandria. Turning my eyes back on the bankbook, I noted the withdrawal I made after high school, $745 to take to college, leaving a $187 balance. With more than ten years of interest, there was probably a little more. Maybe enough to get me to Atlanta without having to shake down my father and Old Man Wickliffe.

I didn't get up right away. One more item remained in the bundle. A little notebook that I had sworn was leather, but time showed it to be vinyl. It was the journal Mr. Fontenot had given me when I thought I was going to be like James Baldwin. I hadn't written more than a handful of entries. Mostly I wrote about trying to get the passport, about buying the money order, and me and Roy going up to Alexandria to get my picture made. The last entry said, "Dear History, The world needs to get ready for Roy Othaniel Hamilton Jr.!"

⎯⎯

THERE ARE TOO many loose ends in the world in need of knots. You can't attend to all of them, but you have to try. That's what Big Roy said to me while he was cutting my hair that Monday afternoon. He didn't have a set of clippers, so he was doing it the old-school way, scissors over comb. The metallic slicing was loud in my ears, reminding me of the time before I knew that a boy could have more than one father. This was back when the words in the front of the Bible told the whole story, when we were a family of three.

"Anything you want to tell me?"

"No, sir," I said, my voice squeaking.

"What was that?" Big Roy laughed. "You sound like you're four years old."

"It's the scissors," I said. "Reminds me of when I was little."

"When I met Olive, you had one word you could say, which was 'no.' When I came courting your mother, you would holler 'no' whenever I got near her and ball up your little fist. But she made it clear to me that what she was offering was a package deal. You and her. I teased her and said, 'What if I only want the kid?' She blushed when I said that, and even you stopped fighting me. Once you gave your seal of approval, she started coming around to the idea of being my wife. You see, even before she said it, I knew that you were the one I was going to have to ask for her hand. A big-headed baby.

"I was just out of the service. Just back. I met Olive at the meat-and-three. My landlady pushed me to steer clear. For one, she was trying to find husbands for her own daughters— might have been six of them. So she whispered to me, 'You know Olive has a baby,' like she was telling me she had typhus. But that made me want to meet her more. I don't like it when folks mutter against other folks. Six months later, we were married at the courthouse with you riding her hip. As far as I was concerned, you were my son. You will always be my son."

I nodded because I knew the story. I had even told it to Walter. "When you changed my name," I asked, "did it confuse me?"

"You could barely talk."

"But I was old enough to know my name. How long did it take me to straighten it out in my mind?"

"No time at all. It started as a promise to Olive, but you're my son. You're the only family I have left now. Have you ever felt like you didn't have a father? Has there ever been one time when you felt like I didn't do all I could do?"

The scissors stopped their clacking and I swiveled in the chair to face Big Roy. His lips were tucked under and his jaw was tight. "Who told you?" I asked.

"Olive."

"Who told her?"

"Celestial," Big Roy said.

"Celestial?"

"She was here when your mother was in hospice care. We had the hospital bed set up in the den so your mother could look at TV. Celestial was by herself, not with Andre. That's when she gave Olive the doll she wanted so bad, the one that favors you. Olive wasn't getting enough oxygen, even with the mask on. Still, your mama was fighting. Hanging tough. It was terrible to watch. I didn't want to tell you about all this, son. They say it was 'quick.' Two months from when they tested her, she was gone. What we call 'Jack Ruby cancer.' But it was a slow two months. I'll say this for Celestial, she came twice. The first time was when she first got the news. Celestial drove all night and Olive was sitting up in bed, more tired than sick. She came back again, right at the end.

"On the last time, Celestial asked me to leave the room. I thought she was helping Olive clean up or something. After about fifteen minutes, the door opened and Celestial held her purse like she was leaving. Olive was lying in the bed so still and quiet that I was scared that she had passed. Then I heard that struggling breathing. On her forehead was a shiny place where Celestial kissed her good-bye.

"After that, I coaxed Olive into letting me give her a dose of morphine. I squirted it under her tongue, and then she said, 'Othaniel is in there with him.' This wasn't her last words. But it was the last thing she said that really mattered. Then, two days after, she was gone. Before Celestial's visit, she was fighting it. She wanted to live. But after that, she gave up."

"Celestial promised to keep it to herself. Why would she do something like that?"

Big Roy said, "I have no idea."

ANDRE

When I was sixteen, I tried to fight my father, because I thought Evie was going to die.

The doctors had said this was it, that lupus had finally gotten her, so we were going through the phases of grief in double time, trying to come out the other side before the clock ran out. I got as far as anger and drove to Carlos's house and punched his jaw as he worked in his front yard, clipping the shrubbery into globes. His son—my brother, I guess you would call him—tried to jump in and help, but he was small and I pushed him to the grass. "Evie is dying," I said to my father, who refused to lift his fists to hit me back. I punched him again, this time in the chest, and when I pulled my arm back again, he blocked the blow, but he didn't strike me. Instead, he shouted my name, freezing me in place.

My little brother was on his feet now, looking from me to our father, awaiting instructions. Carlos, in an affectionate tone I'd never heard from him, said, "Go on in the house, Tyler." Then to me he said, "Time you wasted driving over here and fighting me, you could be spending with Evie."

I said, "That's all you have to say about it?"

He spread his hands like suffer the little children. At his neck, I made out the glint of a braided chain. Hidden under his shirt was a gold disc the size of a quarter. His mother had given it to him a lifetime ago and he never took it off.

"What do you want me to say?" He asked the question mildly, like he actually wanted to know.

And it was a good question. After all these years, what could he say? That he was sorry?

"I want you to say that you don't want her to die."

"Jesus, boy. No, I don't want Evie to die. I always assumed that eventually we would work it out, get back to being friends some kinda way. I thought that down the line we could patch things up. She's a remarkable woman. Look at yourself. She raised you. I'll always owe her for that."

I know it's a very humble declaration, but it felt like a gift.

A week later, Evie rallied and was moved out of ICU to a regular room on the hospital's third floor. On her night table rested a cheery bouquet, a half-dozen pink roses and some green leaves. She invited me to read the card. *Feel better. Sincerely, Carlos.* After that, things between us improved a little. Out of kindness, he now extends invitations to holiday dinners, and out of kindness, I refuse. Any day now, I should receive a Christmas card, and tucked inside will be a chipper letter from his wife. I don't read these annual bulletins; I can't stomach her reports on how healthy and thriving her children are. I don't begrudge them anything, but I don't know them.

This is one thing I envied Roy: his dad. It wasn't that I had never seen anybody with a responsible father before. After all, I grew up right next door to Celestial and Mr. Davenport. But a man who is a father to a daughter is different from one who is a father to a son. One is the left shoe and the other is the right. They are the same but not interchangeable.

I don't think about Carlos all the time, like some kind of tragic black man who grew up without a daddy and is warped for life. Evie did right by me and I'm a basically solid person. But sitting behind the steering wheel of my truck, stranded in the middle lane of an eight-lane highway, I wanted to talk to my dad. Roy Hamilton was out of prison, seven years early. Not that this changed the dynamic tremendously, but the accelerated clock churned my guts and spun my head.

I longed for a mentor or maybe a coach. When I was a kid, Mr. Davenport would step in from time to time, but now he acts like he can't stand my face. Evie clucked her tongue and said that no man likes the rusty-butt who is laying up next to his daughter. I tried to explain to her that it was deeper than that. Evie said, "Was he loving all over Roy before he got sent away?" No, he hadn't been, but that was irrelevant. Now Mr. Davenport was loyal to Roy above his own daughter. In a way, the whole black race was loyal to Roy, a man just down from the cross.

"Stop by anytime," my father had said casually last year when I ran into him and his wife in Kroger on Cascade Road. He was pushing a buggy heaped with chicken, ribs, Irish potatoes, brown sugar, red soda pop, and everything else you need for a barbecue. He saw me before I saw him, or else we never would have talked. As his wife conveniently drifted off to the salad bar, Carlos placed his hand on my arm and said, "It has been too long."

How does this happen to families? I've seen the pictures. There I am, riding on his shoulders, afro like Little Michael Jackson. I remember day-to-day things like him teaching me how to pee without splashing the floor. I even recall the sting of his belt against my legs, but not often. He used to be my father, and now we never talk at all. It occurs to me that maybe a man can love his son only as much as he loves the mother. But no, that couldn't be true. He was my father. I wasn't his junior, but I wore his last name as easily as I wore my own skin.

"You're always welcome in my home," he had said.

And so I decided to take him at his word.

I don't believe that blood makes a family; kin is the circle you create, hands held tight. There is something to shared genetics, but the question is, what exactly is that something? It matters that I didn't grow up with my father. It's kind of like having one leg that's a half inch shorter than the other. You can walk, but there will be a dip.

CARLOS LIVES ON Brownlee Road in a house almost identical to the one where he lived with my mother and me. It was like he wanted the same life, but with different people. His wife, Jeanette, even favored Evie a little bit, redbone with a generous build. When they first got married, Jeanette somehow managed to make a living making ice sculptures for weddings and such. Back then, she had been much younger than Evie, but after all these years, their ages have come together in that uncanny way of passing time.

Carlos answered the door shirtless, with his bald head covered with shaving foam. As he used a nubby towel to blot his forehead, the gold Saint Christopher medal gleamed bright against his dark chest hair. "Andre, everything okay, my man?"

"Yeah," I said. "I was wondering if I could talk to you right quick." When he paused, I added, "You said I could come by anytime."

He opened the door wide to let me in. "Of course. Come on in. I'm getting dressed." Then he announced to whoever was home, "Andre's here."

I stepped inside and was met with the scent of breakfast—bacon, coffee, and something sweet, like cinnamon buns. Before me in the foyer stood a

Christmas tree, pine-scented and littered with shiny silver balls. Already, dozens of glittery gifts rested upon a red cloth trimmed in white, like Santa Claus. And like a child, I worried that there wasn't a present there for me; then like an adult, I worried that I shouldn't have come by empty-handed.

"Nice tree, isn't it," he said. "I let Jeanette handle the decorations. I haul it in, that's all a man can do." He bent and connected a green wire to the wall and the tree was ablaze with white lights so clean and radiant that they glowed, even in the sunny room.

Just then Jeanette appeared, dressed in a kimono the color of peacocks. Arranging her hair, she said, "Hello, Andre. It's nice to see you."

"It's nice to see you, too, ma'am."

"Don't 'ma'am' me," she said. "We're family. Will you join us for breakfast?"

"No, ma'am," I said.

She kissed my father on the cheek, as if to remind me that this is her house, her husband, and the father of her children. Or maybe it was affection, still blooming after all these years. Whatever it was, I felt disloyal to Evie just being there, even though my mother has been much more relaxed on the subject now that she has found true love of her own.

"C'mon with me while I finish up with this head." He pointed at the froth on his dome. "When I was young, ladies knew me for my hair. Half black and half Puerto Rican? Jet black and waves for days. A little pomade and a wet comb? Perfection. But now?" He sighed as if to say, *Nothing lasts.*

I trailed him through the house, which was quiet but for the pots and pans clanging in the kitchen.

"Where are the kids?" I asked.

"College," my father said. "They both get in tonight."

"Where did they go?"

"Tyler is at Oberlin and Mikayla is at Duke. I tried to get them to go to black schools, but . . ." He shook his head as though he didn't remember agreeing to pay for my college only if I went to the school of his choice.

In the bathroom he situated himself between two mirrors and carefully scraped the foam from his head. "Michael Jordan was the best thing that ever happened to black men my age. We can shave our heads and say we're bald on purpose."

I studied our reflections in the mirror. My father was a good-size man. There is a picture of him holding me as a newborn, and against his chest, I look to be no bigger than a hickory nut. He must be sixty by now. His muscular bulk has softened some. On his chest, on the left side, is a keloid scar to honor his fraternity. Seeing me looking at it, my father covered it with his hand. "I'm embarrassed by this now."

"I'm embarrassed that I didn't pledge," I said.

"Don't be. I've learned a few things over these last thirty years."

He returned to the business of shaving his head, and I regarded myself in the mirror. It was as though God knew that Evie would end up raising me alone, so he made me entirely in her image. Wide nose, healthy lips, and hair the color of cardboard but nappy as Africa. The only trait I picked up from my father was cheekbones that jutted like collarbones.

"So," he said, stretching the word out like a drum roll. "What's on your mind?"

"I'm getting married," I said.

"Who is the lucky lady?"

I stumbled, surprised that he didn't know, probably in the same way he was surprised that I didn't know where his kids were in college. "Celestial. Celestial Davenport."

"Aha!" he said. "I peeped that when you were babies. Did she grow up fine like her mama? But wait a minute. Wasn't she married to some dude that ended up being a rapist? Morehouse cat. Was he Greek?"

"But he was innocent."

"Who said he was innocent? Her? If she's still claiming he didn't do it, then you have a real problem." Meeting my eyes in the mirror, he adopted a thoughtful tone. "Forgive me for being such a straight shooter. Nowadays they say it's *being direct*, but your mama called it *being an asshole*." He chuckled. "I've been down here in the South thirty-eight years, but I still run my mouth like a New Yorker."

When he said *New Yorker*, he switched his accent like he was speaking a word in another language.

"You don't have all the details," I said, feeling defensive of both Celestial and Roy. "That's what I'm here to tell you about. The lawyer got his conviction overturned. He's out right now. I'm on my way to Louisiana to see him."

My father put down the razor, rinsed it at the sink. He closed the lid on the toilet and sat upon it like a throne. He beckoned, so I sat opposite him on the rim of the spacious bathtub. "And you're talking about marrying his ex-wife. I see the challenge."

"She's not his ex-wife," I said. "Not technically."

"Whoa, doggie," Carlos said. "I knew it had to be *something* to bring you over here to talk to me."

I told him the whole story from soup to nuts, and when I was done, my father pinched the bridge of his nose like he felt a migraine coming on.

"This is my fault," he said with closed eyes. "This never would have happened if you were trained up under me. I would have taught you to steer clear of a snake pit like this. There can't be a winner. First off, you should have sense enough not to mess with that man's wife. But," he said with a courtly nod, "who am I to judge? When I got with Jeanette, I didn't have no business doing it. Evie put me out. Granted, I had someplace to go, but it was her call. You know that, right? I didn't leave her." He ran his finger over his damp head, feeling for stubbly patches that he skipped over with his razor.

"This isn't what I came over here for."

"Then what *did* you come for?"

"Obviously, I need advice. Guidance. Words of wisdom, something."

"Well," he said, "I have been one of the legs in a love triangle, this you know. You also know that there isn't a happy ending for anyone. I miss your mother every day. We grew up together, too. But she can't be in the same room with Jeanette and—"

"You could have come to visit us by yourself."

"Jeanette is my wife now. Then we had Tyler and Mikayla. You can't say that I made a choice, because your mother was the one who put me out. Don't forget that."

"Enough," I said. "Enough of this historical shit. She put you out because you were chasing tail. She put you out and you married tail, and then you want to blame it on her. What about me? I didn't put you out. I was in second grade."

The air in the closed bathroom was warm, despite the noisy exhaust fan. His shaving cream smelled like cloves and made me feel nauseous. What was I even doing here? My father didn't know me, he didn't know Celestial, and he didn't know Roy. How could he steer me in this storm?

From the other side of our silence, Jeanette sang, "Breakfast is ready!"

"C'mon, Dre," my father said. "Have some eggs and bacon."

"I didn't come here hoping for a seat at your table."

Carlos stuck his head out into the hallway, "I'm coming, Jeanette." Then he turned to me, with a buzz of urgency like he had bought himself only another minute or so. "Let's start over," he said. "You say you want my advice. Here's what I have. Tell the truth. Don't try to cushion the blow. If you're bad enough to do it, you're bad enough to tell it. You can ask your mama. She'll tell you she was so unhappy because I didn't drop lies into her morning coffee. The whole time, she knew exactly who she was married to.

"You go let that man know what you have done, what you're still doing. That's all he's entitled to. You don't tell him with your chin on your chest. You tell him to inform him, for him to see the kind of man you are—however he sizes it up."

"Then what do I do?"

"Depends on what he does. My guess is that he gets physical. I don't think he'll kill you over it. He's not trying to get reincarcerated. But, son, you got a real ass whooping coming. Just take it and get on with your life."

"But—"

"Here's the 'but,'" he said. "The good news is that he can whip your ass all up and down the state of Louisiana, but it doesn't matter. He can't beat Celestial out of you. It's not a to-the-victors proposition."

Then he laughed. I didn't.

"Okay, son, I'm going to get serious. Just because I think you deserve what you're about to go to Louisiana to get, it doesn't mean that I don't wish you well with Celeste. Every relationship requires that you go through some shit." He ran his fingers over the figure scarring his chest. "This was stupid. We branded each other like cattle. Like slaves. We beat the shit out of each other. But it bound us together. I love every single one of them. When I tell you we went through it, I mean it. Maybe what has held me and Jeanette together all these years is what I had to go through and give up to be with her."

And with that, he opened the bathroom door and we walked out into the cheerful house. In the hallway, I zipped my jacket against December and headed toward the doorway, past the twinkling tree. Something in me that was still very young hung back in case a gift was set aside, in case he had remembered me for the holidays.

"Come back Christmas," he said. "There will be a box under the tree for you."

My face burned at being so transparent, and because I shared Evie's coloring, he could see it.

I turned away, but my father spun my shoulder. "I never forgot about you," he said. "Not during the year and never at Christmas. I just wasn't expecting to see you." Then he patted his pockets like he was hoping to find something there. Downhearted, he lifted his gold necklace over his clean-shaven head. "My ma bought it in Chinatown when I finished high school. Other boys got typewriters to take to college, or maybe a briefcase, stuff like that, and she gives me a saint. Saint Christopher is for safe travels and *buena suerte* for bachelors." He kissed the engraved face before holding it out to me. "I hate that you didn't get to meet her. There is nothing like a Puerto Rican grandmother. A summer or two in East Harlem would have got you right." He bounced the gold in his palm like dice. "Look, it's yours. It says so in my will. But I don't see why you have to wait."

My father took my wrist and forced the jewelry into my hand, squeezing my fingers around it with so much force it hurt.

ROY

ood-bye" isn't my strong suit; I'm more of a "see you later" kind of person. When I left prison, I didn't even say good-bye to Walter. He picked a fight on the yard and got himself put into the SHU the day before my release. As I gathered all my belongings and stacked it all on Walter's side of the cell, I wondered if maybe good-bye wasn't his forte either. Missing him in advance, I wrote a note on the first page of the notebook I was leaving behind.

Dear Walter,

When the door is open, you have to run through it. I will stay in touch. You have been a good father to me these years.

Your son,

Roy

Before this, I had never called myself his son. I meant it, but I was struck by a silly fear that Big Roy would find out or even that Olive would know from the grave. But I let the note stay put. On his pillow, I left a picture that Celestial sent of me and her on the beach in Hilton Head. Other men had pictures of their kids, why shouldn't Walter? Your son, Roy, that's who I was.

Now it was time to pay my respects to Olive, down at what used to be called the "colored cemetery." This graveyard dated back to the 1800s, to right after slavery ended. Mr. Fontenot took me here once to rub etchings off the crumbling tombstones; now he was under this ground himself. There were other places to be buried; these days cemeteries are integrated along with everything else, but I never knew of anyone who didn't choose to lay their family down at Greater Rest Memorial.

Big Roy sent me on my way with a big bouquet of yellow flowers wrapped with green holiday ribbon. I drove the Chrysler along the pot-holed road in the middle of the cemetery and stopped when the pavement ended. Exiting the car, I walked ten paces to the east and then six to the south, with my flowers behind my back like it was Valentine's Day.

I passed trendy grave markers engraved with the likeness of the person buried below. These stones were shiny like Cadillacs, and the faces trans-ferred onto rock were almost all young guys. I paused at one, covered with pink lipstick kisses, and did the math in my head: fifteen years old. I thought of Walter again. "Six or twelve," he sometimes said when he was depressed, which wasn't all the time but often enough that I recognized a blue mood when it was settling in. "That's your fate as a black man. Car-ried by six or judged by twelve."

Using Big Roy's directions like they were a pirate's map, I turned right at the pecan tree and I found Olive's resting place, exactly where he promised it would be.

The dusky gray of her tombstone dropped me to my knees. I landed hard on the packed dark earth where grass grew only in determined little patches. Across the top of the stone was etched our family name. Underneath was OLIVE ANN and to the right of that ROY. I lost my breath, thinking a grave had already been laid for me, but then I realized that this resting place beside my mother was my father's. I know Big Roy and I imagine he figured that he may as well get his name on there since he already hired the stonecutter. When it came time to bury him, I wouldn't be charged for anything but the date. I ran my hands over both their names and I wondered where I would be planted when the time came. It was crowded in the cemetery. Olive had neighbors on all sides.

On my knees, I stuffed the flowers into the tarnished metal vase affixed to the stone, but I didn't stand. "Pray," Big Roy had said. "Tell her what you need her to hear." I didn't even know where to start.

"Mama," I said, and then the crying came. I had not cried since I was sentenced and I had humiliated myself before a judge who didn't care. On that horrible day, my snotty sobbing had merged with Celestial and Olive's mournful accompaniment. Now I suffered a cappella; the weeping burned my throat like when you vomit up strong liquor. That one word, *Mama*, was my only prayer as I thrashed on the ground like I was feeling the Holy Ghost, only what I was going through wasn't rapture. I spasmed on that cold black earth in pain, physical pain. My joints hurt; I experienced what felt like a baton against the back of my head. It was like I relived every injury of my entire life. The pain went on until it didn't, and I sat up, dirty and spent.

"Thank you," I whispered to the air and to Olive. "Thank you for making it stop. And for being my mother. And for taking such loving care of me." And then I was still, hoping to maybe hear something in return, a message in a birdsong. Anything. But it was quiet. I gathered myself and stood up, dusting the dirt off my khakis the best I could. I laid my hand on the tombstone. "Bye," I mumbled, because I couldn't think of anything else to say.

I was at the BP station, filling up my daddy's Chrysler with gas, when I finally heard what I think was my mama's voice in my ear. *Any fool can up and go.* Whenever she started saying what "any fool" could do, she followed up with how a "real man" would handle the problem. Another favorite of hers was talking about what dogs were capable of. As in, "Even a dog can make a bunch of puppies, but a real man raises his kids." She made dozens of those observations. She aimed them at me constantly and I did my best to be the real man she had in mind. But she never told me anything about saying good-bye, because as far as she was concerned, real men didn't have any need for farewells because real men stay.

With the gas nozzle in my hand, I paused to hear if she had any more wisdom to share, but apparently that was all I was going to get.

"Yes, ma'am," I said aloud, and turned the Chrysler in the direction of the Hardwood.

I OWED DAVINA HARDRICK a real good-bye and some kind of thanks, too. Maybe I should give it to her straight and point out that she would be smart to rid herself of me, damaged goods that I was. I wasn't what they call "relationship material." All that was the truth, and I wouldn't even have to mention Celestial. But even as I was going over this in my head, I knew it wasn't going to be as easy as that. What transpired between Davina and me was sexual, but it was more than that. It wasn't on the level of me and Celestial when we were trying to have a baby. It was kind of like dancing late at night when you're so drunk that the beat is in charge, so you look the woman in the eyes and you both move to the music the same way. That was part of how it was, and the other part was that she fucked me back to health. I would never actually say that—some words women don't care to hear—but that's what happened. Sometimes the only thing that can cure a man is the inside of a woman, the right woman who does things the right way. This is what I should thank her for.

When I arrived at her place, I rang the doorbell and waited, but I knew she wasn't there. I contemplated dropping a note, kind of like the one I left for Walter, but that didn't feel right. A Dear John was bad, and a Dear Jane was worse. This wasn't about me trying not to be cliché. It was about me trying to remember how to be a human being. How would you go about paying somebody back for reminding me what it felt like to be a man and not a nigger just out of the joint? What kind of currency would make us even? I didn't have anything to give but my sorry self. My sorry married self, to be a little more exact.

I went back to the car, turned over the ignition, and flipped on the heat. I couldn't sit there until she got back, wasting time I couldn't afford to lose and burning gas I couldn't afford to waste. I rummaged through the glove compartment and found a golf pencil and small pad. I should at least use a full-size sheet of paper if I was going to leave a note. I got out of the car and searched the trunk, but there was nothing in it but my duffel bag and an atlas. I sat on the fender, using the palm of my hand as a desk as I tried to think about what to write. *Dear Davina, Thank you very much for two days of restorative sex. I feel much better now.* I knew better than to even press pencil to paper with that idea.

"She at work," said a voice behind me.

There stood a little knucklehead about five or six years old, a felt Santa hat crooked on his peanut head.

"You talking about Davina?"

He nodded and forced a candy cane into a sour pickle wrapped in cellophane.

"You know what time she's coming back?"

He nodded and sucked on the pickle and peppermint.

"Can you tell me what time that is?"

He shook his head no.

"Why?"

"Because it might not be your business."

"Justin!" said a woman from the porch next door, where the French teacher once lived.

"I wasn't talking to him," Justin said. "He was the one talking to me."

To the woman on Mr. Fontenot's porch, I explained, "I'm trying to find Davina. Justin said she's at work and I was wondering what time she would be home."

The woman, whom I took to be Justin's grandmother, was tall and dark-skinned. Her hair, white at the temples, was braided across the top of her head, like a basket. "How do I know it's your business?"

Justin smirked at me.

"She's my friend," I said. "I'm leaving town and I wanted to say good-bye."

"You could leave her a note," she said. "I'll give it to her."

"She deserves more than a note," I said.

The grandmother raised her eyebrows like she figured out what I was talking about. Not a see you later but a true farewell. "It's Christmastime. She won't get off until midnight."

I couldn't spend the whole day waiting for the opportunity to dis-appoint Davina in person; it was 4:25 p.m., and I needed to get on the road. I thanked the grandmother and Justin before getting back in the car and headed toward Walmart.

I walked through the store, scanning all the aisles until I found Davina in the back, near the craft supplies, cutting off a length of something blue and fuzzy for a thin man wearing glasses. "Give me another yard," he said, and she flipped the bolt a couple of times and whacked at it with a pair of large scissors. She noticed me as she was folding the fabric and attaching the price tag. Handing it to the man, she smiled at me, and I felt like the worst person in the world.

When the man walked away, I advanced to the table like I, too, needed something measured and cut.

"Can I help you, sir," she said, smiling like this was some kind of holiday game.

"Hey, Davina," I said. "Can I talk to you for a minute?"

"You okay?" she asked, eyeing my dirty clothes. "Did something happen?"

"Naw," I said. "I just didn't get a chance to change. But I need to talk to you right quick."

"I don't have a break coming up, but grab some fabric and come back. I can talk to you here."

The fabrics, arranged by color, reminded me of Saturdays with my mother, the way she would drag me to Cloth World in Alexandria. Grabbing a bolt of red fabric flecked with gold, I returned to the cutting table and handed it to Davina, who immediately started pulling the cloth free.

"Sometimes people ask how much we have so we have to measure it all. So I'll do that while you talk. What's up? You here to say you miss me?" She smiled again.

"I'm here to say that I'm *going* to miss you," I said.

"Where you going?"

"Back to Atlanta."

"For how long?"

"I don't know."

"You going back to her?"

I nodded.

"That was your plan the whole time, wasn't it?"

She snatched hard at the cloth until the spool was bare and the fabric was stretched out on the table, looking like a movie-star red carpet. She measured it against the yardstick at the edge of the table, counting under her breath.

"I don't mean it like that," I said.

"I distinctly asked you if you were married."

"And I told you I didn't know."

"You didn't act like you didn't know."

"I want to say thank you. That's why I'm here, to say thank you and good-bye."

Davina said, "I want to say fuck you. How about that?"

"What we did was special," I said, feeling like a jackass, although I had not uttered a single lie. "I care about you. Don't be like this."

"I can be however I want." She was mad, but I could see that she was trying not to cry. "Go on then, Roy. Go on back to Miss Atlanta. But I want two things from you."

"Okay," I said, eager to do something and show her that I was cooperating, that I didn't want to hurt her.

"Don't scandalize my name by talking about how when you got out of jail you were so desperate that you knocked off some girl from Walmart. Don't say that to your friends."

"I wouldn't say that. It wasn't like that."

She held up her hand. "I mean it. Don't taste my name in your mouth. And Roy Hamilton, promise me you will not ever come banging on my door."

CELESTIAL

I s it love, or is it convenience?" Gloria asked me that Thanksgiving Day after my father had stormed upstairs and Andre went to gather our coats. She explained that convenience, habit, comfort, obligation—these are all things that wear the same clothing as love sometimes. Did I think this thing with Andre was maybe too easy? He is literally the boy next door.

If my mother were here now, she would see that what we had chosen was anything but convenient. It was Christmastime, and I own a business with a staff of two, and now my wrongfully incarcerated husband is released and I have to tell him that I'm engaged to another man. The situation was a lot of things—tragic, absurd, unlikely, and maybe even unethical—but it was not convenient.

As Andre ran his lines, rehearsing the speech that we agreed would explain ourselves to Roy as gently as possible, I looked up into the empty branches and wondered aloud how long Old Hickey had been here. Our houses were constructed in 1967. As soon as the last brick was mortared into place, our parents moved in and commenced making babies, but Old Hickey predated all of that. When workers cleared the land to build, scores of pine trees were cut down and the stumps blasted from the ground. Only Old Hickey had been spared.

Andre slapped his hand against the rough bark. "Only way to tell is to cut it down and count the rings. I don't want to know that bad. The answer is *old*. Hickey has seen it all."

"You ready?" I asked him.

"There's no ready," Dre said, leaning back on the tree and pulling me close. I didn't resist and pushed my fingers through his dense hair. I leaned to kiss his neck, but he gripped my shoulders and held me away so we could see each other's faces. His eyes reflected back the grays and browns of winter. "You're scared," he said. "I can feel shaking beneath your skin. Talk to me, Celestial."

"It's real," I said. "What we have is real. It's not just convenience."

"Baby," Dre said. "Love is supposed to be convenient. It's supposed to be easy. Don't they say that in First Corinthians?" He held me close against him again. "It's real. It's convenient. It's perfect."

"Do you think Roy will come back with you?"

"He might. He might not," Andre said.

"What would you do if you were him?"

Andre let me go and stepped over the raised roots of the tree. The air was chilly but clean. "I can't say because I can't imagine being him. I've tried, but I can't even walk around the corner in his shoes, let alone a mile. Sometimes I think that if I were him, I would be a gentleman, wishing you well and letting you go with dignity."

I shook my head. Roy wasn't that type of man, although he had dignity in spades. But for a person like Roy, letting go wasn't a self-respecting option. Gloria once told me that your best quality is also your worst. For herself, she identified her ability to adapt. "I've likely rolled with punches when I should have hit back," she said. "But I rolled my way into a life I love." She told me that since I was very small, I have embraced my appetites. "You always run toward what you want. Your father always tries to break you of this, but you are just like him, brilliant but impulsive and a tiny bit selfish. But more women should be selfish," she said. "Or else the world will trample you." Roy, in my mind, was a fighter, a characteristic whose double edges were gleaming and sharp.

"But I don't really know," Andre said, thinking aloud. "He feels like everything was taken from him—his job, his house, his wife—and he wants all his shit back. He can't get his job back; corporate America waits for no man, let alone a black man. But he's going to want his marriage back, like you have been in cold storage all these years. So now it's my job to snatch the fantasy away." He motioned to take in our houses, our bodies, maybe even our city. "I feel guilty as hell. I can't lie."

"Me, too," I said.

"For what?" he asked, slipping his arms around my waist.

"Since I could remember, my father has told me how lucky I was. How I never had to struggle. How I eat every day. How nobody has ever called me 'nigger' to my face. He used to say, 'Accident of birth is the number one predictor of happiness.' Once Daddy took me to the emergency room at Grady, so I could see how poor black folks are treated when they got sick. Gloria was mad when I came home, eight years old, shook to the bone. But he said, 'I don't mind living in Cascade Heights, but she needs to know the whole picture.' Gloria was furious. 'She is not a sociological test case. She is our daughter.' Daddy said, 'Our daughter needs to know things, she needs to know how fortunate she is. When I was her age . . .' My mother cut him off. 'Stop it, Franklin. This is how progress works. You have it better than your daddy and I have it better than mine. Don't treat her like she stole something.' To which my daddy said, 'I'm not saying that she stole it. I just want her to know what she has.'"

Dre shook his head as though my memories were his own. "You deserve your life. There are no accidents—of birth or anything else."

Then I kissed him hard and sent him on his way to Louisiana, like I was sending him off to war.

ROY

PO Box 973
Eloe, LA 98562

Dear Walter,

Hello from the other side. Ignore the return address on this letter because I don't know where I'll be by the time you get this. Right now, I'm in a rest stop outside of Gulfport, Mississippi, where I'm going to get a room for tonight. Tomorrow morning, I'll head to Atlanta to find Celestial and see if I have any life left there. It could go either way. I don't think I'm making too much of the fact that she didn't divorce me, and this time tomorrow I will know.

I have money in my pocket, and I'm grateful for that. When I was a boy, I had a little savings account. I went to the branch this past Tuesday to clean it out, and there I experienced a minor miracle. Olive stopped adding to my commissary after it was clear that Celestial was handling that, so she started saving for my future. The money she made from selling cakes on Saturdays, she put away for me, so I have nearly $3,500. This means I don't have to show up on Celestial's doorstep like a homeless person. But that's what I am, I guess. But at least I don't have to be a *broke* homeless person.

Celestial doesn't know that I'm coming and I'm glad that I don't have to hear your wisdom on that! It's complicated, but she sent Andre to Eloe to come and collect me. By my calculations, he should be hitting the highway first thing tomorrow morning. This is why I didn't tell her I was coming. I need to see her by herself, not with Dre hanging around. I'm not saying that there is anything between them, but I'm saying that there has always been something between them. You know what I mean? Or am I the one being a Junior Yoda? But the point is that I need to talk to her without anyone blocking. So if he drives way out to Louisiana, it will take him another day to get back. So that gives me two days to get done what I need to do.

Admit it. It's a smart plan.

Maybe I am your kid after all.

Anyway, I'm going to put some of this money on your books. Don't spend it all in one place (ha!). And take care of yourself. And if you can, pray for your boy.

Roy O.

THREE

---+---

Generosity

ANDRE

We were not abandoning him. We were not telling him that he was unwelcome. I was to go to Eloe, and we were going to sit down, alone, and talk. I would explain that Celestial and I had been seeing each other for the last two years, that we were engaged. But this didn't mean he didn't have a home to go to. If he wanted to settle in Atlanta, we would set him up with an apartment, whatever he needed to get on his feet. I was to stress how glad we were that he was out and how grateful we are to finally see justice done. Celestial suggested the word *forgive*, but I couldn't give her that. I could ask for understanding. I could ask for temperance, but I wouldn't ask him to forgive me. Celestial and I were not wrong. It was a complex situation, but we were not on our knees before him.

Right before we drifted off to sleep, Celestial murmured, "Maybe I need to go, be the one to tell him."

"You got to let me do this," I said.

It wasn't much of a plan, but it was all I had, that and a Styrofoam cup leaching chemicals into my truck-stop coffee.

Once I exited the interstate, I handled my vehicle like I was taking my driver's exam. The last thing I needed was to attract police attention, especially on the back roads of Louisiana. If it could happen to Roy, it could happen to me. Besides my conspicuous skin, my car was a stunner. I'm a humble man about most things; I care nothing for kicks, and Celestial sometimes throws away my favorite old shirts when I'm not looking. But I do like myself a fine vehicle. The truck—Mercedes M-Class—had gotten me pulled over a half-dozen times in the last three years, and once I was even slammed against the hood. Apparently, make plus model plus race equaled *drug dealer*, even in Atlanta. But this was mostly when I drove through neighborhoods that were all-out hood, or hood-ish, although tony suburbs like Buckhead weren't safe either. You know what they say: if you go five miles outside of Atlanta proper, you end up in Georgia. You know what else they say? What do you call a black man with a PhD? The same thing you call one driving a high-end SUV.

I almost didn't recognize Roy's house without the Chrysler parked in the yard. I circled the block twice, confused. The Huey Newton chairs on the porch convinced me that I was in the right place. As I pulled in close to the house, my bumper kissing the porch, a bank of floodlights hit me, and I shielded my eyes like I was staring into the sun.

"Hello," I called. "It's me. Andre Tucker. I'm here for Roy Junior." The neighbors played music, zydeco, loud and jaunty. I walked slowly, like I was worried that someone might want to shoot me if I made any sudden moves.

Roy Senior stood behind a screen door, wearing a striped butcher's apron. "Come on in, Andre," he said. "You eat yet? I'm fixing to make some salmon croquettes."

I shook his hand and he led me to the built-on living room I remembered from the last time I was here. The hospital bed was gone, and the green recliner looked new.

"I'm here to pick up Roy, you know."

Big Roy walked toward the center of the house with me close behind. In the kitchen he readjusted his apron strings, knotting them around his barrel torso. "Little Roy is gone."

"Gone where?"

"Atlanta."

I sat down at the kitchen table. "What?"

"You hungry?" Big Roy asked. "I could fix you some salmon croquettes."

"He's gone to Atlanta? When did he leave?"

"A while ago. Let me get you something to eat. Then we can talk about the details." He handed me a glass of purple Kool-Aid, which tasted like summertime.

"Thank you, sir. I appreciate your hospitality, but can you give me the broad outline? Roy is gone to Atlanta? How? Plane? Train? Automobile?"

He pondered this like a multiple-choice test as he cranked the lid off of a can. Finally he said, "Automobile."

"Whose car?"

"Mine."

I pressed the heels of my hands to my eyes. "You've got to be kidding me."

"Nope."

I took my phone out of my pocket. We were probably a hundred miles from the nearest cell tower, but I had to try.

"Cell phones don't work so well out here. All the kids want them for Christmas, but it's a waste of money."

I checked the screen. My battery was good to go, but there were no signal bars. I couldn't shake the feeling that I was being set up. On the wall was mounted a green phone, rotary model; I nodded toward it. "May I?"

Crumbling Ritz crackers, he slumped his shoulders and said, "They cut it off yesterday. With Olive gone, it has been hard making ends meet."

I was quiet as he worked over the little bowl, cracking an egg and then stirring the mixture with slow, careful strokes, like he was afraid to hurt it.

"I'm sorry to hear this," I said, embarrassed for even asking about the phone. "I'm sorry to hear it has been so hard."

He sighed again. "I get by, mostly."

I sat down at the kitchen table and watched Big Roy cook. The years had clearly grabbed him by the throat. He was the same age as my own father, give or take, but his back was stooped and wrinkles pulled at the corners of his mouth. This is the face of a man who has loved too hard.

I compared him with my own father, vain and handsome, complexion as smooth as glass. Carlos's signature gold chain was sort of *Saturday Night Fever*, at least that's how I always thought of it. But maybe he treasured it as his mother's gift of protection. I wasn't sure yet what it meant to me.

Plunking the fish patties into a skillet of hot grease, Big Roy said, "You're going to have to stay the night. Gets dark so early in the winter. It's too late to get back on the road. Besides, you don't look like you got another seven hours in you."

I crossed my arms on the table to make a nest for my heavy head. "What is going on?" I asked, not really expecting an answer.

Finally, the simple meal was served. Salmon croquettes and a side of sliced carrots. The croquettes were edible, if not good, but I didn't have much appetite. Big Roy ate his entire meal with a short fork, even the carrots. He smiled at me from time to time, but I didn't quite feel welcome. After dinner, I washed the dishes while he carefully poured the used cooking grease into a tin jar. We dried the dishes and put them away tag-team style, with me pausing every few minutes to see if a signal had somehow made it to my phone.

"What time did Roy leave?" I asked.

"Last night."

"So . . ." I said, doing the math.

"He made it to Atlanta right about the time you were leaving."

Once everything was clean, dried, put away, and wiped down, Big Roy asked me if I drank Johnnie Walker.

"Yes, sir," I said. "Might as well."

At last we settled ourselves in the den, glasses in hand. I sat on the firm sofa, and he chose the big leather recliner.

"When Olive first died, I couldn't bring myself to lay in my own bed. For a month, I slept in this chair, leaned it back and put the footrest up. Pillow, blanket. That's how I spent the whole night."

I nodded, picturing it, remembering him at the funeral, destroyed but determined. "Next to him," Celestial had said, "I felt like a fraud." I didn't tell her, but Big Roy provoked the opposite reaction in me. I felt his emotions, deeper than the grave, and I understood his hopelessness, too, his longing for a woman you could never hold.

"It took me a year to learn how to sleep without Olive, if you call what I do at night sleeping."

I nodded again and drank. Photos of Roy at various ages watched me from the dark-paneled walls. "How is he?" I asked. "How is Roy making out?"

Big Roy shrugged. "As good as you could expect having spent five years locked away for something he didn't do. He lost so much, and not only Olive. Before this, Roy was on the track, you know. He did everything he was supposed to do, got way farther than me. And then . . ."

I flopped back in the seat. "Roy knew I was coming. Why did he take off on his own?"

Big Roy took a judicious sip and bent his expression into something similar to a smile but not quite. "Let me start by saying that I appreciate you playing a role in my wife's home-going. When you grabbed that other shovel, I know you were sincere. I appreciate you for that, too. I am honest right now in thanking you."

"You don't have to say thank you," I said. "I was just—"

But then he cut me off. "But, son, I know what you're doing. I know what you came to tell Little Roy. You got a thing going on with Celestial."

"Sir, I—"

"Don't try to deny it."

"I wasn't going to deny it. I was going to say that I didn't want to discuss it with you. It's between me and Roy."

"It's between *her* and Roy. They are the ones married."

"He has been gone five years," I said. "And we thought he had about seven more to go."

"But he's out now," Big Roy said. "Those two are legally married. Young people don't respect the institution. But I'll tell you, back when I married Olive, marriage was so sacred that everyone aimed for a wife that was fresh, just out of her father's house. They tried to warn me away from her because she had a child, but I didn't listen to nothing but my heart."

"Sir," I said. "I can't say what I think about the institution in general, but I know where things stand with me and Celestial."

"But you don't know where things stand with Roy and her. That's the only thing I care about. I don't give a damn about you and your feelings. Only thing that matters to me is my boy." Big Roy shifted forward; I thought he was going to hit me, but he reached for the remote and activated the television. On the screen, a chef was demonstrating some kind of miracle blender.

I didn't say anything for maybe a minute until the phone rang, long and loud like a fire alarm.

"I thought you said it was disconnected."

"I lied," he said, raising his eyebrows.

"I wouldn't have figured you for this," I said, betrayed. I was tired of being subjected to the whims of fathers—Roy's, Celestial's, and my own. "I thought you were about honor. Your word is your bond, all of that."

"You know"—this time he *was* smiling—"I felt bad about telling you that lie, until you believed it." Now the smile bent into a smirk. "Tell me, do I look like someone who can't pay my bills?"

He chuckled, low and slow, but built up momentum with every breath. I swiveled my head, looking around for hidden cameras. This day was unspooling like a romantic comedy, one in which I don't get the girl.

"Come on," Big Roy said. "Sometimes all you can do is laugh." And I did. At first, I was driven by an urge to be polite, to humor an old man, but something in my chest lubricated and I cackled like a crazy person, the way you let loose when you suspect that God isn't laughing *with* you but laughing at you.

"But let me tell you one thing more," he said, cutting off his chuckle like water at a tap. "I'm happy to let you stay the night, but I'm asking you not to use my phone. You have been alone with Celestial for what, five years? You had all that time to make a case for yourself. Give Roy this one night. I see that you feel the need to fight for her, but let it be a fair fight."

"I want to check and make sure she's all right."

"She's all right. You know Roy Junior isn't going to harm her. Besides, she knows the number. If she had something to say, she would have called you."

"But that could have been her calling a little while ago."

The elder Roy picked up the remote again like a gavel. When he shut off the television, the room was so quiet that I could hear the crickets outside. "Listen, I'm doing for Roy what your own father would do for you."

CELESTIAL

I used to see him sometimes, so I had become accustomed to the stuttered breath, the dancing hairs on my suddenly cold arms and neck. You can live with ghosts. Gloria says that her mother returned to her every Sunday morning for over a year. Gloria would be looking in the mirror rouging her lips, and over her left shoulder was her mother, freshly buried, but alive again in the glass. Sometimes she hoisted me on her hip. "Do you see your nana?" All I could see was my own reflection, ribboned and ready for Sunday school. "It's okay," Gloria said. "She can see *you*." My father thinks this is ridiculous. His denomination, he says, is Empiricism. If you can't count it, measure it, or gauge it with science, it didn't happen. Gloria didn't mind that he didn't believe her because she enjoyed having her mirror mother all to herself.

I never glimpsed Roy's face in a pan of water or scorched into a slice of toast. My husband's ghost showed itself in the guise of other men, almost always young, haircuts Easter sharp year-round. They didn't always share his physical attributes; no, they were as diverse as humanity. But I recognized them by the ambition that clung to their skins like spicy cologne, the slight breeze of power that stirred the air, and finally, a mourning that left my mouth tasting of ash.

On the eve of Christmas Eve, Andre was burning up the interstate heading west, then south, to do my duty. I should have known better than to send a man to do a woman's job. But he insisted, "Let me do this for you," and I was relieved. I don't know what has happened to me. I used to be brave.

As we danced at my wedding reception, my father had said, "Let the man be the man sometimes."

Giddy with love and champagne, I laughed at him. "What does that even mean? Let him stand up to pee?"

Daddy said, "At some point you will come to accept your limitations."

"Do you accept yours?" I asked, with challenge in my voice.

"But of course, Ladybug. That's what marriage teaches you."

And I laughed at that, too, as he spun me dizzy. "Not my marriage. It's going to be different."

ON THE EVE of Christmas Eve-Eve, I packed Andre's overnight bag with clean clothes, blister packs of remedies in case he was struck with a headache, insomnia, or flu. Early the next morning I stood in the driveway as he rolled away, careful not to cut his wheels and hurt the lawn, December brown but alive underneath. My legs tensed like they wanted to chase him and bring him back to my warm kitchen, but my arm waved and my lips said good-bye.

And then I went to work.

POUPÉES OCCUPIED PRIME real estate, where Virginia Avenue crossed Highland. This neighborhood was a kind of Candy Land populated by renovated manors, adorable bungalows, cute cafes, and pricey boutiques. The ice cream parlors served generous scoops, hand-dipped by college-bound teenagers who spoke through colorful orthodontia. The only inconvenience was parking, and that was just trouble enough to make you appreciate the rest.

Southwest Atlanta was my home, no later accidents of geography could ever change that, but sometimes I could picture Andre and me living on the northeast side of town or even in Decatur. I didn't want a fresh start, but maybe a little breathing room would be nice. We'd have to leave Old Hickey behind, but antique magnolias thrived in the Highlands, a different energy, but we'd adjust.

When I arrived at the store, my assistant was already there. As I booted up the computers, Tamar fitted little antlers and red noses on the *poupées* in the front window. I watched her steady concentration, her attention to detail, and I thought that maybe she was my better-case scenario. Prettier and ten years younger, she could play me in the movie of my life. Tamar created intricate miniature quilts for the *poupées*, and I told her to sign each one. They hardly sold because they were as expensive as the dolls, but I refused to let her lower the price. *Know your worth*, I told her. The mother of a son born the week before she finished her master's degree at Emory, Tamar was slightly to the left of respectability, exactly where she liked to be.

This close to Christmas, the dolls remaining in the store were like the kids who didn't get picked for kickball. Some of them were flawed on purpose; I made the eyebrows too thick or gave the doll a long torso with short stubby legs. Somewhere out there was a girl or boy who needed to treasure something not quite perfect. These dolls, as crooked as real children, lined the shelves like eager orphans. Only one beautiful *poupée* remained, adorably symmetrical, chubby-cheeked and shiny-eyed. Tamar fitted him with wings and a halo and then suspended him from the ceiling using fishing line.

Once the display was situated, Tamar said, "Ready to rumble?"

I consulted my watch, a gift from Andre. Old-fashioned, I wound it every morning. As pretty as a baby, it was heavy and noisy, jerking slightly as the seconds ticked. I nodded and unlocked the glass door and we were open for business.

The store became busy, but sales were sluggish. Often someone held a doll and couldn't quite figure out what was so disquieting and returned it to the shelf and looked away. But, as they say, I couldn't complain. By the 25th, they would all be cozy under somebody's tree.

After lunch, Tamar was antsy, fluffing and patting the dolls like pillows. "What's wrong?" I asked at last.

She used her hand to indicate her magnificent bosom. "I need to pump. Seriously. In five more minutes I'm going to pop a button."

"Where's the baby?"

"He's with my mother. I tell you, the thrill of grandbabies will make even the most refined mother forgive you for getting knocked up." She laughed, happy with the cards in her hand.

"Okay," I said. "Go home and feed him. I'll be okay here till close. But do me a favor and pick up some muslin and bring it by my place. We'll have a holiday toast."

I wasn't even done talking and she was already struggling to button her coat.

"Do not buy the baby a pair of three-hundred-dollar sneakers," I told her, handing over a holiday bonus. She laughed, all Christmas and light, and swore that she wouldn't. "But I can't promise not to buy him a leather jacket!"And then I watched my delighted could-have-been self walk out the door.

A few hours later, I was almost ready to close when a good-looking man dressed in a tan wool coat walked into the shop, announced by a jangle of bells. He was 100 percent Atlanta, his shirt still immaculate at the end of the business day. He seemed tired but upbeat.

"I need a gift for my daughter," he said. "Her birthday is today. She's seven; I need to get her something nice and I need it fast."

He didn't wear a ring, so I figured him to be a weekend dad. I walked him around the shop and his eyes bounced off all the remaining dolls, the cheerful ragamuffins.

"Are you from here?" he asked suddenly. "Are you a native?"

I pointed at my chest. "Southwest Atlanta: born, bred, and buttered."

"Same here. Douglass High," he said. "So these dolls, they look kind of 'flicted. Remember when we used to say that? I can't put my finger on it, but all of them are kind of off. Are these the only ones you have?"

"They are all one of a kind," I said, protective of my creations. "There are going to be variations . . ."

He gave a little laugh. "You can save that lie for the white people. But seriously . . ." Then he turned to the ceiling like he was searching for words and his eyes landed on the doll boy floating over our heads. "What about the one up there, dressed like an angel?" he said. "Is it for sale?"

Before I could answer, a movement across the street caught my eye. There, across busy Virginia Avenue, stood a Roy-ghost. I had learned to suppress the startle, but this one caught me unaware because he actually looked like Roy. Not Roy when he was young. Not Roy in the future. This looked like Roy would have looked if he had never left Eloe. The never-left Roy-ghost crossed his arms over his chest like a sentry. I kept my eyes on him as long as I could, knowing that if I turned away he would vanish.

"Do you have a ladder?" said the man. "If it's for sale, I can pull it down."

"It's for sale," I said.

Suddenly he sprang up like a basketball player and brought the angel to the ground. "I guess I still got it," he said. "You wrap, right?"

The doll favored Roy, like a lot of them do. There are some as well that look like me, that look like Andre, that look like Gloria, and Daddy. As the tall man watched, I laid the doll in a box lined with soft tissue paper. I paused, but the impatient tapping of his keys on the counter spurred me to take a breath and fasten the lid in place. It came in stages, this panic that started at my center and fanned out to the rest of me. I had just cut a length of ribbon the color of clean river water, when I couldn't stand it any longer. Using my fingernail to break the tape, I opened the box, snatching the angel boy from the paper, and held his firm body to my chest.

"You okay?" the tall man said.

"I'm not," I admitted.

He looked at this watch. "What the hell," he said with a sigh. "I'm already late. What's going on? My ex says I suck at emotions." Mimicking her, he squeaked, "'I can't teach you how to feel feelings!' So I want to warn you that I'm probably about to say the wrong thing, but my intentions are good."

"My husband is getting out of prison."

He cocked his head, "Is this good news or bad news?"

"It's good," I said too quickly. "It's good."

"You sound like you're on the fence," he said. "But I feel you. It's always a positive development for one more brother to be free." He then quoted his favorite rapper: "'*Open every cell in Attica, send 'em to Africa.*' You remember that?"

I nodded, holding on to the angel boy.

"Take somebody like me," he said. "Aside from a couple of knucklehead cousins, I don't know nothing about that incarceration life. But I know about being married. Divorced people, we are the ones who know. Forget the happy ones; they have no clue. How long has he been gone?"

"Five years," I said.

"Shit. Okay. That's a long time. I went to Singapore for six months. For work. I was trying to make a living. She acted like the mortgage was going to pay itself. When I got home, the marriage was shot. Only six months."

He shook his head. "I'm just saying, don't get your hopes up. Incarceration aside, *time* is the quintessential mother." Then he held his hands out. "Can I get the doll? It's the only good one left."

I ushered him out, wondering if he wasn't a ghost, too, the ghost of what could have happened but didn't. He was my last customer for the evening. Foot traffic out front was brisk, but no one else entered the shop or even paused at the fanciful front window. I left a message for Tamar and then I closed the store early, cutting the lights as my watch jerked the minutes away.

I glanced across the street as I lowered the grate. No one was there besides the parking attendant, who pulled his hat down over his eyes.

ROY

When I was a kid, I collected keys. You'd be surprised at how many are lying around once you learn to notice them. I stored them in jelly jars on the top shelf of my closet. After a while, Olive and Big Roy started bringing me keys they found, too. Mostly, my collection consisted of tin suitcase keys and quick-cut keys that could be replaced for less than a dollar at the hardware store. Once, at a flea market, I bought a Ben Franklin key, long-shafted with two or three teeth at the bottom. But I didn't discriminate, appreciating the idea of holding the means to open dozens of doors. I imagined myself to be in a movie or a comic book. In the fantasy, I would have to unlock a gate and I would try every key in my possession, finding the right one just in the nick of time. I probably kept this up from when I was eight until I was about twelve, when I realized that it was stupid. When I went to prison, I envisioned those keys every day.

WHEN I ROLLED into Atlanta, I entered the city up I-75/85 to see the skyline before me like the Promised Land. I know it's not like seeing the Empire State Building in New York or the Sears Tower in Chicago. As far as I know, Atlanta doesn't have any famous buildings. You might even say that there are no skyscrapers. Sky *reachers* maybe, not sky *scrapers*. Regardless, the city is as enchanting as my mother's face. I lifted my hands off the wheel, rolling under the I-20 bridge with my palms to the sky like a brave kid on a roller coaster. I wasn't *from* this city, like Celestial, but I was *of* it, and it was thrilling to be home.

She told me that Poupées was in Virginia-Highland, exactly where I had suggested that she set up shop, back when we were only dreaming. It was the perfect location: in the city, where black folks could reach it easily, but in a zip code that made white people feel at home. I paid ten dollars to park my car in a lot across the street from her plate-glass window. She had done well for herself, I had to give her that. Her daddy's money may have made it attainable, but she put in the work. The dolls in the window were of all shades—another one of my ideas. *Benetton it up*, I told her—and they looked to be having themselves a merry little Christmas. I stared at the display for fifteen minutes, maybe more, maybe less. It's hard to mark time when your heart is a pinball in your chest.

I thought I saw her standing on a ladder, attaching a winged doll to the ceiling, but that girl was too young. She looked like Celestial did when I first met her, when she wouldn't give me the time of day. I watched for a while longer while the look-alike folded the ladder and disappeared into the back. Then Celestial emerged from behind a hot pink curtain, like she was walking onto a stage.

She had cut her hair, not like a trim or a slightly different style. This new Celestial had almost no hair at all, rocking a Caesar, like mine. I stroked my own head, imagining the feel of hers. It didn't make her look mannish; even from across the street I could see her big silver earrings and red lipstick, but she did seem more firm. I gazed, hoping to catch her eye, but she didn't feel my stare. She walked around her store pointing at things and helping people choose gifts, smiling. I watched until I got cold, then I went back to my car, stretched out on the backseat, and slept like I was dead.

When I woke up, I saw her again, but her look-alike was gone. She was by herself until a tall brother walked in, looking like a cross between *Vibe* and *GQ*. I watched Celestial chat with him, but then she pitched her gaze in my direction, and her smile slid away like it was greasy. I don't exactly believe in telepathy, but I know that I used to be able to talk to her without talking, so I asked her to come outside, to cross the street, to meet me on the sidewalk. I had her for a few seconds, but she pulled away. I waited, hoping that she would restore the connection, but she returned her attention to the task at hand, suddenly clutching the doll to her chest. The brother smiled, and even though I couldn't see, I knew he flashed a mouthful of flawless teeth. Without my permission, my tongue went to the blank place in my lower jaw. But also without my permission, my hand visited the key ring in the front pocket of my pants.

The key ring was among the things I carried out of prison in a paper sack. The rubber-topped car key would fit the family-ready sedan. I didn't know if Celestial kept it, but wherever it was, this key would turn over the ignition. The thick, toothless key used to open my office door, but you could bet dollars to donuts that a locksmith remedied that faster than you can say "guilty as charged." The last key, a copy of a copy of a copy, matched the front door of the pleasant house on Lynn Valley Road. I wondered about that key more than I should have. Once or twice, I opened my mouth and stroked the jagged edge against my tongue.

On paper, it had never been my house. When Mr. D deeded this property over to Celestial, the only string attached was that Old Hickey couldn't be cut down. It was like the way movie stars die and leave their fortune to a French poodle. The tree was mentioned by name, but "Roy Hamilton" was nowhere on the thick stack of documents that sealed the deal. This "home," she promised, was a wedding gift to us both. "The key is in your pocket," she said.

And the key was in my pocket now, but would it work?

Celestial didn't file for divorce. After the first year of no visits, I asked Banks if she could end the marriage without informing me, and he said, "Technically, no." I know she Dear Johned me, but that was two years ago, when I was facing a lot more time. But two years gave her ample opportunity to divorce a brother if that's what she wanted to do. And plenty of time to hire a locksmith.

With the keys in my pocket tinkling like sleigh bells, I returned to the Chrysler, cranked the engine, and headed west. Pressing the accelerator, I kept my mind on one thing, the worn brass key, as light as a dime and labeled HOME.

CELESTIAL

I know this house as I know my own body. Before I opened the door, I felt the presence within the walls the way the tiniest cramp in your womb lets you know to get ready even though it has only been three weeks since the last time. As I stepped into the vestibule, the skin on my arms puckered and pilled, sending rapid sparks crisscrossing along the pathways of my blood.

"Hello?" I called, not knowing what to expect but sure I was not alone. "Who's there?" I may see ghosts, but I don't believe in haints. A ghost is a memory made solid, while a haint is a human spirit got free from the body but traveling this earth just the same. "Hello?" I said again, not sure what I believed in now.

"I'm in the dining room," boomed a man's voice that was definitely of this world, familiar and foreign at the same time.

There sat Roy at the head of the table with his fingers laced and fitted into the cave between his chin and chest. My arms were full of silly groceries for my planned evening with Tamar: lime sherbet, prosecco, chocolate blended with cayenne pepper, and Goldfish crackers for the baby.

"You didn't change the locks on me." Roy rose from his seat, his face glowing with wonder. "After all of everything, you made sure my key would still work."

He took the bags from my arms as though it were the most natural thing in the world, leaving me standing there with nothing.

"Dre is on his way to get you," I said, following Roy to the kitchen. "He left today."

"I know," he said, the bag of food between us like a truce. "It wasn't Dre I wanted to talk to."

I rubbed my arms to quiet the tingling as he set the bag down on the counter and then spun toward me and spread his arms, grinning, showing the dark space in the bottom of his smile. "You don't have love for a brother? I went through a lot of trouble to get here. Don't give me that Christian side hug. I want the real thing."

I walked toward him on legs that didn't feel like my own. He closed his arms around me, and I knew that this was my husband, not some sleight of mind. This was Roy Othaniel Hamilton. He was bigger now than when he lived in this house, his body harder and more muscular, but I recognized his energy, almost on the verge of action. Unaware of his own strength, he grabbed me so hard that I felt a little dizzy.

"I'm home, Celestial. I'm home."

He released me and I filled myself up with greedy gulps of air.

Roy's face was broader and more lined than when I last saw him, two years ago. I let my hand go to my own face, smooth with makeup, and then I remembered my head, almost clean shaven. I almost felt that I should apologize, remembering how he used to roll a single strand of my hair between his fingers. Sometimes he said out loud that Roy III should inherit his eyes but my hair.

He was prepared for this encounter; the starch scent of his new shirt mingled with the sweet fragrance of barbershop ointment. I was caught flat-footed, looking and feeling like the end of a long day.

"I didn't plan on waylaying you like this," he said.

There should be a word, I thought, for this experience when you're surprised but at the same time the moment feels completely inevitable. Sometimes you read about these sixties radicals who accidentally killed a cop, or maybe they did it on purpose, I don't know. But they run away, get a new name, and lead a clean, boring existence. They put on weight; they shop at Macy's. But one day, they come home and there is the FBI. Their faces, flat on newsprint, always look astonished but not surprised.

"I missed you," Roy said. "I have a lot of questions, but I need to say first that I miss you."

I could recite Andre's speech like lines from a play, these words he and I determined *had to be said.* And wasn't Gloria right when she said that telling this particular truth was a woman's work? But I stood in the shade of my husband returned home, and I couldn't bring myself to speak a single necessary word.

He led me to the living room, like this was still his house. He looked around. "This room didn't used to be turquoise did it? It was yellow, wasn't it?"

"Goldenrod," I said.

"All this African stuff is new. I like it, though."

Along the walls were masks, and on nearly every flat surface was a carving, all keepsakes from my parents' travels. He picked up a small ivory figurine depicting a woman ringing a bell. "This is real, isn't it? Poor elephant."

"It's antique," I said, a little defensive. "From before elephants were endangered."

"Not that this would make a difference to the elephant in question," he said. "But I get your point."

We sat down on the leather sofa and looked at each other. We let the silence grow thick, waiting for the other to break the peace. Finally, he scooted so close that our hips touched. "Tell me, Celestial. Tell me whatever it is that you have to say."

I shook my head no. He carried my unguarded fingers to his lips and kissed them twice, then he rubbed my hands over his fresh-shaven face. "Do you love me? Whatever else is details."

I moved my lips as wordless as a goldfish.

"You do," he said. "You didn't divorce me. You didn't change the locks. I had my doubts. You know I did. But when I was on the front porch, I decided to try my key. It slid in easy and turned slippery like WD-40. That's how I knew, Celestial. That's how I knew.

"I didn't walk all over your house. I waited in here because I know you don't use these rooms. Whatever it is, I want to hear it from you."

When I didn't say anything, he said it for me. "It's Andre, isn't it?"

"It isn't yes or no," I said.

Then he surprised me by laying his head in my lap, reaching for my arms and closing them around himself like a blanket.

ROY

She wasn't like how I remembered her. It wasn't just her man-short hair or the spread in her hips, though these are things I noticed. She was different now, sadder. Even her scent was altered. The lavender endured, but behind it was something earthy or woodsy. The lavender was from the oils she kept in a crystal bottle on the dresser. The wood-chip scent radiated from beneath her skin.

I recollected Davina, who welcomed me with accepting arms and a feast fit for a man home from the war. Celestial didn't know I was coming, but I wanted her to sense I was on my way and prepare a table for me. I fell asleep in her lap, and she let me rest until I opened my eyes of my own accord. Night falls early in the winter. It was around eight o'clock, and outside it was as black as midnight.

"So," she said. "How do you feel?" Then she looked embarrassed. "I know it's a basic question, but I don't know what I'm supposed to say."

"You could say that you're glad to see me. That you're glad I'm out."

"I *am*," she said. "I'm so happy that you're out. This is what we've all been praying for, why we kept Uncle Banks working on it."

She sounded like she was pleading with me to believe her, so I held my hand up. "Please don't." Now I sounded like I was the one on my knees. "I don't want for us to talk like this. Can we sit in the kitchen? Can we sit in the kitchen, talk to each other like a man and his wife?" Her face lost its softness as her eyes darted around the room, suspicious and maybe frightened. "I won't touch you," I said, though the words were as bitter as baking chocolate. "I promise."

She moved toward the kitchen like she was marching toward a firing squad. "Did you eat?"

The kitchen was how I remembered. The walls were the color of the ocean, the round table a pedestal topped by dark glass. Four leather chairs were evenly spaced. I remembered when I assumed those seats would be occupied by our children. I remembered when this was my house. I remembered when she was my wife. I remembered when my whole life was ahead of me and this was a good thing.

"I don't have anything to cook," she said. "Not over here. I usually eat . . ." She trailed off.

"Next door?" I asked. "Let's get this part over with. It's Andre. Say yes, so we can go from there."

I sat in the chair that I used to think of as my spot, and she perched on the countertop. "Roy," she said like she was reading a script. "I am with Andre now. It's true."

"I know," I said. "I know and I don't care. I was away. You were vulnerable. Five years is a long time. If anybody knows how long five years is, it's me."

I went to the counter where she sat, positioning myself in the V of her legs. I reached for her face. She closed her eyes, but she didn't pull away.

"I don't care what you did when I was gone. I only care about what our future is." I leaned in, kissing her lightly.

"That's not true," she said as I felt the brush of her dry lips. "That's not true. You do care. It matters. Everybody cares."

"No," I said. "I forgive you. I forgive you for everything."

"It's not true," she said again.

"Please," I said. "Let me forgive you."

I angled toward her again, and again she didn't move. I placed my hands on her defenseless head, and she didn't stop me. I kissed her every way I could think of. I kissed her forehead like she was my daughter. I kissed her quivering eyelids like she was my dead mother. I kissed her hard on her cheeks like you do before you kill someone. I kissed her collarbone the way you do when you want more. I pulled her earlobe with my teeth the way you do when you know what someone likes. I did everything, and she sat as pliable as a doll. "If you let me," I said, "I can forgive you." Starting my circuit of kisses again, I made my way to her neck. She shifted her head slightly so I could touch my nose where her pulse beat close to the surface. But the thrill wore off fast, like the rush of a homemade drug, the way the cheap stuff hits you hard but leaves you hungry in an instant. I moved to the other side, hoping she would tilt her head the opposite way, allowing me access to all of her. "Just ask me," I said, my voice barely more than a rumble in my chest. "Ask me and I will forgive you." I held her now; she was limp, but she didn't resist. "Ask me, Georgia," I said. "Ask me so I can say yes."

———

THE BELL RANG seven times, one after the other, with no break in between. I jumped at the first note, and so did Celestial, righting herself quickly, like she had been caught. She slid off the counter, all but sprinting to the front door, throwing it wide for whomever she might find there. It was the girl from the shop, the one who looked like the past. She was holding a baby who enjoyed mashing the doorbell. He was a plump little fellow, bright-eyed and pleased.

"Tamar," Celestial said. "You're here."

"Didn't you tell me to come by with the muslin from the wholesale place?" The shop girl stepped into the foyer as the little boy reached for her hoop earrings, the left one dangling a key like Janet Jackson's back in the day. "Jelani, you want to say hello to Auntie Celestial?" She shifted the baby in her arms. "I hope you don't mind me bringing him."

"No," Celestial said in a rush. "You know I'm always tickled to see this little man."

"He wants his uncle Dre," Tamar said, struggling with the squirming baby. "You okay, girl? You look stressed, like this is a hostage situation." She laughed a merry little laugh, until she noticed me standing there in the hallway. "Whoa," she said. "Hi?"

Celestial paused before pulling me into the room by my arm. "Tamar, Roy. Roy, Tamar. And Jelani. Jelani is the baby."

"Roy?" Tamar scrunched her pretty face. "Roy!" she said again once she ordered the details.

"Here I am," I said, smiling my salesman's smile. But then I noticed her eyebrow creep, reminding me that I was missing a tooth. I covered my face like I was coughing.

"Nice to meet you." She extended her hand, tipped with blue-green fingernails, the same as the shimmer on her eyelids. Tamar was more like Celestial than Celestial herself. She was the woman I held in my mind when I slept on a dirty prison mattress.

"Sit down," Celestial said. "Let me get you something." Then she disappeared into the kitchen, leaving me alone with this girl and her baby boy.

On the floor, she spread a quilt of various shades of orange and set the baby on top of it. Jelani arranged himself on all fours, rocking. "He taught himself how to crawl."

"Does he take after your husband?" I asked, trying to make conversation.

"Hypereducated single mother here," she said, raising her hand. "But yes. Jelani is the spitting image of his daddy. When they are together, people make jokes about human cloning."

She lowered herself onto the floor beside her son, then unwrapped a paper packet to reveal brown fabric the same color as her skin. She opened another, several shades darker, and then a third that was the peachy white that crayon companies used to call "flesh."

"We are the world," she said. "I believe this is enough to get us through to the new year. Inventory at the shop is pretty low. Celestial is going to have to be a lean, mean sewing machine if she wants to restock. I stay, trying to tell her to let me help, but she says that it's not a *poupée* if she doesn't sew it herself and write her John Hancock on the booty."

I joined her on the floor, dangling my key ring to get the baby's attention. He laughed, reaching for it. "Can I hold him?"

"Knock yourself out," she said.

I pulled Jelani onto my lap. He struggled against me and then relaxed. Not having much experience with babies, I felt awkward and silly. The scene reminded me of a photo taped to Olive's mirror—Big Roy carrying me when I was little like this. My father looked apprehensive as if he were cradling a ticking bomb. I bounced Jelani, wondering if this was the age I was when Big Roy made me his junior.

Celestial returned from the kitchen with two champagne flutes with tiny scoops of ice cream floating atop the bubbly. I took a sip and was reminded of Olive. On my birthday, she used to pull out her punch bowl to mix a ginger ale punch with gobs of orange sherbet bobbing on top. Greedy for the memory of it, I tipped the glass again. When Celestial returned with her own glass, mine was almost finished.

We sat there, the three of us, four if you counted the baby. Celestial and Tamar talked about fabric while I kept busy with Jelani. I tickled him under his chin until he gave his little baby laugh that sounded slightly hydraulic. It was amazing to think that here, in my arms, was an entire human being.

The son that Celestial and I didn't have would have been four or five, I think. If a kindergartner slept in the back room, there is no way Celestial would be talking about how she's with Andre now. I would say, "A boy needs his father." This is a scientific fact. There wouldn't be anything else to talk about.

But as things were, there was a lot to talk about, more words than could fit into my mouth.

CELESTIAL

Eventually, Tamar gathered up her little boy, zipping him into a puffy coat that looked like something an astronaut might wear. Roy and I were both sorry to see her go. It was as though we were her parents, and she our busy, successful daughter who could spare only a few minutes for a visit, but we were grateful for every single second. We stood in the doorway, waving as she looked over her shoulder to ease out of the driveway. As she pulled away, her headlights became two more glowing lights on this block bedazzled for the holidays. My own house was dark; I didn't even bother to hang the spruce wreath I'd bought a month ago. Old Hickey was festive, though. A string of lights candy-caned up the thick trunk. This was Andre's work, his effort to assure himself that everything would be all right.

Even after Tamar was long gone, I stared down the quiet street and worried about Andre. He was in Louisiana now, trying to do the noble thing. I'd rung him from the store while he was on the road, making his way south. *We're worth it,* I told him. How had so much changed in the span of a couple of hours? Absently, I reached in my pocket for my phone, but Roy swept my hand to the side. "Don't call him yet. Give me a chance to speak my piece first."

But he didn't say anything. Instead, he guided my hands across the break in the bridge of his nose, along the scar at his hairline, small but punctuated twice on each side by pinpoint-raised scars. His face, the total-ity of it, rested in my palms, solid and familiar. "You remember me?" he asked. "You recognize me?"

I nodded, letting my arms hang at my side as he explored my features. He closed his eyes as though he couldn't trust them. When his thumb passed my lips, I caught it in a light pucker. Roy responded with a re-lieved sigh. He led me through the house without turning on the lights, like he wanted to see if he could find his way by touch. A woman doesn't always have a choice, not in a meaningful way. Sometimes there is a debt that must be paid, a comfort that she is obliged to provide, a safe passage that must be secured. Every one of us has lain down for a reason that was not love. Could I deny Roy, my husband, when he returned home from a battle older than his father and his father's father? The answer is that I could not. Behind Roy in the narrow hallway, I understood that Andre had known this from the start. This is why he raced down the highway, to keep me from doing this thing that we all feared I would have to do.

How, then, should I classify what transpired between my husband and me the night he returned to me from prison? We were there in the kitchen, me with my back against the granite counter, melted sorbet soaking my clothes.

Roy snaked his hands under my blouse. "You love me. You know you do."

I wouldn't have answered even if he hadn't cut off my breath with a kiss that tasted like desire streaked through with anger. Yes means yes and no means no, but what is the meaning of silence? Roy's body was stronger now than it was five years ago when he last slept in this house. He was a commanding stranger breathing hot on my neck.

When he moved us in the direction of the master bedroom, the corner room that had originally belonged to my parents and was the space where Roy and I slept as husband and wife, I said, "Not in there." He ignored me, leading me as though we were dancing. Some things were as unavoidable as the tide.

He removed my clothes as easily as you might peel an orange, then he leaned over to switch on a bright lamp. I was ashamed of my body, five years older than when he last saw me this way. Time can be hard on a woman. I drew my knees up to my chest.

"Don't be shy, Georgia," Roy said. "You're perfect." He gripped my shin, gently tugging my legs straight. "Don't hide from me. Uncross your arms, let me see you."

In the private library of my spirit, there is a dictionary of words that aren't. On those pages is a mysterious character that conveys what it is to have no volition even when you do. On the same page it is explained how once or twice in your life you will find yourself bared, underneath the weight of a man, but a most ordinary word will save you.

"Do you have protection?" I asked him.

"What?" he said.

"Protection."

"Don't say that, Georgia," he said. "Please don't say that."

He rolled away from me and we lay parallel. I shifted, looking out the window at Old Hickey, ancestral and silent. Even when Roy planted his weighty hand on my hip I didn't turn. "Be my wife," he said.

I didn't answer, so he flipped me over like a log and pushed his face into the hollow of my throat, wedging his hands between my thighs. "Come on, Celestial," he said. "It's been so many years."

"We need protection," I said, filling my mouth with the word, feeling its weight on my tongue.

He guided my hand below his rib where the skin was knotted and rubbery. "I got stabbed," he said. "I never did anything to this dude. Never even looked at him, and he sharpens a goddamn toothbrush and tries to kill me with it."

I let my thumb travel over the scar.

"You see what I've been through?" he said. "You didn't know what was happening to me. I know that if you knew, you wouldn't have done me like that."

He kissed my shoulder and up toward my neck. "Please."

"We have to use protection," I said.

"Why?" Roy said. "Because I was in prison? I was innocent. You know I was innocent. When that lady got raped, I was with you. So you know I didn't do it. Don't treat me like a criminal, Celestial. You're the only one that knows for sure. Please don't treat me like I got some kind of disease."

"I can't," I said.

"Well, can you at least listen?" He lifted stories from his box of memories, each one making the case for why he shouldn't be forced to put a barrier between us.

"I accidentally killed a man," he told me. "I've been through a lot, Celestial. Even if you go in innocent, you don't come out that way. So, please?"

"Don't beg me," I said. "Please don't do that."

He moved closer, pinning me to the bed.

"No," I said. "Don't do this."

"Please," he said.

Picture us there in our marriage bed. Me, fixed to the mattress, completely at his grace. But is there any other way, even when love is true and pure, not dirty with time and betrayal? Maybe that's what it means to be in love, to willingly be at the mercy of another person. I closed my eyes, feeling his weight above me, and I prayed like I was supposed to when I was a little girl. *If I should die before I wake.* "Protection," I whispered, knowing there was no such thing.

"I'm in pain, Celestial. Can't you tell?"

And so I laid myself back again, seeing how he had suffered these years, seeing how he suffered then, with his head against the pillow. "I know," I said to Roy. "I know."

He turned to me. "Is it because you think I got something, that I did something while I was in there? Or is it because you don't want to get pregnant again? Because you don't want to have a baby for me?"

There was no acceptable answer to this question. No man welcomes this way of doing it but not doing it. Coming close but only so close.

"Tell me," he said. "Which one?"

I flattened my lips, sealing the truths into myself. I shook my head.

He turned, pressing my chest with his own. "You know," he said, with a trace of menace. "I could take it if I wanted to."

I didn't struggle. I didn't plead. I braced myself for what seemed fated from the moment I entered my own home and felt that it was no longer mine.

"I could," he said again, yet he raised himself from the bed, wrapping the sheet around himself like a winding cloth, leaving me cold and exposed. "I could, but I won't."

ROY

Davina didn't do me that way. When I came calling, she opened her home. She opened herself. Celestial, my lawfully wedded, is playing me like Fort Knox. Walter tried to warn me. I was prepared to stomach that there had been another man, maybe even other men. *A woman's only human.* I'm not naïve. Nobody survives prison being cute. But when a woman doesn't divorce you, puts money on your books, and doesn't change the locks on you—under these circumstances a man might think that he has a chance. And when you lean in to kiss her, she lets you, when you lead her by the hand to a bedroom, you know that you weren't imagining the whole thing. I've been away five years, but not so long that I don't remember how the world works.

Do you have protection?

She knew I didn't. I came to her ready but not prepared. She is my wife. How would she feel if I broke out with a rubber? She wouldn't take it that I was being considerate; she would take it that I thought she had been sleeping around. Why couldn't it be like it was in New York, when we were almost strangers? How many times, when I was away, did I recall that first night? I flicked through all the details, a silent movie in my mind, and I guarantee there was no latex on the set. That night in Brooklyn, I felt like Captain America; I didn't even care that I lost my tooth defending her honor. You don't get that many opportunities to be a hero like that. Now she wants to act like it never happened.

I threw the bedsheet to the floor and straggled the house in the buff, searching for somewhere to lay my nappy head. The master bedroom was out of the question for obvious reasons, so I settled myself in the sewing room and flopped on the futon, although it was a little short for a man my size. The room was cluttered with *poupées* in various stages of creation. Beside the sewing machine was a cloth head, box brown, and a few pairs of arms topped with waving hands. I won't lie and say it wasn't disturbing. But I was already disturbed when I stormed in there.

The finished dolls sat up on a shelf, looking patient and friendly. I thought of Celestial's assistant—was her name Tamara? I thought of her big, healthy boy. When Celestial left the room to get their coats, the girl touched my arm with her blue-green fingernails. "You are going to have to let her go," she said. "Break your own heart, or they will break it for you." My anger rose up the way smoke does, thick and suffocating. There was only one thing to say, but it wasn't fit for polite company. "I'm telling you," she said. "Because I know what you don't. It's not going to be on purpose, but you're going to get hurt." I was trying to figure out what kind of game this little girl was playing when Celestial returned with the coats and kissed the baby like he was her own.

It was maybe three o'clock in the morning; these were drunk thoughts, even though I wasn't drinking. I reached up on the shelf, pulled down one of the dolls and punched it in the face. The soft head dented before it sprang back, still smiling. I stretched out on the futon, with my feet hanging over the edge, but I couldn't get comfortable. I got up, crept down the hallway and stood outside the room where Celestial was sleeping, but I couldn't bring myself to try the knob. If she locked the door against me, I didn't want to know.

Back in the workroom, I picked up the phone and dialed Davina, who answered sounding frightened, as anyone would be at this hour.

"Hey, Davina, it's Roy," I said.

"And?"

"I wanted to say hello," I told her.

"Well, you just did," she said back. "Satisfied?"

"Don't hang up. Please stay on the line. Let me say how much I appreciate you spending time with me. For being so nice."

"Roy," she said with a little melt in her voice. "You safe? You don't sound solid. Where are you?"

"Atlanta." After that, I didn't have much in the way of words. There's not many women who will hold the phone and listen to a grown man cry over another woman, but Davina Hardrick waited until I was able to say, "Davina?"

"I'm here."

She didn't say, *I forgive you.* But I was grateful for those two words just the same.

"I don't know what to do," I said.

"Go on to sleep. Like they say, weeping endures for a night."

"But joy comes in the morning," I finished. This is the promise spoken at every Baptist funeral. I thought of my mama, and I asked Davina if she had been there for her home-going.

"Did you see Celestial and Andre? Were they together then?"

Davina said, "Why do you care so much?"

"Because I do."

"I'll tell you this. I saw them afterward when I was picking up some hours at the Saturday Nighter for my uncle Earl. They came in and started getting drunk in the middle of the day, her especially. I don't think they were together, but it was coming. You could taste it on the breeze, like rain on the way. When he went to the bathroom, she leaned across the bar and said to me, 'I am a terrible person.'"

"She said that? My wife?"

"Yeah. That was her exact words. Then old boy came back and she got herself together. Five minutes later, they were gone."

"Anything else?"

"That's all. Later on, your daddy came in. Black dirt on his clothes from head to toe. People say he buried your mother with his own two hands."

I held the receiver hard, pressing it against my ear, like that would make me less alone. I wasn't even a week out of prison and already I felt caged again, like a woman had used a length of clothesline to bind me to a chair. You hear these stories about men who shoplift a beer right in front of the security cameras so they can get sent back to the joint, to get back to where they know what to expect. I wouldn't do something like that, but I'm not mystified by the choice. Pulling a soft lap blanket over my hips, I thought about Walter, my father the Ghetto Yoda, and I wondered what he would say about all of this.

Davina said, "You there?"

"Yeah," I said.

"Get some rest. It's hard at first, for everybody. Take care of yourself," she said with a calming voice like a lullaby.

"Davina, I was thinking to tell you something. I've been thinking back."

"Yeah?"

"I remember a boy named Hopper."

"Was he okay?" Her voice was so low that I couldn't say for sure that I actually heard it, yet I knew what she said.

"He was doing okay. That's why I didn't remember him, because there wasn't much to remember."

When I hung up, the large orange clock over the sewing machine announced that it was three thirty, a perfect right-angle o'clock. I figured Andre was at my father's house, likely sleeping in my bed. In the dark, I smiled a little bit, picturing Andre's expression when Big Roy told him I was gone to Atlanta. He was probably dressed in jeans and a T-shirt like an average person, but in my mind's eye he was always wearing that skinny gray suit he wore for my mother's services. *Oh Mama*, I thought. What would she think if she could see me now, sleeping on the couch in my own house, surrounded by happy baby dolls that Celestial was going to sell for $150 a pop?

"Only in Atlanta." I said it out loud before I finally figured out how to sleep.

ANDRE

Roy's father and I slept in the living room, with me on the couch and him in his recliner chair, like he didn't trust me not to make a break for the door. He didn't need to worry. By the time I covered myself with the crisp sheet and soft blanket, I was tired and ready to close the book on this insane day. The room was quiet except for the hiss of the gas heater in the corner, glowing blue and running hot. Still, we woke up several times in the night and shared a few words.

"You want kids?" he asked me, just as I had fallen asleep.

"Yeah, I do," I said, hoping to return to my dream.

"Roy, too. He needs that new beginning."

Feeling claustrophobic under the covers, I wondered if Big Roy knew how close he had come to being a grandfather. I recalled driving home with Celestial, miserable and exhausted. "I don't know about Celestial, though. She might not want them."

Big Roy said, "She just thinks that she doesn't. Babies bring the love with them when they come."

"You and Ms. Olive decided to stop after Roy?"

"I would have kept going," Big Roy said, through a yawn. "Fill up the house. But Olive didn't trust me enough. She was scared I would get my own offspring and forget about Little Roy, but I wouldn't do that. He was my junior. Still, she went to the doctor and got that taken care of before I even had a chance to bring it up."

Then he was asleep again or at least not talking. I lay there counting the hours until morning, fingering my father's chain, doing my best not to think about Roy making his way home.

It was dark out when Big Roy rose from his recliner and pointed me in the direction of the bathroom, where he set out fresh towels and a toothbrush. Before I headed for the road, we ate breakfast: coffee and dinner rolls slick with butter. The weather was cool but not cold. We sat on the front porch, our legs dangling.

"You want her," Big Roy said, fiddling with the strings on his hooded sweatshirt. "But you don't *need* her. You see what I'm saying? Little Roy needs his woman. She is the only thing he has left of the life he had before. The life he worked for."

The coffee, laced with chicory, gave off a sweet tobacco-smoke aroma. Although I usually take mine black, Big Roy lightened it with milk and sweetened it with sugar. I drank it down, then set the cup on the concrete floor beside me. I stood up and extended my hand. "Sir," I said.

He shook my hand in a manner that felt both formal and sincere.

"Stand down, Andre. You're a good man. I know you are. I remember how you carried Olive. Do the decent thing and stay away for a year or so. If she wants you after a year, and you still want her, I won't object."

"Mr. Hamilton, I *do* need her."

He shook his head. "You don't even know yet what need is."

He waved like he was dismissing me, and without thinking, I moved in the direction of my car, but then I turned back. "This is bullshit, sir."

Big Roy regarded me with a confusion, as though a stray cat suddenly started quoting Muhammad Ali.

"I'll admit that I have had it better than some, but there are a whole lot who have it better than me, and there are some out there who have it worse than Roy. Be honest. You have to see my point, too. I saw you out there that afternoon in the hot sun struggling with that shovel. You know exactly what it is that I feel."

"Olive and I were married more than thirty years; we went through a lot."

"It doesn't give you the right to talk to me like this, to act like you're God up on a throne. Do I have to go to jail to have a right to try to be happy?"

Big Roy scratched his neck where the hair was growing in tight gray curls, then swiped at the standing water in his eyes. "You have to understand, Andre. The boy is my son."

ROY

Morning came gently. I slept deep and hard until the sound of frying bacon woke me up. I always started the day achy. Five years lying on a prison bunk will ruin your body. In the light of day, I still found the dolls to be unsettling but less mocking than they had been at night.

"Good morning," I called out in the direction of the kitchen.

After a beat, she said, "Good morning. You hungry?"

"After I have a bath I will be."

"I put some towels in the yellow bathroom," she said.

Looking down, I remembered that I was as naked as a newborn. "Anybody here?"

"Just us," she said.

Treading down the hall, I was aware of my body: the puckered scar below my ribs, my prison muscles, and my penis, morning strong but still disappointed. Celestial was busy in her kitchen, rattling pots and pans, but I felt something like surveillance as I made my way. Safe in the washroom, I saw that she had set my duffel bag on the counter so I would have clothes to wear. Hope woke up with a growl like a hungry stomach.

Waiting for the water to heat up, I checked under the sink and discovered some kind of manly shower gel that I figured must belong to Dre. It smelled green, like the woods. I kept rooting around in the cabinet, looking to see what else belonged to him, but I found nothing, no razor, no toothbrush, no foot powder. So hope gave another little growl, like a rottweiler puppy this time. Andre didn't live here either. He had his own separate house, even if it was right next door.

Under the hot shower, I preferred not to use Dre's soap, but the only other option smelled like flowers and peaches. I cleaned my whole body, taking my time, sitting on the side of the tub, scrubbing the bottoms of my feet and between my toes. I squeezed some more soap and used it on my hair, rinsing myself in water so hot it hurt. Then I dressed myself in my own clothes bought with my own money.

When I got to the kitchen, she had positioned the plates and glasses in front of the chairs that we never used to use.

"Good morning," I said again, watching her pour batter onto the waffle iron.

"Sleep well?" Celestial's face was bare, but she wore a dress made out of sweater material that made her look like she was going out.

"Actually, I did." Then the hopeful rottweiler puppy started his thing again. "Thank you for asking."

She served waffles, bacon fried crisp, and a fruit cup. She made my coffee black with three spoons of sugar. When we were still normal, we sometimes ate brunch at trendy restaurants, especially in the summer. Celestial wore tight sundresses and flowers braided into her hair. With my eyes on my wife, I would tell the waitress that I liked my coffee like I liked my women, "black and sweet." This always got me a smile. Then Celestial would say, "I like my mimosa like I like my men: *transparent*."

Before we ate, I opened my hand. "I think we should say grace."

"Okay."

With bowed head and closed eyes, I spoke. "Father God, we ask you today to bless this meal. Bless the hands that prepared it, and we ask you to bless this marriage. In the name of your son we pray. Amen."

Celestial didn't say "Amen" back. Instead, she said, *"Bon appétit."*

We ate, but I couldn't taste anything. It reminded me of the morning before my sentencing hearing. The county jail served a breakfast of powdered eggs, cold bologna, and soft toast. For the first time since I had been denied bail I cleaned my plate, because this was the only time that I couldn't actually taste it.

"Well?" I said, finally.

"I have to go to work," she said. "It's Christmas Eve."

"Let your twin mind the store."

"Tamar already agreed to open for me, but I can't leave her by herself the whole day."

"Celestial," I said, "me and you need to talk before—"

"Before?"

"Before Andre gets here. I know he's on his way."

"Roy," Celestial said. "I hate the way this is happening."

"Listen," I said, hoping to sound reasonable. "All I want is a conversation. I'm not saying that we need to take it to the threshing floor. I want things to be cool between us. If we play our cards right, tell each other the truth, I can be gone before Andre even gets . . ." I hesitated. I didn't want to say *home*. "I'll be gone before he even gets back."

Celestial stacked my scraped-clean plate on top of hers, which was half full of breakfast. "What is there to say," she said, sounding fatigued. "You know everything that there is to know."

"No," I said. "I know what you've been doing, but I don't know what you want moving forward."

She nibbled her lip like she was thinking, walking through every scenario in her head. When she was finally ready to speak, I wasn't ready to hear it. "Let me get my stuff first," I said. "Just let me collect my things."

Startled, she said, "The clothes went to charity, one that helps men dress for interviews. Everything else I boxed up. I didn't throw out anything personal." Celestial looked deflated. I missed her defiant cloud of hair. I wanted her back to the way she was when I met her, pretty and a little outrageous. I smiled at her to tell her that I could still see the young lady that she used to be, but then I remembered my jack-o'-lantern grin.

My missing tooth was part of my body that should have been with me forever. Teeth are bones at the end of the day. And everyone has a right to their own bones.

"Is there anything in particular you need? I made a little inventory sheet on the computer."

All I wanted to take with me was my tooth. For years, I stored it in a velvet box, like what a ring comes in. I couldn't tell her because she would think that I was being sentimental, that I was turning the memory of our first date over in my mouth like a mint. She wouldn't understand that I couldn't leave without the rest of my body.

SHE HAD MADE her choice. I could see it in the determined square of her shoulder as she washed my plate and cup. She had chosen what it was going to be and that was that. Just like a jury in a prefab courtroom had decided that I was a rapist and that was that. Just like a judge in another shabby courtroom decided I was going to prison and that was that. Then a compassionate judge in DC agreed that the prosecutor set me up, so I got free and that, too, was that. For the last five years, people have been telling me what my life is going to be. But what could I do about it? Tell the judge that I'm not going to jail? Tell the DA that I decided to stay? What could I tell Celestial? Could I demand that she love me again? Last night when we were in bed, when she was chanting "protection, protection," for a moment, less than a moment, a micro-moment, a nano-moment, I thought about showing her that it wasn't up to her. Five years ago, I swore to a jury that I never violated any woman. Even in college, I never wrestled with a date until things went my way. My boys, some of them, talked about how when you find out a girl has done you wrong, you get her in bed one more time for one last angry fucking. I was never into beating somebody up with my dick, but I considered it last night for a flash of an instant. I think that's what prison did to me. It made me a person who would even entertain such a thought.

THE WAY TO the garage is downstairs and then through the laundry room, where a stainless-steel washer and dryer hummed, modern and efficient. I entered the garage and flipped a switch, raising the large paneled door. The metal-on-metal noise made me swallow hard. When we first were married, Celestial said that the screech of the garage door made her smile because it meant that I was home from work. In those days, we had been right in there, together on all the levels—mental, spiritual, and yes, physical. But now, it's like she doesn't even know me. Or even worse, it's like she never knew me. What about this, Walter? Nobody prepared me for this.

The light of the day brightened the space a little bit. It was Christmas Eve, regardless of what was happening to me. Across the street, a stylish woman moved a dozen poinsettias onto the porch. Kitty-corner, lightbulb candelabras winked on and off. In the bright of day, I could barely make out the bulbs, but when I squinted, there they were. Directly in my view was that tree that Celestial tended like a pet. It's not like I couldn't appreciate vegetation. When I was a boy, I was partial to a pecan tree, but for a reason. It dropped premium nuts that sold for a dollar a sack. Olive cared for a stand of crape myrtles in her backyard because she delighted in butterflies and blossoms. It was different.

Turning my attention back to the great indoors, I saw that the garage was well maintained, and I figured this was Dre's doing. He was always organized. The garage had a showroom vibe to it, too clean for anything to actually have been used. When I lived here, you could smell the dirt on the shovel, the gas in the mower, and the broken-twig scent on the clippers. Now each tool was hung on a peg, polished like she was trying to sell it. Everything was labeled, like you needed a little tag to tell you what an axe was.

Along the south-facing wall was a cluster of cardboard boxes. Clear block letters: ROY H., MISC. I would have preferred to see only my name, ROY. Or ROY'S STUFF. Even ROY'S SHIT would have been a little more personal. When I left the prison, they gave me a paper sack labeled HAMILTON, ROY O. PERSONAL EFFECTS. In that bag was everything I had on me when I went in, minus a heavy pocketknife that belonged to Big Roy's uncle and namesake, the first Roy. Now I was looking at six or seven not-big boxes. All of them could easily fit in the Chrysler. Smarter men, like Big Roy or Walter, would load it all up and hit the highway. But no, not me. I hauled the stack of boxes out and sat them on the half-circular bench at the base of Old Hickey.

Returning to the garage, I searched for something to cut the packing tape, but unless I was willing to use a double-sided axe, there was nothing. I made do with my keys, the very same ones that opened the front door, giving me a bellyful of false hope.

The first box contained everything that had been in my top dresser drawer. Things weren't arranged in any kind of order, like she and Andre had opened up the box, pulled the drawer, and poured everything in. A small bottle of Cool Water cologne was packed along with a few buckled snapshots from my childhood and some pictures of Celestial and me, taken at the beginning. Why wouldn't she at least save the photos? At the bottom of the box were the seedy remnants of a dime bag of weed. In another carton I found my college diploma, safe in its leather case, which I appreciated. But an egg timer and half-empty prescription for antibiotics? I didn't see the logic in it all. A glass paperweight was cushioned in a purple-and-gold sweater, which I pulled over my head. It smelled like a thrift store, but I was glad to have something between me and the chill.

I didn't care about any of this stuff anymore, but I couldn't stop myself from ripping open box after box, pouring the contents out on the grass and, sifting through, hunting for a tiny chip of bone. Looking at the house, I noticed some movement at the window. I imagined Celestial peeking out. Over my shoulder, I felt the eyes of the lady across the street. There was a time when I knew her name. I waved, hoping that she wasn't getting antsy, thinking of calling the police, because a close encounter with law enforcement was the last thing I needed. She waved back, placed a stack of envelopes in her mailbox, and lifted the red flag. Between Big Roy's Chrysler riding up on the curb and me out here ripping open boxes and trash flying everywhere, it must be the type of ghetto scene they are not familiar with on Lynn Valley Road. "Merry Christmas," I called, and offered another wave. This seemed to put her at ease but not enough that she went back into her house.

HIGHLIGHTS FROM THE final box included a mason jar containing bicentennial quarters that had been with me since I was six, along with a couple of stray keys, but I didn't find my original tooth. I ran my fingers under the cardboard flap in case it was hiding there, but what I found instead was a pale pink envelope bearing my mother's schoolgirl writing in sky-blue ink. I sat down on the cold wooden bench and unfolded the page inside.

Dear Roy,

I am putting this in writing so that you can take this message to heart and not cause confusion with backtalk because you are not going to like what I have to say. So here it is.

First, I want to say that I am very proud of you. I may be *too* proud. There are many at Christ the King who are tired of hearing me talk about you because so many of their youngsters are not doing well. Boys are in jail or headed that way and the girls all have babies. This is not true for *everyone*, but it's *true enough* for there to be a spring of jealousy and envy against me and mine. This is why I pray a prayer of protection for you every single night.

I am happy to hear that you have found someone that you want to marry. You know I have always wanted to be a grandmother (tho I hope I look too young to be a "granny"). You do not ever have to worry about taking care of your father and me. We have set aside money since the beginning so that we can manage our bills in old age. So do not think that what I have to say has anything to do with any type of money consideration.

What I want to ask you is if you are sure that she is the woman for you. Is she the wife for *the real person who you are*? How can you know if you have not even brought her to Eloe to meet your father and me? I know that you have been spending time with her family and you are very impressed by them, but we need to meet her, too. So come pay us a visit. I promise that we'll make everything look nice, and I also promise that I will behave.

Roy, I cannot say an ill word against a woman that I have not met, but my spirit is troubled. Your father says that I do not want you to grow up. He points out that a lot of spirits were troubled when him and myself "jumped the broom." But I would not be your caring mother if I didn't tell you that my dreams have come to me again. I know you don't believe in signs, so I am not going to tell you the nitty-gritty. But I am so worried about you, son.

Your father could be right. I admit to holding you a little too close. Maybe when I meet Celeste I'll rest easy again. She does sound nice from what you say. I hope her parents won't think your father and me are a couple of little country mice.

Read this letter three times before you tell me what you think. I am also including a prayer card, and it would do you some good to pray on this *every night*. Get on your knees when you talk to the Lord. Do not call yourself praying by lying in the bed *thinking*. Thinking and praying are two different things, and for something this important, you need *prayer*.

Your loving mother,
Olive

I folded the letter and slid it into my pants pocket. The breeze bit, but my body was sweaty. My mama tried to warn me, tried to save me. But from what? At first, she was always trying to save me from two things—prison and fast-tail girls. When I finished high school without catching a charge or getting anyone pregnant, she felt like her work was done. Putting me on that Trailways bus to Atlanta with those three brand-new suitcases, she held up her fists, crowing, "We did it!" I can't say she worried about me again until I told her I was getting married.

I sat myself down on the bench to read the letter again. I didn't believe in Olive's "prophetic dreams"; besides, it wasn't Celestial that was my undoing, it was the State of Louisiana. Still, I took some comfort in the tenderness lacing my mama's words, but I was cut to the quick remembering how I'd reacted all those years ago. I responded, hemming and hawing, but I was a hit dog, hollering. *Don't be ashamed of us*, she said without saying.

I read the letter over again and again, each word a lash. When I couldn't take it anymore, I slid it back into my pocket and looked at the mess I'd made with the boxes. Something as small as a bottom tooth could be easily lost among the rubble, easily hidden between blades of grass. Maybe it was only fitting that I move into this uncertain future without it. The grave robbers of the next millennium would find me incomplete for all eternity, the story of my life there in my jaw.

I swear to God my plan was to leave right then. I would gas up Big Roy's car and get back on the highway, taking nothing with me but my mama's letter.

But then I thought I spotted a tennis racket in the garage. It had been expensive, and more important, it was mine. Maybe I would give it to Big Roy; when I was little we used to hit tennis balls at the rec center in town. I walked up the sand-white driveway, thinking of Davina and what Celestial told her after Olive's funeral. "Georgia," I called to the air, "you are not the only one who's a terrible person."

I scanned the garage wall. Sure enough, the racket dangled from a little hook. I pulled it down and found it to be warped with age and disuse. When I bought this racket, it was the finest to be had in all of Hilton Head. Now it was reduced to corroding metal and catgut. The grip had gone gummy, but I mimed my backhand, butting up against the bumper of Celestial's car. The first blow was an accident. The second, third, and fourth were more purposeful. The car alarm squealed in protest, but I didn't stop until Celestial entered the garage with her bag on her shoulder and her keys in her hand.

"Honey, what are you doing?" She used a little remote to silence the alarm. "You okay?"

The pity in her voice scraped over my skin.

"I'm not okay. How am I supposed to be okay?"

She shook her head, and again there was that soft sadness. I have never struck a woman. Never have I wanted to. But at that moment, my hand itched to slap all that concern off her lovely face.

"Roy," she said. "What do you want me to do?"

She knew full well what I wanted her to do. It wasn't that complicated. I wanted her to be a proper wife and provide a place for me in my own home. I wanted her to wait for me like women have been waiting since before Jesus. She kept talking, but I didn't have any patience for damp cheeks or noise about how she *tried*.

"Try spending some time as a special guest of the State of Louisiana. Try that. How hard could it be to stay off your back for five years? How hard could it be to make a tired man feel welcome? I picked soybeans when I was in prison. I have a degree from Morehouse College and I'm working the land like my great-great-granddaddy. So don't tell me about how you tried."

She was sniffling when I attacked the car again. The tennis racket wasn't much match for the Volvo. I couldn't even bust out the windows. I did get the alarm to wail, but Celestial silenced it immediately.

"Roy, stop it," she said, sighing like an exhausted mother. "Set down that tennis racket."

"I'm not your child," I said. "I'm a grown man. Why can't you talk to me like I'm a man?" I couldn't stop seeing myself through her eyes: hot and funky in my Walmart clothes and high school sweater and swinging a raggedy tennis racket like some kind of weapon. I dropped it to the floor.

"Can you please calm down?"

I scanned the neatly labeled rows of tools, hoping to find a heavy wrench or a hammer that I could use to bust out every window on that vehicle. But there, just at arm's length, was the double-sided axe and I liked the look of it. Lo and behold, as soon as I got my hand around that thick wooden handle, the room leaned in a different direction. Celestial sucked in her breath, and there was raw fear on her face. This grated, too, but it was better than her pity. I lifted the axe as best as I could in that cramped space between the Volvo and the garage wall. The window burst, sending safety glass everywhere. But even though she was terrified, Celestial had the presence of mind to again turn off the alarm, keeping things quiet.

Still gripping the axe, I walked toward her as she shrank back.

I laughed. "You think I'm dangerous now? Do you know me at all?" I walked out of the garage with the axe slung over my shoulder like Paul Bunyan, feeling like a man. Stepping out into that cold sunny day, I was set to head back to Eloe with nothing but the axe, my mama's letter, and the fear in my wife's eyes.

Isn't there something in Genesis about not looking back? A stupid glance over my shoulder showed her expression relaxing, glad I wasn't taking anything that couldn't be replaced and glad I didn't destroy anything that couldn't be repaired.

"Do you care for me, Georgia?" I asked her. "Tell me you don't and I'm out of your life forever."

She stood in the driveway with her arms wrapped around herself like she was freezing. "Andre is on his way."

"I didn't ask you about no Andre."

"He'll be here in a minute."

My head hurt, but I pressed her. "It's a yes-or-no question."

"Can we talk when Andre gets back? We can—"

"Stop talking about him. I want to know if you love *me*."

"Andre . . ."

She said his name one time too many. For what happened next, she would have to take some of the blame. I asked her a simple question and she refused to give me a simple answer.

I turned from her and made a sharp left turn, pounding across the yard, feeling the dry grass crunch under my shoes. Six long strides put me at the base of the massive tree. I touched the rough bark, an instant of reflection, to give Old Hickey the benefit of the doubt. But in reality, a hickory tree was a useless hunk of wood. Tall, and that's all. To break the shell of a hickory nut, you needed a hammer and an act of Congress, and even then you needed a screwdriver to get at the meat, which was about as tasty as a clod of limestone. Nobody would ever mourn a hickory tree except Celestial, and maybe Andre.

When I was a boy, so little I couldn't manage much more than a George Washington hatchet, Big Roy taught me how to take down a tree. *Bend your knees, swing hard and low, follow up with a straight chop.* Celestial was crying like the baby we never had, yelping and mewing with every swing. Believe me when I say that I didn't slow my pace, even though my shoulders burned and my arms strained and quivered. With every blow, wedges of fresh wood flew from the wounded trunk peppering my face with hot bites.

"Speak up, Georgia," I shouted, hacking at the thick gray bark, experiencing pleasure and power with each stroke. "I asked you if you loved me."

ANDRE

I expected to come home to psychological chaos. But when I pulled my truck to the end of Lynn Valley Road, what I encountered was more physical than emotional. The yard was strewn with cardboard and other garbage; Celestial was standing in the driveway dressed for work, sobbing into her fists, while Roy Hamilton was hacking away at Old Hickey with my double-sided axe. I hoped that I was hallucinating. After all, I had been driving for a long time. But the piercing thwack of metal against green wood convinced me that the scene was real.

Celestial and Roy both spoke my name at the same time, striking a peculiar chord. I was torn, not sure which of them to respond to, so I asked a question that either of them could answer: "What the hell is going on?"

Celestial pointed at Old Hickey as Roy gave another gutsy swing, leaving the axe buried in the tree, like a sword stuck in a stone.

In the driveway, I stood midway between them, two separate planets, each with its own gravitational pull and orbit. The sun glinted overhead, giving light, but not heat.

"Look who's here," Roy said. "The third most terrible person in the world." He picked up the tail of his shirt to mop his perspiring forehead. "The man of the hour." He smiled broadly, looking snaggle-toothed and unscrewed. The axe jutted from the tree, immobilized.

I don't know that I would have recognized Roy if I had run into him on the street. Yes, he was the same Roy, but prison made him bulky, deep grooves creased his forehead, and his shoulders caved a little toward his overdeveloped chest. Although we were roughly the same age, he seemed much older but not in that elder-statesman way like Big Roy; he was more like a powerful machine that was wearing out.

"What's up, Roy?"

"Well . . ." He looked up at the sun, not bothering to shield his eyes. "I got locked up for a crime I didn't commit, and when I get home, my wife has hooked up with my boy."

Celestial walked toward me like this was any other day and I had just returned from work. By habit, I curled my arm around her waist and kissed her cheek. The touch of her was reassuring. No matter what had happened in my absence, I was the one holding her now.

"You okay, Celestial?"

"Yes, she's okay," Roy said. "You know I wouldn't hurt her. I'm still Roy. She may not be my wife, but I'm still her husband. Can't y'all see that?" He held his hands up as if to show he was unarmed. "Come talk to me, Dre. Let's sit down like men."

"Roy," I said. "Everybody can see we got a conflict here. What can we do to squash it?" After I released Celestial, my arms felt useless. "It's all right," I said to her, but I was really trying to convince myself. Joining Roy in the "don't shoot" salute, I advanced toward Old Hickey. The odor of the exposed wood was oddly sweet, almost like sugarcane. Displaced chunks of wood littered the grass like misshapen confetti.

"Let's talk," Roy said. "I'm sorry about what I did to your tree. I got carried away. A man has feelings, you know. I have a lot of feelings." He swept the wood chips from the seat.

"My father built this bench," I said. "When I was little."

"Dre," he said. "Is that all you got?" He popped up, snatching me into a back-clapping man-hug, and I was embarrassed at how I balked at his touch.

"So," he said, releasing me and plopping down on the bench. "What you know good?"

"This and that," I said.

"So are we going to talk about this?"

"We can," I said.

Roy patted the space next to him and then leaned back on the tree, stretching his legs in front of him. "Did my old man tell you how we set you up?"

"He mentioned it," I said.

"So what was it? I need to know that, and I promise I'll get out of your way. What was it that made you say, 'Fuck ole Roy. I'm sorry he's sitting in prison, but I think I'll help myself to his woman'?"

"You're misrepresenting," I said. "You know that's not how it went down." Because it felt dirty leaving Celestial in the driveway, out of earshot, I beckoned to her.

"Don't call her over here," Roy said. "This is between me and you."

"It's between all of us," I said.

Across the street our neighbor straightened several poinsettias, placing them into a row. Roy waved at her and she waved back. "Maybe we should invite the whole neighborhood and let it be between everybody."

Celestial sat on the bench between us, clean like rain. I circled my arm around her shoulder.

"Don't touch her," Roy said. "You don't have to pee on her like a dog marking your territory. Have some manners."

"I'm not territory," Celestial said.

Roy got up and began an agitated pacing. "I'm trying to be gracious. I swear to God, I am. I was innocent," he said. "Innocent. I was minding my business and next thing I know I got snatched up. It could happen to you, too, Dre. It takes nothing for some he-say she-say to go left. You think the police are going to care that you got your own house or that you got that Mercedes SUV? What happened to me could happen to anybody."

"You think I don't know that?" I said. "I been black all my life."

Celestial said, "Roy, not one day went by when we didn't talk about you, didn't think about you. You think we don't care, but we do. We thought you were gone for good."

I was silent as Celestial explained. Her words were those we agreed upon, but now they rang less than true. Were we saying that our relationship was an accident of circumstance? Were we saying, too, we loved each other only because Roy had been unavailable? That was a lie. We loved each other because we always had, and I refused to ever claim anything different.

"Celestial," Roy said. "Stop talking."

"Look," I said. "Roy, you have to see that we're together. Full stop. Details are not important. Full stop."

"Full stop?" he said.

"Full stop," I repeated.

"Listen," Celestial pleaded. "Both of you."

"Go in the house," Roy said. "Let me talk to Dre."

I pressed my hand to the small of her back to urge her toward the door, but she was adamant. "I'm not going," she said. "This is my life, too."

We both turned to her. The admiration I feel for her flashed on Roy's craggy face. "Listen if you want to," he said. "I told you to go in the house for your own benefit. You don't need to hear what me and Andre need to talk about. I'm trying to be a gentleman."

"It's her choice," I said. "We don't keep secrets."

"Oh yes you do," Roy sneered. "Ask her about last night."

I asked her with my eyes, but her expression was blank, shuttered down against the sun.

"I'm telling you that you don't want to be out here," Roy said to Celestial. "When men talk, it's not a pretty kind of conversation. That's really the main thing about being in prison. Too many men in one place. You're stuck in there knowing that there is a world full of women who are putting out flowers, making things nice, civilizing the whole planet. But there I was stuck in a cage like an animal with a bunch of other animals. So I'm going to give you one more chance, Celestial. Take your pretty little self in the house. Go sew some baby dolls or something."

"I'm not going," she said. "Somebody has to be out here who has some sense."

"Go on in the house, baby," I said. "You had your chance to talk to him all day yesterday." I tried to make the word *talk* sound neutral, not like I was wondering what they did beyond conversation.

"Ten minutes is enough," Roy said. "This won't take long."

Celestial stood up. I watched her back, smooth and muscular, as she walked away. Roy looked across at the neighbor who was watching openly now, not even bothering to fiddle with her flowers.

After Celestial finally disappeared, he said, "Like I said. The world is full of women, Atlanta especially. You're black, employed, heterosexual, unincarcerated, and into sisters. This shit is your fucking oyster. But you had to go for my wife. That was disrespectful to me as a person. It was disrespectful to what I was going through, what all of us are going through in this country. Celestial was *my woman*. You knew it. Hell, you're the one that introduced us." Now he was standing before me, his voice not so much raised but going deeper. "What, was it just convenient? You wanted some pussy next door so you wouldn't have to bother getting in your car?"

Now I got to my feet, because there are some words that a man can't take sitting down. When I stood up, he was waiting on me and thrust his chest against mine. "Get out of my face, Roy."

"Tell me," he said. "Tell me why you did it."

"Why I did what?"

"Why you stole my wife. You should have left her alone. She was lonely. Fine, but you weren't. Even if she was throwing it at you, you could have walked away."

"What about this is so hard for you to comprehend?"

"That's bullshit," Roy said. "You knew she was my wife before you got caught up with this love stuff. You saw your opportunity and you took it. Long as you got your dick wet, you didn't care."

I pushed him because there was no other option. "Don't talk about her like that."

"Or what? You don't like my language? We are not all that PC in prison; we say what's on our mind."

"So what do you mean? What do you want me to say? If I tell you she was a piece of ass, you would want to fight. If I tell you I want to marry her, it won't be any better. Why don't you just hit me and cut the chitchat? The bottom line is that she *doesn't* belong to you. She *never* belonged to you. She was your wife, yeah. But she didn't *belong* to you. If you can't understand that, kick my ass and get it over with."

Roy paused for a minute. "That's what you have to say? That she doesn't belong to me?" He let out a stream of spit through the space where his tooth used to be. "She doesn't belong to you either, my friend."

"Fair enough." I walked away, hating the questions twining up my legs like a barbed vine. It was doubt that did it, that left me exposed, not watching my own back. Roy's laugh shook me up, made me forget that I trusted her like I trusted my own eyes.

He struck me from behind before I had even taken a step. "Don't walk away from me."

This is the violence my father promised me. *Take it*, he had said. *Take it and get on with your life.* I offered my face and Roy hit me squarely in my nose before I could even ball my fists. I felt the impact first, then the hot gush over my lip, followed by the pain. I got in a couple of strong blows, a low hook to the kidneys, and drove my head into his chest before he wrestled me to the ground. Roy spent the last five years in prison while I'd been writing computer code. Up until this very instant, I was proud of my clean record, my not-thug life. But on the grass beneath Old Hickey, shielding myself from Roy's granite fists, I wished I were a different type of man.

"Everybody is so calm, like this is only a little speed bump." He panted. "This is my life, motherfucker. My life. I was married to her."

Have you ever stared fury in its eyes? There is no saving yourself from a man in its throes. Roy's face was haunted and wild. The cords of his neck muscles were like cables; his lips made a hard gash. The unceasing blows were fueled by a need to hurt me that was greater than his own need for oxygen or even freedom. His need to hurt me was greater even than my own desire to survive. My efforts to protect myself were ritualistic, mannered, and symbolic, while his fists, feet, and needs were operating from a brutal code.

Had he learned this in prison, this way of beating a person? There was none of the stick-and-move that I remembered from school-yard brawls. This was the nasty scrapping of a man with nothing to lose. If I remained on the grass, he would stomp my head. I raised myself, but my legs failed me. I fell first to my knees, like a building being demolished, and then I was on the lawn, the odor of dry grass and wet blood in my nose.

"Say you're sorry," he said, his foot poised to kick.

This was an opportunity. A chance to wave the white flag. It would be easy enough, to spit out the words along with the blood in my mouth. Surely I could give him that, only I could not. "Sorry for what?"

"You know what for."

I looked into his eyes narrowed against the sun, but I didn't see anyone that I recognized. Would I have surrendered if I thought it would have saved me, if I believed that he was intent on anything other than killing me? I don't know. But if I were going to die on my front yard, I would die with the taste of pride in my mouth. "I am not sorry."

But I *was* sorry. Not for what was between Celestial and me, I would never regret that. I was sorry for a lot of things. I was sorry for Evie, suffering from lupus for so many years. I was sorry for elephants killed for their ivory. I was sorry for Carlos, who traded one family for another. I was sorry for everyone in the world because we all had to die and nobody knew what happened after that. I was sorry for Celestial, who was probably watching from the window. Most of all, I was sorry for Roy. The last time I saw him on that morning before his mother's wake, he said, "I never had a chance, did I? I only thought I did."

There was pain, yes, but I figured out how not to feel it. Instead, I thought about Celestial and me and how maybe we just *thought* we could weather this calamity. We believed we could talk this out, reasoning our way through this. But someone was going to pay for what happened to Roy, just as Roy paid for what happened to that woman. Someone always pays. *Bullet don't have nobody's name on it*, that's what people say. I think the same is true for vengeance. Maybe even for love. It's out there, random and deadly, like a tornado.

CELESTIAL

I wonder about myself sometimes. Roy and Andre circled each other, radiating locker-room energy: violence and competition. They told me to leave, and I did. Why? Was I afraid to bear witness? I'm not an obedient person, but on that Christmas Eve, I did as I was told.

They must have grabbed each other as soon as I shut the door. By the time I made it to a window—peeking through a curtain like a silly southern belle—Roy and Andre were rolling around on the dry lawn, a tangle of arms and legs. I watched for what must have been only several seconds, but whatever the duration, it was too long. When Roy gained the upper hand and pinned Andre to the ground, straddling and punishing him with windmilling fists and rage, I pulled open the window. The lace curtain floated from the thin rod, covering my eyes like a veil. I yelled their names to the wind, but they either wouldn't or couldn't hear me. The grunts of exertion and satisfaction both layered over the gasps of pain and humiliation. All these noises floated up to my window, moving me to run outside with the intention of saving them both.

Stumbling and quaking, I reached the lawn. "November 17!" I yelled, hoping the memory would reach him.

He did pause but only long enough to shake his head in disgust. "It's too late for all of that, Georgia. No magic words for us anymore."

Now I had no choice. I pulled the phone from my pocket and aimed it like a gun. With whatever air I could gather, I screamed, "I'm calling the police!"

Roy froze, pulled up short by the threat. "You would do that? You would, wouldn't you?"

"You're making me," I said, fighting to steady my shaking. "Get off him."

"I don't care," Roy said. "Call the law. Fuck you, fuck Andre, and fuck the police." Andre struggled to free himself, but Roy, as if to underscore his point, delivered a close-fisted blow. Andre shut his eyes but didn't cry out.

"Please, Roy," I said. "Please, please don't make me call the police."

"Do it," Roy said. "Do I look like I care? Call them. Send me back. There's nothing for me here. Send me back."

"No," Andre managed to say. His pupils, dark and wide, edged out light irises. "Celestial, you can't send him back. Not after everything."

"Do it," Roy said.

"Celestial." Andre's voice was resolute but distant as an overseas call. "Put the phone down. Right now."

Kneeling, I set it carefully on the lawn like I was surrendering a weapon. Roy released Andre, who rose only to his knees, his body at half-mast. I rushed over to him, but he sent me away. "I'm fine, Celestial," he said, although he wasn't. Wood chips clung to his clothes like mites.

"Let me look at your eye."

"Stand down, Celestial," he said softly, his teeth streaked pink.

Only a few yards away, Roy flexed his hands in time with his steps. "I didn't kick him. When he was on the ground, I didn't kick him. I could have. But I didn't."

"But look what you *did* do," I said.

"What about you?" Roy was pacing now, back and forth over a short distance, like he was covering the floor of a narrow cell. "It wasn't supposed to be like this," he said. "I was just trying to come home. I wanted some time to talk to my wife and figure out what was what. Dre wasn't supposed to have nothing to do with it."

I DIDN'T CALL the police, but they came anyway, with strobing blue lights but no sirens. The officers, a black woman and a white man, acted put upon to be working on Christmas Eve. I wondered what they were thinking as they regarded us. Both men were bruised and bloody, and I was dressed like holiday cheer, whole and unhurt. I felt like a mother of newborn twins, hurrying from one man to the next, making sure neither was neglected, that both had a piece of me.

"Ma'am," said the woman cop. "Is everything all right?"

I had not been this close to a police officer since the night at the Piney Woods when I had been pulled from my bed. My body memory smarted as I fingered the scar underneath my chin. Despite the December chill, I felt the spectral heat of that August night. Roy and I had been ordered through crosshairs not to speak and not to move, but my husband reached for me anyway, tangling our fingers for one desperate instant before a cop separated us with his black boot.

"Please don't hurt him," I said to the policewoman. "He's been through a lot."

"Who are these men?" the white cop asked me. His accent was thick and gooey, all Marietta, turn left at the Big Chicken. I tried to connect with the woman, but she fixed her eyes on the men.

With the voice I used on the telephone, I said, "This is my husband and my neighbor. We had a little bit of an accident, but everything is fine now."

The woman looked to Andre. "Are you the husband?"

When he didn't answer, Roy spoke. "I'm the husband. It's me."

She nodded at Andre for confirmation. "So you're the neighbor?"

Rather than say yes, Andre recited his address, pointing at his own front door.

Once the police satisfied themselves, their Merry Christmases resonated like a dark omen. They left without blue lights, just the exhaust souring the air. Once they were gone, Roy sat heavily on the half-moon bench. He gestured toward the seat beside him, but I couldn't go to him, not with Andre standing a few feet away, his face purpling around the eyes and his split lip showing red meat.

"Georgia," Roy said, and then his body contracted dry heaving, his head between his knees. I went to him and rubbed his twitching back. "I'm hurting," he said. "I'm hurting all over."

"You need to go to the hospital?"

"I want to sleep in my own bed." He stood up, like a man with somewhere to go. But he only turned toward Old Hickey. "It's too much." Then quickly—it must have been quickly, but I somehow took notice of each move—Roy tucked his lips against his teeth, gripped the tree like a brother, and then tipped his head back, presenting his face to the sky before driving his forehead against the ancient bark. The sound was muted, like the wet crack of an egg against the kitchen floor. He did it again, harder this time. I found my feet, and without thinking, I positioned myself between my husband and the tree. Roy craned his head back again, cocked and ready, but now if he chose to drive his skull forward, he would strike me instead.

He executed a little twitch of his knotted shoulders. Then he surveyed Old Hickey, the wood chips scattered in the grass, Andre, me, and lastly himself. "How did this happen?" Roy touched his forehead; the small cut leaked blood over his eyebrow.

Then he sat down on the grass, smoothly but with a sense of mission. "What do you want me to do?" he asked. He turned to Dre with the same curious tone. "Seriously. What do you think I should do?"

Andre sat himself gingerly on the round bench, tensing himself against his injuries. "We'll help you get set up. If you want, you can stay in my house."

"I'll stay in your house and you will stay in my house with my wife? What kind of sense does that make?" Then he looked to me. "Celestial, you knew that wasn't going to work. You *know* me. How could I go for that? What were you expecting?"

What did I expect? The truth is that before Roy materialized in my living room, I had forgotten that he was real. For the last two years, he was only an idea to me, this husband of mine who didn't count. He had been away from me longer than we had been together. I'd convinced myself that there were laws limiting responsibility. When I sent Andre to Louisiana, I hoped that maybe Roy would choose not to come to Atlanta at all, that he would send for his things, that I would be a memory to him in the way that he was a memory for me.

"Roy," I said, wondering aloud. "Tell the truth. Would you have waited on me for five years?"

He twitched that same shrug. "Celestial," he said, like he was talking to someone very young, "this shit wouldn't have happened to you in the first place."

Andre made a move as if to join us on the dry grass, but I shook my head. His breath escaped his mouth in exhausted puffs of white.

"How does it feel to make all the decisions?" Roy said. "It's been up to you for the last five years. When we were dating, it was up to me. You had a finger that needed a ring. You remember that? Remember when I was a fiancé you could be proud of, flashing that rock like a searchlight. I won't lie and say I didn't get off on it. But now I don't have anything to offer you but myself. But it's better than it was last year, when I couldn't even give you that. So here I am." He looked to his left. "Your turn, Dre. What do you have to say for yourself?"

Andre spoke to Roy, but he looked at me. "I don't have to tell Celestial what I feel. She already knows."

"But tell me," Roy said. "Tell me how you ended up with your head on my pillow."

"Roy, man," Dre said. "I'm sorry for what happened to you. You know I am. So don't take this as disrespect, but I'm not going to discuss this with you." He touched his busted lip with his tongue. "You had a time when we could have talked, but you wanted to fight. Now I don't have anything to say to you."

"What about you, Georgia? Do you have anything to say? How did you end up picking Dre over me?"

The true answer was that Olive had settled it by lying in her coffin as Big Roy showed me what real communion looked like, what it sounded like, even what it smelled like—fresh earth and sadness. I could never tell Roy that by his parents' measure, what we had wasn't a connection for the ages. Our marriage was a sapling graft that didn't have time to take.

As if he could hear the murmur of my thoughts, he said, "Was Dre just at the right place at the right time? Is this a crime of passion or a crime of opportunity? I need to know."

How could I tell him that desire didn't work the way I thought it did when I was younger, my head turned by the electricity of attraction. Andre and I had an everyday thing. We moved each other like we had done it forever, because we had.

When I didn't answer, Roy pressed on. "How did we end up here? My key works, but you won't let me in."

He gathered his body up and plunked down on the bench, blank-eyed and miserable. I turned to Andre, who didn't meet my gaze. Instead, he studied Roy, broken and shivering.

"You didn't do this to him," Andre said. "Don't let him set that at your feet."

And he was right. All around Roy were the shards of a broken life, not merely a broken heart. Yet who could deny that I was the only one who could mend him, if he could be healed at all? Women's work is never easy, never clean.

"You know where I'll be." Andre turned toward his own house.

Andre went his way; Roy and I went ours, me leading Roy the way you would provide assistance to a man who has been shot or has lost his sight. As we climbed the stairs to the front walk, I heard Andre's calm words. "He hit his head pretty bad. He might be concussed. Don't let him go to sleep right away."

"Thank you," I said.

"Thank me for what?" said Andre.

IN THE BATHROOM, Roy let me clean his wound, but he refused to go to the emergency room. "I know you can take care of me."

But there was little to do besides apply antiseptic. As the night stretched on, we asked one another questions to keep sleep at bay, even though both our eyelids hung low, as though weighted down by coins.

"What were you looking for?" I asked him. "When you were going through all the boxes?"

Roy smiled and snugged the tip of his pinky in the gap in his mouth. "My tooth. It wasn't trash. Why did you throw it out?"

"No," I said. "I have it."

"It's because you love me," he slurred.

"Stay awake," I said, shaking him. "People with concussions can die in their sleep."

"Wouldn't that be some shit," he said. "I get out of prison. Come home, find my wife with another man, win her back, and then get in a fight with a tree and wake up dead." He must have sensed a change in me, even in the dim light. "Did I speak too soon? I didn't win you back?"

Each time his eyes drooped, I shook him back to life. "Please don't," I whispered, opening myself to him, undoing a rusted latch. "I can't lose you like this."

ANDRE

This is how I am lonely.

When Celestial opened my front door with her key and walked into the family room, she had changed her clothes, but I was still wearing the fight-filthy jeans from that terrible afternoon. Even before she got close enough for me to see her swollen eyes, I sensed the salt on her like you can on the beach. It wasn't quite 1 a.m., night but also the next day.

"Hey," she said, lifting my legs and sitting on the sofa. Setting my calves back on her lap, she added, "Merry Christmas."

"I guess," I said, handing her the square glass containing the last of my father's scotch. As she swallowed it, I smelled Carlos in the fumes.

I inched closer to the back of the sofa and made room. "Lie down," I said. "I don't want to talk about this when I can't feel you next to me."

She shook her head and stood up. "I need to walk around." She traveled the room like a ghost, aimless and trapped.

With effort, I pulled myself to a seated position. I'd taped my ribs, but it hurt with every breath. "So I take it that Roy is still alive?"

"Dre," she said. Finding the place in the room farthest from me, she sat on the white carpet and crossed her legs. Her bare feet looked naked and cold. "He's wrecked."

"That doesn't have anything to do with us."

"There's so much that you don't know. Things people like us can't even imagine."

"Is that why you're hiding in the corner? Celestial, what are you doing?" I beckoned to her. "Come here, girl. Talk to me."

She returned to the sofa and we lay down. Celestial fitted herself against me, her forehead against mine.

"I married him for a reason," she said. "You can never really unlove somebody. Maybe it changes shape, but it's there."

"You really believe that?"

"Dre, we have so much," she said, "and he has nothing. Not even his mother. The whole time he was talking, my face was on fire, just like at Olive's funeral. Her handprint stinging on my cheek, making sure I didn't forget. It's hot right now." She reached for my hand. "Touch it."

I nudged her away from me, suddenly irritated by her touch, by the scotch on her breath, even the scent of lavender on her neck. I didn't want to cradle her talk about ghost slaps, dead mothers, and the right thing to do.

"Just go," I said. "If you want to leave me, just do it. Don't try to make it supernatural. You are the one making this choice, Celestial. *You.*"

"You know what I mean, Dre. We've been lucky. We were born lucky. Roy's starting from scratch. Less than scratch. You saw him trying to kill himself up under that tree. He wanted to crack his own skull."

"Actually, I was the one he was trying to kill."

"Dre," she said. "You and me, we are just heartbroken. That's it. Only heartbroken."

"Maybe that's it for *you*," I said.

"Baby," she said. "Can't you see? Whatever I do to you, I am doing to myself."

"Then don't do it. You don't have to."

She shook her and said, "You didn't see him. If you had seen him, I know you would agree with everything I'm saying."

"I need you, Celestial," I whispered. "All my life."

She shifted so that we were touching again. When she closed her eyes, I felt the tickle of her lashes.

"I have to do this," she said.

CELESTIAL OWED ME nothing. A few months ago, this was the beauty of what we had. No debts. No trespasses. She said that love can change its shape, but for me at least, this is a lie. I kept my arms around her, my body aching and cramped. But I held her until muscles failed, because when I released her, she would be gone.

ROY

I woke up at a quarter past eleven and the clean air smelled like trees. Except for her hair, Celestial was my Georgia girl again. I stood up and she embraced me, spreading her fingers across my shoulders. Her skin was warm like a cup of cocoa.

"Merry Christmas, baby," I said, just like Otis Redding.

"Merry Christmas," she replied with a smile.

"With everything, I almost forgot about the holidays," I said, wishing, too late, that I had used some of Olive's money to buy Celestial a perfect gift, a big thing in a small package.

"Don't be silly," she said. "You're safe. In one piece."

She knew this wasn't completely true. I was embarrassed remembering Christmas Eve, not the violence but my desperate confessions as she kept me awake to save my life. When I told her about the pear, she soothed me with a hymn, the same one she sang for Olive. I had forgotten the power of her voice, the way she scuffed you in order to buff you smooth. It made me think of Davina and her means of restoring a man. What would Celestial think if she knew how I had readied myself for this homecoming by breaking a gentle woman's heart? It costs you to hurt people. But I supposed that Celestial knew that already.

"You know what I want for Christmas?" I said. "My two front teeth. Really just that bottom one."

She wiggled away and went to the dresser wearing a slip that made her seem like a virgin. The first time I saw her wear white was our wedding day, and the last time had been the night when the door was kicked open.

On her dresser rested a jewelry case that was a replica of the dresser itself. She opened it and retrieved a little box. She handed it to me; I shook it and was rewarded with the hard rattle of a fragment of lost bone.

"Remember that night? You had me out here trying to be Superman."

"You rose to the occasion," she said. "More than rose—soared."

"I hope this doesn't come off wrong. I know you're an independent woman and everything. You got your own money and your daddy's money, too. But I liked being able to save you. Chasing that kid down the street, I was a hero. Even when he kicked my tooth right out of my head."

"He could have killed you," she said. "I didn't think about that until you caught up with him."

"He could have, but he didn't. No sense worrying about things that didn't happen." I took her hand. "I'm not even worried about what *did* happen. This is a fresh day. A fresh start."

We cooked a late breakfast in our nightclothes. I volunteered to make salmon croquettes. She put herself in charge of grits. As she stirred the pan, a ruby shimmered dark and hot on her right hand.

The phone rang and Celestial answered it "Happy Holidays" like it was the name of a business. From her side, I could tell she was talking to her parents. Mr. and Mrs. Davenport, eccentric genius daddy and school-teacher mama, safe in their haunted house. I missed them, all that comfort and security. I held out my hand, hoping she would pass me the phone, but she shook her head, mouthing, *Shhh.*

"Are we going over there for dinner?" I asked after she hung up.

"We're kind of not getting along," she said. "Besides, I'm not ready to bring the world into this yet."

"Christmas is my favorite holiday," I said, remembering. "Ever since I had teeth, Big Roy would slice up an apple and we'd share it. When he was growing up, all he would get under the tree was the one apple. He didn't know other kids were getting toy cars, school clothes, and stuff. He was excited for what he got—a piece of fruit all to himself."

"You never told me that," said Celestial.

"I guess I didn't want you feeling sorry for us, because really, it's one of my happiest memories. After we got married, I slipped down here on Christmas morning to have my apple."

She looked the way you do when you figure something out. "You could have told me. I'm not how you think I am."

"Georgia," I said. "I know that now. Don't be upset. All that was so long ago. I made mistakes. You made mistakes. It's all right. Nobody is holding anything against anyone."

Seeming to think it over, she pulled open the oven, taking out a pan of toast cooked the way Olive used to make it, soft on the bottom, crispy on the top except for five dots of butter. She held the bread out for my inspection. Her face said, *I'm trying. I am trying so hard.*

I rummaged in the fridge until I found a big red teacher-apple. The knife I pulled from the block was small but sharp. I cut away a thick slice and handed it to her before carving one for myself. "Merry Christmas."

She held the fruit aloft. "Cheers. *Bon appétit.*"

That was the first moment when it felt right, when true reconciliation seemed possible.

The taste of the apple, sweet chased by a twinge of tart, reminded me of Big Roy. I pictured him all alone on this holiday. Wickliffe would be off with his daughter and grands, and Big Roy didn't much truck with anybody else.

"Celestial," I said. "I know I said we weren't going to get stuck in the past. But I have one more thing I need to talk about."

Chewing her apple, she nodded, but her eyes were afraid.

"I'm not trying to fight," I said. "I swear I'm not. This isn't about Andre, and it's not about having kids. It's about my mother."

She nodded and covered my hand with her own, sticky with apple juice.

I took a breath. "Celestial, Big Roy told me that you told Olive about Walter. He said it killed her. Actually killed her. He said she was getting better, but when you told her about Walter, she gave up. She couldn't see the point anymore."

"No," she said as I pulled my hands from hers. "No, no, no. It wasn't like that."

"Then what was it like?" I promised her that I wasn't mad, but maybe I was. The apple in my mouth tasted like dirt.

"I did go see her at the end. She wasn't dying soft, Roy. It was bad. The hospice nurse tried, but Olive wouldn't take the pain medicine because she thought it would kill her faster, and she was trying to live for you. When I went there, her lungs were so full of cancer that I could hear the clogging in her chest like when you blow bubbles in a glass of milk. She was fighting it hard, but she couldn't win; her fingers were tinted blue and her lips, too. I asked your father to leave the room, and I told her everything."

"Why? How could you do that? She didn't last another day." Olive died alone while Big Roy was off to the 7-Eleven to get her some applesauce. *I missed her,* he told me. *I got back and she was already gone.* "My mama didn't deserve that."

"No." She shook her head. "You can blame me for a lot but not for that. When I told her, she shook her head, looked up at the ceiling, and said,

'God sure is funny. Sending Othaniel to the rescue.' Your daddy thinks she gave up, but that's not what it was. When she knew you weren't by yourself, she could finally let go."

Celestial crossed her arms over her chest like she was holding herself together. "I know you said not to. But if you had been there . . ."

And now I held myself with the same posture, arms crossed and gripping my sides. "It wasn't my fault that I wasn't there. I would have been there if they had let me."

We sat at that table, neither able to comfort the other, her remembering being a bystander to my mother's suffering and me suffering because I was denied the experience.

She composed herself first, took the apple from the table, and sliced off another piece for herself and one for me. "Eat," she said.

Night followed day, as it always does, and each night promised a day soon to come. This is something I took comfort in these last bad years. While Celestial showered, I called Big Roy, and I could hear the melancholy in the way he spoke our mutual name.

"You okay, Daddy?"

"Yes, Roy. I'm okay. Got a little indigestion. Sister Franklin brought me a plate, but I ate too much of it, too fast maybe. She's not a cook like your mama but not half-bad."

"It's okay to enjoy it, Daddy. Go ahead and like her."

He laughed, but he didn't sound like himself. "You trying to marry me off so you don't have to come home and take care of me?"

"I want you to be happy."

"You're free, son. That makes me happy enough for the rest of my days."

Next, I rang Davina as the steam from Celestial's shower wafted into the bedroom.

"Merry Christmas," I said to her. In the background was music and laughing. "Is this a bad time?"

She hesitated, then said, "Let me take the phone outside." As I waited, I imagined her with a tuft of tinsel glinting in her hair, her hand on her hip. When she came back, I tried to sound casual.

"I just want to say Merry Christmas." I held the phone with both hands like I was worried that somebody was going to snatch it from me.

"Roy Hamilton, I have one question for you. You ready? Here it is: *something* or *nothing*. This could be the eggnog talking, but I need to know. What happened with us, was it *something* or *nothing*?"

This is how it was with women, pop quizzes with no right answer. "Something?" I said with a little question curling up like a tail on a pig.

"You're not sure? Listen, for me, Roy Hamilton, it's something. It's something to me."

"Davina, don't make me lie. I'm *married*. I found out that I'm still married."

She cut me off. "I didn't ask you all that. All I asked is *something* or *nothing*."

Twisting the phone cord, I recalled our time together. Could it have been only two nights? But those two nights were the start of the rest of my life. I crawled to her door, but I walked away on my own two feet. "Something," I said, leaning in. "Definitely something. I wish I could say what."

I hung up as Celestial emerged, looking herself like a Christmas present, dressed in a little lace-nightie thing that I recognized as something that I'd bought for her. She had complained that it looked itchy, meaning that it looked cheap. I had paid good money for it, but now that she wore it, I could see her point. She twirled. "Like it?"

"Yeah," I said. "I do. For real."

She lay back on the pillows like a goddess on her day off, her chest dusted with fine flecks of gold. "C'mere," she said, sounding like someone on television, not like a real person in real life.

I went to her, but I didn't hit the light.

"One more thing," I said. "One more thing to clear the air. Okay? Before we do this, okay?"

"You don't have to. Didn't you say we're starting fresh?"

I smarted at the word *fresh*. Back in Eloe, it meant not getting ahead of yourself. But I knew how she intended it. Fresh was this fantasy of entering a clean, uncluttered room and shutting the door behind you. "I don't want to start fresh. I want to start real."

"Tell me then."

"Okay," I began. "When I was in Eloe for those few days, I was in a hard place. It was a lot to deal with. There's a girl. Someone from high school. She invited me to her place for dinner, and one thing led to another." Strange as this may seem, my confession felt familiar, like a favorite pair of jeans. This dynamic was a holdover from before, when we quarreled as only lovers do. This time, Celestial had no right to be jealous, but since when do you need a right to feel the way you felt? I smiled a little, remembering the time that she threw away my slice of wedding cake and drank the rest of the champagne by herself. Maybe I missed the fighting as much as the loving, because with Celestial, I had never known one without the other. Our passion was powerful and dangerous as an unstable atom. I'll never forget our kiss-and-make-up when she bit my chest, leaving a purple ring that gave me a good hurt for a day and a half. With a woman like that, you knew you were *in something*.

Celestial said, "How could I be mad at you? I'm not a hypocrite."

I studied her face, which reflected only weariness. She may as well have shrugged. I had been gone a long time, but I still knew her a little bit. There are things in a core of a person that didn't change. Celestial was an intense person. Yesterday under the tree, she fought to maintain her composure, to keep her fire in check, but I could feel her burning. "Georgia, do you know what I'm trying to say?"

"I know," she went on. "You had been through a lot. I know it didn't mean anything. That's what you're about to say, right?"

"Celestial," I said, catching her up in my arms. I was wearing my trousers and socks, while she was nearly nude. She smelled of glitter powder and soap. "You don't care, do you?"

"It's not that I don't care. I'm trying to be an adult about it."

"I called her a second ago while you were in the shower." I slowed my delivery, letting each word land hard. I didn't enjoy unspooling the details. I swear, I didn't want to hurt Celestial, but I did need to know if I *could*. I had to know if I still had that kind of power, that kind of sway. "When I was with her, she showed me how to be myself again, or maybe she introduced me to my new self, the person I have to be from here on out. It wasn't purely sexual. I can't lie and tell you that it's nothing. She treated me like a man, or maybe just a human being."

Celestial's look was as blank as an egg. "Well, what's her name?"

"Davina Hardrick. She asked what was up with the two of us. I mean me and her, not me and you."

"What did you say?" Celestial sounded merely curious.

"I told her I was married."

Celestial nodded as she killed the light and pulled me to the bed. "Yes, you are a married man."

I lay in the dark, feeling unsure, as if I had forgotten my own name.

Davina said that the only question is *something* or *nothing*, but that's as much a fantasy as a fresh start. For the rest of our lives there would be *something* between me and Celestial. Neither of us would ever enjoy the perfect peace of *nothing*. After the clock by the bed flashed midnight and Christmas was over, I felt my wife nibbling kisses across my shoulders. I smelled unhappiness on her breath, but she continued caressing me, saying my name in a mournful whisper. I turned to face her; Celestial's head in my hand was as fragile as a lightbulb. "You don't have to, Georgia."

She shushed me with a kiss I wasn't sure I wanted. In the light of the night table clock, I made out her taut brow and quivering eyelids. "We don't have to," I said. "We could just go to sleep."

Her skin was hot against my thigh as I fingered the lace trim of her nightie. My hands, on their own, sought the rest of her, but her muscles tensed in the wake of my fingers. It was as though I were turning her to stone, cell by cell.

"This is how I love you," she said, laying herself on the bank of pillows. Even in the dark, I could make out the rapid rise and fall of her chest, her bird-in-the-hand breaths. "Please, Roy. Please let me make this right."

WHEN I WAS in prison, Olive visited me every weekend until she was no longer able. I was always glad to see her but always humiliated for her to see me. One Sunday, she was different, but I couldn't quite say how. She must have known about the cancer, but she didn't tell me. What I noticed was her breathing; Olive was aware of it and her attention was catching. She took in air then like Celestial did now, up tempo and afraid.

"Little Roy," Olive said. "There is no doubt in my mind. I just need to hear from your own lips that you didn't do it."

I leaned back, flinching as though she'd spit in my face. Olive reached for me the way you would lunge for a glass tumbling from the table. "I know you didn't," she cooed. "I know you didn't. Please let me hear you say it."

"I was with Celestial the whole time. You can ask her."

"I don't want to ask her," my mother said. "I want it from you."

I can't remember this day without hearing the air around her words, without imagining the tumors multiplying, consuming her body. Olive was dying and I spoke to her with bitterness in my mouth. That I didn't know makes no difference.

"Mama," I said, talking to her like she was slow or didn't speak English. "I am not a rapist."

"Little Roy," she began, but I cut her off.

"I don't want to talk anymore."

When she left, she said, "I believe you."

As I watched her walk away, I made note of everything about her that I didn't admire. I ignored the devotion that she wore like a cape, I paid no heed of her strength or hardworking beauty. I sat there thinking of all I didn't love about her, too angry to even say good-bye.

IN THE QUIET room, my wife lifted her lovely arms, encircling my neck, pulling me to her with a power I didn't know she had. "I want you to be okay." Her voice was brave and determined.

"I didn't do it," I said. "I never touched that lady. She thought it was me. You couldn't tell her that I didn't break into her room and hold her down. When she was on the stand, I couldn't even look in her face, because in her eyes, I was a barbarian, worse than a dog. When I looked at her looking at me, I became what she thought I was. There's nothing worse that you can say about a man."

"Shhh," Celestial said. "All that's over."

"Nothing is ever over," I said, unwinding her arms from my shoulders. I lay beside her, remembering us sprawled on the asphalt, forbidden to touch. "Celestial," I said, surprised by the bass of my own voice in my chest. "I am not a rapist. Do you hear what I'm trying to tell you?"

"Yes," she said, but she seemed confused. "I never thought you did it. I know who I married."

"Georgia," I said. "I know who I married, too. You're *in* me. When I touch you, your flesh communicates with my bones. You think I can't feel how sad you are?"

"I'm scared," she said, her fingers transmitting a miserable willingness. "It's hard to start over."

THE VAST GENEROSITY of women is a mysterious tunnel, and nobody knows where it leads. The writing on the walls spells out trick questions, and as a man, you must know that you cannot reason your way out. What unkindness showed me that she loved me by revealing the ways that she didn't love me? Celestial was offering herself to me like a banquet prepared in the presence of my enemies, like a flawless red pear. What cruelty revealed that she cared by making me understand the limits of the same?

"Listen," I said with what threatened to be my last breath. "Listen, Georgia. Hear what I'm about to say." I made my words hard and she stiffened against them. To make amends, I spoke tenderly like I was addressing a butterfly. "Celestial, I will never force myself upon a woman." I removed her two frightened hands from my body and held them between my own. "Do you hear me? I will not force you. Even if you let me, even if you *want* me to, I will not do it."

I kissed her finger near the base, where my ring once rested. "Georgia," I said, beginning a sentence I couldn't bear to complete.

"I tried," she began.

"Shhh . . . Just sleep, Georgia. Just sleep."

But neither of us closed our eyes against the immeasurable dark of that silent night.

Epilogue

Dear Celestial,

People around here think that I got saved in prison. But prison is a haunted house of mirrors; it was impossible for me to come to the truth there. When I try to explain this, they turn around and ask me if I am a Muslim, since I don't belong to a church, but they know that I think of myself as a man of God. I can't really break it down to them because I can't really break it down to myself. Who would believe that what happened to me came to pass in the holy dark of our bedroom?

I'm ashamed to think about what I did to Andre. I swear to you that I never hurt another human being like that before. Even when I was incarcerated, I never brutalized anyone. I get hit by a sharp pain behind my eyes to think of how close I came to killing him. Dre didn't fight me back hard. That made me feel like he didn't think I was worth the effort. Maybe I wanted you to see him suffer because it didn't seem like you cared if I was in pain or not, but I knew you cared about him. I know that none of this makes sense, but I'm trying to express my emotions at that time. I was out of my head. I was even jealous of that tree. I felt forsaken. That is the only word for it. When you said you were going to call the police, I was glad. That phone in your hand was a pistol and I was hoping that you would fire it. Then you would have to live with that and I wouldn't have to live at all. This is how my mind was working. This is how my heart was pumping. I was ready to die and take

Dre with me. I was going to kill him with only the hands God gave me.

I used these same hands to sign the documents your uncle Banks drew up. Davina is a notary, so you will see her name as well. I know this is the right thing to do, but I hated seeing my signature on that dotted line. We tried. I guess that is all we can say or do.

Sincerely,
Roy

PS: The tree? Did it make it?

Dear Roy,

Seeing your handwriting feels like a brief encounter with a friend you know you may never see again. When you were away, the letters made me feel close to you, but now they remind me how far we have traveled away from each other. I hope that one day you and I can get to know each other again.

Now that I have the papers, you probably think that Andre and I will be on the next bus to the justice of the peace, but we don't feel the need to get married. My mother, his mother, even strangers—they all want to see me in a white dress, but Dre and I like what we have, the way we have it.

At the end of the day, I don't want to be anyone's wife. Not even Dre's. For his part, Dre says he doesn't want a wife who doesn't want to be one. We're living our lives together, a communion.

Thank you for asking about Old Hickey. We had a specialist out last week who told us that you can tell the age of a tree just using a measuring tape and a calculator. According to the expert, Old

Hickey is about 128 years old. They say he has another 128 in him, assuming that nobody else comes after him with an axe.

And this is the news: I am having a baby. I hope you will be happy for Andre and for me. I know it is painful, too, and don't think that I have forgotten what we went through all those years ago. It may be unreasonable for me to ask this of you, but will you pray for us? Will you pray every day until she is born?

Always,

Georgia

Dear Celestial,

Don't laugh, but I'm the one running to the JP. Davina and I are not trying to have a baby, but I would like to try my hand at marriage again. You say that you are not cut out to be a wife, but I disagree. You were a good wife to me when conditions were favorable and for a long time when they were not. You deserve more respect than I ever gave you and more than you give yourself.

As for me, I would like to be a father, but Davina already has a son and that situation is very unhappy. She doesn't want to start over, and truthfully, as much as I used to fantasize about my little "Trey," I don't want to jeopardize what I have with her over a dream that may not even fit me anymore. I wish I could be like Big Roy and take her son as my own, but he is an adult. She and I are enough to be a family. If you need a kid to keep you together, then how together are you? That's what she says and she is probably right.

Of course I will pray for your family, but you make it seem like I'm a preacher! I'm not trying to minister to anyone but myself.

I have found myself a small plot of sacred ground by the stream. Do you remember that spot? I go out there early in the morning and listen to the wind play that bridge music while I think or pray. Everyone knows that this is my morning routine. Occasionally I invite one or two to come along. Big Roy has joined me and sometimes Davina. But mostly it's me alone with my own head and my own memories.

And speaking of heads, Big Roy and I have gone into business. We have a barbershop called Locs and Lineups. You know I always had that entrepreneurial streak. Picture a traditional barbershop complete with pole but with a lot of 2.0 amenities and services. We're making decent money, not Poupées level (yet), but I'm content.

My prayer for you is for peace, which is something you have to make. You can't just *have* it (words of wisdom from my Biological, who I go visit most Sundays—he's getting old in there and it is hard to watch).

But mostly my life is good, only it's a different type of good from what I figured on. Some days I get antsy and start talking to Davina about pulling up stakes and starting over in Houston, New Orleans, or even Portland. She humors me, but when I'm done, she smiles because we both know I'm not going anywhere. And when she smiles at me, I can't help giving one back. This is home. This is where I am.

Sincerely,
Roy

ACKNOWLEDGMENTS

There were many moments in the composition of this work when I feared I would not be able to resolve the thorny conflicts that both bind and separate these characters. I offer bottomless gratitude to the people and institutions who believed in me during the dark moments in which I struggled to believe in myself.

In particular, I owe thanks to my friends and family who assisted me by reading early drafts, unwittingly providing crucial dialogue, challenging me to think more expansively, and helping me right the ship: Barbara and Mack Jones, Renee Simms, Camille Dungy, Suheir Hammad, Shaye Arehart, Maxine Clair, Denis Nurkse, Maxine Kennedy, Neal J. Arp, William Reeder, Anne B. Warner, Mitchell Douglas, Jafari S. Allen, Willie Perdomo, Ron Carlson, Ginney Fowler, Richard Powers, Pearl Cleage, Lisa Coleman, Cozbi Cabrera, June M. Aldridge, Alesia Parker, Elmaz Abinader, Serena Lin, Sarah Schulman, Justin Haynes, Beauty Bragg, Treasure Shields Redmond, Allison Clark, and Sylvia Jenkins.

As we witness dramatic decreases in funding for the arts, I'm grateful for the generous support of the following organizations: the National Endowment for the Arts, the Ucross Foundation, the MacDowell Colony, Rutgers University–Newark, and the Radcliffe Institute for Advanced Study at Harvard University.

Jane Dystel, my brilliant agent, has been with me since the beginning; not even Dante was blessed with such a charming and capable Virgil. Lauren Cerand is my publicist and confidante. Bridgett Davis listened to me tangle with this story for years with a patient and gracious ear. Jamey Hatley kept the faith. Terraine Bailey, Ronald Sullivan, and James Tierney are fluent in both letters and the law. Thank you for helping me get the details straight. My editor, Chuck Adams, is a sharp collaborator and a very nice man; Algonquin Books is a true friend of the arts. Jeree Wade knows the way to the answers. Tom Furrier is the world's greatest typewriter doctor and quite the gentleman. My fast-friend, Amy Bloom, was kind enough to shine a light in the dark. Claudia Rankine and Nikki Giovanni allowed me to borrow their verses, and I strive to follow their sterling examples. Dr. Johnnetta B. Cole told me to keep going, and I was powerless to disobey. Andra Miller pushed me to finish, while Elisabeth Scharlatt cooed, "No book before its time." They were both right, and to both I extend great thanks.

Sweet, sweet Lindy Hess was my dear friend, mentor, and champion. I'm devastated that she didn't live to see this book in print.

READING GUIDE

1) Do you feel that the title *An American Marriage* accurately represents the novel? Why or why not?

2) There are two father figures in Roy's life: Big Roy is the one who shepherded him into adulthood and helped him grow into a responsible, capable person, but Walter is the one who taught Roy how to survive. Do you feel these men deserve equal credit? If not, which was the more important figure in Roy's life and why?

3) When Celestial asks Roy if he would have waited for her for more than five years, he doesn't answer her question but reminds her that, as a woman, she would not have been imprisoned in the first place. Do you feel that his response is valid, and do you think it justifies his infidelity? Do you believe that he would have remained faithful if Celestial had been the one incarcerated? Does this really matter, and if so, why?

4) The story is told through three characters' points of view. The author originally wrote it from Celestial's perspective and then tried a second version from Roy's point of view. Do you agree with her decision to tell it from all sides? Why was it important for us as readers to have the three first-person perspectives? What did it reveal about each character's intentions?

5) You may not have noticed that Tayari Jones does not specify the race of the woman who accuses Roy of rape. How did you picture this woman? What difference does the race of this woman make in the way you understand the novel's storyline?

6) Roy is hurt when Celestial, in discussing her career as an artist, doesn't mention him or the role he played in giving her the encouragement and freedom to follow her dreams, but Walter argues that she is justified in her silence. Do you agree? Do you think her silence is due to shame, or is she just being practical in how she presents herself to advance her career?

7) In her 'Dear John' letter to Roy, Celestial says, 'I will continue to support you, but not as your wife.' What do you think she means by this statement? Do you feel that Roy is wrong to reject her offer?

8) Do you think that Andre strategized to get Celestial to fall in love with him, or did it happen naturally? Do you feel that it was a surprise to them that their relationship developed after all those years of friendship?

9) Andre insists that he doesn't owe Roy an apology for the way his relationship with Celestial changed. Do you agree? Why or why not?

10) Do you understand Celestial's impulse to seek companionship and love with Andre in Roy's absence, or do you think she should have stayed true to Roy no matter what?

11) When Roy is released from prison, he first goes to his childhood home and almost immediately makes a connection with Davina. Do you feel that given the tenuous relationship he has with Celestial – who is still legally his wife – he is cheating? Why or why not? And when Roy announces to Davina his intention to return to his wife, do you feel that her anger is justified?

12) It is obvious that Andre is different from Roy in many ways. Do you feel that he is ultimately a better match for Celestial? If so, why?

13) If Roy had never gone to prison, do you think their marriage would have survived? Why or why not?

14) After Roy is released from prison, Celestial eventually feels she must return to Roy because he is still her husband. Do you think this was the right decision? And do you think she should have given the marriage more of a chance?

15) The author set out to write a book that explored some of the inequalities related to race and the legal system in a way that these issues would resonate with readers who might think, 'This couldn't happen to me'. Do you think she succeeded?

How About Railway Modelling

by

John Craven

and

John Cockcroft

ep

EP Publishing Limited

First published in Great Britain 1979 by EP Publishing Limited,
Bradford Road, East Ardsley, Wakefield, West Yorkshire, WF3
2JN

The publisher would like to thank Mr John Priest and James B.
Wright for allowing their photographs to be reproduced.

ISBN 0 7158 0677 7

Part One Copyright © John Craven, 1979

Part Two Copyright © John Cockcroft, 1979

Printed and bound in Great Britain at The Pitman Press, Bath

Contents

Gauges and Scales

Gauge Name	Gauge Between The Tracks	Scale of Modelling (to the foot)	Notes
Z	6.5mm	1/220	Commercially made by one manufacturer.
N	9mm	1.9mm	The smallest of the popular gauges.
TT	12mm	3mm	The original table-top model railway, designed in America. Kit form only.
HO	16.5mm	3.5mm	Used mainly for Continental and American models.
OO	16.5mm	3.5mm for track. 4mm for the models.	Used only for British prototypes (engines and stock). The most popular of all the gauges. Vast selection of readymade items.
EM (stands for Eighteen Milli-metre)	18.2mm	4mm	Items like wheels, axles and now track are made by the trade.
S4, or Scale Four	18.83mm	4mm	Dead accurate modelling. Everything is to the scale of 4mm, even the height of the rails.
P4, or Proto Four	18.83mm	4mm	Ditto. One firm supplies components.
S	⅞in	³⁄₁₆in	No commercial support. Halfway between 4mm, which some people think is too small, and 'O' gauge.
O	32mm	7mm	Used to be much more popular — now generally regarded as too big, and expensive.
1	45mm	10mm	The biggest of the normal gauges, and the only one that still can work on steam. Really a model engineering gauge.
H09, or 009	9mm 9mm	3.5mm 4mm	Most popular of the Narrow Gauge models. Large vehicles on very narrow track.

A Hobby for Schoolboys, Super-stars and Bishops

There are some places in the world, so I am told, where you run the risk of being lynched if you suggest that model railways are nothing but toy trains. During my investigations into this very special hobby that grips millions of enthusiasts in just about every country of the world, I have so far managed to stay in one piece!

So, thank goodness, have the countless tiny trains that I have tested on all kinds of tracks, and thanks to the help of many model railway 'freaks', I now know that their precious models are far from being playthings. Even though an amazing variety of people, from schoolboys to bishops to super-stars, seem to get endless pleasure from what the rest of us would honestly consider to be playing with them.

Somebody told me, when I asked him what he thought was the great attraction of model railways, that it was like building a three-dimensional moving picture. That might sound a little grand, but I can see what he meant. For, to be a true enthusiast, you do not just put models together. You try to make them *live*, in a Lilliput world that you have built for them. I reckon that to get the most out of this hobby, you need to be a bit of an engineer, as well as an artist, an historian and a showman!

Engineer because obviously the building of the models calls for that particular kind of mental application; artist because you need a flair for designing the landscape through which your trains will run; historian because, if you choose to operate a railway that is based on one of the old steam companies, you will want to know all about that company; and finally showman, because when you have got it all working together, you will want to display your very own creation, in action, to other people.

Hang on a minute, though. I do not want to make it all sound too tough. There are hundreds of thousands of railway modellers in Britain alone who do not regard themselves as any of those things, and yet they get a vast amount of satisfaction and *fun* out of their hobby. The important qualification that they do all share is an amazing dedication.

The ones I have met will talk about the hobby till the steam runs out. They have, quite literally 'one-track minds'. That track has model trains running on it! Many of them would give up everything they have for a chance to run a real-sized railway of their own. But they do not have a few

1

A part shot of the early layout 'Piper's Mead' by Allan Downes. The materials used are commercially made stone and card wallpapers, window and doors. The trackwork, the locos and rolling stock was all handbuilt

million pounds to spend, so they scale their ambitions down to size. For them, there are still the problems and the excitement of the real thing. The 8.03 is dead on time, there seems to be some kind of problem down in the marshalling yards, and watch out . . . the London Express is coming in too fast! But it is all happening in miniature.

One of the country's top modellers explained it to me this way, 'People build model railways for all kinds of reasons. Because they like creating things with their hands, because they want to bring back to life what they think of as the golden days of the railways — the days of steam — and because there's a great kick out of running your own line.

'Let's face it,' he went on, 'any hobby is an escape — a pleasant way of passing time. A schoolboy gets home in the evening, he's had a tough day at school, but when he sets up his railway, he is in a different world completely.

'It is the same for all of us — schoolboy, factory worker, businessman. With model railways, we create our own little world. It can open up new horizons in life for people with boring, routine jobs — and for those with very demanding jobs, it can help to keep them sane.'

2

Whether they are building and operating the modern diesels of British Rail, or the glamorous steam trains of the old private railways, today's railway modellers are carrying on a craft that began two hundred years ago. The early pioneers of the real-life railways used to build models to see whether their inventions would actually work, or just explode. Back in the 1760s, an instrument maker called James Watt was asked to repair a model of one of the very first steam engines.

He quickly realised what was wrong, and why it would not work properly. He set about to improve the design, and started on a career that revolutionised the whole of industry and transport, by harnessing the power of steam.

It was his assistant, William Murdoch, who made the first working *model* of a locomotive, in 1784. When it was run one night, in a dark avenue leading to the Redruth church, the parson suddenly came across it and was frightened out of his wits! Murdoch was threatened with the sack if he continued such experiments. I found that story in a book called *Model Railway Engines* by J. E. Minns (Weidenfeld and Nicolson), which has many fine illustrations of steam engines, right from the earliest days.

Mr Minns explains it this way, 'Since civilisation began, man has shown a longing to spend time and patience recreating in miniature the objects surrounding his life.

'As technology advanced, a new use for modelling appeared, since it was so much easier and less expensive to build a working model of a theory, rather than risk life and limb with a full-size machine or apparatus.'

And Mr Minns has a nice description of the relatively short life of the steam locomotive. He says, 'At a time when practical space travel is a normality, it is already fantastic to look back on machines so incredibly crude in conception.

'In fifty years, people will be trying to explain to their incredulous children that for a century and a half man rushed about filling metal containers on wheels with water, lit a fire underneath, waited an hour and a half for steam to be produced, and then careered off at speeds in excess of a hundred mph — with smoke, steam and cinders flying out of a hole in the front of the machine, totally obscuring their line of vision . . .

'At all stages of development they were larger than life, almost living, machines, presenting an image of great power and beauty.'

And that is what today's model railways are all about — trying to recapture, in scaled-down size, the magic of that era. Strangely, events have now turned full circle, and the National Railway Museum at York plans to use scale models of classic engines which, themselves, have not survived the years. Certainly, Messrs Watt and Murdoch, and George Stephenson with his Rocket, started not only a whole new way of travelling, but a vast new hobby as well.

It was some years after the first steam trains started operation that men decided it would be fascinating to model them just as a hobby, for no practical purpose. The first ones were powered by steam, by clockwork, or they were just pushed along. Towards the end of the last century, model railways started to go electric — and that is the way many of them have been, ever since.

Meeting Modellers

Not so long ago, I went down to one of the country's top model railway exhibitions, at Bristol, and joined in the crowd of fascinated onlookers as two friends of mine, Clive Cobley and Peter Jessop, operated their extensive layout.

What staggered me was that everything is done so realistically. They run their trains, some of them modelled on the engines of the 1860s, along a mock-up section of the old London, Brighton and South Coast Railway from Selsey-on-Sea to a station just a little further up the track.

Not only are all the details faithfully accurate — or 'prototype' in the lingo of the railway modellers — but the trains run to a carefully-worked out timetable, and they even ring the bell when a train is requesting permission to leave the station. When permission is given, the trains set off through a cardboard-and-paste countryside, past copses of trees made from sticks and lichen-moss, and over a river made from plastic resin. But everything is so real I even wanted to dip my finger in the river, just to check it was not really water!

For a little while, they let me take over control at Selsey station, and it was only then that I got a taste of what running your own railway is all about. When I was young, I did not have an electric train set — I had a clockwork one which I thought the world of, but I missed out on the world of Hornby and Scalextric. Don't let me sound like a deprived child, I was far from that, but I can now understand why normal, sensible grown men

4

do behave a bit like children when they operate an electric train set for the first time.

First of all, there is a strange feeling of power. Your fingers on the control box can make an engine and five carriages begin to move — forwards, backwards, sideways if you are not careful!

A deft movement along the box that controls the points and you can switch them over, electrically, without moving from the spot. John Cockcroft will be going into details about how it is done later on, and he will also be giving tips on how to make his lifelike scenery, as well as instructions on how to build your own engine, coaches, wagons, and of course, the vital baseboard on which everything will run.

Basically, I am not what you could call electrically minded. I can change a plug, but that is about my total knowledge of the workings of electricity. To me, the electrical aspect of model railways is the least interesting, so do not expect me to dwell on it. My colleague will do that in Part 2 when he explains how your baseboard should be wired up. All I need to know is that the power goes from the control box into the rails on a 'flow' and 'return' system, and the engine picks up the current so that it can operate its electric motor.

Peter, who was operating the Selsey-on-Sea section while Clive was looking after the other half of the layout further up the track, told me that not all the line is electrified all the time. There are many sections that can be cut off when not in use, and they can be switched on or off from the control point. When an engine or some wagons are 'unwanted' in a siding, then they are deprived of the power to move.

Back at my control box, though, all kinds of things were happening. I had to send off the next passenger train to London, but I could not do that until Clive had rung his bell to say he was ready to accept my train into his 'patch'. That would not happen, of course, till the signals were set to 'go' — a task that I left Peter to work out!

Meanwhile, I had to send a shunting engine on to the turntable, because it was facing the wrong way for its next mission. That meant isolating the express train, still on the platform, while we switched power to the little shunter. It was all tremendous fun, and I can understand why people feel mentally exhausted after a couple of hours operating a layout that has been built to exhibition standards. I narrowly avoided a collision after only a few minutes!

Now, before we get to the practical side of things I want to tell you more of what I have learnt about this fascinating hobby. Everyone seems to start in the obvious way — by getting a model train set ready-made, either as a present while young, or as a 'treat' to oneself later on in life. From those beginnings, people build up their collections. At first, maybe, they buy more ready-made engines, carriages and wagons, but later they could branch out into making their own, either from kits or from plans and materials that they have collected themselves. Modellers call the latter 'scratch' building, because they are starting from scratch.

There are a dozen different sizes when it comes to building model trains, and they are identified by their different gauges. In the days when people had large houses, with lots of space for the railways to run around, the most popular gauge was 'O'. Engines and carriages in 'O' gauge are approximately 48 times smaller than the real thing — the scale is approximately 7mm (¼in) to the foot. 1.6km (1 mile) of real railway line would cover 36.8m (121ft) in 'O' gauge.

Apart from its size — many modellers find 'O' to be more suitable to garden layouts because of that — another disadvantage of the 'O' gauge is its cost. It tends to be expensive — when you are building it from 'scratch', even things like wheels are rather pricey.

By far the most popular gauge in Britain, outstripping all the others, is 'OO', known as Double O. All the big manufacturers cater for this gauge, and nearly all modellers have started out with a train set like the famous Hornby Double O. Many other makers also offer a wide variety of choice in engines, coaches, wagons, and all the paraphernalia — and, of course, the track. With such a wide choice, it is the difference in cost between the various models and manufacturers that generally decides the issue. But if you want something really unusual, you will probably have to build it yourself.

Double O is almost half the size of 'O' gauge. The scale is 4mm to the foot for rolling stock, and 3½mm to the foot for the actual track. Don't let that confuse you, though — the system works very well.

Maybe its great popularity is that it is not too big and not too small. One expert told me, 'The very small gauges, like N gauge at a scale of 1.9mm to the foot, are tremendous space-savers, because you can get a complete layout in a space smaller than a coffee table. But because the engines and coaches are so small, many people find them very hard and fiddly when it comes to hand building.

'As a general rule with the smaller gauges, people don't bother to put lots of detail on the individual vehicles — you would need a microscope! Instead, they model for the general, overall effect.

'With Double O and the other middle-sized gauges, you can model each individual vehicle, and as you get better, you can add all kinds of touches,

NORTH WEST KENT

E M GROUP

The North West Kent EM Group's layout at the 1978 Bristol Exhibition visited by John Craven

like decorating the insides of carriages, and putting details into the inside of the cab.

'Often when you have finished, you can't actually see what you have done inside, but there is a tremendous sense of achievement in knowing that everything is exactly right, outside *and* in.

'When you get to the big stuff, like the O gauge, you then model every individual *part* on the vehicle.'

On page iv you will find a full list of all the different gauges.

Once you have got your first train set — probably a steam-type loco-motive with some carriages and a few metres of track — the important thing to do, straight away, is to turn it into a properly functioning railway.

This is the advice I was given, 'The worst thing you can do is to set up the track in a loop, and have the train chasing its tail. You'll go bonkers after half an hour, and you will never want to see a model train again.

'What you must do immediately is to give yourself, and your railway, some challenges. Make sure you have sets of points, so that you can shunt in and out of sidings. Whatever you do, don't run it around in a simple circle.'

Once you have decided that you enjoy model railwaying, and that there *is* something rather special about the hobby, there are several ways in which you can start building your own little 'empire'.

If you simply enjoy the pleasure of operating the trains, and do not wish to make anything yourself, then you can gradually buy more ready-made stock and track, and then decorate your layout with ready-made stations, signals, scenery and people. Obviously, this is the most expensive way of doing things, and it means that you will not have any really rare trains because they are not manufactured. I would class this hobby as 'model railways', rather than 'railway modelling'.

For those who wish to expand both by adding to their ready-made collection and by building their own, there are lots of surprises and challenges in store. Once you have chosen your gauge, the next thing to do is to choose your railway.

Choosing a Railway

There is certainly no lack of choice when it comes to picking the railway company you want to 'adopt'. You have the whole world to choose from. There are very few countries without railways of some description — some of them stayed primitive all their days, others were always technically advanced.

The most popular foreign railways among modellers in this country have always been the Continentals — French, German and Swiss — and the Americans. The popularity is reflected in the fact that the big manu-facturers see them as good business, and make the locomotives and coaches of those railways, either ready-built or in kit form. But for obvious reasons, most modellers in Britain choose to model British prototypes. While older modellers remember seeing them in action, younger modellers can still go to special working displays of old British steam engines, or readily get hold of information about them.

More and more these days, people are modelling the up-to-date diesels of British Rail. There was a time when diesels were almost a dirty word among modellers, but not any more, and many young modellers find it easier to relate to trains they can see every day than to the massive steam giants of the past.

Some enthusiasts model British Rail as it is today, others specialise in the times and the trains of 1947 when it came into operation. Prior to that, from 1923, there was a great era in steam which thousands of modellers like to try and re-create, the era of the Big Four. These were the four companies that dominated rail transport in Britain — the London, Midland and Scottish (LMS); the London, North Eastern Railway (LNER); the Southern Railway; and the Great Western Railway.

They were formed, in 1923, from the amalgamation of a great number of smaller railways, so modellers who want to concentrate on the early days of steam have a vast choice of companies. For instance, the Southern Railway swallowed up the following smaller companies: the South Eastern Railway; the London, Chatham and Dover Railway; the London, Brighton and South Coast Railway; the London and South West Railway; the Isle of Wight Railway; the Isle of Wight Central Railway; the Freshwater, Yarmouth and Newport Railway; the Lynton and Barnstaple Railway, and quite a number of other minor lines. The same thing applied to the other three in the Big Four, and the only one that did not change its name in the amalgamations was the Great Western. But it, too, took over the duties of other, smaller lines, including most of the Welsh railways — like the Taff Vale — and many small mining railways.

So, there is a bewildering choice when it comes to 'adopting' your railway, and here is what Clive Cobley and Peter Jessop did. They picked one of the small outfits that was later merged into the Southern — the London, Brighton and South Coast Railway.

Clive told me, 'All the big old railways, and many of the smaller ones, have societies that support them, and it's a good idea to join the particular society that cares about the railway of your choice.

'They will help you with historical information about the way things used to look. They have masses of books, drawings and photographs covering everything you can think of about the old companies, and if they cannot help you, no one can.

'When you are trying to follow the 'prototype' as closely as possible, you are led into historical research, not only into the railways themselves, but into the areas through which the railways used to run.

'For instance, it is important to know the produce of the area, because that is what would be carried in the wagons. It would be very wrong, say, to put masses of coal wagons into a model station in Sussex, which is a market gardening area.

'Instead, there should be plenty of vans, and wagons carrying timber and shipments from the docks, if the station was on the main line.'

Clive added, 'The buildings, as well, should be of the right style for the area in which your railway is set. Different companies constructed their buildings in different ways, and research will show which style would be best for your chosen railway.

'It is also very important to get your model people right. They bring life to your platforms and layouts generally, and women's fashions, in particular, changed over the years.

'I find that when I look at the old photos, read the books and look up the timetables of years ago, everything comes alive again, and I can imagine how it was in the days of steam.

'The London, Brighton and South Coast was a small company — it ran in a triangle from Waterloo to Portsmouth to Hastings. But it would take four large filing cabinets to store every photograph that was taken of the railway. That gives you some idea of how well documented were many of the old companies.'

While they were browsing through all the records to make sure their layout around Selsey had the right atmosphere, Clive and Peter discovered all kinds of fascinating stories. Stories like Queen Victoria's last ride. Apparently, the Queen did not like to travel fast, and she was far from amused if the Royal train travelled any quicker than fifteen miles an hour. The driver had orders never to exceed that speed, and he kept this Royal Command — until the Old Queen died. She was at her home at Osborne, on the Isle of Wight, when she died, and her body was brought by boat to Portsmouth, where the train was waiting to carry the coffin to London. But the weather was bad, the boat was delayed, and people were already gathering at Waterloo to pay their last respects to their monarch. When the coffin was finally put aboard the Royal train, the driver was given special permission to open up the throttle. With the coffin probably bouncing about in the coach, the Royal train reached London in record time. Queen Victoria had travelled faster in death than ever she had in life. The new King, Edward the Seventh, was on the platform to meet the train, and he obviously had not been kept waiting for too long, because later the driver was awarded a medal!

Queen Victoria was not the only Head of State who chose to travel slowly on the London, Brighton and South Coast line. In 1870, the Shah of Persia was returning from Portsmouth after a visit to Queen Victoria at Osborne. The Shah complained bitterly about the high speed of the train, and later requested that the driver be beheaded. Fortunately, he did not get his way.

Stories like that might have been forgotten forever had not modellers like Clive and Peter come along and started to dig away the past so they could build their 'toy trains'.

Peter says, 'Many people who do not pick a particular railway when they start modelling later regret it. Often, they find themselves with all kinds of different rolling stock in the markings of several railways, and it is always a great problem deciding what to keep and what to sell.

'I would recommend a line like the Great Western to new modellers. The colours are attractive, and it never changed its name or its markings. The engines always stayed green, and though the coaches were red for a short time, they soon went back to being chocolate and cream.'

He added, 'You do get very involved in the history of a railway, and although you set out to find more about, say, the markings of the Royal train, you end up uncovering little stories which show you things that really mattered in those long gone days.'

Joining a Club

Now that you have decided on your gauge, and your railway company, the next thing is to get building! As you are likely to come across all kinds of problems as a newcomer to the hobby, the best thing to do is to join a club.

There are model railway clubs in every town and city, and more than a hundred of them are affiliated to the oldest and best known of them all, the Model Railway Club itself. The club has its own custom-built premises near Kings Cross Station in London. Some of the affiliated clubs are specialist ones representing the different gauges, such as the Gauge O Guild, and the EM Gauge Society, but most of them are ordinary model clubs around the country. If you have decided to model in Double O, it is useful to know that every club or society, apart from the specialist ones, has its own Double O section.

The affiliation to the Model Railway Club (MRC) is a very loose one, with no rules or regulations, but through it the MRC has contacts with model-makers all over Britain, and right across the world. A new club can become affiliated providing it has been going for more than 12 months, and it holds regular meetings.

To find out more about the MRC, I went along to meet two of its senior members, Jonathon Abson and Ron Parren. They told me the MRC was founded in 1910, and now has about five hundred members of its own. Most of them live in the London area, and the subscription is cheaper for country members — people who live and work more than thirty-five miles outside the capital.

Jonathon told me, 'The club is a real focal point for the hobby. Hundreds of people come to our clubhouse, either as members or visitors, to get information, make models and talk over problems.

'Every Thursday evening, we have a club-night, and there is a Saturday morning meeting every month, so that country members and guests from other clubs can take part.

'In addition to that, there's always activity going on in our layout room, which is always a big shambles with new ones being built and old ones being dismantled.'

It is during club-nights, all over the country, that modellers un-stick their problems, and create a kind of teamwork that you rarely find in other hobbies.

Says Ron Parren, 'You can get one chap who is marvellous at making engines . . . he does nothing else. To him, it is like shelling peas. Then there is another chap who is a wizard at building scenery, but he can't use a soldering iron for love or money.

'But when you get a group of a dozen of those types all coming together, they can produce the most exquisite layout using their collective talents.'

The MRC's library is one of its great prides. The room is set out like the reading room of any public library, with tables and chairs down the middle. The only difference is that the only thing to read about is railways. The metal book cases are crammed with about three thousand volumes. One case is devoted entirely to all the books that have ever been written about model railways. Three other cases contain the history of the railways themselves, and there are draughtsmen's cabinets filled with original drawings from the various railway companies.

Also in this room there are all the model railway magazines, dating back to their first numbers, and all of them bound into annual editions. The place is run like a normal library, with tickets and fines, and with such a vast collection to which to refer, the members have got no excuse at all for getting things wrong! It is probably the finest library in the country on railway topics.

Members of the MRC are nearly all adult, though people over the age of fourteen can join. There are some younger ones around, I was told, but they do not have to pay!

One of the MRC's big responsibilities is to run the National Model

Railway Exhibition every year at the Central Hall, Westminster, in London. Club members work hard to set up the exhibition, and run it during the big week. Officials go 'talent-spotting' to clubs all around the country, looking for new and interesting layouts to put on show.

There are dozens of model railway exhibitions every year, and the National was the first — it has been going for more than fifty years — and it is one of the best, if not the best. The day that I was there, the building was bursting at the seams — and most of the crowd seemed to be genuine enthusiasts, not just people who had come in out of the cold. In every corner — and there are lots of those at Central Hall — there were fans shop-talking, and hundreds of people pressed around the demonstrations, trying to get a closer view.

Lots of noise, lots of fun and — it seemed to me — a very masculine affair. I noticed the same thing at the Bristol exhibition a few days later. Model railways do not seem to interest the female of the species. True, they were there in largish numbers at both exhibitions, but they were either mums or sisters being dragged around, or else they were wives or daughters of club members, helping out.

At both exhibitions, I admired the careful balance between com- mercialism, with the trade stands of the makers and the suppliers, and the working layouts for the public to watch. Jonathon Abson of the MRC told me, 'At our exhibition, the traders cater for the serious modeller who is graduating from taking everything out of a box . . . not that there aren't plenty of ready-made models on display'!

For visitors who had a technical problem, or just felt that there must be a better way of doing something, the MRC ran non-stop 'problem bureaux' all through the week of the exhibition. Half a dozen experts sat behind their tables, working on an assortment of models, and handling thousands of queries. The same thing happens at other exhibitions.

Said Jonathon, 'The experts are happy to spend as long as you like showing you how they do it, and discussing possible answers to your problems. And there is no charge!'

The experts learn a thing or two themselves during the week. One of them told me he was just about to start cutting out a coach at his table when a visitor let out a sudden gasp.

'You're not going to do it like that,' he said, looking at the drawing of the coach, which happened to be from the Glasgow and South Western Railway.

The expert looked hard, and said, 'Well yes, I was'.

'Good heavens,' said the man, who turned out to be a former locomotive foreman from Inverness. 'I can tell you that they weren't like that.' He went on to tell the expert how the carriage should have been, and the result was that everyone is now a little wiser.

Wandering around the National exhibition, I noticed that there were no prizes or trophies. Ron Parren, the vice-president of MRC, explained, 'Competitiveness is something of an anathema to the MRC. We have four trophies in the club office which were competed for until ten years ago, but nobody really is interested in them.

'It seems to be different in other parts of the country. In Manchester, they are highly competitive, and they really covet the trophies they award. You see them being handed out at their exhibition time.

'They all seem to vie with each other there for these positions of prestige. Maybe it's got something to do with people's attitudes in various regions, but here in London we cannot get this competitive element off the ground.'

But with or without the 'knock-out' competition, all the clubs are anxious to stress that no one is ever turned away because he is not an ace modeller. Says Jonathon Abson, 'With very few exceptions, almost any club will let you do your own thing your own way. Where there are trophies, the entry conditions are often very loosely termed, so that no one feels rejected.'

The National Exhibition

One of the great thrills for me, as a newcomer to model railways, was to see a real steam engine working at the National Exhibition. Here was the original reason for it all — the model that proved it could actually work using steam as a propulsion — brought right up to date.

The layout was built by members of the Gauge One Model Railway Association, the largest of the gauges in model railways and the only one in which live steam can really be used effectively. Gauge One works out at a scale of 10mm to the foot, so the engines, with their steam boilers running on meths, butane gas, and sometimes even on coal, are much too big for the average house. It is only at exhibitions that most modellers get the chance to see these big brothers of the hobby in action.

The layout at the exhibition had a double-track main line circling the stand, with a station on one side and a country setting on the other. The steam trains pulled their loads in truly realistic style, after being prepared for duty in the loco depot at one end of the stand, while groups of children watched in wide-eyed wonder. It was strange to think that this demonstration could be the first time they had ever seen a real steam engine 'in the flesh'.

Slightly smaller, but no less impressive, was another display put together by one of Scotland's leading modellers, Nigel McMillan. He builds in O gauge, the great favourite earlier this century, which works out at 7mm to the foot. Unlike many layouts I have seen, there was nothing romantic or glamorous about Nigel's setting — it was based around a colliery slag-heap.

He told me, 'The railways in the west of Scotland did not make their money out of carrying passengers, they made it out of carrying coal. The typical train on the Caledonian Railway wasn't a smart blue engine with a stream of blue and white carriages. It was a dirty long coal train with a black engine.

'To try and recapture that, I have got more than a hundred coal wagons on this layout, running either empty back to the pit, or coming down loaded.'

It is a massive display twenty-two feet long, and a great deal of research went into the planning of the Lyoncross colliery layout. But then, Nigel has an MSc degree in coal mining history, and the whole layout is modelled on actual sites.

As well as the colliery line, there is a bogie-way taking waste to the slag-heap, a narrow gauge railway running to serve the next-door drift mine, and a rather flashy main line running straight through.

Nigel is a stickler for detail — the tatty colliery rails were salvaged from an out-of-doors 'O' gauge line, and they have ten years of genuine rust on them. In sharp contrast, there is the gleaming rails of the main line, kept in good order by a fastidious railway company. There are other neat details — slogans for Home Rule for Scotland and graffiti on the walls in the sidings, and a model railwayman is caught in the act of spending a penny!

The entire layout of Lyoncross Colliery was built in nine months in a space excavated underneath Nigel's house (friends nicknamed it the Colditz railway!) and everything on the display was built by hand. It is one of the few really big layouts around that was started completely from scratch.

Nigel told me, 'This is an exhibition layout. It is not for playing with. The operators have to work very hard. I run a schedule so that the trains change continuously. At an exhibition, the public only stays at one stand for maybe ten or fifteen minutes, so they don't want to see more than two runs of the same train. I try to show them everything we have got in that time.

'Personally, I don't like the smaller gauges. Because I build everything myself, I find it much more satisfying to make them in this large size. I have built smaller ones for other people, but I could not take them seriously.

'I can put more detail into these engines, and when it is finished they are big enough to see properly — and they sound like real trains!'

Nigel is one of the great enthusiasts of the hobby, but in his choice of gauge, he is now very much in the minority. Double O is the runaway success of the century — a fact that is proved by the vast number of displays and trade stands at all exhibitions which cater for the average modeller with his averaged-sized models.

Designing your Layout

Gone are the days when serious model-makers would run their track round the front-room floor, risking the wrath of their womenfolk if they did not remove all trace of trains when the room was needed for something else.

Now, modellers run their tracks on what they call baseboards, which can, if necessary, be folded up and stacked neatly away in a matter of minutes. So, as a new modeller, one of your tasks will be to build your own baseboard, and you will find the technical details and instructions for this later on in the book from page 37 onwards.

Your aim should be to create, on your baseboard, a little bit of the British countryside, with a railway line running through it. You can try to make a townscape if you want, but generally that is much more complicated and difficult.

I noticed that, among the dozens of layouts I inspected, not one of them depicted a big, main-line station. The reason, of course, became obvious. If you wanted to model Kings Cross station and its network of lines and sidings in the 4mm gauge (Double O) you would need a baseboard the size of a tennis court!

So, generally speaking, it is more practical as well as more romantic to base your railway on a little branch line, or a small station on a main line. Even then, modellers find they have to compromise. Platforms of small country stations can well be four hundred feet long, and scaling them down in Double O would make them almost six feet long. That is far too large for the average layout, so people find themselves buying or making stations, platforms and other buildings which may not be exactly to scale, but which fit happily and realistically on to their baseboard thus allowing them to model more accurately. But if you want greater variety of stock and more excitement from the operation of the layout, choose a main line station.

Now, to the baseboard itself. The ideal board for the standard gauge sizes such as Double O is about four feet long, and between eighteen inches and two feet wide. Much wider than that, and it is too easy to knock things over when you stretch across the board. For material the experts recommend half-inch chipboard, not hardboard. Hardboard can twist and

Clive Cobley controlling his layout with an electric pencil. Note how the track plan is reproduced on the control panel

distort, which is the last thing you want when you have delicate tracks running across it. Also, you cannot pin things easily into hardboard, and modellers are forever sticking extra bits into their boards.

The chipboard needs to be supported by a strong frame (50mm (2in) deal is best), with three cross-bars, and you can screw and glue the chipboard to the frame. Remember, this baseboard needs to be sturdy, so that it can be taken almost anywhere and stand up to a fair amount of bashing without your display being damaged.

It is best to make two boards, so that you can have about eight feet of layout to work on, and the boards can be joined together with flat-back hinges. This makes sure that every time you open the board, the two halves meet exactly, and where the rails meet you get a positive join. When the boards are folded up, one fits neatly on top of the other. Later, you can add more boards to meet the needs of your expanding railway.

If you have room in your house, a permanent or semi-permanent installation is best. But, remember, you may have to move, so plan everything accordingly.

In addition to the baseboards, you will need what I think is the nicest description in the whole of model railways — the Fiddle Yard. This is an extra piece of board which attaches to the end of your layout, though technically it should be out of sight of any spectators. The Fiddle Yard is the place where anything goes! On its board, there are lines of sidings, and this is where, quite literally you do your fiddling ... preparing the engines, coaches and wagons for their journeys on to your layout. It is also the only place where you can actually lift things up and turn them round — on the layout proper, that kind of behaviour leads to raised eyebrows.

When you are designing your board, it is a good idea to build a bridge, covered by hills, between the fiddle yard and your display so that in your imagination, and in the imagination of anyone else who is watching, your trains come through a tunnel from the fiddle yard just as though they were arriving at your station from any destination, anywhere in the British Isles. Your station is 'real' — the fiddle yard represents the rest of the world!

Clive Cobley and Peter Jessop gave me some tips about what you might call their 'philosophy of baseboards'. First of all, they said, plan your layout on paper before you start to build anything. If you want, use graph paper with its marked-out squares, so you can be sure your measurements are right.

When it comes to laying the track, you will need a main line running into your station; a runaround loop so that the engine that pulled in a train can nip round and pull it out again; what is called a head shunt — a shunting line that leaves the main line clear, so that shunting work can proceed happily without fouling the main line and blocking passenger trains; and perhaps a couple of sidings.

In their opinion, what you do *not* need is an old-fashioned circuit. To many modellers, that does still smack of toy trains, and there would not be room for it on your layout, anyway. It is possible, on larger layouts to use a circuit where the trains are out of sight for part of their journey round.

When you have drawn your plan, cut out some little pieces of paper or cardboard, and pretend they are your engines and carriages. Slide them around the plan of your track (they will need to be roughly the same scale) and make sure that everything will run smoothly, that the trains can get in — and out — of everywhere. After all, it is no good having the prettiest layout ever, if the thing does not flow. Even the experts have been stumped at times with engines trapped against the buffer stops, so you might as well start with a fool-proof system. And another piece of advice: do not make it too simple.

Anything less than a main line, a head shunt, a loop, and two sidings and you will be bored within five minutes of running your first engine.

Try to make your layout as quiet as possible, otherwise everyone else in the house will rapidly get fed up with your railway. Many top modellers use sound-aborbing cork as the working surface on top of the chipboard. But, if you are running out of money, you could always use cardboard.

When you reach the stage of putting up buildings, you can if you wish buy plans of real stations, just to give you some idea of how things should be laid out. If there is a local station within easy reach, even a derelict one, why not take a close look round. You might be able to soak up the atmosphere, and transfer it to your baseboard. When you are building your display, I am sure you will find you have a marvellous chance to project your imagination. You are on your way to building your ideal railway.

Rolling Stock

Before you get too advanced with your buildings, perhaps you should be adding to your rolling stock. You can buy modelling kits for engines, carriages and wagons in either plastic or white metal. All the pieces are already cut out for you in the box — you have to assemble them, glue them together, and paint the finished model. These kits remove what some people would call the drudgery of model making. There is no need to buy a plan, no need to cut out all the individual pieces and panels. That has already been done for you.

Even so, many expert modellers prefer to do those 'drudgery' jobs themselves anyway — it gives them the satisfaction that everything really is their own work. But there is no doubt that the upsurge in recent years of the model kits has enabled thousands of people to make the kind of equipment that is just not available in ready-made form.

For instance, one kit manufacturer offers seven different LMS coaches, and you can personalise each one of them by, say, leaving some of the windows down, or putting passengers inside. All the good quality kits have detailed instructions about the painting schemes of the various railway companies and they will give you the correct serial numbers to paint on . . . a very important point for the purists!

One of the top kit manufacturers, Bob Wills, who started in business back in 1959, told me, 'The great thing about kits is that modellers can take their hobby just as far as they want, and as far as they are capable.'

He has noticed that, over the years, the kits are featuring more and more detail. That, he thinks, is partly because the modellers are getting keener, and partly because the manufacturers get great personal enjoyment from getting the details exactly right. One of Bob Wills' latest kits is of the handsome Wainwright Class C steam engine, that is still running on the famous Bluebell Line in Kent. So they had the opporunity to go along to photograph every detail and the result can be seen in things like the rivets. On this Double O gauge model, the rivets are so small you can hardly see them anyway. But in fact there are three different sizes of rivets, because that is how many different sizes there are on the real loco.

On the Wainwright's draw-bar, for instance, there are precisely the right number of rivets, in precisely the right size, in precisely the right place. That kind of detail might not have been found a few years ago.

When you are building an engine from a kit, you can either build it on to a ready-made chassis which has the electrical parts already assembled,

Three decades of OO gauge model coaches. From right to left, a printed tin plate Hornby-Dublo LNER 1st/3rd (made 1950s); centre an early P.C. models kit-built LNWR Brake 3rd (late 1960s); left a superb Mainline ready-to-run LMS 57ft 1st/3rd (introduced 1978)

or you can build the chassis as well. As with more simple kits, the manufacturers supply full instructions for assembly.

Jonathon Abson, of the MRC, says, 'The great thing about kits is that the finished product looks good if you put it together just as the manufacturer tells you.

'But you can, if you wish, spend a lot of extra time putting the details on, and turning the model into something that would not disgrace itself in a competition.

'If you were to assemble the basic kit for a carriage it would probably take you three nights work, including the painting, if you knew what you were doing. If not, say a week.

'The experts can scratch-build their own, cutting the pieces out of board, in about the same time. The kit might cost three times what the experts would spend on their materials.'

Generally, model makers go on to 'scratch' building once they have developed their confidence. If they make their models well enough, they will always find a ready market should they want to sell. One modeller I met built a loco for a total cost in parts of £8. He put a lot of time and effort into it, but the finished product was immediately valued at £155. Not a bad investment!

Allan Downes' Scenery

Not everyone heavily involved in model railways likes trains. That might seem an astonishing statement, but it is true, especially as far as Allan Downes is concerned. Allan is one of the country's leading scenery builders for railway layouts, yet he admits that he cannot tell one engine from another.

He told me, 'I realised that model railways provided a great excuse for building very large models, and you can't build those kind of things without an excuse.'

Allan lives in High Wycombe in Buckinghamshire, and he drives a van for a living. But his mind is nearly always on his models. His latest triumph is a 4mm scale model of a Cotswold village, called Candleford Mill, in which the main street winds past farms whose barn doors have seen better days; past thatched cottages, some of them modernised, others in need of attention. There is a quaint little pub and, of course, the required railway station. The whole place breathes life, reality and beauty. I have spent a lot of time driving through villages in the Cotswolds, and to me, Candleford Mill is real.

An Allan Downes' model village scene from an extensive exhibition layout

So it came as a great surprise to learn that Allan Downes has never been to the Cotswolds. He dreamt the whole place up after looking at a series of colour photographs of the area on a calendar!

When new modellers start to build the scenery for their baseboards, they will work strictly to plans if they want to make their creation look believable. But, after a time, they will be able to take the same attitudes to their hobby as does Allan.

He told me, 'When you build a village like Candleford Mill from your imagination, you can put up the kind of buildings that you think *ought* to be there. How many times in real life have you seen a beautiful place that has been spoilt by a few ugly buildings?

'When you are modelling, you put all your dreams into the place, shuffle them around a bit, and you don't get any eyesores. On the other hand, if you visit an actual place and get taken over by it, then you feel you have to get it exactly right in the model, and you start to measure distances, and things like that.

'Then, when you are modelling it, those details are in your mind. They get in the way, and they slow you down. You could be making a door, and you think to yourself: "I'm only making it two foot wide, and really it should be three feet. That was the measurement." I'm sorry, but that is not for me — I like to work from impressions in the mind.'

Allan Downes is a master builder of dreams, but he is a practical man when it comes to the actual business of modelling. He believes, basically, that all cottages and houses look the same. The things that make them different in various parts of the country are the colours of the stone and the brick, and the roofs.

'Cotswold stone has a very definite greyish hue,' he said, 'and if you can get that hue on to your model, then you have a Cotswold cottage. In my models, nothing is perfect, nothing is quite square.

'Because, you see, in real life nothing is shaped quite perfectly, except the Pyramids, and nobody knows how they managed that. It is easier to sit down and build models of places that look a bit rough than it is to create something that looks perfect, and at the same time, you are being true to life.' And nothing is imperfect enough to make it an eyesore!

Candleford Mill took six months to build in Allan's spare time. The buildings are all hand-made from 1mm thick card, using Peco scene modelling texture spread over the card. The stone effect is then worked in, and all the roof tiles — thousands of them — were individually cut and laid. The tiles took about a third of the construction time, and they are twice as big as they should be. The excuse, says Allan, is artistic licence. If

An Allan Downes' watermill scene in 4mm scale where the wheel is seen hopelessly trying to churn away in a polyurethane river

they were to the correct scale, nobody would be able to see them.

'Don't go for scale, go for effect,' is his advice. 'There is no given height for a tree or a hedge, or for the angle of a railway cutting. Choose one that feels right to you, and looks good on the model. On a house, put in an extra door if you want — or take one away if you don't like it.

'Once you have made your first model, the second comes much easier, the third is better still, and so on. You find you have to think much less, and it becomes 90 per cent application. Instinctively, things are right, and now I can make a Cotswold cottage in an evening, while watching television!'

Allan believes he has really succeeded with a layout when it is photographed and afterwards people think it is a real place, and not a model. He has always been unorthodox — he laid out his first scenic model in a pig-sty! And he is used to awful things happening to his models. He built a Gothic castle for one of the Pink Panther films, and it was blown to pieces in the last reel!

Not many people can hope to emulate his talents, but at least they can now find out how he operates, and learn some of his secrets. He is printing details of how to make various types of buildings in a series of books called Downesplans.

It took me about twenty minutes to walk along the layout for Candleford Mill. With every pace, there are fresh things to see, clever techniques to admire. It seemed to me to be almost a coincidence that the village had a railway line running through it. But no model railway could have a better setting.

Thomas the Tank Engine

Creating a model village based on calendar pictures of a place in the Cotswolds is really like weaving your own bit of magic. Even more magical, though, is the setting dreamed up for his model railway by one of the great characters of the hobby, and one of the greatest children's story-tellers of the century, the Reverend W. Awdry.

There can be very few people who have never heard tell of Thomas the Tank Engine, the hero of a million bedtimes. Thomas, the tough little engine who gets into great escapades, was invented by the Reverend Awdry many years ago, and the books that tell the deeds of Thomas and his friends delight every new generation.

For some reason, model railways have a great following among the clergy, the Reverend Awdry is a classic kind of enthusiast — tall, lean and craggy, with what seemed like a total involvement in his trains, and the island he has invented to run them on.

Yes, he has dreamt up his own island. It is called Sodor, and it is off the north-west coast of England, between Barrow in Furness and the Isle of Man. To him, the island is so real that he showed me a map of the place. It looked like a real Ordnance Survey map, and it carefully charts the towns and villages, the rivers and hills, and the railway lines along which Thomas, Daisy the Diesel, Duke the Lost Engine and all the others have their adventures.

'Actually,' he told me, 'the isle of Sodor is a development of a real island called Walney. When you cross over the bridge from Barrow in Furness and go to what you think is the far side of Walney island, you apparently see what you believe to be the sea.

'But that's an illusion,' he said, with a twinkle. 'What you are really seeing is the island of Sodor.'

Let me tell you a little more about the Reverend Awdry and his mythical island, because it seems to me that his ideas are the perfect way of breathing life and realism into a model railway layout. They may seem a little cranky to some people, but he gets a great deal of fun out of his trains, and it is far better to create a 'world' for your railway than to run it coldly round a carefully laid track.

In the Reverend Awdry's world, the island of Sodor has two narrow gauge railways, the Mid-Sodor and the Skarloey (that, apparently, is a native word meaning 'lake in the woods'). The railways serve towns like Peel Godred, Arlsburgh, and Wellsworth. The Skarloey railway runs up to the mines in the hills, and there is even a scenic loop line round the lake there, which was opened to mark the railway's centenary.

Reverend Awdry is a keen railway modeller, and he works in the tiny 009 gauge, just about the smallest possible. He showed me one of his layouts, a magnificent cut-out section of the Mid-Sodor railway where it climbs, in a series of loops, to the summit of the line. Devotees of his books might like to know, incidentally, that this was the stretch of track featured in the drama of Duke the Lost Engine.

Reverend Awdry told me, 'The most difficult thing about such a small gauge is getting things back on the track again. It can be quite infuriating.'

So, to spare his anger, he uses a small, oblong piece of plastic board which, at one end, has a small triangle stuck on in the middle, just big enough for the bogies to pass over the top. He puts the vehicle on to the board, and slides it over the little triangle and on to the tracks. A useful tip for people planning to build in small gauges.

When I asked why he had chosen such a fiddly size in which to work, he replied with typical logic. 'I knew it would have to fit into the boot of an 1100 car,' he said. 'So the layout couldn't be more than 3ft 6in (106cm) wide and 2ft deep (60cm).' Therefore, it had to be 009.

And how, I wondered, did he come to discover Sodor? It turned out to be a long story, all tied up with Viking legend. In olden times, the Isle of Man and the Hebrides were part of the Norwegian Empire, and the Vikings called the Hebrides, Sodor. When they were Christianised, they appointed a Bishop to Sodor and Man.

When Alexander the Third of Scotland drove the Norse out, he appointed the Bishop of Argyle to take over the Hebrides. To this day, he calls himself the Bishop of Argyle and the Islands. Sodor ceases to exist.

'But possibly in the hope of a comeback, the Bishop on the Isle of Man continued to call himself the Bishop of Sodor and Man. He's Church of England now, but he keeps the title, and I decided to find the other half of his diocese for him!'

The Reverend Awdry finds himself believing in his mythical island, and he is able to convince other people, too. 'I give lectures about the island,' he said. 'I call them Pages of Sodor History. After one of these lectures, someone came up to me and said that because I talked so freely about the island and its people and its railway, wasn't I laying myself open to libel!'

It is no wonder that people find it hard to tell where fact ends and fiction begins, because the Reverend Awdry has even weaved Sodor's own Saga — a mixture of Manx and Norse legends blended together with heroic figures and stirring events of his own invention. To confuse things even more, he lives in Sodor — it is also the name of his house!

But why, I wondered, had he bothered to spin all this magic. The Reverend Awdry had a practical answer. 'To be viable, a railway has to serve towns and villages, and industries, and they all have to have a reason for existing. The places need names, and names are all wrapped up in history.'

So, the island of Sodor was invented to provide a background of reality for Thomas the tank engine and his friends. While we had been talking, I had looked in vain around the layout for Thomas.

'He's not here,' said his inventor. 'People are always asking to see him, but at the moment he's under the bed in the spare room.' Even the glittering stars of the model railway world have their unglamorous moments!

Conclusion to Part One

So, like me, you must now realise that model railways *are* much more than just toy trains. They are the basis of an absorbing hobby, and they help transport their followers into a rose-tinted world of make believe where steam trains are not noisy monsters that belch their dirty smoke across the countryside.

Instead, they are the handsome heroes of a golden age of transport. Purists can though, if they wish, now buy 'dirty black' paint to add a touch of realism! Most do not bother.

The people who get hooked by model railways fall into two main age groups. First, there are young men, from enthusiasts in short trousers to experienced modellers up to about the age of 24. After that, they tend to get married, and have other interests — for a while, at least! The other main group is of men who discover, or re-discover, the hobby as their children start to grow up.

As for me, I somehow escaped its attractions, until now! But, after taking a long look at the hobby and meeting some of the people who are deeply involved in it, I am ready to 'have a go' at starting my own railway. So I will read along with you as John Cockcroft takes over, and tells us how it really should be done.

Planning a Layout

In the first part of the book John covered the different aspects of modelling in the various scales. Much depends on the amount of room and money you have available, and your preference of prototype. If you like making very detailed locomotives and stock, and are not too bothered about scenery, 'O' gauge is suitable. N gauge is for the person with little room, or one who likes to see his railway in a landscape.

For the person who likes all aspects of modelling, from track and scenery to locomotives and rolling stock, 4mm scale is the best compromise in normal circumstances. OO gauge has, as John said, swept the board this century.

Most comments in this book apply to all scales, but where measurements are quoted they refer to 4mm scale. For N gauge modellers the rough guide is to halve 4mm scale dimensions, for 'O' gauge double them and knock off an inch or so in every foot and you will not be far off.

Consistency and Standards

I have kept this section separate from the scale/gauge part because of its importance to successful running. Without doubt, more layouts in any gauge have come to grief through not sticking to one track and wheel standard than through anything else.

In Fig. 1.1 are shown the essential measurements of wheels and track. Track gauge is only one of them and obviously needs to be accurate. It is not too difficult to get most wheels to run on plain track, provided the flange depth is not greater than the rail height. The problem comes when point work is encountered, because here the wheels have to be controlled, or checked, from taking the wrong direction and derailing. This checking is done by check rails which are placed so as to hold the inside of the flange to prevent the wheel from drifting away from the running rail. Obviously the gap between the running rail and the check rail have to be wide enough to let the flange pass through, but not so wide that no control is exerted, this I have called check rail clearance in Fig. 1.1. Problems will also occur if the distance between the two inside faces of the wheel, the back-to-back gauge, is smaller than the distance between the faces of two check rails, the check rail gauge. Wheel profiles and track gauges and clearances *must* be constant on any layout or bad running will result.

When modellers talk about fine scale they mean nearer the prototype which in model form means very small flanges and treads. All ready-to-run stock in OO gauge has wheel and track standards quite a bit heavier than true scale so that the stock stays on track laid on an uneven carpet if necessary.

The big manufacturers have a tendency to make their stock with finer scale wheels than previously, and there is quite a lot of consistency between makes. Peco universal pointwork copes well with most ready-to-run stock, and the new Peco fine scale pointwork will deal with all but the coarsest wheels. Peco fine scale will also accept the finer wheels supplied with loco kits such as K's and Romford wheels, which often run rather lumpily over universal pointwork.

One final point about track standards: rail height is classified by codes, in 4mm scale standard British bull head rail is code 65. Most universal

Fig. 1.1
Wheel profile

back to back gauge
flange width
flange depth
flange
tread

Check rails

check rail gauge
check rail clearance
Track gauge
rail height usually referred to as Code

Fig. 1.2

| Storage siding | Station | Storage siding |

a) End to end layout

| Station | Storage siding |

b) Terminus to storage sidings

Station

c) Continuous layout

Storage siding

Station

Storage sidings

d) Continuous layout with terminus, there are many possibilities using split levels running tracks under parts of the layout

29

track uses code 100 rail and is greater than scale height; the higher the code number the higher the rail.

Realities and Compromises

What are some common compromises made in model railways? Firstly, you can limit the amount of real railway you attempt to model; in the first section John noticed this problem and offered one solution by modelling small stations. Branch lines, particularly branch termini, were some of the smallest and simplest of real railway stations. They were, however, laid out in a fairly spacious and straggling manner, and a scale OO gauge model can require more than fifteen to twenty feet in some cases.

Therefore, we came up with another compromise, that of compression.

As John noted, platform lengths can usually be reduced without losing too much effect. I would say four feet in OO gauge is as long as a small branch platform need be. You can get away with less but be careful not to lose the *feeling* of spaciousness so peculiar to a rural branch. On a more important station I usually think five-foot platforms are a minimum, and prefer six foot if possible. Remember to allow about one foot of platform for each coach, so your train lengths will be dictated by your platforms. Another thing to think about when planning a layout is to allow for trains of suitable length in all parts of your system. It is not very railway-like if your ten-coach express can only go into six foot storage sidings!

It is quite possible, therefore, to reduce the length needed to give a good impression of a branch terminus from twenty feet to twelve feet or less, including a small storage yard.

Rural branches are all very well, but they are very limited in their operation and variety of locos and stock. Another solution to this problem of space is to model a type of real station in a cramped site, such as a small city terminus. This is an ideal prototype for someone who is interested in running intensive passenger services. I would recommend anyone interested in town stations to look at the famous 'Minories' design by C. J. Freezer in *60 Plans for Small Railways* published by Peco. Of course there are very limited opportunities for modelling trees etc., in this type of layout, so if you find rural scenery attractive this is not for you.

Planning

Now that you have decided on scale and gauge and what sort of railway you would like to model it is time to get it down on paper. You know more or less the size and shape of the area you have to work in, so start by doing a few sketches of the sort of scheme you imagine will suit you. Then stop and think whether you like the idea before going on to details.

This has got you as far as deciding whether you want an end-to-end, or continuous layout and how many stations you think you can have. Though Clive Cobley and Peter Jessop recommend against having a continuous run or circuit, such a design has some advantages. Firstly, it is useful as a test track for locos; most end-to-end layouts are not long enough for a loco to get really run in. Secondly, a continuous run gives you an opportunity to see your trains running without having always to be watching your control unit. In other words, it can be relaxing just looking at your train from different locations. Thirdly, unlike an end-to-end layout you do not have to turn each train round or move the engine to the other end once it has left the station and entered the fiddle yard. Finally, there is nothing you can do in an end-to-end layout that you cannot do in a continuous one, because if you like, you can run a continuous layout on an end-to-end basis. Fig. 1.2 shows a few types schematically. Which you choose will often be decided by the shape of the area you have to work in.

Radius of Curves

The next stage is to find out whether your sketch plan can be fitted into your space. Firstly, let us think about the main lines, especially if there are curves involved. To measure a curve we use its radius; this is explained in Fig. 1.3. Many model railway locomotives are not happy on curves of two foot radius or under; indeed three foot radius is a much more desirable minimum if you plan to use kit-built models with finer wheels. This means that you have to have an area at least four feet wide to allow a two foot radius circuit to run to the very edge of the baseboard. For easier curves correspondingly wider space is needed.

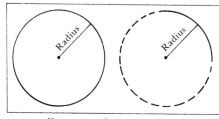

Fig. 1.3
Radius is: the distance from the centre of a circle to the rim. Curves are parts of circles and are measured by radius also

On all parts of the layout that are not hidden in tunnels, etc., try to make the curves as wide as possible because on real railways they hardly ever scale down to even three foot radius. Fig. 1.4 shows a useful trick which also improves running — the transition curve. Instead of a train

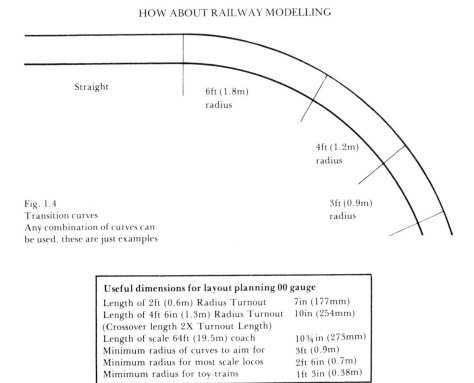

Straight

6ft (1.8m)
radius

4ft (1.2m)
radius

Fig. 1.4
Transition curves
Any combination of curves can
be used, these are just examples

3ft (0.9m)
radius

Useful dimensions for layout planning 00 gauge	
Length of 2ft (0.6m) Radius Turnout	7in (177mm)
Length of 4ft 6in (1.3m) Radius Turnout	10in (254mm)
(Crossover length 2X Turnout Length)	
Length of scale 64ft (19.5m) coach	10¾in (273mm)
Minimum radius of curves to aim for	3ft (0.9m)
Minimum radius for most scale locos	2ft 6in (0.7m)
Mimimum radius for toy-trains	1ft 3in (0.38m)

suddenly hitting a tight curve with a bump, it is eased into it gradually as in real railways. Finally, try to hide all your tight curves or at least disguise them. Put them in a tunnel or screen them with a cutting, even put a bridge over them to break up the image and distract the eye. Avoid siting them in a place where it is possible to look along the tracks. A tight curve is not as obvious when seen from the side.

Fitting things in

Once you know whether you can fit the main lines into your room it is time to start more detailed planning. For this I usually start with a drawing at about 25mm (1in) to 300mm (1ft) scale. The table above gives a few dimensions which help in the accurate planning of a layout, and Fig. 1.9 shows clearances and height restrictions. It is also useful to buy a few items which you may use on your layout, a couple of yards of track, a couple of points, a wagon and a coach, for example. These enable you to visualise more clearly the space required for your proposed stations.

Train Lengths

I have already mentioned the importance of planning your layout as a whole, keeping the lengths of trains in mind. At every place where a train has to stop there must be adequate room for normal operations to be carried on. Places to watch for this include platform lengths and, very importantly, run-round loops as illustrated in Fig. 1.5. These enable a locomotive to change from one end of a train to another. They are used for passenger trains in most termini and by goods trains when shunting is to take place. Adequate provision must also be made in hidden storage sidings or 'fiddle yards'; nearly every train which leaves your station must go there, so there must be room for it.

Sidings are another place where you must think how much room you require for stock. It is no use allowing a long loop for dealing with goods trains if your siding space is inadequate to deal with all the wagons.

Fig. 1.5
A run round loop

Length of train which can be run round

Loco spur must be long enough for longest loco to clear the points

Traffic Flows

Once you have decided on your train lengths and made adequate provision for them in your mind, you must set about arranging the point work and running lines in such a manner that trains can move from one place to another relatively freely. I say 'relatively' because particularly in smaller layouts a little complication adds to the operating interest.

Fig. 1.6 shows an efficiently arranged goods yard using a head shunt so that the through line is uninterrupted by shunting. Provided the head shunt is long enough, wagons can be sorted into and out of the sidings without interference to passing trains.

Fig. 1.6
Goods yard with headshunt

Main line

head shunt

run round loop

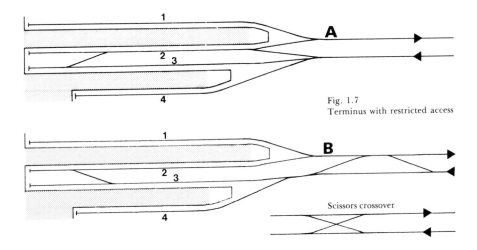

Fig. 1.7
Terminus with restricted access

Scissors crossover

Another feature to try to include in a terminus is the maximum availability of platform roads for each incoming and outgoing track. Fig. 1.7 shows the situation and the solution by using cross-overs. In station A, trains can only arrive at platforms 2, 3 and 4 and depart from platforms 1 and 2. By moving one cross over and adding another access is achieved to all platforms for both departures and arrivals. The inset shows a space-saving alternative, the scissors cross-over.

Finally, one last bottleneck is shown in Fig. 1.8. Here the locomotive shed has been located in a suitable corner of the baseboard with access from the end of platform 1. The problem is that unless platform 1 is very long, all but a short train would block it, and seal up all your locos. So if you have a kickback access make sure you do not want to use it for anything else, or it will prove a false economy.

Fig. 1.8
Kickback access to loco shed

Platform 1

Kickback
access

Loco shed

Split levels

It is often the case that more room can be gained by running one track above another. This is particularly so where a station can be built over part of a low level circuit or storage yard. To get one train over another requires, in 4mm scale, a clearance of 75mm (3in) above the lower set of tracks. If you add the thickness of the upper baseboard and its framing, it means you require a minimum rise of four and a half inches.

A model railway locomotive will have its train loadings severely limited by a rising gradient. A maximum gradient of 1 in 30 is desirable if running is not to be badly affected. This means a rise of 25mm (1in) for every 750mm (2ft 6in) of track. Allowing for smoothing out the change from horizontal to slope at both top and bottom of the rise, it will take about 365cm (12ft) of track to get up to our 115mm (4½in) high baseboard.

The distance required for the high level gradient can be halved if the low level track can fall at 1 in 30 at the same time. In any event try to keep your gradients as shallow as possible, and always avoid gradients near points where locomotives are uncoupled from trains or you will find your stock in a heap at the foot of the hill!

Finishing off your Plans

When you have drawn up your first plan, it is a good idea to re-draw it to a larger scale with greater accuracy. I use a 50mm (2in) to 300mm (1ft) scale, with larger plans than that for the difficult parts. As John found out, this plan can be used to try out your possible train movements using card cut-outs. Some ideas for the landscape and buildings can be sketched in, and a start made on thinking in detail about baseboard construction.

The cardinal rule of baseboard joints is never put them through your point work. All points must be either one side or the other of a joint. Many people advocate standard length boards for ease of storage and, indeed, with portable layouts this is a considerable advantage. But it does mean that your point work is rather dominated by the baseboard design. Another thing to ensure is that baseboard frames are positioned away from the point operating units at the toe of the point, so if there is a heavy concentration of points at a particular location, juggle points and frames about until they are clear of each other.

If you have any choice in the matter, try always to keep the pointwork down to basic turnouts with the occasional diamond crossing. Elaborate points and crossings can cause trouble both with running and electrically, and if you buy them they are expensive, getting on for £7.00 at 1979 prices for a double slip, so try and avoid them unless you have no alternative.

If you have tunnels and long cuttings make sure you can get to any train that gets stuck in them. Either make lift off sections or cut a suitable hole in the baseboard under a tunnel so that you can get your arm in, and the stock out without resorting to the fire brigade (see Fig. 1.10)!

Finally, try and think about yourself, your size, your odd angles and big over-scale hands. It is no good making your operating space so confined that you spend half your time demolishing your scenery with your elbow.

A Full Size Plan

The final stage in layout planning before actual construction is to make a full size plan. I think most households will have spare rolls of old wallpaper which can be reversed and the back used for the design. This stage is really confirmation of the feasibility of the design and helps greatly in the cutting out of baseboards and in laying track.

Despite all this planning, there are usually a few alterations made when actually laying the track so it is time to leave the drawing board and get on with the real work.

Fig. 1.9   Some useful measurements in 00 gauge (in N gauge halve the measurements)

Baseboard Building

Baseboards

Baseboards are the foundation of all you will build later, they must be built strongly and rigidly. A poor baseboard will spoil the running of your trains, so take the time to make it properly.

Materials

Wood and wood products are the only materials suitable for baseboard construction.

Chipboard, as John found out in part one, is a good material for baseboard surfaces. Being the largest single part of your baseboard, the surface is the most affected by expansion and contraction. Because chipboard is made up of lots of chips of wood stuck together, they can expand and contract in different directions as the temperature changes but do not distort the overall shape very much. It also has the advantage of being strong, but not so hard that you have difficulty sticking things into it. One disadvantage is its weight, but as 12mm (½in) thickness is adequate, this is not usually a problem. By the way, as John noted, never use hardboard.

Despite its stability, a chipboard surface requires bracing to stop it flexing about as you move it, lean on it, and abuse it in other ways when building your layout. Normal cheap softwood bought from timber merchants or do-it-yourself shops is adequate for most of the bracing and other under-baseboard work. The bulk of the framing will be strong enough if made up from 5cm × 3cm (2in × 1in) strips, but odd sizes may be required in places.

To stick the baseboard together it is best to use both screws and glue. Screws should be 40mm (1½in) wood screws in a hole drilled through the baseboard into the frame, with the heads countersunk or recessed into the baseboard surface. When buying screws, ask the shopkeeper what size drill is necessary to make suitable holes, Fig. 2.1 shows the technique. As for the glue, any reputable woodworking glue is suitable. White glues such as Resin W or Evostick woodworking glue are easy to use, efficient, and can be used in modelling later.

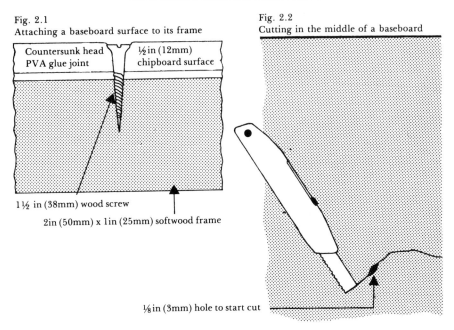

Fig. 2.1
Attaching a baseboard surface to its frame

Fig. 2.2
Cutting in the middle of a baseboard

Countersunk head
PVA glue joint

½ in (12mm)
chipboard surface

1½ in (38mm) wood screw

2in (50mm) x 1in (25mm) softwood frame

⅛ in (3mm) hole to start cut

Cutting out the Surface

As John noted in part one, it is unwise to have portable baseboard sections larger than about 120cm (4ft) by 60cm (2ft). This is a useful size for buying chipboard because it comes to the timber merchant in 240cm (8ft) by 120cm (4ft) sheets and can thus be easily divided. In fact you may be able to get him to do the cutting for you on his circular saw and save a bit of work; make sure he is fairly accurate though.

If you do not have standard shaped boards, mark them out yourself using a full-size plan of the railway (see page 36) and saw them with a handsaw. Make sure all edges adjoining another board are absolutely straight. If they are not, use a Surform or plane to smooth them out. For curved and other more complex cuts in sheet chipboard, a piercing saw is needed. There is a good cheap version that fits into a Stanley knife handle. If you cannot start a cut at a baseboard edge, drill 3mm (⅛in) hole through the baseboard and start from there as in Fig. 2.2.

Making the Frames

Always cut the frames to fit the baseboard surface. This avoids a lot of trouble if your carpentry is somewhat crude and if your work needs 'adjustment' to fit your plan, the surface acts as an accurate template. It is recommended that for a well-made baseboard the frames should be 30cm (1ft) apart in both directions. In fact, a solid surface of chipboard really only needs frames about 45cm (1ft 6in) apart.

If it is possible, the arrangement of framing should be based on rectangles as shown in Fig. 2.3. Odd corners and triangles can be supported by adding to the basic grid as in Fig. 2.4.

What happens when two braces intersect? You can saw one to fit in between the others, but in that way much of the strength is lost. It is much better to use a simple halving joint which preserves the continuity of both braces. Fig. 2.6 shows a halving joint, which consists of two saw cuts 25mm (1in) apart and 25mm (1in) deep, in each brace, with the wood between the cuts removed with a wood chisel.

Marking out is simple. Lay all the long braces on the underside of the baseboard as in Fig. 2.7 and lay all the cross braces over them. Then, using a sharp pencil draw a line across the long braces where each side of a cross brace passes over them. Using a square and a rule, mark in the 25mm (1in) deep cuts on the sides and cut out that half of the joint.

Then by fitting the cross braces into the slots, and making sure everything fits onto the baseboard, mark the cross braces in the same way and cut the joints out. Everything should fit after a little cleaning out with the chisel. It does not matter if there is some slop because you can pack big gaps with a spare bit of wood and glue. Before assembling the frame, drill some large holes through each brace between the joints. These can later be used to pass wires through when the electrical work starts.

Always assemble the frame under the baseboard surface, never try to build up the frame and attach it later. There are, however, exceptions to this when using open top baseboards as we shall see later.

Mark out the line of the frame on the surface and drill for screws approximately every 30cm (1ft). Then cover both sides of the join with glue, and screw the first brace in position. Remember that all those braces with their halving joints on the side away from the baseboard must be attached first, or you will not be able to get them under their opposite halves later. Finally, when all is assembled and the glue has dried, clean off any untidy ends with a Surform or chisel.

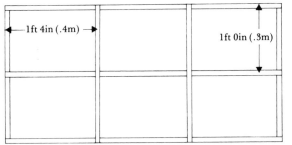

1ft 4in (.4m)

1ft 0in (.3m)

1ft 6in (.45m)

1ft 0in (.3m)

Fig. 2.3 Framing for simple rectangular baseboard 4ft (1.2m) x 2ft (0.6m)

Fig. 2.4
Frames on a corner baseboard 3ft (0.9m) x 3ft (0.9m)

Fig. 2.6
Halving joint

Fig. 2.5

More complex shapes require as many as possible of the braces to stretch the full length of the board

1in (25mm)

1in (25mm)

2in (50mm)

Fig. 2.7
Setting out the braces for marking

Mark here on each joint

Baseboard Joins

If your layout is permanently set up, joins between baseboards are not such a problem because you can drill and screw them together, or bolt them with 100mm (4in) coach bolts. It does not matter if the system you choose takes a bit of time to pull apart, or if you lay your track across the joint without a break.

Things are not so easy for owners of portable layouts. Joints have to be assembled and taken apart frequently, but always remain accurately in alignment to ensure smooth running over them. There are many ways of joining baseboards together; I will only deal with a few well tried methods.

Bolts and Dowels

Fig. 2.8 shows a typical bolt and dowel join. It is best to make a card, or plywood template for drilling all the holes in both baseboard ends to ensure that they are identical. The template should only have small holes in it so that at first only small pilot (or starting) holes are drilled in the baseboard end. These pilot holes are drilled out progressively to the correct diameter for the 100mm (4in) coach bolts and the 12 or 20mm (½ or ¾in) diameter dowels. After lining everything up and checking for errors, the dowels are glued into the holes on one side. They need only project 25mm (1in) or less because the bolts will hold both sides together quite firmly.

Hinges

Hinges are frequently used to join baseboards together, either as folding joints or as devices to align boards.

A pair of baseboards hinged together with face fixing or flat back hinges can be folded over each other and stored or transported easily, see Fig. 2.9. If the model railway is between them when folded, it is also well protected from damage. Obviously if the hinges are flush with the baseboard surface one half of your layout will squash the other when the boards are folded, so the hinges have to be raised to clear this. In a fiddle yard all that is needed is for the hinge to be screwed onto a piece of ⅛in ply and it will clear the rails. Do not forget to add some matching packing pieces at the other end of both boards to give clearance there.

If you wish to use this method on a scenic section of your railway, adequate clearance must be given for the highest features on both boards. The situation can be eased by siting scenery and buildings so that they

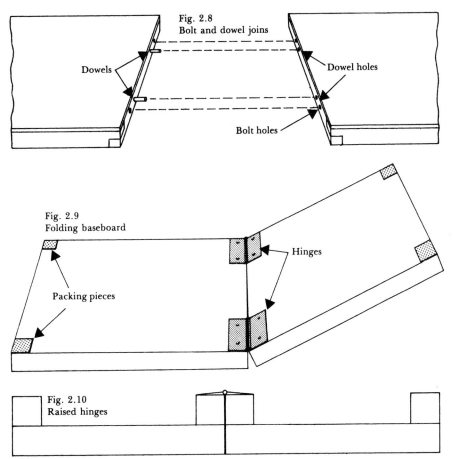

Fig. 2.8
Bolt and dowel joins

Dowels

Dowel holes

Bolt holes

Fig. 2.9
Folding baseboard

Hinges

Packing pieces

Fig. 2.10
Raised hinges

interlock when folded together, and taller items can be made removable. However, it is still desirable to to have at least 100mm (4in) between them, and this means raising the hinges on blocks by 50mm (2in) on either side as in Fig. 2.10. You must think of this before the baseboard is made because merely screwing the blocks onto the surface will not be strong enough to withstand the stresses imposed on them. They must be shaped and firmly attached to the frame below as in Fig. 2.11.

If the hinge-pin is removed from a hinge by filing off the head at one end, the hinge will come apart. As the two halves fit together closely and accurately they can be used to align two baseboards. To do this two hinges are attached to the baseboard frames across the join, one at each side, see

Attachment of hinge block for 2in (50mm) x 2in
(50mm) hinge

Fig. 2.11

Block glued and screwed
to frame corner

Surface of board cut away
for clarity

replacement for
hinge pin

Fig. 2.12
Split hinge baseboard joins

Fig. 2.12. It is easy to align them by attaching half the hinge to one board, lining the boards up and attaching the other half of the hinge to the other board. The hinge-pin is then removed and the boards will come apart. If you can find one, a long nail or piece of metal rod of the correct diameter, bent over as in Fig. 2.12, can be used to replace the hinge-pin and is much easier to remove.

Legs and Brackets

The first thing to decide before making legs for your layout is what height above the floor it is to be. There are no clear rules about this, usually about 100cm (3ft) to 106cm (3ft 6in) is chosen. Some people like to operate their railway from eye-level when sitting down — it looks more realistic that way. So they set their layouts 120cm (4ft) high or even more, above floor level. However, if your board is too high, it makes working on it difficult, and the problem of elbows doing demolition work crops up more often!

Again, things are far more simple for those who have a permanent layout site because the legs can be screwed to the baseboard frame, or the layout attached to the wall as in Fig. 2.13. With a portable layout the legs have to be kept out of the way when the layout is moved. This can be done by making them either detachable or folding. Folding legs made up of stripwood and hinges as in Fig. 2.14 seem at first sight to be neater.

But they are far more complex and difficult to make, and the layout has to be tilted about quite a lot to close them, thus increasing the risk of damage.

This leg can be a wall post if convenient

Wall

Wall bracket for layout

2in (50mm) x 1in (25mm) full width of layout

Wall post 2in (50mm) x 1in (25mm) rawlplugged and screwed to wall

2in (50mm) x 2in (50 mm) leg screwed to frame with 2in (50mm) x 1in (25mm) tie at bottom

Fig. 2.13
Permanent layout legs and wall mountings

Fig. 2.14
Folding legs

2in (50mm) x 1in (25mm) wood

Arrangement of leg hinge

Location of hinges

Fig. 2.15
Trestles

Width of baseboard

3in (75mm) x 1in (25mm) — stripwood

Legs 2in x 1in stripwood

Clothes line knotted at each end when correct height reached. Make sure it is tight

I prefer simple detachable trestles as in Fig. 2.15 because they can be adjusted to suit the layout, and the layout's location. All that is required is to alter the length of the rope to raise or lower them if you have a lumpy floor. Once you have got them adjusted for the usual location of your layout, number them and always use them in the same positions.

Open-Top Baseboards

An open-top baseboard is one which has part of its area consisting only of framework without a solid surface. This can save both weight and money in places where you only have a few tracks going across a wide area as in Fig. 2.16. While it is essential to always have solid board under the tracks, scenery can have less rigid support and considerable savings of chipboard can be made. Obviously the framework has to be made separately from the baseboard, so care will have to be taken to ensure all is accurate and square.

Track

Scenery

Fig. 2.16
Open top baseboard

Raised Baseboards and Gradients

Many model railways have more than one level (see page 35) and the amount of trackage that is raised affects baseboard design. If, for example, a couple of tracks are to be on an embankment, then the arrangement illustrated in Fig. 2.17 can be used. 12mm (½in) chipboard is quite strong enough only to require support every foot or so, and this can be given by 50mm × 25mm (2in × 1in) blocks. The blocks can be attached to a solid baseboard below, or to the open-top frame as in Fig. 2.17.

Gradients are made in exactly the same way by varying the height of the support blocks. In some situations a gradient can be started by cutting the baseboard surface at each side of the track bed, and bending the rise upwards with chocks as in Fig. 2.18(a). If, however, the gradient is too steep for such a gradual rise, a wedge shaped piece of wood can be used to ease the start of the climb. See Fig. 2.18(b).

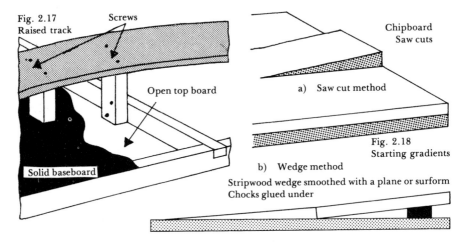

Fig. 2.17
Raised track

Screws

Chipboard
Saw cuts

Open top board

a) Saw cut method

Solid baseboard

Fig. 2.18
Starting gradients

b) Wedge method

Stripwood wedge smoothed with a plane or surform
Chocks glued under

High-level baseboards which can be lifted from above low-level tracks should be made in exactly the same way as normal baseboards, using 50mm × 25mm (2in × 1in) framing. This is because to all intents and purposes they are independent structures, subject to all the normal stresses. They can be supported on blocks which are attached to the lower baseboard in the normal way making sure that clearances for trains below are adequate. Some form of ensuring alignment will have to be used, such as split hinges as in Fig. 2.19. Permanently attached high level baseboards can have much lighter framing, consisting of 25mm × 25mm (1in × 1in) strip.

46

Fig. 2.19
Securing a high level baseboard using split level
hinges

Hinges with removable pin

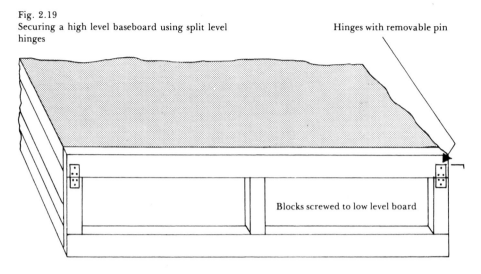

Blocks screwed to low level board

Finally, always ensure that there is adequate access to the underside for working on wiring and point motors. Therefore, only have a permanently attached upper board if there are few tracks below and the lower board can be of an open-top design.

At last we are able to get to a stage which involves real railway modelling. The baseboards are made, the plans are drawn, it is time to get the tracks down and see things begin to look like a railway.

Track Laying

Track Standards

Before you start, have a look again at page 28 and remember that your chosen track and wheel standards *must* be compatible.

Generally speaking a manufacturer's stock will run well on his own track. But few modellers want to get everything from one source, and like to mix stock from different manufacturers on their layout. One of the best makes of ready made pointwork sold in Britain is Peco Streamline; there are two sorts, Universal and Fine. Both use Code 100 rail, but the Fine pointwork is for anyone wanting good running with wheels such as those sold for use with loco kits, like K's and Romford. It will also take Airfix and Mainline stock and the finer Hornby Silver-Seal wheels.

If you intend using only ready-to-run locos and stock, Peco Universal is probably the most suitable. It will accommodate most of the models currently produced by the big manufacturers, such as Hornby, Lima, Airfix, Mainline and Wren. Be careful of some old products sold second-hand, which have very crude wheels indeed.

Though all these points and wheels are to the same gauge (OO) there is a marked difference in standards. From left to right they are: SMP point with ultrascale wheels; Peco steamline point with mainline wheels; and Lima point with obsolete Tri-ang wheels

Plain Track

Practically everyone modelling in the popular gauges such as N and OO will buy ready made track whatever the standard he works to. There are two types, rigid track which comes in short lengths set into straights and curves of various radii, and flexible track which comes in yard lengths and can be bent to any reasonable curve you choose. Both types have a plastic base in the form of sleepers and rail chairs which hold the rails to gauge.

Rigid track is sold with most train sets; its main purpose is for laying on the floor or other temporary sites where quick assembly and removal are necessary.

Flexible track can be made to suit your design and does not impose restrictions. Wide curves can be formed and made to flow in a railway-like manner. It does require more care when laying, but as we shall see, it is really quite simple and very effective.

rail section

Fig. 3.1
Track laying

⅛in cork sheet
underlay stuck with Evo-Stick

Track stuck with white woodworking glue and held with temporary track pins

Cork cut with sloping edge about 2mm from sleeper ends

Laying Track

Before laying anything, it is best to get an outline of your track plan onto the baseboard. I grid the design off the full size plan by measuring the distance from the baseboard edge to the track, at one foot or six inch intervals, then filling in using actual pieces of track and points. This may sound crude after all your planning, but small improvements and alterations can be made at this stage.

It is always best to start with some form of underlay for your track, it keeps down noise and adds a certain springiness. I prefer to use ⅛in cork sheet, which can be bought from most model shops quite cheaply. Because it comes rolled up and is springy, it is best to use an impact adhesive such as Evo-Stick, which holds it down instantly and firmly. Make sure that the room is well ventilated, because Evo-Stick fumes are dangerous when concentrated and *never* smoke when using Evo-Stick. Before laying, cut the cork sheet roughly to shape with a Stanley knife, and only trim off to a sloping edge when the track is laid, see Fig. 3.1. Where two or more tracks run closely parallel use one sheet of cork for all of them.

3.2
Reinforcing rails at baseboard joins

Track pins with rail soldered on

Fig. 3.3

break

Plastic track

Couple of copper clad sleepers with rail soldered on

Plastic based track is best glued down, but track pins or drawing pins can be used temporarily while the glue sets. White woodworking glue such as Evo-stick woodworking adhesive is useful because if a mistake is made, the track can be lifted using a thin knife.

The most important thing to aim for when laying any track is smoothness, both vertically and horizontally. So before you fasten any track down, make sure that there are no bits of cork or other rubbish under it and that the under-lay is absolutely flat and free from bumps.

Most makes of track have suitable rail-joiners, Peco sell metal and plastic ones for code 100 rail, plastic joiners being used for insulated rail breaks (see page 61). To test each rail joint use a light unweighted wagon, run it over the joint at speed in both directions; if it bumps or derails find where the irregularity is and file it smooth.

If you have a portable layout, extra strength is needed to protect vulnerable rail ends when the layout is taken apart. One way of doing this is to knock in a track pin at the side of each rail end and solder the rail to it as in Fig. 3.2. Alternatively a couple of copper-clad paxolin sleepers, such as those sold for building your own track, can be glued to each side of the baseboard join with Evo-Stick and the rail soldered to them, as in Fig. 3.3. But always make sure an insulation gap is made in the copper, between the rails. In either case, it is better to lay the track over the join first, secure it, and saw it apart after.

Pointwork

Fig 3.4 shows the different parts of a point as commonly named in model railways. The important parts are the blades and the frog. Both blades are tied together by a tie bar which is arranged so that movement to one side or the other causes the wheels of a passing train to be directed up one or other of the switch rails. How this movement can be arranged is discussed on pages 53 to 57.

Where the two routes finally diverge, one rail must cross another, this is the frog, and really is the most important and difficult part of all pointwork. For a short distance between the knuckle and the nose (see Fig. 3.4) one wheel of each passing vehicle is unsupported by solid rail. The check rails and wing rails guide its passage through, and prevent it taking the wrong direction. Obviously with such an arrangement there is a limit to the amount of variation in flange size and back to back gauge that will pass through unbruised (see pages 28 and 29). All parts of the point have to line up and be accurately gauged, so if you plan to build your own points, make sure you know the standards you are going to use, buy the gauges, and stick to them.

Another thing about point frogs in model railways is that if you use two rail electrification, one rail crossing the other causes a short circuit. This is overcome in two ways, the dead-frog and the live-frog. Leaping ahead to the chapter on Electrical Work (page 59), so to speak, I will deal with these here.

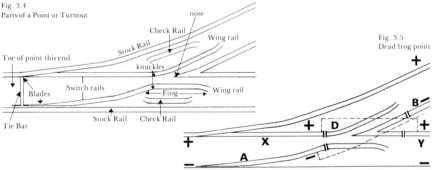

Fig. 3.4
Parts of a Point or Turnout

nose
Check Rail
Wing rail
Stock Rail
Toe of point this end
knuckles
Blades
Switch rails
Frog
Wing rail
Tie Bar
Stock Rail
Check Rail

Fig. 3.5
Dead frog point

Some people, including the vast majority of ready made point manufacturers believe that the only good frog is a dead one, as in Fig. 3.5. Here the problem of the conflict of polarity at the frog is avoided because the frog is neutral. Switch rail A is wired to rail B at the other side of the frog, by the same token switch rail X is wired to rail Y, and never the twain shall meet. The one objection to this system is that, in practice, slow running of locomotives over the frog is impaired by loss of pick-up on the dead spot. Theoretically there should be no difficulty if more than one pair of wheels is used for pick-up, but in practice there are often problems.

Fig. 3.6
Live frog points   Double rail break if a feed is located in this direction   Feeds

a)   Point set for straight road

Switch on tie bar or operating mechanism

b)   Point set for diverging road

If there are no feeds in this direction there is no need for a double rail break

To avoid the problem of jerky slow running, most scale modellers use live frogs. Peco cater for this demand by producing 'Electrofrog' points (their dead frog version is called 'Insulfrog'). In this system, instead of having nothing to do with the conflict of polarity, the frog has to change sides every time the blades are moved, see Fig. 3.6a and b. A switch is built in to the point operating mechanism which ensures that the frog is of the same polarity as the switch rail on which the train will run.

This means that *both* rails on the route which is *not* set are of the same polarity; no train can run, but as it is only half a current no short circuit will occur. A short *will* occur if these two rails receive current of both polarities from another source beyond the frog. Therefore, as mentioned in Chapter 4 *never* have a source of current beyond a live-frog point *unless* there is a double rail break after the frog but before the track feed. See Fig. 3.6a. You can, however, feed any number of live frog points from one source provided it is on the toe end of all of them.

There is one exception to this. In places where it is unimportant to have electrical isolation of the route the point is set against, a compact method of wiring round a live frog can be used, as in Fig. 3.7. Here the frog is

Fig. 3.7
Non-isolating wiring of live frog point

Track feeds can be on either branch but
will feed both branches

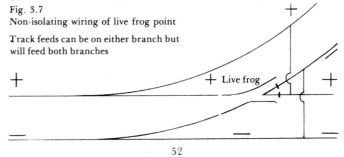

+ Live frog

switched as a live frog, but otherwise is treated almost as a dead frog, and both branches are fed current at the same time. This method is useful at cross-overs, and loco spurs where an isolation facility is not required, and avoids the necessity of a terminal at the toe end of the point. Practical applications of this can be seen in Fig. 4.6 on page 64.

Points can be laid in exactly the same way as plain track, with pins and glue. I think it is best to leave in a few track pins near the tie bar if an electric point motor is used. This will help stabilise the point against the shock of the motor as it changes. Be particularly careful not to get glue on the switch mechanism or the frog, or dire results will follow which are difficult to remedy without replacement.

One thing you must do is make provision for whatever operating mechanism you are going to use, before the point is put in place. This usually means cutting away the cork underlay and drilling holes, or cutting small sections from the baseboard. The nature of the preparation will depend on which operating method you use, and this will be discussed in the next section.

More complex types of pointwork such as crossings, slip points and three way points should only be used where absolutely necessary. There is not space here to discuss their problems and complications, but Peco make plain crossings, in N and OO gauge and a double slip in OO gauge only. These types use dead frogs; with live frogs, fairly complicated switch-ing of various parts of the track including frogs is involved. This should not be tackled by a beginner unless he is particularly inclined towards wiring and electrics.

Point Operation

The vast range of methods fall basically into two categories, electrical and manual operation. Each point on the layout can be operated in either manner, you do not need to only stick to one system.

Manual Operation

Manual operation means that your fingers provide the switching force to move the tie bar. Obviously the simplest method is to change the blades over with your finger. This is the most efficient method of all, provided the blades stay where they are supposed to, and they are within easy reach. Most modellers dislike this system because of the 'big overscale hand' reaching down from above, and operate the point from the base-board edge or a lever frame as do real railways.

The limits to manual operation are two-fold, firstly it is difficult to

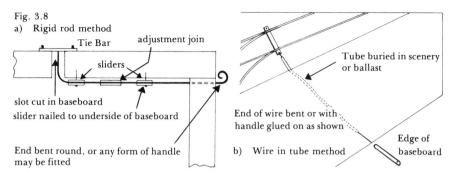

Fig. 3.8
a) Rigid rod method

Tie Bar   adjustment join

sliders

Tube buried in scenery or ballast

slot cut in baseboard
slider nailed to underside of baseboard

End of wire bent or with handle glued on as shown

Edge of baseboard

End bent round, or any form of handle may be fitted

b) Wire in tube method

arrange efficiently over distances greater than about six feet, secondly there are very great problems when crossing joins between baseboards which are regularly dismantled. So use manual operation only where the pointwork to be operated is fairly close, and then only if no baseboard joins are in the way.

You do not need to operate all your points from a lever frame or signal box as do real railways. If your layout is quite small you can work the point from the nearest place on the baseboard edge. Fig. 3.8 illustrates two methods, (a) having rigid rod under the baseboard surface, (b) having more flexible rod working through a tube above the surface. In (a) the rod consists of 20 standard wire gauge (s.w.g.) piano wire, sliding in brass sliders. The sliders are made by soldering 20 s.w.g. inside diameter brass tube onto a piece of brass strip which is drilled and fastened under the base-board with track pins. At the tie bar the piano wire is bent up through a slot in the baseboard and passed through a small hole drilled in the bar. To enable the parts to be put together more easily there is a join near the tie bar end which is made by soldering some 20 s.w.g. inside diameter tube over the break in the wire.

Using wire in tube operation as in Fig. 3.8b, there is no need to go under the baseboard, but the cork underlay has to be cut away where the tube is to pass under nearby tracks. This method can be made fairly flexible so that the operating point need not be exactly opposite, and can be hidden in a suitable building or hill. When all is working, the tube can be buried under ballast and other scenic features. Wire and tube are sold at good model shops, though cheap alternatives have been used by some modellers.

Despite the practical advantages of having point operation at the near-est place on the baseboard edge, many modellers find that a lever frame is more realistic and satisfying to operate. Here all points on one baseboard are operated manually from a row of levers located together. This introduces more complications than with the previous system because the movement of the lever has to be carried along the baseboard to the tie bar, and this usually involves two changes in direction. The best way to turn the movement through a right angle is by using bell-cranks.

In Fig. 3.9 is shown a practical rodding system which uses paxolin bell-cranks as made by Keil-Kraft for use in radio controlled model aircraft. They are very cheap and have enough holes in them to accommodate most adjustments, but are easy to drill for the odd unusual fitting. Rodding is 18 s.w.g. piano wire for longer runs, but 20 s.w.g. is better for the tie-bar operating wire due to its greater flexibility. Sliders are used which are identical to those described on page 54, and the brass tube joiners permit adjustment and ease of assembly. There is only one suitable lever frame now on the market, called the Addlever, which often needs the bearings strengthening for long service but is otherwise very good. It is wise to anticipate the use of this system during baseboard construction and provide suitable gaps under the frames through which the rods can pass.

If any manual system is used to operate live frog points, polarity switching will have to be incorporated in the system. Fig. 3.10 shows a simple sliding switch made from a piece of copper clad sleeper, glued to the point rodding. The small brass screw is located, touching the copper in such a position that when the rod moves, contact is made on one side or other of the gap. If each side of the gap is wired to a different polarity, the frog will receive current only from the side which is in contact with the screw.

Electrical point operation

A large number of modellers use electrical operation for all their points. This is probably because once they have mastered the technique, electrical operation is easier to set up than a manual system in which each point is different. Other advantages are its long range and lack of problems with baseboard joins, making it the obvious method for the more remote points on your railway.

Fig. 3.11 shows the basics of a point motor. It consists of two electrical windings called solenoid coils which when electrified, tend to pull an iron bar in one direction. So if one is energised the bar moves one way, if the other is energised the bar moves back. This movement, if connected by linkages to the tie bar, will operate your points at the flick of a switch.

How you connect the motor to the point tie bar depends on where the motor is to be sited. Some locations enable the motors to be hidden in buildings or under scenery, and work the tie bar by a small wire across the baseboard surface. Many locations, however, make this impossible and the motor has to be sited under the baseboard and a wire has to protrude up through a slot as in the manual system. Whenever a point motor is used, a way of reducing the suddenness of the movement on the tie bar has to be used. Fig. 3.11 shows one such method, by including a V-shaped bend in the operating wire. This sort of bend can be fitted in most locations, and adds enough spring to the wire to save broken joints on the tie bar.

How do we deal with the wiring and operation of these motors? Firstly, you must have a power control unit which has an uncontrolled 16 volt a.c. (alternating current) output, see page 59. Then you need only three wires,

Fig. 3.9
Point Rodding system using Bell Cranks, as seen from the side

Fig. 3.10
Polarity changing switch attached to point rodding for use with live frog points

Fig. 3.11
Solenoid Motor

as in Fig. 3.10. One is a negative wire which goes to both coils and acts as a common return for both of them. The two other wires are both positive and one goes to each coil by way of a switch, which permits only one of them to be energised at one time.

Obviously, the coils only need to be energised briefly. So the switch must only permit a short pulse of power, and then break the circuit again. There are two widely used ways of achieving this. One is by the electric pencil method as in Fig. 3.12. Here the wire from each coil is taken to one of a pair of screws located in a diagram of the layout. The wire from the control unit is taken to a probe, which can be touched against one screw or the other, to activate whichever coil is required to set the point. Suitable pencils, or probes, can be bought from model shops, but any piece of metal can be used. There is no danger of electric shock by the way, voltages are far too low.

An alternative method of operating electric points is by buying a flash switch. Unlike most switches, which leave a current flowing when they are thrown, the flash switch has two passing contacts which feed pulses of current to the point motor solenoids. Because the coil you wish to activate is always the last of the two to receive power, the point is always set in the direction in which you want the train to go. Flash switches are fairly expensive because their use is very limited outside model railways, and advantage cannot be taken of the economies of mass production to keep their price down.

A note about Signals Operation

Space does not permit detailed discussion of signal operation. Basically though, signals require an up and down movement, rather than the side to side movement of points. Fig. 3.13 shows how to fit a simple bell-crank under a signal which turns the movement in the direction you desire. All the methods of operation described in this chapter can be used to work semaphore signals. Colour light signals need a constant current, which can be directed to the appropriate bulb by means of multiple throw switches.

Ballasting

It is best to leave ballasting until after the wiring is installed because this enables you to hide some of the connections under the chippings.

Ballast on most railway track since before the war, means granite

Fig. 3.12
Electric pencil point operation

Track diagram on control panel

Screws, each wired to the appropriate coil of the motor

Electric pencil or probe wired to the 16v A.C. output of the control unit

Fig. 3.13
Bell crank mounted vertically to work a signal

pivot point

chippings. Ballast is used to provide a firm track bed and allow adequate drainage. Firstly, spread the ballast around the track, and then when everything is tidy mix some white woodworking glue with water until it is very runny. Then add a few drops of washing-up liquid. This breaks the surface tension and permits the mixture to flow into the ballast. Using an old washing up liquid container drip the glue onto the ballast — which you can buy from model shops — until it is fairly well soaked. Leave overnight and all should be solid. Be very careful near the frog and toe of points or you could jam them up or cause obstruction.

The painting of track is a matter of taste. Some people paint everything with a uniform brown colour, others only paint the sides of the rail brown and leave the rest natural. I can only advise you to go and look at some real track, or colour photos, and copy them. One last word, do not paint the rail surface. If you do accidentally then clean it again because electrical contact at 12 volts d.c. has enough problems without paint insulation! Keep rail surfaces clean at all times, preferably by wiping with a track cleaner before every operating session.

Electrical Work

Power supplies and the mains

The first thing to do is to get the electricity fairly near your layout, and down to a less lively voltage than 240 volts a.c. You can use batteries but in the long run it is expensive, and irritating when they wear out. It is better to use one of the many good mains transformer control units that are on the market, all of which do the job safely and reliably.

All transformers sold in Britain have to comply with stringent safety regulations, and are completely safe, unless you run your trains from the bath or something equally stupid. But do beware of secondhand units, especially if they are old and battered. Always ask for evidence of safety checks, and if in doubt leave them alone.

Normally, control units take mains current at 240 volts a.c., transform and rectify it, and output a controlled variable supply at up to 12 volts d.c. suitable for running your trains. On most types there is also a 16 volt a.c. uncontrolled output for powering point motors and other accessories. Sometimes, also, there is an uncontrolled 12 volt d.c. output which can be used to feed a second variable output controller without bothering to have another transformer. To make sure look at the top of the control unit, or on the box for *output*, and all the things it does will be listed for you.

There are many different types of transformer control units available. Some use simple resistance devices to alter the output; some use transistors to control output and give smoother train running. There are more complex devices which simulate the weight of a train and make stopping more interesting and realistic — in a frightening way — while other units make whistle noises.

Usually, though, you get what you pay for. Cheaper units are certainly adequate for a beginner who is not yet concerned that slow running is very slow, and starting and stopping very smooth. You can always get a better unit later when you have gained experience and feel it worth the investment.

The transformer/rectifier part can be purchased separately, and located away from the control panel to save weight and bulk. With this arrangement panel-mounted or hand-held control units can be used.

59

Make sure, however, that your control unit is compatible with your trans-former, or it may suffer an expensive death!

Safety

Although you have little to do with mains current, there are a few points to note :

1. Make sure there is no damage to the cable, and *never* ever touch a bare wire unless it is physically disconnected from the wall socket.
2. Ensure that the plug is properly and firmly wired up, and that if it is fusable, the fuse is of the correct amperage for your control unit.
3. Do not tamper with the mains electricity of the house, and *always* switch off at the mains switch box if the socket on the wall is suspect.
4. When the layout is not in use, unplug the lead from the transformer.
5. Do not allow water or other liquids anywhere near the mains supply.
6. Never use mains-type cable for low voltages. One day you might get mixed up and, if you are lucky, merely melt your trains.

Sections

In Fig. 4.1 is shown the basic circuit used to make a model locomotive move. All that is required is to take a wire from one of the control unit terminals to one rail, and likewise wire the other terminal to the other rail; one becomes the feed, the other is the return. It does not matter which you regard as feed, provided the locomotive goes in the required direction. Nor does it matter which is return — but you *must* be consistent throughout the wiring of your layout.

All modern locomotives work on the two-rail principle as seen in Fig. 4.1. Current passes from one rail, via the wheels, to the motor, then via the opposite set of wheels to the return rail.

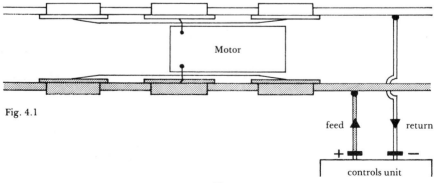

Fig. 4.1

feed ▲   ▼ return

+ ▬▬   ▬▬ −

controls unit

On layouts with only one loco operating all rails can be live, and the loco will go anywhere provided the points are set correctly. If that is all that is required then you need read no further and can forget about sections.

But as soon as you buy a second loco, as you almost certainly will, you will find it very annoying if you have to take one of them off the tracks in order to run the other.

One development is worth mentioning before we go into any detail. During 1979 and 1980 there are being introduced a number of electronic control systems. These work by punching out codes on a control console which activates and varies the speed of any one or more locos on a layout, even though power is supplied to all the tracks. If you use this system, all that I am going to say about sections and control is irrelevant. But for those who continue to use conventional methods, probably the majority for some years yet, read on.

Isolating Sections

There are two types of sections, isolating sections and full sections. On a very simple layout, a few dead end isolating sections would be enough to keep quiet any locos not in use. In Fig 4.2 a dead end isolating section is shown. All that is required is a saw-cut break in *one* rail and a wire from each side of the break connected to an on/off switch on your control panel.

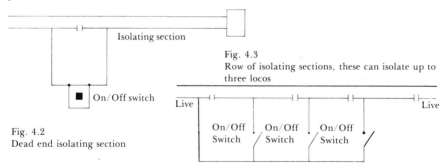

Isolating section

Fig. 4.3
Row of isolating sections, these can isolate up to three locos

On/Off switch

Live

On/Off Switch   On/Off Switch   On/Off Switch

Live

Fig. 4.2
Dead end isolating section

You can put an isolating section on a through line by making two breaks nine inches or more apart and wiring in the same manner as a dead end. Make sure there is a feed at the other side of your section or it will be permanently dead. In places like locomotive sheds you can really go to town with rows of isolating sections for engine standing, as in Fig. 4.3.

61

Full Sections

On any but a very simple layout, it is much easier to operate if larger parts of the trackwork can be isolated than just odd bits here and there. These larger divisions are called full sections and are capable of being operated when all the rest of the layout is electrically dead, so obviously they each have to have their own feed from the control unit.

It is always best to have a break in *both* rails at the ends of a full section. It makes it easier to understand your section divisions and eases fault tracing on the return side. Fig. 4.4 shows the arrangement for wiring up two full sections so that a train can move on either, or from one to the other.

It may seem daft to cut a break in the rail, then wire across it as in Fig.4.4 but it halves the wiring you will have to think about later. This wire, which is connected from one terminal of your control unit, and goes to all sections without any switching, is called the 'common return' wire. Once you have a common return, you only need think of one wire to all your section switches. You can even use one common return for more than one control unit, as we will find out later.

It is, however, unwise to use common return wiring on really complex layouts, where each section is best made completely independent, with positive and negative feeds. Throughout this chapter I will refer to the wiring as though common return were in use. All that is necessary to install double pole feeds is to substitute 'double pole' wherever I have written 'single pole', and in the diagrams assume *two* wires on each circuit where I have shown only a single wire.

Fig. 4.4

common return wire

Section 1

Section 2

On/Off Switch for Section 2

On/Off Switch for Section 1

Control unit

Where to put Sections and track feeds

Before you start wiring your layout, think about what you want your trains to do. It is no good having a station which gets all its electrical power via another station down the line, and then plan to operate locomotives independently in each.

One thought about points, especially the live frog variety is, as we have explained on page 52, the necessity for the current to be fed from the toe end of the point, and never from beyond the frog. So if you find you have to have a track feed which leads directly to the frog of a point, as, for example, in a simple oval track with a siding, or at the end of a run-round loop, cut *both* rails just beyond the frog, and if necessary connect a new feed before the toe. There are exceptions to this where only a short loco spur or siding are connected via a live frog point. Here, as we saw on page 52, simple jumper wires can avoid a separate feed beyond the toe. This makes them non-isolating, and no loco can stand beyond them unless a separate isolating section is arranged.

Even with dead frog points it makes things easier to understand if feeds only come from the toe end, and also avoids sudden rogue influxes of current when the point is set one way. Fig. 4.5 gives a few examples and also shows a few simple symbols used in track diagrams. You can supply any number of points from one feed provided it is at the toe end of all of them.

What are good candidates for sections? This depends on the size of a layout and its complexity.

Fig. 4.6 shows a fairly extensive layout for a beginner, incorporating a main line circuit with a junction station and a branch rising to a high level terminus. Either of the two stations could be modelled independently with the tracks coming from a fiddle yard.

As can be seen, there are quite a number of feeds, and all point frogs are protected by double rail breaks from feeds beyond them except where I have indicated. Not all feeds and rail brakes need to be full sections. Some can be wired together and controlled by one switch. For clarity, therefore, I have drawn rail breaks between sections with a double line, even though they are not physically any different from ordinary gaps.

I would recommend that the up and down main lines be each one section thus allowing independent running on either line. To permit storage of trains in the tunnel while shunting is carried out in section A, I have made all the tunnel tracks into one long isolating section. A few sidings in the tunnel would be a great advantage in the operation of a varied train service.

Another section should be branch platform and goods sidings in Station A. The goods sidings alone are too limited to warrant separation by themselves, but by including the branch platform track this part of the station could be quite interesting to operate.

Now to the branch, which as I said earlier could be made into a layout

A Electrical symbols used in track diagrams

Fig. 4.5

Track feed One rail break Two rail break

isolating break with on/off switch

B Wrong Right

Normally never have a track feed beyond a live
frog point unless there is a double rail break

C

Cross overs should always have a double rail
break between them

STATION A

D F A

E

Fig. 4.6
Points A,B,C,D,E,F have jumper wires after the
frog and can have feeds beyond the frog

Storage lines

isolation switches

Storage lines under

B C

STATION B

by itself by running all trains into a fiddle yard. Station B is best divided into two sections, one for the main line and passenger side, and another for the goods yard and head shunt. Passenger trains can arrive, the engine run round and depart without affecting the goods yard in the slightest. A goods train arrives in the platform loop and the loco pulls the train back into the head shunt after running round. As the yard and head shunt are one section, shunting can be carried out there independently of passenger trains on the branch.

More than one Control Unit

It has probably occurred to you that it seems a bit pointless having a layout, such as shown in Fig 4.6, if you only have one control unit. What is the good of being able to shunt the yard at station B without hindrance to other trains, if you cannot run more than one train, anyway? A way of using more than one control unit must be found.

A cowardly way out, which is full of limitations, would be to have the layout divided between two or more control units and leave it at that. In effect this would become two or more separate layouts. Undoubtedly the biggest difficulty in this system would be moving trains from one section controller to another. Some method of enabling either or any control unit to control trains over all or part of the layout at some time is necessary; this is the principle of cab control.

Cab control

As its name implies, cab control is a method of driving a loco anywhere on the layout as if you were in its cab. It is basically simple to set up, with two control points, as would be convenient (with one at each station) in the layout in Fig.4.6. Both control panels would have five section switches, one for each section on the layout as outlined above. Fig. 4.7 shows the arrangement. A common return for both panels is quite safe, and if both are mistakenly connected to one section at the same time the automatic cut-out built into all control units comes into operation and all trains stop. The basic rule when operating this system is *always* return the section switches to *off* when not in use and no embarrassment will ensue.

Partial Cab

For a layout such as that in Fig. 4.6, though, it may prove unnecessary to have all sections controlled by both control panels. For example, the operator at station B will rarely need to run trains round the up and down

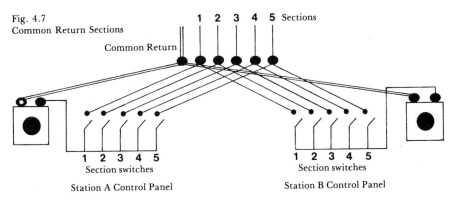

Fig. 4.7
Common Return Sections

1 2 3 4 5 Sections

Common Return

1 2 3 4 5
Section switches
Station A Control Panel

1 2 3 4 5
Section switches
Station B Control Panel

main lines. By the same token, the operator at station A will not be able to see well enough to shunt the yard at station B. So it may be better only to have the branch platform and goods sidings at station A, and the branch line and passenger station at B on the cab system, and leave the other sections under the exclusive control of one or other of the operators. Thus the operator at A will still be able to drive a train out of station B into station A, and on to the main line if he wishes, and the operator at B will be able to drive trains from the branch platform at A into station B. However, only B will shunt the goods yard at station B and only A will drive trains on the main line. It is possible to have two control units at station A by using single pole, double throw switches. This would enable both main lines to be used at once, or a main line and the branch at once. However, you will need your wits about you if you want to control two trains at the same time.

There are many permutations of cab control most of which involve different switching systems, but require no alteration of the feeds and sections. A booklet well worth buying if you wish to go a little more deeply into cab control systems, is a Railway Modeller 'Shows You How Booklet No. 4, Cab Control' by C. J. Freezer published by Peco.

Practicalities of Wiring

It is all very well working out all your circuits and wiring places, but if you cannot understand what wire is what under the baseboard much of your effort is wasted. Also, once your wiring is finished, alteration and fault-finding become a nightmare among festoons of cable. It is best to be organised at the outset. As with all aspects of model-making the extra time spent on a thorough job will pay you back many times over.

Wire and wiring

Wire is readily obtainable from radio shops and model shops, though usually you pay more at the latter. The best sort is called single core multi-strand bell-wire and comes in a wide range of colours. As I said earlier, do not use any type of mains cable for low voltages because of the fatal danger of confusion. A colour code or system of tabs can be used to identify wires. These can be made from a bit of paper stuck on with sello-tape. All the circuits should be drawn in a little note book with any number codes, etc., listed or indicated on a diagram. While you are there it is a good idea to mark each wiring hole in the baseboard with an indication of where it goes.

When you have a number of wires heading for a similar destination tape them together as a cable. If they have to go a long way under the baseboard, either feed them through holes in the framing or screw a few hooks of the appropriate size into the underside of the board and hang the wire from them as in Fig 4.8.

Soldering is the only reliable way of attaching wires to the track. Fortunately, the joint required is simple to make, provided the bit of your iron is small enough. Fig 4.9 shows the arrangement. Drill a hole, just adequate for clearing the wire, as close to the rail as possible. It is a good idea to melt some solder on to the wire before pushing it through the hole. It adds rigidity and makes it easier to form a good joint. When the wire appears above baseboard level bend it at right angles under or alongside the rail, which should be cleaned first with a glass-fibre brush.

Fig. 4.8   Fig. 4.9

sellotape or insulation tape

Hole in frame support

hook support

Use of rail
joiner

Usual result

Best result

approx 6in (150mm)

67

Quickly apply the soldering iron and then some multicore solder, which should melt and flow into the joint. If the solder will not flow and forms a grey globule, the joint should be re-cleaned and another attempt made. Try to be as quick as possible or you may melt the plastic track base. A good method, if it is possible at the location chosen, is to use a rail joiner with the wire soldered in it, or under it as in Fig. 4.9.

Terminal Strips

If your layout is divided into a number of baseboards, try and arrange all incoming wires to arrive at a terminal strip, as in diagram 4.10. It is then necessary to have only one wire for each section, and one common return to leave the baseboard. All the track feeds for each section can radiate from the terminal strip. Even if your layout is not divisible it is still better to have terminal strips located at various points to economise on wiring.

Another advantage of terminal strips is that faults can be isolated and tracked down by following the circuits from one terminal strip to the next. Alterations are much easier to make both at the control panel and base-board end of the circuits. Make sure, however, that all alterations are noted in your wiring note book.

The best terminal strips are made using solder tag strips. They are fairly easy and cheap to obtain from radio shops and army surplus electronics stores.

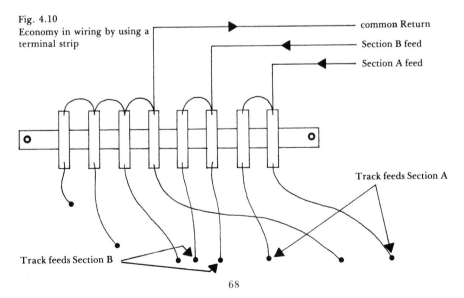

Fig. 4.10
Economy in wiring by using a
terminal strip

common Return

Section B feed

Section A feed

Track feeds Section A

Track feeds Section B

Fig. 4.11 Multi pin plug and socket

Crossing Baseboard Joints

The best way to cross baseboard joints is to use multi-pin plugs. These consist of a varied number of pins projecting from a plug, which fit into a matching socket. Fig 4.11 shows a typical design. A wire is connected to a tag at the back of one of the pins and the circuit is continued by another wire attached to the matching tag in the socket half. As many wires as there are pins and sockets can be joined and pulled apart quickly and easily.

There are only two problems with multi-pin plugs, price and availibility, so it is best to keep their numbers to a minimum.

Control panels

I always think that a railway feels better if it is operated from a neat control panel. I am in favour of a separate panel, detachable from the layout, which can be re-used in a later scheme. This type is easily the best for portable layouts, the extra cabling and multi-pin plugs required are a small price to pay for the convenience of the arrangement.

Laying out a control panel is usually done in one of two ways; firstly as in Fig 4.12 by having all the switching located on a diagram of the layout, with each section identified by a different colour. This is the usual design used by people who operate points by the electric pencil method (see page 57). All or part of the switching for sections and isolating sections can be located on the diagram, enabling the layout to be understood fairly easily by a visitor unfamiliar with its operation. This system has the disadvantages that alterations to the track layout are difficult, and as the panel is 'tailor-made' for one layout, extensive alterations are necessary if it is to be used again.

Neither of these disadvantages applies to the type of control panel shown in Fig. 4.13 which has all switches located in ranks, numbered and identified. Above is mounted a track diagram with all points and signals numbered and track sections drawn in different colours. I find this method more railway-like, and after getting used to it, more pleasurable to operate, but that is a personal opinion. It has the advantage that track alterations are relatively easy; a new diagram can be made if necessary and switches added or changed with little difficulty. Consequently, it is possible to transfer this type of control panel to a new layout, provided it is of a similar size and complexity to the old. A newcomer does have to work harder to understand it, however, and this system is not usually used on club layouts which are operated by many different people.

On a practical level a control panel is best surfaced with something strong yet thin so it can be easily drilled; ¼" (6mm) plywood is a good choice. It is up to you what angle of slope, if any, you give the panel, but it must be hinged along one long side like a desk so that easy access to the wiring is available. It is also a good idea to fit a chain or tape to prevent the lid falling right over the back pulling your wiring apart in the process.

Sources of materials

I have mentioned the expense of buying electrical equipment made specially for model railways. Most of the switches you will need, the wire, multi-pin plugs, and other items are not unique to model railways. Many have their uses in warfare and other activities hopefully outside model railways. So if you can find a source of military surplus electrical equipment, many items can be obtained at a fraction of the cost of specially produced material bought in model shops.

Another useful source, though less cheap than army surplus, are radio and hi-fi dealers. Their customers are not usually bemused by jargon, and know the worth of an on/off or single pole, double throw switch, and pay a lower price accordingly. The one switch not readily obtainable, except at model railway shops, is the point operating passing contact or 'flash switch' — mentioned on page 57. For the other switches, etc., I wish you good hunting and hope you bring in a bargain.

Fig. 4.12

Track plan type control panel

Fig. 4.13

Switch box type of control panel

Making Scenery and Buildings

Scenery and Buildings

Now that your layout has reached the stage where everything works, it is time to clothe the bare boards with the trappings of reality, scenery and buildings. It is a fact that no matter how well made are the locos and track, the realism of a model railway rests on its buildings and scenery.

For the purposes of model railways it is easier to split up techniques used to make the box-like buildings from those used to represent their natural surroundings. They need to be planned as one, and allowance made for the buildings in the scenery and vice versa, but because scenery is more adaptable it is best to make at least the more important railway buildings first, so I will start with building construction.

Buildings

Unlike real buildings which, if badly constructed fall down in a heap, model buildings have an unpleasant tendency to bend and warp in a most embarrassing manner, if care is not taken to make them rigid enough. Fortunately, because we are only really interested in the outside, compromises can often be made inside. This applies to both kit-built and scratch-built buildings, because many kits as supplied do not have enough rigidity and added strength is of great benefit.

Kit-Built Buildings

There is a growing range of kits for buildings to be found in model shops these days.

Most British kits are made from pre-printed card, examples include those made by Prototype and Builder-Plus in both N and OO gauges and Superquick in OO gauge only. They are punched and creased ready for assembly and go together easily and well. It is, however, of benefit if strength can be given by adding stripwood braces at the corners and along the top and bottom of the walls as in Fig. 5.1, this prevents the sides from bowing inwards towards the middle.

When the kit is finished there are often white edges showing where the card has been cut — these should be carefully touched-in with suitable

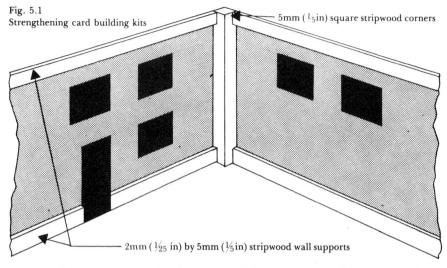

Fig. 5.1
Strengthening card building kits

5mm ($^1\!/_5$in) square stripwood corners

2mm ($^1\!/_{25}$ in) by 5mm ($^1\!/_5$in) stripwood wall supports

water colour paint. One disadvantage of these kits is the flat texture of the finish, devoid of any relief at brick joins or between slates. You can scribe the brick courses before assembly but this can lead to distortion. Most people accept this shortcoming, which is only evident at close range.

Scratch-Built Buildings

With the exception of certain types of railway buildings and some housing, there are no standard structures which can be found everywhere. Therefore, if you do not want your layout to look like anyone else's, with kit-built buildings and nothing else, you will have to make some at least from scratch.

The first thing you need is some form of design. There are frequent elevations of railway buildings published in the model railway magazines, and Allan Downes has included plans of many of his fine buildings in two books called 'Downesplans' published by Peco, which are well worth having. Alternatively, you can measure a building yourself and make your own plans. Take a long tape measure and a yard or metre rule, and record every dimension you can find. Take a lot of photos, using the yard rule as a scale, and a reasonable drawing of the building should be possible.

As I said on the last page, model buildings need to be rigid enough to resist warping. When scratch building, the technique is to make a strong box-like basic structure and then add all the detail to the outside, and inside if you wish. Useful materials for making this basic shell include card and plastic, though other materials can be used.

Allan Downes makes the beautiful buildings shown in the photographs around a shell of 1mm card, a technique described by the late John Ahern in his classic book 'Miniature Building Construction' published by M.A.P. When using this technique make sure that the card is of the best quality, soft, cheap card is a false economy.

Plastic sheet is one of the most widely used materials today, the most popular make is 'Plastikard' by Slaters, which is available at most model shops.

Plastikard parts are joined together using a liquid solvent called Mek Pak, which is applied with a small paintbrush, then runs up the join by capillary action and dries in seconds. Always make sure that the room is well ventilated when using plastic solvents such as Mek Pak. This simplicity of adhesion, combined with its clean edges when cut, makes plastic very suitable for model railway use. However, it can sag and bend if not supported adequately, or if too much Mek Pak is used on a join. So it is best to make the shell of a building from 50 or 60 thou Plastikard to give sufficient strength.

Fig. 5.2 shows a basic building shell, no details other than window and door openings need be included, but remember that the shell is the inner-most layer, so using your design, you must work out its size allowing for the thickness of the surface layers. If the building includes a large area, put in some cross-walls for added support, and remember that the roof will also need supporting. I like to make an inner roof skin of the same materials as the walls. This makes a very firm foundation which will not warp or bend, undoing all the work you put into the detail.

Fig. 5.2
Basic shell of building

Make additions as a separate box

cut ends to fit between
sides and under roof

Detailing a Model Building

Because of the many different finishes you will need to represent various building materials, it is impossible here to give more than a few guide-lines. There are, for example, a number of different stick-on wall

Fig. 5.3
Cutting out overlays at windows

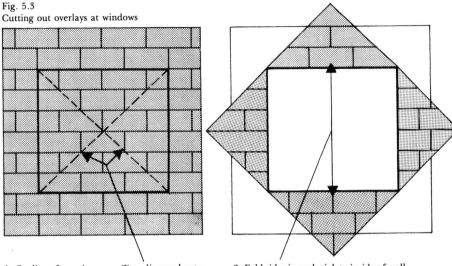

1. Outline of opening   Two diagonal cuts   2. Fold sides in and stick to inside of wall

coverings on the market, papers, plastic sheets and moulded plaster sheets. Printed paper is the cheapest, though some makes are unembossed and have the same problems of flatness as card kits (see page 72). Some stone papers, however, are very good, notably those made by Faller which are embossed and slightly textured. They can be attached with a PVA glue, or Mek Pak if a plastic base is used.

Plastikard make a number of embossed plastic sheets which can be stuck to a Plastikard shell with Mek Pak. These or any plastic sheet can be attached to wood, card or metal by first covering the non-plastic surface with a thin coat of Evo-stick, which is allowed to dry. The plastic sheet can then be placed over the surface and Mek Pak run into the join. Do not use Evo-Stick in the normal way or it will melt through the plastic, or grossly distort it. Like plastic kits, these embossed coverings do need to be toned down or painted if they are not to be too glaring and bright.

Moulded plaster can be bought in fabric reinforced sheets, and is stuck with Evo-Stick, or woodworking glue.

With all the overlay sheets it is possible to cut them roughly to shape, attach them to the building shell and trim them with a sharp craft-knife. Windows can be cut out as in Fig. 5.3 so that the wall covering goes round the sides of the window opening.

Allan Downes uses Peco Scene Texture or Pyruma to make the magnificent stone walls on his buildings. After a preliminary layer of white wood-

74

working glue on the card base, he spreads the plaster-like texture thinly over the wall surface. Then, while still soft, he carves the courses in a random manner, or uses a press-on mould to give a stone effect. For more precise cut stones such as often found on railway buildings, the plaster can be scribed when dry.

Roof slates can be made in the manner shown in Fig. 5.4, using strips of postcard. These can be painted later with a suitable grey poster paint, or oil paint. Alternatively, if you are not bothered about the overlaid effect, suitable papers can be bought and stuck on to the roof. This latter method is best for N gauge where slates made by the first method would be too thick anyway.

Windows are best made from 1mm perspex or there are clear sheets of glazing sold by Plastikard, but they can warp and bend if not held securely with Mek Pak. Window frames in N gauge are best scribed and the lines filled with paint. This method is also suitable for 4mm scale, but some modellers prefer to attach thin paper or Plastikard frames to their windows to give a more realistic relief effect.

Scenery

There are many types of scenery in Britain; this variety makes each part of the country distinctive and individual. Therefore, if you are going to base your model on a particular part of the country get a lot of photographs, or go and see it, and look for the colour and shape that make it what it is.

Once you have decided on the sort of landscape you intend to model, think about how the railway would fit into it. Railways were built into a landscape that was already there, so your cuttings and embankments have to look as if they *had* to be built, and were not just put there. Think about the slopes and streams, the roads and cottages, as if the railway was not there — do they still make sense or does your stream flow uphill?

Scenic Foundations

Fig. 5.5 illustrates a popular method of making a scenic foundation using a chicken wire skeleton on rough frames, or crumpled newspaper. Then over this is laid a surface of plaster-soaked bandage, which can be bought commercially. If you cannot get a supply of chicken wire, pieces of newspaper glued with paper glue can be used, but these require more continuous support, and take a lot longer to put on than chicken wire. Plaster-soaked bandage can be replaced by any thin cloth, with Polyfiller or a similar plaster worked onto and into it. Avoid over wetting plaster and make the first layer quite thick, then add a thinner layer later.

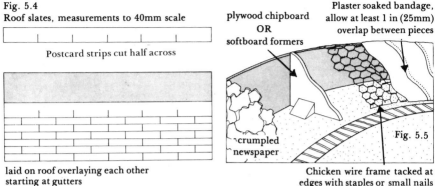

Fig. 5.4
Roof slates, measurements to 40mm scale

Postcard strips cut half across

laid on roof overlaying each other
starting at gutters

plywood chipboard
OR
softboard formers

Plaster soaked bandage,
allow at least 1 in (25mm)
overlap between pieces

crumpled
newspaper

Fig. 5.5

Chicken wire frame tacked at
edges with staples or small nails

Expanded polystyrene such as is used as packing can be used. It is easily worked with woodworking tools to form rough contours for the hills and cuttings, it can then be used as a basis for the final layers of textured scenery.

Scenic Details

Ground surfaces

There are obtainable from model shops a wide and expanding range of scenic materials mostly consisting of coloured powders of various sorts. These powders are really for finishing off a surface, and need textures under them if they are not to look like a mowed lawn.

Plaster can be textured by stippling it with an old brush while it is still sticky, or mixing cork granules into it before application, or by a combination of both techniques. In either case it is a good idea to add some powder paint to the mix to give a basic brown or dull green ground colour. Besides giving you a start with colouring, chips in the plaster do not show glaringly white.

Various sorts of cloths have been used to represent grass. On one layout I know, babies' old nappies are used effectively as rough grass. Supplies of old nappies tend to be rather variable, however!

H. J. Topping in his superb Pendlebury layout uses surgical lint in a very effective manner. After making a textured coloured surface of plaster and cork mix, he spreads thin layers of glue on places where he wishes to represent grass. The surgical lint, obtainable from chemists, is laid over this and pressed lightly down. When the glue has set, the lint is carefully ripped off leaving a realistic grass effect of small hairs, which is then spray painted with an airbrush.

Trees and Bushes

Trees are particularly difficult to make effectively; there are a number of commercially made types on the market.

To make trees yourself, a number of ways can be used depending on how much time and effort you are prepared to put into making them. By far the most common method is to use dried lichen as a basis for twigs and foliage. This is then stuck to a trunk made from twisted wire covered with paper or plaster, and painted thickly to hide the seams. This is illustrated in Fig. 5.6. Lichen is stuck to the twigs, lightly glued and then covered with a sprinkling of flock powder, or even dyed tea leaves. When everything has set, highlights can be picked out with a little artists' oil paint of suitable colours.

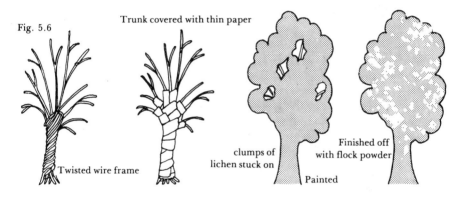

Fig. 5.6

Trunk covered with thin paper

Twisted wire frame

clumps of lichen stuck on

Painted

Finished off with flock powder

Water

Because of its constant movement it is not possible to make totally realistic water. The easiest water to represent, therefore, is deep still water. Plain glass or perspex, painted or left clear on the underside is suitable. If clear water is to be modelled, the river bed will have to be painted in muted green/brown colours before the 'water' is added, see Fig.5.7.

For shallow or moving water the best material is polyurethene varnish. A river bed is modelled first, and then fairly thin layers of varnish poured over and allowed to dry each time. Tints of brown or green oil paint can be added to the layers to give a greater effect of depth. The top layer has to be quite thick, and while it is drying, the surface is teased into ripples with a piece of wood, keeping this treatment up until you are certain that the ripples will not sink out as the varnish dries. Finally, a thin coat of varnish is painted over the whole to give it a wetter appearance.

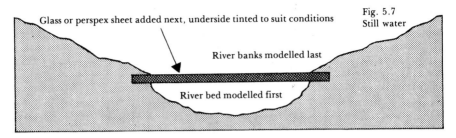

Glass or perspex sheet added next, underside tinted to suit conditions

Fig. 5.7
Still water

River banks modelled last

River bed modelled first

Man-Made Items

Essentially, items such as walls and fences can be made in exactly the same way as buildings, using card and plaster. Many details, like telegraph poles, telephone boxes, some fences and people, can be purchased at model shops, and do save a lot of time and trouble, Merit and Slaters both make a wide selection. Roads can be made on a foundation of card or plywood cut roughly to shape and landscaped at the edges. The surface can either be made from fine sandpaper, or fine sand dropped onto wet paint and the surplus brushed off later.

There are a number of bridges and tunnel mouths available commercially; these can be fitted over or under the tracks and landscaped in. Thin card is stuck under the arch and covered with brick paper, but the surface of over-bridges is better made on a more rigid foundation as in Fig 5.8. Under-bridges can be fitted under a raised track as discussed on page 46.

Surface of card
or plywood

Bridge face

Fig. 5.8
Overbridge construction

Thin card lining

Wood blocks

Station Platforms

If you use flexible track and want station platforms on curves, you will have to make your own. Fig. 5.9 shows one method of construction, though a solid chipboard interior can be used. You can have problems with long coaches on tight curves striking the platform edge unless adequate clearance is given. Fig 5.10 shows a simple way of avoiding this; obviously if the curve is very tight the platform will be a long way from the track. So try and avoid this situation, if only for your passengers' sake!

Edging stones, paper

Fig. 5.9
Platform construction

Paper or plastic
sheet coverings

Thin (about 1mm) plywood top and sides

Solid wood ramp   Stripwood spacers every 6in (150mm)

Fig. 5.10
Measuring for clearance on a curved platform

Split a pencil lengthways and hold it against the sides of your longest vehicle at the points indicated. This will mark your clearance along the baseboard.

Locomotives, Rolling Stock and Operation

Rolling stock, particularly locomotives, are the glamour side of model railways. To most of us there is no thrill greater than looking at our latest or newest resident in the loco shed. This popularity is evidenced by the tremendous range of ready-made and kit-built locomotives on the market today. So much so that there is much less scratch building of locomotives in 4mm scale than ever before.

Wheels

Try and decide how much you care about the appearance of your wheels before you invest time and money in track laying. Also, if you have made or intend to make some of your locos and stock from kits such as those made by K's or any which have their own chassis kits, use finer pointwork, for example, Peco Fine. In N gauge it is the norm for people to buy a readymade chassis even if they use kit-built bodies, so wheel problems are not as frequent.

There are three problems commonly associated with wheels: out of gauge, out of true, lack of concentricity (i.e. the axle is not in the middle of the wheel).

● Out of gauge

The back-to-back gauge of a OO wheel should be 14.5mm. Some coarse wheels are narrower and will still go through universal or toy train point-work. However, if you use finer standards it is necessary to have a back-to-back gauge. If you cannot buy one, they are easily made, as in Fig. 6.1, keep on trying if you mess up the first, but for heavens sake *do not* accept anything but absolute accuracy.

● Out of true

This is noticeable as a wobble at the rim when the wheel is spun. With loco driving wheels a wobble can sometimes be eased by carefully adjusting the wheel as you tighten up the fixing, or by using a wheel press, such as made by Hamblings. If the problem is caused by a bent or warped wheel there is nothing you can do except replace it.

Fig. 6.1   Measuring the back to back gauge
Back to back gauge

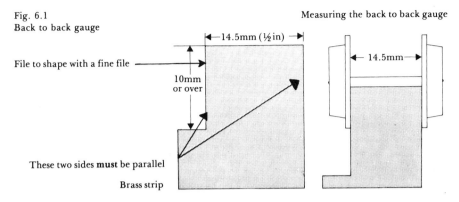

● Lack of concentricity

This is usually only found on wheels with plastic centres. It does not often cause derailments, but is evidenced by your stock wobbling up and down slightly as it runs along. This looks very unrealistic and the pair of wheels and axle should be changed.

Sources of Locomotives and Rolling Stock

Basically, there are three sources, ready to run, kits and scratch building.

● Ready to run

Over the last few years the model train branch of the toy market has exploded into a hive of activity, with three new manufacturers entering the field. There has also been a trend towards better quality and accuracy in the models. Airfix and Mainline both produce superb models, and Lima look like rivalling them soon. This is very encouraging for a beginner because it puts really accurate models in his price range, and starts him off on the right footing. However, it is impossible for these manufacturers to ever satisfy all the range of prototypes demanded by modellers so other sources must be used.

● Kits

Kits cost a lot less to manufacture than do ready-to-run models. They can be made in materials requiring less expensive production methods. Kits now provide the majority of locomotives and stock that most modellers require unless they model the pre-1920's period.

Locomotive Kits

The most common types of loco kit are made from cast white metal. This is a low melting point lead alloy which can be cast accurately into quite intricate shapes. Loco kits made from this can be glued together with epoxy resin adhesives, or soldered with special low melting point solder. Some are made to fit on chassis from ready-to-run models, and these should be attempted first. Others have a special chassis kit, or include a chassis when you buy them.

Always build the chassis first, and get it to work. Then you can build the body, making sure at every stage that everything fits round the motor and wheels and no rubbing or electrical short circuits occur (see page 84). When building a chassis ensure that it is level, with all wheels touching the rail. Fig. 6.2 shows how to do this using a sheet of glass.

There are other types of loco kit, such as those made from etched brass or stamped nickel-silver. These are not recommended for beginners due to the complexity of assembly and the need for fairly skilful use of a soldering iron. An excellent series of articles on kit building entitled 'Confessions of a Lapsed Scratch Builder' by C.J. Freezer started in the September 1978 issue of *Model Railways*, and is well worth reading.

Fig. 6.2
Checking the squareness of a loco chassis on glass

There should be no rocking when any corner of the chassis is pressed

When all is level put a drop of cyno acrylate adhesive on the spacer screws

Coach Kits

There is much greater variety of the types of coach kits than loco kits. They are often made from a mixture of materials though probably the easiest to actually build are those made from plastic. Ratio do a good series of plastic kits but these require painting. Maj make some with a clear plastic shell and stick-on pre-coloured sides. Some are quite advanced and complex. Mallard, P.C. and a number of other firms make kits with many etched brass parts. They assume a fair knowledge of coach construction and are not recommended for the beginner.

I would strongly advise anyone who is really keen to start making coach kits to read a couple of articles entitled 'The Coaching Trade — Coach Kits 78' by Harry Drummond in the November and December 1978 issues of *Model Railways*. These articles review all the major types of coach kits available at that time, and give practical hints on their construction.

Goods Stock Kits

Goods stock tends to be the simplest rolling stock, and usually kits are easier to build than any others. It is a good idea to make your first break from ready-to-run stock with a goods vehicle kit.

Plastic kits are best to start with. Ratio make an excellent range of kits; Slaters, Maj and Three Aitch are others and there are many more to choose from. I would recommend an article by Harry Drummond, 'How Does Your Goods Train Grow? — a survey of 4mm scale wagon kits in the November 1977 issue of *Model Railways*. This covers most of the wagon kit makes available at the time. When building a wagon, always bear in mind the principles outlined on page 88, and keep your wheel standards constant.

● **Scratch Building**

As with kits, start with a wagon and graduate from there. Some kits are a good introduction to the skills of scratch building; coach kits by Roxey Mouldings, for instance, and loco kits by Jamieson.

Two good books on loco construction are well worth reading — *Miniature Locomotive Construction* by John Ahern, published by M.A.P. and *Model Locomotive Construction in 4mm Scale* by Guy Williams, published by Ian Allan. A useful beginners' guide is an article by R. D. Naylor entitled 'Coach Construction' in the February 1979 issue of *Model Railway Constructor*.

Common Running Faults in Locomotives

Jerky running or no running at all are caused either by mechanical obstruction to the free movement of the chassis, or by an electrical fault. Just by watching the problem it is often difficult to tell which of the two it is. If you have some sort of short circuit, or overload indicator on your control unit, or better still an ammeter, it is usually possible to work out the type of fault you are dealing with. Otherwise it is a matter of trial and error.

Electrical Faults

In a loco which has been running well and develops a sudden fault, the problem is likely to be electrical.

● Dirt obstruction of the current

Make sure all wheels with pick-ups on them are clean, both on the back and on the treads, and that the track is clean. Look at the motor (see Fig. 6.3) and make sure the commutator is clean and the brushes not too worn.

Fig. 6.3
Typical Model Railway Locomotive Motor

Spindle

Magnet

Commutator

Armature

Brushes

● Short circuit

If the locomotive has a metal body, such as a white metal kit, and only fails to work when the body is on the chassis but the chassis runs by itself, the fault is almost certainly a short circuit through the body. Look inside the body for any tiny spots that look burnt and file them back. Place the body on the chassis and check that the wheels are clear of the splashers or any other part of the inside. If they are very close file back some of the body, but be careful not to make a hole right through. Another likely place is where the brushes stick out of the top of the motor. If there is trouble there scrape away some metal from inside the top of the boiler. At each stage check whether the fault is cured.

Then look at any bogie or trailing wheels, check that the insulated rims cannot touch either the body or the chassis as they pivot round a curve. A good idea is to stick a very thin piece of Plastikard on any part of the chassis or body where a short circuit may occur. Look particularly at the front steps of a loco where a leading bogie wheel swings sideways round curves.

● Collector faults

Fig. 6.4 shows a conventional phosphor-bronze collector strip arrange-

84

collectors touch back of **rim only**
on **all** driving wheels

Fig. 6.4
Collector arrangements for locomotive

Phosphor-bronze strip soldered to
L-shaped piece of brass

Copper clad paxolin collector block, with saw cut to split copper
into two halves, glued to chassis

ment. It is shown on both sides of the locomotive, but if the wheels on one side are not insulated there is only need to have collectors on the other side. With one side insulation a wire is taken from the collector block to one brush of the motor, the other brush is connected to a convenient part of the chassis. There must be a T.V. suppressor on the motor feed wire — these can be bought at model shops.

When checking collectors, make sure:

i   that they touch the rims of all the wheels that they are meant to touch
ii that they do not touch anywhere else on the chassis or wheels, especially when the wheels are moving
iii that the collector block and motor feed wire are completely insulated from the rest of the chassis and motor.

If all this fails to cure the fault, strip the whole lot down and re-assemble, checking for mechanical and electrical faults at each stage.

Mechanical Faults

● Wheels and Motion

To trace problems in the wheels and motion it is necessary to disconnect or remove the motor from the chassis. This leaves the wheels free to move — or not move if there is a fault.

Starting with the wheels, remove all the motion and see whether the chassis will run freely up and down a bit of rail, sloped gently one way, then the other. If it sticks, check which axle is the problem and gently file out the axle hole (the bearing) with a round needle file until the wheel will turn freely. If the wheels stick because the chassis is a little wide between them, file the face of a bearing gently until the wheels rotate freely, do not overdo this, particularly on a driving axle.

Next, fit the coupling rods (those that join the wheels together). Test the chassis again by rolling on a sloping rail, then lift up each end in turn and push and pull it along the track on its end wheels only. If it sticks or falters, the rods are binding.

There are three reasons for this:

i   If the holes in the coupling rods are spaced differently from the wheel centres. The distance between the wheels and the length of the rods between them *must* be the same. Check with a pair of dividers, or mark the wheel centres and lay the rods on them. Very small differences can be corrected by filing out the holes in the rods slightly, but do not overdo it.

ii If the positioning of the crank pins on the wheels is not identical. This means that you must first check that all crank pins are of the the same throw (distance from the centre of the wheel). A pair of dividers can be used for this, see Fig. 6.5(a).

Secondly, check that all crank pins are perpendicular to the face of the wheel (that means do they stick out straight?) see Fig. 6.5(b).

If the pin is found faulty in either case get a new wheel and start again.

iii The quartering of the pair of wheels on an axle is not correct. When both driving wheels are on the axle of a model locomotive the crank pin on each wheel should be set at a right-angle to the other. This means that one wheel is turned so that the crank is at the nearest point to the rail, the crank on the other side will be level with the wheel centre, this is called quartering, see Fig. 6.6. If any of the pairs of wheels are quartered differently from the others, binding will occur. Most makes of wheels available for use with kits have provision on their fixings for the quartering to be accurate, if they are not accurate take them back to the shop. Some ready-to-run locos have driving wheels on plain axles which can be adjusted by carefully pushing them round the axle. It is not wise to overdo this or your wheels may become loose.

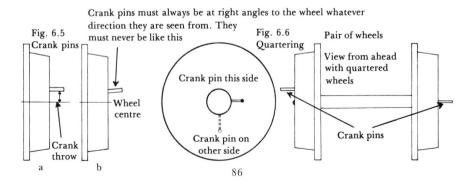

Fig. 6.5
Crank pins

Crank throw

a   b

Crank pins must always be at right angles to the wheel whatever direction they are seen from. They must never be like this

Wheel centre

Fig. 6.6
Quartering

Pair of wheels

View from ahead with quartered wheels

Crank pin this side

Crank pin on other side

Crank pins

Fig. 6.7
Conventional chassis arrangement

● Gearing faults

All motors in kit-built chassis, and some ready-to-run-types, are mounted along the chassis driving the wheels through a worm gear and spur gear, as in Fig. 6.7. A more efficient method now being used extensively by ready-to-run manufacturers is a short motor mounted across the frames driving through a train of spur gears. The worm and spur system give more problems, however, if the mesh is not correct.

To be efficient, the teeth of the worm should be just clear of the bottom of the gaps between the spur wheel teeth. A useful trick is to mesh the two with a piece of tissue between them, and then remove it, leaving a small gap between them. The other method is to use trial and error until the chassis runs most easily. Some chassis have an adjustment screw under the motor to alter the mesh. If not, thin pieces of brass, Plastikard or paper can be added and removed to raise and lower the motor and adjust the gears.

A final point about gears: do not leave much sideplay on the driving axle, and always fasten the gear wheel in the centre of the axle. Any deviation from the centre reduces the efficiency of the gearing.

One thing to remember about a new chassis is that it needs oiling and running-in. Do not expect it to be perfect at first. If it seems generally smooth but a little stiff and noisy, give it a very light oiling with fine oil, and run it for about half an hour round a test track in each direction.

Fault Finding in Rolling Stock

Goods Stock

If you build a wagon kit or find a ready-to-run wagon does not run well or often falls off the track, there are a number of things you can check.

i Check that the wheels are not at fault, see page 80.

ii Are the wheels level? Set the wagon on a piece of glass and test for any rocking. If you are building a wagon, assemble the wheels into the underframe and let the adhesive set with the wagon standing on glass, checking frequently for any rocking.

Alternatively, you can buy a compensation kit which will allow one axle to rock a little to accommodate track irregularities and make levelling unnecessary, see Fig. 6.8.

iii Check that both axles are at right-angles to the rails. If the wagon rolls in a curve on a sheet of glass or if it travels in a slightly crab-wise fashion, they are not. Fig. 6.9.

iv Make sure you have a bit of plasticine or something heavy in the load, or under a plastic wagon to add a little weight. If your wagons are too light, they will bounce about unrealistically and often bounce off the rails.

Fig. 6.8
Compensation allows one pair of wheels to move up and down

Fig. 6.9
Vehicle axles must be at right angles to the track as in (a) not as in (b)

Coaches

Similar comments apply to coaches, though generally they hold the track better than other stock. Often, ready-made coaches rock and wobble excessively on their bogies. It is a good idea to put a couple of pads of Plastikard or brass under the body and on the bogie to prevent excessive movement as in Fig.6.10. Be careful not to make them too rigid, though, or they may derail on curves due to the bogies being too stiff to pivot properly.

Couplings

There are a number of different types of couplings available, it is best to standardise on one type. If you do not mind the rather obvious appearance of the couplings on ready-to-run stock, then choose one make of these and stick to it. Replace all others with the type you choose, all of them are fairly efficient and trouble-free, so the choice is yours.

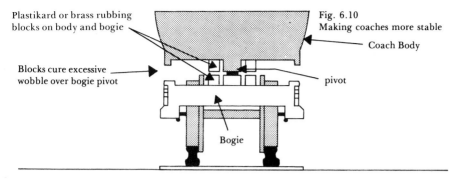

Fig. 6.10
Making coaches more stable

Plastikard or brass rubbing blocks on body and bogie

Blocks cure excessive wobble over bogie pivot

Coach Body

pivot

Bogie

For those who want to make their couplings more realistic or less obtrusive, there are a number of systems. Many scale modellers use three-link couplings, miniature versions of those used on real railways. These neither couple nor uncouple automatically, so they have to be hooked on and off the coupling hook using a tiny wire shunter's pole. There are a lot of laughs to be had watching this activity on otherwise scale, automatic layouts at exhibitions.

Practical alternatives are the fairly unobtrusive magnetic couplings of various types. Of these, one of the most robust and reliable is the Sprat and Winkle Coupling. This consists of an etched brass pivoted hook mechanism, with an iron chain hung below. When the vehicle passes over a magnet hidden under the track, the iron chain is attracted to it and the hook is pulled down and uncouples. Coupling is done simply by pushing two vehicles together so that the hooks lock on a small bar, fastened between the buffers.

Painting

All models can be improved by good paintwork and any model can be spoiled by bad paintwork. Therefore, it is essential that the paint is smooth, thin, and free from brush marks. This can be achieved in two ways:

● **Brush painting**

Always use very thin coats, left to dry for at least a day between each coat. Apply the paint quickly in a completely dust-free atmosphere. If any dust sticks, gently rub the offending surface with the finest sandpaper (called flour paper) after it has thoroughly dried. Use only good quality artists' sable hair brushes, cheap brushes are a false ecomomy. Clean the brushes first with thinners, then with soap and water after use. Always start painting with a coat of primer, and before that clean the model with scouring powder and an old toothbrush, making sure you are not too vigorous. Only add the detail to your model after it is painted; this avoids build-up of paint on and around detail. Before you tackle your best model, practise on an old one, or bits of scrap metal and Plastikard.

● **Airbrush painting**

This uses a fine spray of paint from a specially designed piece of equipment. The cheapest make is by Humbrol and it is good enough for larger surfaces such as the main colour of wagons, coaches and locos. Airbrush painting has the great advantage of eliminating brush marks, and covering all parts of the model equally with a very thin coat of paint. It is much quicker than brush painting but is more cumbersome to set up.

You can pay very large amounts of money for airbrushes that paint thin lines. But here their advantage over a conventional brush is limited, because on small surfaces and thin lines, brush marks are not really noticeable. So you may as well buy a cheaper airbrush and use it only for the larger surfaces where it really has an advantage over brush finishing.

If you want to go further into airbrushing there is an excellent article on all makes of airbrush by John Talbot Jones in the January and February 1978 issues of *Model Railways.*

Operation

Running Correct Trains

A model railway is a complete thing, it is made up of a lot of other models, but to make it realistic, trains must be made up in a realistic manner. This does not mean you cannot run any trains until you have read all the British Railways Rule Books on train formation. But as you add to your knowledge use it in your railway, and slowly things will look better.

Read about train make-up, for example, there have been quite a number of articles on goods trains in the magazine *Model Railways* over the last couple of years. Look at photos of the sort of trains you want to run, look where the brake compartment is placed, what sort of engine is pulling the train, what type of stock is used. It is possible, even with reduced train lengths, to give an impression of a well run railway simply by following a few basic guidelines.

Types of Train

Depending on where you imagine your railway to be, and what sort of line it is, i.e. main line or secondary line, the traffic passing through will vary. To take an extreme example, there will be no china-clay traffic in York-shire, but there are likely to be coal trains, and wagons loaded with wool bales. If the prototype of your layout is near the sea, oil trains and fish vans may be expected, and a fair number of excursion and holiday specials will add to the variety of locos and carriages you can run. In fact it is always possible to run special trains with odd combinations of locos and stock, for example, goods engines were fairly often used on holiday relief trains when the railways were short of more suitable power.

Besides through traffic, your station will have to be served realistically by suitable trains. Passenger services to and from different destinations will have to vary in length, coaching stock and locos. Goods traffic is even more governed by your facilities, cattle trains need cattle docks, heavy loads need cranes, coal needs coal staiths, vans need a shed or platform to unload.

Sequence Operation

Once you have decided on the sorts of trains working on your layout and their formation, it is time to work out how many of each type is required and how often they run. A basic passenger service is the best place to start, then goods trains serving your stations need to be fitted in. Finally include through workings.

The best way to get all of this in order is to start with a list of trains in the sequence you intend to run them. When this list is finished it is time to try out the workings to see if they are possible. For example, do you have enough space in the fiddle yard for all the trains you expect to be there at any time, or have you got enough passenger trains in the right place? It is best to use this stage to make alterations and adjustments, and to try and arrange things so that the locos and stock at the end of a sequence are in the same places as at the beginning. In this way the sequence never really has an end and can be carried over and over without having to move stock by hand at the end of each session.

When the broad outlines of train movements have been worked out, go into details about any shunting and station movements at each station.

Besides having a copy of the full sequence at each operating point, it is a good idea to have there a book of flip-over cards. This enables each operator to see quickly where he is in the sequence, and what he is to do next.

Timetable Operation

In long established layouts, well tried, with operators who are familiar with the line, timetable operation can add a new sense of urgency and excitement to running. It is fairly easy to take a successful sequence, time it, and produce a timetable. This means that if there are delays, or derailments, trains will have to be held, or pass each other to keep to time. An evening of hectic last minute alterations to train movements may be produced by one failed loco, whereas in a sequence everything would just have to wait a bit longer.

It is a good idea to have a separate stoppable clock for use with timetable operation, so that you can break off when you want. Obviously you could work out a strict system based on actual time, but it would be difficult to get all your stock in the right place if you missed the starting time. Because of their short journey times between stations on a model railway, some operators work to a speeded up clock so that their timetable reads more realistically. Unfortunately, though journeys between stations are quicker than reality, station working — shunting, running round, etc. are not. So you have to be very rapid indeed with all the complexities of station work, and often lose all the realism you hoped to gain.

It is best for a beginner, or anyone who has just finished a new layout, to start with a sequence operation and only graduate on to a full timetable when he is familiar with all aspects of operation. It may be that you are happy with a sequence, especially if it keeps you fully occupied and interested. A timetable may only harass and annoy you, which takes away the only reason for having your railway — fun.

I do hope in this small book that John and I have interested you in model railways. It is a wonderful hobby, so full of variety that almost any skills can be accommodated at some point. The most important thing to remember is that is a hobby, and a hobby is for relaxation and entertainment. You will read in magazines of people going to quite extraordinary lengths to get this or that bit of their model absolutely correct. But remember, your model railway is entirely your own, and if you are pleased with the way it is, it is the best model railway in the world.